"Dinnae press me, Ewan; I beg ye. All I can say is that I cannae be a wife to any man."

"Not even me? I'm different from most others. I want more from my wife than to take complete control of her life. I want a companion, a woman who will share in my joys and burdens, who will advise me when it's needed. A woman I can honor and cherish."

And love.

He was not foolish enough to speak the words, for he must have known that any woman would be hard-pressed to believe them upon such a short acquaintance. But he was clever enough to know that was what many females craved most of all—to be loved.

"Ye need a wife with a dowry, who has a family that will accept ye. There are many others that will do."

"Nay, Grace. I only want ye. I cannae promise to be an ideal husband, but I will try to be all that you wish me to be, all that you need."

"Ye are without question the boldest man in the Highlands, Ewan Gilroy."

He grinned at her. Grace felt her heart quicken and her throat go dry. She knew he was going to kiss her even before he leaned close and brushed his mouth against hers. And when he did, she forgot to breathe. . . .

Books by Adrienne Basso

HIS WICKED EMBRACE

HIS NOBLE PROMISE

TO WED A VISCOUNT

TO PROTECT AN HEIRESS

TO TEMPT A ROGUE

THE WEDDING DECEPTION

THE CHRISTMAS HEIRESS

HIGHLAND VAMPIRE

HOW TO ENJOY A SCANDAL

NATURE OF THE BEAST

THE CHRISTMAS COUNTESS

HOW TO SEDUCE A SINNER

A LITTLE BIT SINFUL

'TIS THE SEASON TO BE SINFUL

INTIMATE BETRAYAL

NOTORIOUS DECEPTION

SWEET SENSATIONS

A NIGHT TO REMEMBER

HOW TO BE A SCOTTISH MISTRESS

BRIDE OF A SCOTTISH WARRIOR

Published by Kensington Publishing Corporation

BRIDE
Of A
SCOTTISH
WARRIOR

ADRIENNE
BASSO

ZEBRA BOOKS
KENSINGTON PUBLISHING CORP.
http://www.kensingtonbooks.com

ZEBRA BOOKS are published by

Kensington Publishing Corp.
119 West 40th Street
New York, NY 10018

All Kensington titles, imprints and distributed lines are available at special quantity discounts for bulk purchases for sales promotion, premiums, fund-raising, educational or institutional use.

Special book excerpts or customized printings can also be created to fit specific needs. For details, write or phone the office of the Kensington Special Sales Manager. Attn.: Special Sales Department. Kensington Publishing Corp., 119 West 40th Street, New York, NY 10018. Phone: 1-800-221-2647.

Zebra and the Z logo Reg. U.S. Pat. & TM Off.

First Printing: July 2014
ISBN-13: 978-1-4201-2904-5
ISBN-10: 1-4201-2904-X

First Electronic Edition: July 2014
eISBN-13: 978-1-4201-2905-2
eISBN-10: 1-4201-2905-8

10 9 8 7 6 5 4 3 2 1

Printed in the United States of America

To my beautiful, accomplished, extraordinary nieces,
Jennifer Colucci Dickson,
Allyson Gambarani,
Kerry Ann McBride,
Ashley Casale, and
Courtney Casale.
With love from your favorite auntie!

Chapter One

Scottish Highlands, Dunnad Castle, November 1314

"He's dying," Edna whispered, her voice hushed and reverent.

"I know." Lady Grace Ferguson tore her gaze away from her maid's sympathetic eyes and looked down at her husband. Sir Alastair, chief of Clan Ferguson, lay still and quiet beneath a pile of heavy furs, his ashen face lined with pain, for even in sleep the agony did not leave his broken body.

Grace studied him for a few moments, examining the strong line of his jaw, his crooked nose, the heavy dark stubble on his chin and cheeks. Though his wife for nearly seven years, she found his features were unfamiliar, for Sir Alastair had spent most of the days of their marriage away from her, fighting beside Robert the Bruce as that noble man secured the Scottish crown on his head and independence from the English.

Grace softly stroked Alastair's fevered brow, the skin dry and warm. Instantly his eyes opened.

"Hot," he croaked, attempting to push away the pile of furs.

Grace's heart tightened as she realized he lacked the strength to move them. "Shhh," she purred, sitting on the edge of the bed. "Let me."

She pulled back the furs to his waist, then turned to the bowl of water on the table. Dampening the clean cloth she had brought, Grace slowly, gently brushed it over Alastair's face. As she did so, she could feel the waves of heat radiating from his body.

"He'll catch a deathly chill if ye keep that up much longer," Edna admonished.

Grace nearly smiled. He was dying; they both knew it. Yet Edna still worried about him catching a chill. 'Twas testament indeed to how far the uncertainty and madness was spreading among them all.

"I'll not stop as long as it brings him a small measure of comfort," Grace insisted, running the cloth over his chest and arms. "God knows he's had little peace these past few weeks."

It seemed such a cruel irony that after surviving nearly seven years of warfare, Alastair was going to perish because of a hunting accident. He had been thrown from his horse and attacked by a wild boar while hunting four weeks ago. His leg had been shattered in several places, the bone poking obscenely through the flesh.

Brother John, a monk with renowned healing skills from the Turriff Monastery, had been brought to the keep. Miraculously, the monk had stitched together the worst of the mangled flesh and bound Alastair's leg, but the fever and infection raging throughout his body would not abate.

"Ye've done enough of that fer now, milady. Why

dinnae ye put down the cloth and I'll take this away before anyone sees what ye've been doing?" Edna suggested.

Ignoring her maid, Grace continued with her ministrations, admitting they brought her as much, if not more, comfort than Alastair. With this small task, she finally felt as though she was doing *something*, instead of sitting calmly at his bedside, watching him die.

The repetitious movements soon fell into a rhythm, and with that, the words that followed came naturally. Murmuring soothingly, Grace spoke of how he would be better soon. How the fever would break and his strength would return. Again and again, she dipped the cloth in the water, squeezing it dry, then wiping it over his head, shoulders, chest, and arms, all the while encouraging him to believe the impossible.

"Grace?"

"I'm right here, Alastair."

He squinted at her, his features drawn tightly in confusion. "Drink."

Grace motioned to Edna. The maid frowned again, but refrained from reminding her mistress that Brother John had forbidden his patient any liquids until the sun set. Instead, the maid poured a small amount of ale into a goblet and handed it to Grace.

She shifted so she could support Alastair's shoulders, then held the vessel to his mouth. He sipped slowly. When he was done, Grace laid him gently back on the mattress and once again covered him with the furs. His eyes fluttered closed.

Slowly, as not to jostle him, Grace stood. "Fetch me a chair, Edna."

The maid clucked her tongue. "Ever since the men

carried him home on a litter, ye've spent nearly every waking minute and half the night in this sickroom. Why dinnae ye go to yer chamber and lay down? I promise ye'll be summoned at once if there's any change in Sir Alastair's condition."

"I'm too restless to nap."

"Then go outside and take a walk in the sunshine to stretch yer muscles. 'Tis cold, but the wind is quiet and the fresh air will do ye a world of good."

For a moment Grace was tempted to comply. The days were growing shorter and colder. Soon the icy winds and snow-covered ground would make spending any time outdoors a misery. She glanced down at Alastair, running her hand over his flushed cheeks, and sighed.

Escaping from the suffocating air of gloom in the chamber sounded heavenly, yet she could not abandon her wifely duties. "Nay, Edna, I shall stay by my husband's side."

The maid shrugged with acceptance, then pulled over the requested chair. Grace had just settled herself in it when the chamber door opened.

"Good day, Lady Grace." Brother John glanced around the chamber, his brow drawing into a heavy frown when he spied the bowl of water, damp cloth, and goblet. "Have you been ignoring my orders again?" he asked, huffing with a superior air of indignity. "I have told ye repeatedly that ye must follow my instructions precisely if ye wish Sir Alastair to recover."

Grace clenched the edge of the fur blanket. "I'm only trying to ease his pain."

Muttering beneath his breath, Brother John hurried to his patient's side. Grace forced herself to rise from the chair, so the monk could attend Alastair's leg, which was braced between two long planks of wood and covered in long strips of linen. As Brother John carefully snipped away at the linen, the putrid smell of rotting flesh filled the room.

Grace's stomach heaved. Holding her hand over her nose, she glanced down at the bed. Alastair's entire leg was gray in color, tinged with streaks of bright red surrounding several gaping wounds. She took a step back, almost knocking over the chair.

"Dinnae let the odor distress ye, Lady Grace," Brother John said. "'Tis not obvious to the untrained eye, yet I can see there's been improvement." The monk managed a very slight grin, his thin lips parting to expose long, yellow teeth and a smile so condescending it was clear he thought her a simpleton.

Keeping her composure, Grace answered with a concerned frown. "His fever rages and he suffers mightily."

"'Tis God's will," Brother John replied. He slapped a foul-smelling poultice over an oozing wound, then started to reapply the dirty bandages.

Alastair let out a loud groan. Grace sprang forward, pushing her way between the monk and her husband. "Fer pity's sake, why must ye be so rough? Have ye no compassion at all?" Taking the bandages away from Brother John, Grace turned to Edna. "Fetch the clean linen ye washed yesterday. I'll bind Sir Alastair's wounds myself."

"Lady Grace—" There was a note of annoyance in Brother John's voice.

She turned and faced the monk, her expression set. "I will tend him," she insisted. Brother John's face reddened in anger. Grace could hear him grinding his teeth, but she refused to relent. Enough! How long was she to remain silent and complacent, while her husband was forced to suffer? She might not know as much about the mysteries of healing, but she could apply a dressing without causing undue pain.

The monk stood waiting for several long moments, then realizing her determination, he turned and huffed out of the chamber. Grace listened to the sound of his footsteps on the rough wooden floor until they faded into silence.

"He'll be back," Edna observed wryly.

"No doubt. This time with reinforcements. We must act quickly."

Moving as fast as possible, Grace and her maid wrapped the clean bandages around his shattered leg, struggling to avoid causing Alastair any additional pain. He made no sound while they worked, waking only when they were finished. Knowing she would have but a scant moment alone with him, Grace turned to her husband.

"Can ye tell me where it pains ye the most?"

Alastair's face lit with a ghost of a smile. "Everywhere, milady. Even my hair."

"It will get better," she whispered, hoping the lie did not reveal itself in her eyes.

"Ye've a kind heart, lass. I wish I had known ye better, wish there had been more time. . . ." His voice trailed off with a regretful sigh.

An unbearable loneliness seized her heart, followed by a stab of regret. Regret for all she'd never experienced, never had in her life. A loving husband, a gaggle of healthy children clinging to her skirts, a sense of peace and contentment. Theirs had been an arranged marriage, yet both parties had been willing. If not for the war and the years of separation, they might have had a chance to find happiness together. Or at least a peaceful contentment.

"We'll have more time together than we know what to do with, Alastair, once ye have recovered."

He grimaced. Behind his mask of pain, Grace caught a glimpse of vulnerability and it made her heart ache even more. "'Tis no use. I'm dying and there's naught anyone can do except prolong my agony. A task Brother John seems hell-bent on completing."

"His skill is widely praised," Grace replied, not knowing what else to say, for her husband spoke the truth.

Alastair reached out, his fingers surprisingly strong as they gripped her hand. "I heard him talking with his assistant last night."

"Who?"

"Brother John. My healer." Alastair rubbed his thumb over Grace's knuckles. The intimate gesture brought tears to her eyes. "The monk said as a last resort he'll cut the leg."

Grace gasped. "Ye already have enough cuts upon it. Why would he insist on more?"

"Nay, Grace, ye dinnae understand. He wants to cut the leg *off*."

Grace shook her head vehemently. "Nay, oh, nay. Alastair, ye must have misheard. 'Tis barbaric to even consider such a thing. Besides, no warrior can lead his clan with only one leg."

"Aye." Alastair sighed heavily and closed his eyes. "Ye must stop it from happening, Grace. Ye must allow me to die in peace, with all my limbs still attached to my body."

How? Clasping her husband's palms between hers, Grace leaned forward, pressing their joined hands against her chest. "If ye want to refuse the treatment, then ye must tell Brother John. Loudly. Forcefully. He'll have no choice but to obey."

"Och, lass, most days I lack the strength to open my eyes to see who is tending me." Pain and anguish filled Alastair's voice. "Ye must speak fer me."

Grace attempted a comforting smile through her tears. "They'll not listen to a woman, no matter how loudly I shriek. Can ye not ask one of yer brothers for aid?"

"I dinnae believe they would listen. Besides, 'twould be unmanly, cowardly. I dinnae want that to be my legacy."

Grace's throat constricted. Pride, 'twas always pride when it came to men. Yet while she might not agree, she did understand his feelings. "I'll do what I can," she whispered.

"Pray fer me," Alastair croaked.

"I do. Almost hourly I ask God to bring ye back to health."

A grimace of sorrow stole across her husband's face. "Nay. Pray fer death, as I do. I dinnae fear it; I welcome it. I long fer it."

Grace heard footsteps again, this time more than one set. As she predicted, Brother John had returned, bringing with him Sir Alastair's brothers, Douglas and Roderick. The three entered the room and stared at her, a myriad of expressions on their faces.

Douglas appeared concerned, Roderick wary, and

Brother John smug. Though she believed Alastair's brothers each carried a genuine affection for him, they had clear and differing opinions on his recovery. And their own particular reasons for wanting him to linger or go quickly to his final reward.

Since Alastair had no son of his own, Roderick and Douglas would each fight hard to be the one to lead the clan once Alastair was gone. If the gossip Grace heard around the castle was to be believed, Douglas currently had the most support, though Roderick was making some progress in changing the minds of his clansmen.

Thus Douglas would benefit the sooner Alastair died, while Roderick might be successful in his bid for power if given more time to garner support. 'Twas no surprise that it was Roderick who had insisted that Brother John be fetched to tend to Alastair. Indeed, no expense or effort had been spared, a commend-able occurrence if one did not delve too deeply into Roderick's ulterior motive.

"Brother John says that Alastair is much improved," Roderick exclaimed. "Does that not gladden yer heart, Grace?"

"'Twould indeed make me joyful, if it were true."

Brother John snorted. "Ye lack the knowledge to properly judge," the monk insisted. Yet she heard the clank of glass upon metal as he portioned out the medicine, and she observed his shaking hands. Despite his superior attitude and almost swaggering bravado, the monk was nervous.

They all stood silently as Brother John adminis-tered the medicine, massaging Alastair's throat to help him swallow. Nearly half the liquid dribbled out the side of his mouth. Grace moved forward to wipe it away.

"Will it aid him even if he cannae drink it properly?" Roderick asked.

"Aye," the monk replied. "A smaller amount is actually preferable. Too much might do him great harm." He secured the cork stopper on the glass bottle and it disappeared into the folds of his brown robes. "We shall wait a few more days, but if the flesh on his leg continues to rot, I shall perform the operation we discussed."

Grace turned. "Nay! Ye willnae remove his leg. I forbid it."

The three men turned toward Grace, varying degrees of shock and surprise on their faces. "Ye're too tenderhearted, Lady Grace," Brother John said. "An admirable quality, no doubt, in a female, but one that has no place in a sickroom."

"Ye will not cut off his leg," she repeated.

"I am the one in charge of Sir Alastair's health. Therefore, I am the one who will make that decision." The monk's eyes narrowed. He sounded furious.

But Grace would not relent. Still, she hesitated before speaking again. Men never liked to have their authority challenged. She moved toward Douglas, searching for an ally. "Can we not allow God to decide Alastair's fate?"

Douglas met her eyes, his face scored with genuine concern. "We must do all that we can to save him."

"Butchering him willnae save him," she dared to whisper.

The expression of compassion and concern faded from Douglas's face. "Aye."

"Do ye agree, Roderick?"

Grace could feel her legs shaking, her heart pounding, and she had the distinct feeling that she was turning red. Yet she fought hard to keep her voice calm and firm, lifting her chin in defiance. She would not acquiesce without a fight. Not when so much was at stake.

Shadows of flickering daylight softened Roderick's face and for a moment Grace dared to think he understood why this was so important. But ever the warrior, Roderick bristled against even the smallest hint of weakness. "We must do as Brother John commands."

His words chilled her. They had each acknowledged it was hopeless, yet still refused to allow Alastair a peaceful death. She sank gracefully into the hard, wooden chair and folded her hands on her lap. This battle would not be won with words or reason. She would have to find another way.

Grace sat silently as the men spoke in low tones to each other, and gradually she returned to what they expected her to be. A quiet, placid, and obedient female, content to peacefully accept what she was told, to willingly follow the dictates of men. Yet inside she seethed.

She reminded herself that there would be a price to pay for her interference. In this world and most likely the next, when she would have to stand before God and account for her earthly sins.

Yet was this a sin? Granting her husband's last wish, easing his unbearable suffering?

Three days. She had but three days to figure out a way to peacefully end her husband's suffering and hasten his leap from this life into the next. Her eyes burned and for a brief moment she was afraid she was going to cry. She curled her hands into fists, tightening them until the nails bit painfully into the soft flesh of her palms, blinking several times until the burning vanished.

Brother John turned and she heard the distinct rattle of the bottle of medicine hidden within the pocket of his robes. He had told Douglas that too much of the elixir would cause serious harm. Or perhaps death?

Grace's chest tightened. It was hard to breathe. But she knew now what she had to do.

The sun shone high overhead, yet the warmth of its golden rays did not reach the long line of weary travelers plodding across the barren landscape. The winter cold seeped into their very bones, the chilling wind stinging any exposed flesh. Sir Ewan Gilroy glanced down at the crudely drawn map, searching fruitlessly for the landmarks that would indicate they were getting close to their journey's end.

"We should have turned right at the pile of jagged rocks," an amused male voice declared.

"Shut up, Alec." Ewan squinted again at the map, annoyed to realize his close friend and captain of his guard was right. It would take nearly an hour to turn around, making their arrival before nightfall unlikely.

"The valley below is protected from the wind," Alec mused. "A good place to make camp fer the night. Do ye agree?"

"I suppose," Ewan grumbled.

"Here, let me see." Alec held out his gloved hand and Ewan reluctantly handed him the map. 'Twas a sad man indeed who could not lead his people on a true course, but Ewan was too weary to protest. Alec had ridden at his side through seven years of war and two years before that—he was the closest thing to a true brother Ewan would ever have and he trusted him completely. He also had, to Ewan's great annoyance, a skill in map reading that many, including Ewan, lacked.

"If we turn a mile up ahead, we can easily reach yer land from this side," Alec proclaimed. "Actually, it might even be a shorter route."

"Stop gloating," Ewan said with an affable grin, raising his arm to give the signal to turn.

The long line of exhausted travelers wound around like a giant serpent as they changed course, turning directly into the wind. Heads down, the group plodded onward, Ewan in the lead, Alec by his side.

They remained silent for the next few hours, alone with their thoughts as they battled the elements. At last Ewan caught sight of the five mountains indicating they were drawing near. The news spread quickly down the line, reenergizing everyone. Despite his determination to remain calm and keep his expectations realistic, Ewan's heart picked up speed as he urged his mount forward. Finally he crested the rise and got his first look at the valley below.

The sight took his breath away. Unmoving, he stared silently, barely acknowledging Alec's presence beside him.

"Mother of God," Alec swore beneath his breath.

"Indeed," Ewan answered.

He had not expected King Robert to bequeath him a grand estate. Those riches were rewarded to men of higher standing and legitimate birth. Truth be told, he was humbled to have been given any land by his king, for Ewan was one of thousands of knights who had fought to secure the crown on Robert the Bruce's head. Yet Robert had taken a liking to Ewan and he understood that rather than a trunk of gold, a true reward to a bastard son would be a property to call his own and the chance to create a lasting legacy for his progeny.

Though most of the western Highlands had supported their king's rise to power, some areas had resisted and suffered mightily for it. Apparently Ewan's new holdings had been one of them.

The valley below was stark and barren, the dry, dusty soil swirling like a cloud. On the far side, perched atop a large hill, stood the remains of the small castle, its crumbling stone walls and charred beams visible even from a distance.

"The mountains on either side create a natural defense," Alec offered.

"One would think," Ewan muttered. "Yet clearly they were not enough to hold back Robert's troops."

Blackened areas where cottages had stood marred the peaceful view. Most of the structures that were intact looked as though a strong wind would blow them over. There was no smoke from any cooking fires coming from the cottages, no sounds of livestock or people, no signs of any life at all.

"Do ye think it's entirely deserted?" Alec asked.

"'Tis best to assume that some still reside in this godforsaken place," Ewan replied. "Just to be safe."

Ewan drew his sword. A select band of his best warriors did the same. Falling in beside him, they rode into the valley, leaving the rest of the party to wait until they were summoned.

As they drew closer to the keep, they discovered a cluster of cottages in somewhat better condition, most boasting four walls and sturdy roofs. Without warning, two frightened pairs of eyes suddenly appeared in a cottage window, then disappeared in an instant.

"Did ye see that?" Alec asked.

"Aye," Ewan replied. "There's more than a few pairs of eyes trained upon us. Yet I dinnae fear we are riding into an ambush. From what I can see, 'tis mostly young faces and women peering out."

The slightly improved conditions of the property vanished once they reached the drawbridge of the castle. The thick oak door had been smashed to pieces, most likely with an iron-tipped battering ram. The stone steps leading to the battlements were scattered throughout the bailey, the rooftops of each of the four corner towers charred and splintered. A few rusted swords were ground into the dirt, testament to the fierce hand-to-hand combat that bespoke of the intensity and carnage of the final battle.

The gaping hole at the entrance to the great hall allowed Ewan to see clear through to the other side and he quickly realized it was uninhabitable. Additional holes in the roof had left the interior exposed to the elements for years; it would take a crew of men weeks to make the necessary repairs before anyone could live in it.

Once gathered in the bailey, the men dismounted. Ewan turned in a complete circle to view every inch of his domain. Despite the disappointment at the appalling conditions, his heart pummeled in his chest. *Mine. My castle. My lands. My legacy.* It was exhilarating, intoxicating to realize how far he had risen in the world. From a starving, neglected, discarded bastard son of an earl to a laird of his own lands. An impossible dream for most, yet he had somehow achieved it.

With a blood-chilling battle cry, Ewan thrust his sword into the ground, then lowered himself to one knee and bowed his head. His prayers for the future were silent and heartfelt. *Let us have peace and prosperity and a wee bit of fun.*

When he was finished, Ewan rose and regarded his men. "Ye four go out to the cottages and rouse the village folk. 'Tis time we all met."

One of the men leered a smile. Ewan sent him a warning glare and added, "Dinnae draw sword or dirk unless ye are challenged. We want to live among these people, not scare them witless."

Ewan waited patiently for the men to carry out his orders. It didn't take long for them to round up a sad-looking collection of old men, young children, and frightened women. Dressed in little more than rags, they stood huddled together inside the crumbling bailey, their eyes darting suspiciously in all directions.

"Is this everyone?" Ewan asked one of the old men.

"Aye," he answered, straightening his crooked back. "Though there will be far fewer alive once the winter sets in fully."

A flash of pity burned in Ewan's gut. 'Twas a harsh life, and though he vowed to try his best, he knew he could not alleviate all the pain and suffering that came with struggling to survive in such a brutal place.

"I am Sir Ewan Gilroy, newly appointed laird of these lands and Tiree Keep," he shouted, his deep voice rumbling through the ruins. "At the bequest of our great King Robert, my men and I have come to rebuild this property and renew the bounty of the land. I will accept the pledges of all those who are willing to remain here and swear allegiance to me. In exchange, I vow that ye shall live here in peace and prosperity under my rule and protection."

There was complete silence, then a few murmurs of fear and suspicion rumbled through the air. Ewan stood tall and proud, waiting for the first brave soul to break ranks and declare his intentions. He stared hard in turn at each of the old men, but surprisingly it was one of the women who stepped forward.

"What happens if we choose to leave?"

A raw tension stretched through the bailey at the bold question. "Ye'll have till daybreak to pack what ye can carry and be gone from my land."

"Ye'll not force us to stay?" she asked, the doubt clear in her voice.

"Nay." Some might think that a foolish answer, but Ewan calculated that if they had somewhere better to go, then they would have already fled. Besides, a pledge freely given had far more potency than one forced at sword point.

Nervous whispering among the villagers began and then slowly, one by one, they dropped to their knees and bowed their heads, until each and every one was prostrate. A rush of triumph seared Ewan's soul at this first clear victory, accomplished without harsh threats or bloodshed.

"Wonderful," Alec drawled beside him. "More mouths to feed."

"Ye'll be glad they are here come spring when the

crops need to be planted," Ewan said beneath his breath.

"That's assuming we'll still be alive in the spring," Alec grumbled, yet he smiled in irony as he spoke.

Ewan gave him a sobering look, then turned to the villagers. "Tonight we will feast together on the fresh game my men and I hunted this morning," he announced with quiet authority. "Tomorrow, we will start to rebuild the castle and yer cottages."

The mood of the crowd changed in an instant. The stiff tension eased and cautious smiles appeared. Not a bad beginning, yet Ewan knew he would have to prove his intentions with deeds, not empty promises.

The bailey soon came alive with the sounds of preparations. Carts were unloaded, tents erected, sleeping quarters discussed. Ewan stood in the midst of it all, enjoying the commotion and activity, until he spied his mother gingerly making her way across the bailey, her pinched-faced maid at her side.

"I dinnae understand why you gave the order to unload the carts," Lady Moira Gilroy said with annoyance. "Ye cannae possibly intend fer us to stay here tonight."

"We shall sleep in our tents, as we did on those nights we couldnae find shelter during our journey here."

Lady Moira stared blankly at him for a moment, then laughed aloud. "Surely ye are jesting, Ewan."

"Do I look amused, Mother?"

"Nay, ye look like a simpleton, preening like a proud peacock. Well, 'tis no great favor King Robert has done ye, my son, granting ye a pile of burned out rubbish and calling it a reward. 'Tis disgraceful."

Ewan sighed. "I'll be sure to share yer opinion of his gift the next time I'm in the king's presence."

"This place is a hovel," she declared, turning up her nose. "If you stubbornly insist on staying, then we must take up residency in the cottages. I noticed a few of them were not completely destroyed."

"I'll not be turning folks out of their homes."

"Ye are laird here now." His mother took hold of his arm, her expression anxious. "Ye must establish yer authority or else ye'll never be respected and obeyed."

Ewan gently patted his mother's wrist. Life had been unkind to Moira Gilroy. Raised to be a lady, the life she had envisioned never materialized. It vanished when she became pregnant and bore an illegitimate child. Cast out by her family, disgraced and forsaken by the father of her only child, she had struggled to keep herself and Ewan alive.

"Ye have to trust me, Mother. I know what I'm doing."

Her reply was a disbelieving snort. Ewan refused to acknowledge it. With a reassuring smile, he turned to direct his men, though deep in his gut he was silently wishing he possessed at least half the confidence of success he so brashly portrayed to the world.

Chapter Two

Grace turned at the sound of her bedchamber door opening, relieved to see it was Edna. In her hands the maid carried Grace's midday meal, but Grace had no interest in the food. Even if she had, she knew it would be near impossible to eat, for in the week since Alastair's death her stomach seemed to be tied in a permanent knot.

Sadness, everyone said. The result of respectful mourning from a pious wife and gentle lady. But Grace knew the truth. 'Twas guilt over the part she had played in her husband's demise, mixed with a strong measure of fear, that kept her stomach churning and her nights sleepless.

"Well, 'tis finally decided," Edna huffed, as she set the plate of warm food on a small table. "Douglas will be the next clan chief."

"How did Roderick take the news?"

"Poorly." Edna nudged the bowl of stew closer to Grace. "His face was a thundercloud when it was announced and he stormed from the hall cursing a blue streak. A group of his most loyal men followed behind."

Grace turned her back on the food and sighed. "Will he challenge his brother?"

Edna shrugged. "Who knows? Some say he will, but most dinnae think he will be so foolish."

Grace frowned. She had little faith in the good sense of men, especially when they were angry. Especially when they were denied something they wanted so badly.

A noise at the chamber door distracted her. Lifting her head, Grace barely stifled a shriek at the sight of Roderick in the doorway. He glanced at Grace with narrowed eyes, then gestured to Edna. "Leave us."

The maid scurried closer to Grace. Though grateful for the support, Grace could see the gesture only succeeded in angering Roderick. "Please fetch me some wine, Edna," she said, dismissing the servant.

Roderick moved toward her the moment they were alone. "Ye've heard the news about Douglas?"

"Aye, Edna just told me he'll be chief."

"Does it please ye?"

"I'm glad it has been settled, for the sake of the clan."

Roderick's eyes turned suspicious. "Would ye be as glad, I wonder, if I had been named chief?"

"Of course."

"I dinnae believe it." He leaned in close, his face nearly touching hers. "I've some questions I want answered about the night that Alastair died."

Grace backed away and averted her eyes. "'Tis a raw and painful memory and much too soon to speak of that tragic night."

Roderick reached out, grasping her chin in the

palm of his hand and jerking it upward. "Is that a guilty look I see?"

"Ye are speaking nonsense," Grace bristled. She kept her eyes upon him, though his searing look made her skin crawl.

"I think not." Roderick squeezed his fingers and a sharp stab of pain shot through Grace's jaw. "Tell me true, are ye in league with Douglas?"

"Nay!" Grace shut her eyes to gather her composure. *'Tis no more than I deserve, dear Lord, and yet I ask fer mercy.*

"Dinnae look so surprised by the question." Roderick's face tightened with annoyance. "No one can deny that Douglas benefited from Alastair's quick passing. And ye, milady, were the only one with Alastair when he died."

Grace held back a gasp. *Quick?* The poor man had suffered mightily for weeks. "'Twas hardly unusual that I was with my husband when he died. I stayed at his bedside throughout his illness."

"I spoke with Brother John the morning of the funeral. He told me that ye insisted he leave the chamber that night. Why?"

Grace twisted out of Roderick's cruel grip and stepped away, turning her back to him. It was too hard to answer these questions under his sharp, accusing gaze. "Brother John was clearly exhausted. I merely suggested that he take a few hours to rest before returning to care fer Alastair."

"The monk said ye repeatedly insisted that he leave the sickroom."

"I did no such thing," Grace answered truthfully. It had taken little persuasion that night to get Brother

John to seek the comfort of his own bed. Getting a lethal dose of medicine, however, had been a far more daunting task.

"Brother John said that Alastair was improving."

"Och, Roderick, ye cannae believe it. Ye saw him yerself. Alastair was dying and there was nothing anyone could do to save him."

He moved behind her, put his hands on her shoulders, and forced her to turn. "Are ye speaking the truth?"

"I have no reason to lie."

Roderick's face filled with fury. "Ye've every reason to lie and we both know it. If Alastair had lived but a few more weeks, then I would be chief, not Douglas."

Grace opened her lips to protest, then closed them without saying a word. Jaw set, eyes grim, she saw there was no argument she could present that would sway Roderick from that belief.

"Ye cannae undue the past, Roderick. Best to go forward and accept God's will."

"I cannae. I willnae." Roderick blinked and something dark shifted in his eyes. "Be warned. The longer ye keep to yer lies, the harder it will be on ye when I uncover these falsehoods and take vengeance against my enemies."

Roderick slammed the door hard as he left. It took four deep breaths before Grace could find the strength to guide her shaking legs and collapse on the chair. She didn't even notice that Edna had returned until the maid spoke to her.

"Take a good long drink." Edna held out a wine goblet.

Though tempted, Grace shook her head and woodenly turned to the maid. "Roderick suspects I was involved in Alastair's death. He threatened a mighty vengeance."

The maid paled. They had never spoken of that night, but Grace was aware that Edna knew something was amiss. And the loyal maid refused to judge, an action for which Grace was profoundly grateful.

"'Tis no longer safe fer ye here," Edna whispered. "We need to go home, milady."

Grace swallowed hard. Home. Where exactly was home? Promised to the church as an infant, Grace had been taken to the Convent of the Sacred Heart at the age of five, a few months after her mother had died. The dedicated nuns had raised her, preparing her for a spiritual life that had never come to pass. Her brother, Brian McKenna, had plucked her from the convent when she was barely fifteen and married her to Alastair, to secure an alliance with the Fergusons.

As Alastair's wife she had been treated with respect and deference, but she stood apart from the clan. Young, unsure of herself, and naturally shy, Grace had been unable to form any deep bonds of friendship with the wives and daughters of the clan. Perhaps if Alastair had been there to smooth the way for her, she would have learned how to accomplish that much-desired goal. But the reality remained that despite being married to the clan chief, she was an outsider.

"Do ye think my brother would welcome me if I went to him?" Grace asked anxiously.

Edna nodded. "Ye're his blood. And the McKennas always care fer their own."

"Won't I look guilty if I run?"

"Nay. Ye're a widow with no children. There's no reason not to return to yer family. I think that most would expect it." Edna sat on the edge of the bed, absently taking a sip from the wine goblet Grace had refused. "Ye'll have to ask Douglas fer an escort."

Grace flushed. "What if he commands Roderick to do the deed? I'll not be safe with him and certainly cannae tell Douglas why."

"Aye. Ye'll have to get word to yer brother without either man knowing and ask fer a McKenna guard to be sent here to bring us home."

More intrigue? When would it end? Grace sighed. She was a simple woman, used to living a quiet life of wifely duties, attending to the running of her household, acting with the decorum and piety befitting a woman of her stature. This sort of clandestine behavior went against her experience, as well as her nature. Yet she was quickly learning it was but part of the price she'd have to pay for her actions.

Ewan pulled alongside the small river, dismounted, then casually held the reins while allowing his horse to drink. They had traveled a fair distance this day and the animal deserved a reward. As he waited for the stallion to drink his fill, Ewan lifted his face toward the late afternoon sun and closed his eyes. After all the constant activity and noise at the castle, the silence around him was soothing.

He took a deep breath. The faint hint of heather in the air foretold of the coming spring and the familiar, comforting scent buoyed his spirits.

Somehow they had survived the first winter at Tiree with only a few deaths—three villagers to old age and two of his guardsmen to a mysterious sweating sickness. Food had not always been plentiful, yet

Ewan felt a sense of pride that none had died from starvation or exposure to the harsh winter cold. He had worked hard to do all that he promised, providing food and shelter for everyone, but he also acknowledged they had been lucky.

Spring would bring the rebirth of the land, summer milder weather, and hopefully in the fall, a bountiful harvest. Yet it was essential that they now plant as many fields as possible, hunt as much game as they could find, and store away an abundance of food and fuel in anticipation of the next winter. A man's luck, as Ewan knew all too well, did not last indefinitely.

He heard the sound of footsteps approaching, but didn't bother to open his eyes. He was safe enough on his own land, especially this close to the keep. *My own land. Will I ever get used to saying that, I wonder?*

"I overheard Margaret and Colleen talking in the kitchen this morning," a female voice announced. "They remarked with the snow starting to melt, the priest should arrive earlier than usual, most likely in a few weeks' time."

With an ironic smile, Ewan turned to his mother. "Have ye a burning need to make yer confession and seek absolution fer yer sins? Is that why ye are so anxious to see a priest, Mother?"

Lady Moira drew in a still breath. She had fared well through the harsh winter, losing none of her strength or edge. "I've little use fer men of the cloth, as ye well know. I was referring to yer needs."

Ewan scrutinized his mother in puzzlement. "I'm not in need of a confessor or a priest."

"I never thought ye were." Moira glanced away, looking out at the budding greenery. "But ye need to seriously think about taking a wife, Ewan, and saying yer vows when the priest arrives. It might be as long as a year before he returns. If ye wait much longer, all the good women will be taken."

"All of them?" Ewan answered with a teasing smile, but Lady Moira was not amused. The furrow between her brows, which seemed to be a permanent fixture on her forehead ever since he could remember, deepened.

"Ye can scoff at my blunt tongue as much as ye like, but I'll not soften the truth. Ye need an heir to carry forth yer legacy, and fer that, ye need a wife."

Though he fought against it, Ewan felt his heart start to pound. 'Twas irritating enough having a lecture from his mother; 'twas worse when she was right. He did need a wife and for more than a broodmare.

Since arriving at the keep, he had worked beside his men from dawn till dusk, rebuilding his castle, protecting his lands, and providing for the villagers. Exhausted, he fell into his cold, lonely bed each night, wondering why the sense of accomplishment and pride he felt wasn't enough. Would all of this mean more if there was someone to appreciate his efforts, to benefit from his success, to share in his good fortune?

It seemed such a ridiculous notion, yet alone in the darkness he acknowledged that was what he needed, he wanted. A female companion who would sit at his side in front of the evening fire, listening to his stories with admiration shining in her eyes. A willing lass who would warm his bed and laugh at his jokes. A kind woman who would offer her opinions when asked, and hold her tongue when required.

Who would bare his children and mother their bairns with love and tenderness.

In short, he wanted a woman to share his life.

Shaking his head, Ewan nearly burst out laughing. Ever since he had been old enough to fondle and bed a woman, he had avoided emotional entanglements and commitments. Yet now it seemed as though he thought of little else. *Peacetime must addle a man's brain,* he decided.

"A wife would be useful," he said cautiously. "Yet it is neither a decision I'll make hastily nor an obligation I'll take lightly."

His mother nodded with approval. "I'll not have a son of mine treat any woman with disrespect. 'Tis part of the reason I encouraged ye to order yer men not to force any of the village women into their beds."

"That decree has hastened several marriage proposals."

"Aye, that's why I'm pressing ye to make yer choice," Lady Moira exclaimed. "Besides, the castle needs a woman to run it properly."

Ewan was surprised by that revelation, for his mother seemed to relish taking charge of his household. After decades of being treated as a disgraced, fallen woman, Lady Moira was finally being given the respect she was due and she appeared to relish the role. How would she truly feel if a younger woman replaced her?

"I've no complaints with the job ye're doing," Ewan said.

"I've earned a rest," Moira snapped. "'Tis yer wife who should be running yer household and seeing to the welfare of yer people, not yer mother."

Knowing he shouldn't encourage her, yet unable to stop himself, Ewan asked, "I suppose ye've already decided which woman I should marry."

Moira's face brightened. "There are many worthy women in the village, but I've noticed that Margaret often gives ye special looks."

Ewan shook his head. "Margaret gives all my men special looks."

Moira shrugged. "Aye, I had noticed that she can be a bit bold at times. How about Deirdre? She's not afraid of hard work and seems to be a natural leader among the other women."

"Deirdre is a fine lass, but surely ye've noticed how Alec cannae keep his eyes from straying toward her every time she walks into a room."

Moira waved her hand dismissively. "No matter. Ye're the laird of these lands, the leader of all who reside here. If ye want her, then ye should have her. I'd wager she'd much prefer her position as yer wife than Alec's."

Ewan jerked his head toward his mother. "I've too much respect fer Alec to take something he wants from under his nose. Especially since she means little to me and a great deal to him."

Ewan heard his mother sigh. "If not the fair Deirdre, then who?" she asked.

Ewan squashed the urge to turn and stomp away. 'Twas none of his mother's business who and when he married, but he would have to be a blind fool to miss the hard determination shining in his mother's eyes. Moira Gilroy was not going to be denied; she intended to discuss the matter here and now.

"I plan to travel south to find my bride."

Lady Moira shook her head. "It will be hard fer a

village lass to be accepted here. Many willnae want to leave their families, either, no matter how much ye sweet talk them."

"I'm flattered by yer confidence in my abilities to charm a woman. The truth is I'm going to search fer a female who expects to leave her home."

His mother's deepening frown of confusion forced Ewan to elaborate—something he had hoped to avoid. "I'm going to wed a woman raised to be a lady."

"None will have ye."

Ewan glanced at her in irritation. Honestly, should he have expected anything less than her full censure? "Class lines have been a bit blurred with the war. I'm a knight, trusted by my king, and a man of property."

"Ye are a bastard, first, last, and always. No chief or laird will offer ye anything but the dregs, the impure, unfit females in his family, those that no others will have or want."

As much as he longed to deny it, Ewan knew there was some truth to his mother's cruel words. Yet he refused to believe the situation was so dire. Standing in the valley, surveying the land he now owned, Ewan renewed his resolve to achieve all that he desired, all that he dared to dream.

Including a noble wife.

Alec approached on horseback. Ewan noticed him pull back on the reins and slow his mount when he caught sight of Lady Moira. His mother must have also seen Alec approaching, for she let out a most unfeminine snort and began walking away.

After a few steps she halted, then turned to face Ewan. "I'm feeling desperate enough over the matter that I'd even considered asking Alec to talk some sense into ye, but I know it would be a waste of my breath. He only echoes yer opinions and never expresses his own."

"Perhaps in this instance his opinion is in agreement with mine," Ewan replied.

Lady Moira let out an even louder snort, then turned and walked away. Expression puzzled, Alec dismounted and came to stand beside Ewan.

"I believe I've just been insulted by yer mother," he said. "Again."

"Pay it no mind." Ewan snatched a flat rock from the riverbed and flung it into the water. "My mother and I have been discussing my future wife."

"Yer scowl tells me it wasnae a pleasant conversation."

"Is it ever?" Ewan picked up a second rock and let it fly. "I must make a match with a woman who possesses a substantial dowry. We need seeds, grain, livestock, and coin in order to survive another winter."

"Aye. But does it have to be a bride bringing it all to ye?"

"Who else?"

"Ye could ask the earl fer a loan," Alec suggested.

Ewan frowned at the mention of his older half brother. "I'd rather eat my sword than go to Kirkland fer help," he stated emphatically.

"Och, now dinnae be shy. Tell me what ye truly think of my advice."

Ewan laughed appreciatively. "There's no other way, Alec. I've thought long and hard about it and I know what needs to be done. 'Tis a wealthy bride I seek and I'll not be complaining if she's fair to look at and siren in my bed. Will ye accompany me on my quest?"

"Aye. I cannae miss the chance to see ye make an arse of yerself over a woman, now can I? When do we leave?"

The squeal of childish laughter rang through the solid timbers of the McKenna great hall and bounced off the stone walls. Malcolm McKenna, age six, oldest son of the laird and the acknowledged ringleader of his siblings, pressed his younger brother and sister closer behind his aunt's skirts. Grace smiled down at the trio and obligingly moved into position, willingly acting as a human shield.

"Ye'll never find us now, ye mighty dragon," Malcolm called out with bravado, then tried unsuccessfully to hush his sister's nervous giggles.

The mighty dragon—Sir Brian McKenna, chief of the clan, laird of these lands and father to this raucous brood—crouched low and let out a fiendish growl. "Ye cannae hide from me! I'm coming to get ye and woe to the first lad or lass I capture in my evil grip."

More nervous giggles followed as Brian stomped about the great hall, slowly circling toward Grace. She could feel the back of her skirt being pulled by anxious little fists as the mighty dragon came nearer and nearer.

Baring his teeth, the dragon let out an exaggerated roar. At the fierce noise the children broke ranks and ran in three different directions. Brian winked at Grace before reaching out a long arm and scooping up his daughter. Katherine let out an ear-splitting squeal, causing Brian to roar louder, making the child burst into excited giggles.

The capture brought her brothers, along with two of the castle hounds, into the fray. Malcolm jumped on the dragon's back, while James clasped his arms around the dragon's leg, hanging on tightly even as the leg was lifted in the air and swung in a circle. One hound began barking, the other howled, and all three children screamed. The din was so loud several servants in the hall moved to cover their ears.

'Twas chaos, pure and simple. And Grace loved every minute of it.

The game continued. Brian released his prey and the children ran for cover, imploring Grace to save them. Smiling, she pointed to the best hiding spots, then stood in front of her brother and made a great show of trying to hold him back.

He neatly sidestepped her and soon had all three of his youngsters once again hanging off his solid frame, their screams and laughter filling the entire castle.

"Och, Brian McKenna, have ye lost what little sense the good Lord gave ye?" Lady Aileen asked as she entered the great hall, her protruding belly leading the way. "I thought ye were out on the practice field with yer men, but instead I find ye racing around the hall like a half-wit, screeching at the bairns until they are near to having fits. I ask ye, how are we ever going to get them to settle down fer an afternoon nap?"

"I'll tire them out with play," Brian answered.

"I'm too old fer naps," Malcolm declared, poking his head out from behind his father's shoulder.

"Me, too," James piped up.

"Mind yer tongues when speaking to yer mother, lads," Brian lectured, a trace of laughter in his voice.

Arms on her hips, Aileen McKenna glared at her husband and children. "Well now, we'll see just how funny ye think this is when they're whining through their evening meal and then they crowd into our bed in the middle of the night because nightmares about dragons are keeping them from a peaceful slumber."

Brian's expression sobered. He swung Malcolm off his back, then pried James from his leg and carefully set Katherine on her feet. Lining the trio up in size order, he glanced down at his children. "There'll be no crying and no nightmares from any of ye tonight. Understood?"

The three little heads bobbed in unison. Grace moved her hand to her mouth to hide her grin. Brian turned toward his wife with a satisfied air, as if the matter had been neatly settled, but his victory was interrupted by his wife's smirk.

"They'd agree to eat a dragon to keep the game going. Am I right, Grace?"

"Aye, Aileen." In the six months that she had lived with her brother and his family, Grace had learned 'twas always best to agree with her sister-in-law. Brian McKenna might rule his men and his lands with a mighty fist and a strong will, but Aileen McKenna ruled her husband. "They'll give any excuse to keep playing with their da."

"That's 'cause he's the biggest bairn of all," Aileen said.

"'Tis true—and ye love me fer it, lass." Brian grinned unapologetically.

Aileen slapped her husband on the shoulder. Brian reached out, snaking his arm around her rounded waist, pulling her forcefully against his chest. Aileen made a great show of resisting, until Brian leaned down and whispered in her ear.

Aileen's lips parted in a radiant smile. The mother of three, with another on the way, she glowed with a special inner beauty. Yet it always seemed to shine brightest when her husband was near.

"He thinks to sweet talk me into letting them continue with their play," Aileen said wryly.

"Aye, 'tis how a proper husband acts, right, Grace? And something that I know ye'll be sorely missing if ye keep to yer plan to return to the convent."

Grace worked hard to keep her face impassive. It was hardly the first time she had heard a similar comment from Brian. With her mourning ending, her brother often made reference to the delights of marrying again.

Grace swallowed hard. Brian and Aileen had done so much for her. The last thing she wanted was to insult or offend them. But marriage? Never again.

"We've agreed that Grace will make the decision about her future when she is ready," Aileen lectured, glancing pointedly at her husband.

"Aileen."

"Ye heard me."

"I dinnae agree to allow Grace to make the decision all on her own," Brian insisted.

"Aye, ye did."

"I've changed my mind."

"Ye cannae," Aileen huffed. "And that's final."

Brian tilted his head and stared at his wife until she broke into a slow grin. The love between them was so open and tangible it filled the room. Grace quickly lowered her chin, feeling as though she was spying on something private, intimate. She fought the tightness in her throat, suppressing the envy she felt.

No man had ever looked at her that way. And no man ever would.

The matter of Grace marrying again was dropped. The debate over whether or not the children should continue with their boisterous play took its place, until they were interrupted by a soldier entering the great hall. "Riders approach."

Brian's entire demeanor instantly changed. Gone was the carefree father amusing his children and in its place was the forceful leader. "Can ye see their colors?"

The soldier shook his head. "They're too far away. The sun's at their backs and in our eyes."

"Raise the portcullis and have our best archers posted on the battlements."

Grace felt her heart accelerate and she chastised herself for being foolish. Her brother would keep them safe. The McKenna Castle was well fortified, well armed, and filled with some of the fiercest warriors in the Highlands.

"Are ye expecting a visit from yer father or any of yer kin?" Brian asked his wife.

"Nay. They know I'll send word once the babe is born and that willnae be fer at least another month." Aileen looked at Grace. "Perhaps it's one of yer brothers-in-law? 'Twould be a fitting show of respect if Douglas or Roderick came to see how ye're faring, Grace."

Grace's heart froze at Aileen's innocent remark, and a sharp sense of foreboding ran through her. She had said nothing to her brother or sister-in-law about the nature of Alastair's death. An unexpected appearance by either Douglas or Roderick could only mean trouble for all of them.

"We shall hope that it is a friend and not an enemy approaching," Brian said. "But until I know fer certain, I want both of ye and the bairns to stay in the third-floor solar."

"I'd like—"

"No arguments, Aileen," Brian admonished. Softening, he touched her cheek with the back of his finger. "I'll send word as soon as I know 'tis safe."

Heavy broadsword in hand, he gave his wife a swift kiss on her brow and hastened from the room.

Chapter Three

The sunshine bathed Ewan's head in pleasant warmth, almost as though it were trying to offer him comfort against the effects of the cool wind blowing through his body. Looking over his shoulder, he glanced down the line at the mounted men who rode behind him, their expressions tired and bored. They were a rather sorry-looking group, yet he could not fault them for their lethargy. He had never imagined his quest south to find a bride would have taken so long—and been so fruitless.

Oh, he had been received with courtesy, if not enthusiasm, at each castle he visited. But the friendly welcome quickly turned to mistrust when he declared his intentions to wed, and one by one the female relations of the family became mysteriously absent. A few of his noble hosts had made the effort to avoid insulting him directly, but the message was clear—his suit was not looked upon with favor or enthusiasm.

Despite his determination not to, Ewan was unable to dispel the sense of unworthiness that stirred within him. Would he never be judged as a man, on the strength of his merits? Would he always be tied to his illegitimate birth—examined and found wanting no matter how much he accomplished or how high he rose?

He didn't know what annoyed him more—the fact that he had been rejected or the realization that he couldn't easily disband the notion of wedding a lady from a good family. 'Twould truly be much easier if he followed his mother's advice and married a simple village girl.

Ewan sighed. The truth was he might very well be doing just that if Brian McKenna could not provide him with an alternative. After the last disastrous attempt at making a match, Ewan decided to seek out his friend. He was hoping Brian might know of a clan with a marriageable female that would be amenable to forging an alliance with him. Hell, he was even willing to swallow his pride and ask the McKenna to broker the marriage if necessary.

Though another part of him was tempted to turn tail and run. To return home still unwed and think about getting married next year. Or the year after.

A faint ringing sound vibrated through the still air. Raising his head, Ewan caught sight of their destination on the horizon, a mammoth structure of stone towers, battlements, and protective walls.

"It appears that we have been sighted," Alec commented, bringing his horse alongside Ewan's. "And considered to be hostile, judging by the sound of those alarm bells."

"I dinnae understand why. The castle is as well fortified as McKenna always bragged," Ewan observed, his eyes trained upon the tall towers and high stone curtain wall, with a second wall behind it.

Ewan gave the order for his men to close ranks. He slowed their approach, but the warning bells continued to ring out. In fact, the ringing seemed to be spreading from one tower to the next, until a steady chime blanketed the land.

"The McKennas dinnae appear to be a friendly sort," Alec commented as several archers took up positions on the battlements, their arrows already notched and ready to fly. "Having fought beside Brian McKenna for the king's cause for many years, I willnae be surprised to discover they are the kind of warriors who will shoot an arrow first and ask questions later."

For the first time that day, Ewan smiled. "We are a small group of men. I understand the need to be suspicious of strangers riding up to yer gates, yet 'tis clear we pose no grave threat. Even McKenna knows it will take far more than this sad lot to successfully storm his walls."

Ewan's words proved to be correct. After giving his name to the captain of the guard and requesting to speak with the McKenna, the thick oak drawbridge was slowly lowered. As they rode into the bustling bailey, Ewan spotted Brian McKenna standing in the arched doorway to his great hall. A tall, broad, heavily muscled warrior, the McKenna broke into a genuine grin when he recognized his friend.

"Have ye already grown tired of living among us, in the deepest part of the northern Highlands?" Brian asked.

"Aye. That's why I've rode south, to see how soft and easy life is fer all of ye."

"Och, 'tis the Lowlanders that live a life of ease, as ye well know. After all, that's where ye were raised."

Ewan smiled, taking the jest in the good humor it was intended. He swung himself over his horse and landed neatly on his feet. The men embraced, leaving Ewan surprised at how much seeing Brian lightened his dark mood.

"I've a warm hearth, plenty of ale, and a hearty meal to bid ye welcome," Brian said as they entered the great hall.

"It sounds heavenly, but I need to ask if yer wife knows that it's me who's come calling."

The question stopped Brian in his tracks. "I'd forgotten that ye're acquainted with my Aileen."

"I'd hardly call it an acquaintance, dear husband." Aileen Sinclair McKenna emerged from the shadows, bristling with indignation. "Sir Ewan and I spent a most unpleasant afternoon together a very long time ago."

Brian's puzzled frown slowly cleared as comprehension dawned. "Aye, that's right. I'd forgotten that as a wild young lad ye kidnapped my wife."

"I haven't forgotten," Aileen bit out, coming to stand toe-to-toe with her unexpected guest.

Ewan barely managed to keep from fidgeting. It had been nearly eight years since he had last seen her, but time had been kind to Aileen. Her features were still as pretty, her complexion just as fair, her hair an enticing shade of red. Even heavy with child, she had a fresh, girlish way about her. Well, except for the sparkling eyes that were now shooting daggers at him.

"'Tis a delight to see ye, Lady Aileen," Ewan drawled. "May I say ye are looking just as beautiful and radiant as I remember?"

"Ye may say whatever ye wish, but dinnae think yer winsome smile and blatant flattery will change my mind about ye, Ewan Gilroy. Ye're a scoundrel and a rogue from the top of yer head to the tip of yer toes."

For a moment Ewan didn't reply. Then he took a step closer and cleared his throat. "Guilty as charged, milady. Yet ye must admit that ye came to no real harm when ye were in my uhm . . . care. In fact, one could say ye have me to thank fer yer current happy circumstance. Ye might very well have ended up married to my half brother if not fer my timely intervention."

"Och, now dinnae be getting all full of yerself," Aileen scoffed, returning his stare without flinching. "I've the brains and courage to find my own path in life and that never included being the wife of the Earl of Kirkland."

Time, it appeared, had not dulled any of Lady Aileen's spirit. Remembering all too well the experience of witnessing her temper, Ewan strove to change the direction of their conversation. "Aye, the McKenna are lucky indeed to have ye as their lady. While on campaign, Brian was near pitiful, complaining constantly of missing his beautiful wife."

The edge of a smile crept onto Aileen's face, though she tried to hide it. Seizing the moment, Ewan reached for her hand. Raising the back to his lips, he pressed against her knuckles in a courtly gesture of honor and respect.

"Ewan speaks the truth," Brian said cheerfully, as he pointedly maneuvered himself between Ewan and his wife, effectively breaking their physical contact. "Though there were some who thought it unmanly to hear me pine fer my bride so openly, none dared to challenge the depth of my discomfort."

Aileen raised a disbelieving eyebrow. "Enough. Both of ye. Sir Ewan is welcome in our home as long as he gives his word he will act with knightly honor."

Ewan held up his hand. "I shall."

"And I will make certain that he does," Brian said as he put his arm around his wife.

Aileen's expression softened and she leaned back into her husband's embrace. He whispered something in her ear and she shook her head, then lowered her chin. Knowing Brian's bawdy nature, along with the telltale blush on Aileen's cheeks, left little doubt in Ewan's mind that the comment had been sexual in nature. And most likely inappropriate.

Still blushing, Aileen left, promising to send in refreshments. At Brian's urging, they climbed the dais and sat at the long wooden table. Though they had not seen each other for over a year, it took no time at all to reestablish their friendship. They spoke of shared memories and recollections of the men they fought with and exchanged information about the king.

As they talked, Ewan noticed two young boys sneaking peeks at him from behind a tapestry. Apparently, Brian did also.

"No need to be skittish, lads," Brian bellowed. "'Tis not the damn English come to murder ye in yer beds, but Sir Ewan Gilroy, a knight brave and true and a favorite of King Robert. Come and meet him."

With a familiar swagger that clearly labeled them Brian's sons, the two youngsters approached. The pride in the McKenna's voice was unmistakable as he introduced the lads, then sent them scampering off with orders to see what had happened to the promised refreshments. Obeying their father with worshipful enthusiasm, the boys nearly collided with the servants bringing in the trays as they left.

Trays piled high with food and pitchers of ale were placed in front of them. Ewan glanced at the opposite end of the great hall, pleased to see Alec and his men were also being served refreshments and were joined by a cordial-looking group of McKenna soldiers.

Ewan took a few minutes to consume a good portion of the simple fare, deciding that food eaten in the home of a friend had a far better taste and lay warm and comforting in his stomach. Feeling relaxed for the first time since starting his journey, he allowed himself to savor the restful feeling.

A log popped and shifted in the enormous fireplace, sending sparks flying. Ignoring the noise, Brian poured another tankard of ale for each of them.

"Why are ye not up in the north, freezing yer arse off at the keep the king gifted ye?" he asked. "What is it called? Tirra?"

"Tiree. 'Tis a fine piece of land, with a small village of folk and a strong, fortified keep. Well, fortified now that we've rebuilt most of the walls." Ewan leaned back, sinking into the thick pillow that covered the seat of his chair. "I'm surprised to realize how much I miss it, but this journey is important. I've come south in search of a bride."

Brian's brow lifted in surprise. "As I remember, ye never had to go very far to find a willing lass, and that was only fer a dalliance. Dangle the prize of being yer wife and they'll be lining up all the way down to the border."

"If only it were so simple." Ewan grimaced. "I've

discovered that many a good man looks down his nose at someone of my birth."

"Yer father was an earl."

"Aye. An earl who refused to marry my mother."

Brian tipped back his tankard and finished it. Wiping his sleeve across his mouth, he broke into a friendly grin. "Do ye have any special requirements fer yer bride?"

Ewan shrugged. "I'd like to find a lady of good birth, young enough to bear children, mature enough to have some experience of life, who possesses a sizable dowry and a forgiving nature. Mayhap, do any women of yer acquaintance spring to mind?"

"Nay." Brian rubbed his chin thoughtfully. "Though there is my sister, Grace. As I think about it, I realize that she fulfills all yer wants."

Ewan stared at his friend. "Grace? Isn't she married to Alastair Ferguson?"

"She's a widow. Alastair died last winter."

"I dinnae know. My sympathies."

Brian nodded. "He was a good man and a fine warrior, but his passing has left Grace adrift in the world, without a proper home of her own."

"There must be many eligible men who are interested in being tied to her."

Brian stared into his tankard and grunted. "Dinnae ye mean being tied to me and the McKenna Clan?"

"Aye, well, that too."

"There's been interest. A few offers as well."

"Yet ye've refused them?" Ewan folded his hands and waited. There had to be more, something Brian wasn't telling him. He shuffled through his mind for anything he could recall about Grace, yet found nothing.

Brian never spoke of her and Ewan had spent no significant time in the company of Alastair Ferguson during the king's campaigns for Scottish independence. There had been no talk of his wife, no gossip surrounding her person or actions. Yet clearly something was wrong with the lass or Brian wouldn't be suggesting this alliance.

Brian regarded him with shrewd eyes. "Steady, Ewan. By all rights I should be insulted by that look ye're casting my way."

Ewan frowned uneasily. "I've been turned away by each and every family I've approached fer a bride and those were all minor clans. Naturally I'm a bit suspicious of an offer from ye."

Brian leaned forward, his expression serious. "I cannae lie to ye, my friend. It willnae be easy to win my sister's hand."

Ewan bit back an oath. *I knew it!* Still, there was good reason to stay calm and hear the rest. An alliance with a clan as important and powerful as the McKenna's was far more than he had dared to hope. "I've dealt with prickly females before and managed them well. I'm sure I can do the same with Grace."

"There's nothing prickly about Grace," Brian insisted. "She's the very model of female decorum, refinement, and obedience."

"Are ye sure she's really yer kin?" Ewan joked.

Brian grinned. "Aye, though she's as different from the rest of the McKennas as chalk to cheese."

Ewan leaned back and folded his arms across his chest. His patience for riddles was quickly fading. Thankfully, Brian was a forthright man who appreciated honesty.

"So, then, what's wrong with her?" Ewan asked bluntly.

The McKenna's features darkened like a thundercloud, but he somehow managed to hold on to his temper. "In honor of our friendship I'm going to pretend I never heard that insult."

Ewan opened his mouth to apologize, but Brian glared forcefully, sending a clear message. Ewan shut his mouth and waited.

"Grace was promised to the church as a babe. She was raised there and would have taken the veil had I not needed her so desperately," Brian explained.

"Fer an alliance with the Fergusons?"

"Aye. 'Twas a good match and not an unhappy marriage." Brian sighed. "I believe she was content." He shook his head vigorously, as though trying to clear it, then spoke in a deliberate tone. "She came to live with us shortly after Alastair died. Fer the first time in my life, I've gotten to know my sister. She's a wise, calm female, sweet and loving, with a fine sense of humor. Any man would be proud to have her fer his wife and mother of his bairns."

"Then what's the problem?"

Brian hung his head sheepishly, then picked up a large wedge of hard cheese and popped it into his mouth. "Aileen has become very fond of Grace, as have I. Above all else, we desire her happiness."

"A fine sentiment."

"'Tis. Yet Grace has a very different idea of what will bring her joy and peace."

"She's acting rebellious?" Ewan asked, having difficulty believing anyone, least of all a female relation, would be able to effectively deny Brian McKenna.

"Rebellion is not a part of Grace's nature."

"Then she'll willingly do as ye command?"

Brian cleared his throat. "Well, the trouble is, I cannae exactly command Grace to do what I want."

"Why not?"

The McKenna shifted in his seat, looking more uncomfortable than Ewan had ever seen him. "I promised Aileen I'd not force Grace into an unwanted marriage. The choice must be left to Grace as to which path she will follow."

Ewan felt his jaw drop open. 'Twas madness to leave a woman solely in charge of her fate. It went against human nature, the laws of God and man. Women needed to be cared for, guided, protected. That McKenna, one of the most traditional, duty-bound men he knew, would allow such a travesty was nothing less than shocking.

"Wipe that smirk right off yer face, Ewan, before I do it fer ye," Brian reprimanded. "God's teeth, I've lived with her long enough to know there's hell to be paid when Aileen is crossed, and I'm not about to stick my neck out and let my head be chopped off. And it's always more difficult when she's carrying a babe. At times her moods can be downright terrifying."

Ewan spared a slight smile for his friend. "Is the man Grace has decided she wants to marry someone ye find unsuitable?"

"She does not want to remarry. She speaks of returning to the convent where she was raised and living out the rest of her days inside those walls." Brian's jaw bulged as his body tensed with emotion. "But Grace is not a woman meant to be locked away. She deserves more. Having a family to fill her day, children of her own, a life that revolves around people and happiness, not quiet and prayers."

"And ye think I can give her that life?" Ewan asked, humbled, as well as slightly unnerved, by the challenge.

"I think ye're the only one I'm willing to let try.".

Grace had just gotten the children settled on their pallets when Edna entered the chamber. "Sir Brian is asking fer ye in the great hall, milady."

"Och, but she cannae leave now! Aunt Grace is going to tell us a story," Malcolm exclaimed.

"About knights and maidens," Katherine piped up.

"And dragons," James added, his eyes wide with excitement.

"If I'm summoned, then I must go," Grace said regretfully, though she was not surprised by the request. She'd much rather stay with the children than greet whoever had come to see her brother, but duty demanded she obey.

"Do ye know the story Aunt Grace was going to tell us, Edna?" Malcolm asked hopefully.

"I dinnae," Edna confessed. "But I do know a tale of goblins and fairies."

"Is it scary?" Malcolm asked.

"Aye, but it all turns out right in the end. Would ye like to hear it?"

Promptly forgetting their aunt, the children turned their complete attention to Edna. As she slipped out the door, Grace heard her maid telling the children to gather close. Grace smiled, knowing that Edna's story would likely be equal parts noble and gruesome. Grace would certainly have to be far more imaginative the next time she told the children a tale in order to compete with Edna's epic adventure and keep the wee one's attention.

Grace arrived at the hall, but halted the moment she saw a young page struggling to carry in a laden tray that was almost twice his size.

"Let me help, Connor," she said, reaching for the full pitcher of ale before it tumbled to the floor.

"Oh, thank ye, milady." Connor grinned, straightened the now-lighter tray, and hurried to the dais. Grace followed slowly, squinting at the two seated men. One was her brother—the other unknown to her. Yet she knew by the tingling feeling climbing up her spine that the stranger was watching her.

Why?

She ventured closer, keeping her eyes trained on the edge of the table. When she reached the dais she had no choice but to look up. Her brother's scowl immediately turned to an overly bright grin. Grace's stomach tightened with suspicion.

"Grace, there's someone I'd like ye to meet," Brian bellowed. "Sir Ewan Gilroy has come to pay us a visit."

Dressed in a well-made green tunic and leather trews, Brian's guest sat with one ankle crossed casually over the other knee, as relaxed as he might have been in his own hall. He came to his feet and stepped close when they were introduced, an imposing warrior of solid muscle and brawn.

With slightly trembling hands, Grace placed the pitcher of ale on the table. Standing so close meant she had to tip her head back to meet Sir Ewan's gaze. He was tall and broad-shouldered, a dark-haired man, with piercing blue eyes, a wide mouth, and a square jaw.

"Lady Grace."

"Sir Ewan."

"'Tis an honor to meet such a fair and lovely lady."

Uncertain how to respond to such a flirtatious compliment, Grace simply curtsied. She supposed Sir Ewan was trying to be polite, but then she noticed that he was staring at her intently, in a way that no man ever had.

It made her nervous.

Grace smoothed a hand over the top of her wrinkled skirt and wondered what he saw when he looked at her. Nothing extraordinary, to be sure. Her petite frame lent itself to a younger appearance, but her face possessed the maturity of her years. Her auburn hair, said by many to be her best feature, was plaited and pinned to her head, and covered with a veil. Her gown was plain, serviceable, and loose-fitting, just as she preferred.

Yet for some unexplained reason, Sir Ewan seemed to find her fascinating. His gaze drifted from her face to her breasts to her hips to her feet. Grace's breath quickened and her heart thumped wildly against her rib cage. *'Tis a delayed reaction,* she told herself sternly. *I'm merely relieved it's not Roderick, come to make trouble.*

She forced herself to relax. She was perfectly safe, here in McKenna hall, with her brother at her side. The realization bolstered her courage. She took a step closer.

The spicy, masculine scent of leather surrounded her. Grace inhaled slowly, allowing it to linger in her nostrils. It was pleasant, oddly comforting, and unsettling all in the same moment.

She could tell by the rising heat in her cheeks that her face was flushed. Embarrassed by this reaction, she shifted on her feet, feeling utterly foolish for having such a girlish reaction to a handsome stranger.

And then Sir Ewan did the most amazing thing. He smiled. If she thought him handsome before, he was heart-stopping now. That smile brought a twinkle of mischief to his eyes and revealed a dimple in his unshaven cheek. For just a moment, receiving that mesmerizing smile did funny things to her stomach and knees, but Grace soon pulled herself back to reality.

Ewan Gilroy possessed the dangerous, manly good looks that left women stumbling on their feet. Probably since he was old enough to shave off his whiskers. Oh, yes, there was no doubt that Sir Ewan was the kind of man who delighted in tempting women with his handsome face and promising smile, but she was immune.

Or so she told herself.

"What brings ye to the Highlands, Sir Ewan?"

"A quest, milady. That might have just come to a very satisfactory end." He took a step closer and she swore she could see the remnants of his smile lurking in his eyes. "That is, if ye look kindly upon me."

"Me?"

"Aye. Shall I tell ye the details?"

Grace shivered. His voice was deep and rich, an intoxicating sound she could listen to for hours. A vision of herself sitting at his feet, her head resting on his knee as he regaled her with tales, invaded her mind.

Shaking herself out of that ridiculous stupor, Grace looked beyond Sir Ewan to her brother. "How long will yer friend be visiting with us?"

Her brother's eyes narrowed with caution. He paused, almost as if weighing the words in his mind before speaking. "Ewan has journeyed here fer more than a visit."

"Oh?" Grace struggled to remain calm, but she felt her distress start to bubble to the surface.

"Aye. A most important reason has brought him to us." Brian cleared his throat loudly. "Ewan is in search of a bride. And I've suggested that ye would do nicely."

Chapter Four

Ewan could have sworn Lady Grace did not move an inch, yet somehow she conveyed both shock, disdain, and disapproval. Of him? Or the suggestion of their marriage? Or perhaps 'twas both?

The reaction bothered him more than he cared to admit. He hadn't been dismissed so quickly and thoroughly by a female since he was a lad. True, all his offers of marriage had been rejected these past few weeks. But it had been the male leaders of the clans saying nay to him, not the women. 'Twas one of the few things that salvaged Ewan's pride in this whole sordid mess, knowing he could have charmed the women, if given the chance.

He studied Lady Grace's face. She was pretty enough, but not an exceptional beauty. She was delicate and petite, with a fair complexion and pouty lips. Her eyes were gray, like her brother's, with an intelligent and quiet composure lurking in their depths.

Lady Grace was nothing like the usual woman who

caught his eye, for he generally preferred tall, curvy brunettes. Yet why did his heart beat so much faster when he gazed at her?

Ewan continued his inspection. Though of good quality, her gown was simple and loose. In his experience, noblewomen tried to make themselves as attractive as possible, dressing in soft wools and vibrant colors. Yet Lady Grace wore a plain gown of rough cloth, the dull gray fabric washing out any hint of color from her face, the loose folds hiding her female curves.

Ewan offered her an encouraging smile. She appeared startled. Her eyes traveled over him, from the top of his head to the tips of his soft leather boots. He found himself squaring his shoulders and puffing out his chest. The gesture did not go unnoticed; Lady Grace's eyes narrowed shrewdly and her mouth tugged into a disapproving line.

God's wounds, now he felt like a perfect arse.

Quickly recovering, Ewan leaned forward, smoothly insinuating his mouth beside her ear so that she'd be forced to acknowledge him.

"Will ye join us at the table, milady?" She pulled back, but he was prepared for that reaction, neatly taking her right hand and raising it to his lips. "'Twould be an honor."

Her fingers were cold, although the room was stuffy and overly warm. She did not pull away from him, but stayed quiet and still. Her worried gaze slid to her brother.

The sight bothered Ewan, leaving him with the most ridiculous urge to put his arms around her and cradle her close. To assure her that all would be well, that he would protect her, honor her, cherish her, make her happy.

If only she'd allow him.

"Aye, join us, Sister."

Her eyes opened wider. She stepped back from Ewan, but was still close enough that he could feel her warmth. Shooting a daggerlike glare at her brother, Lady Grace dipped into a low curtsy. "Ye must excuse me. I've duties to attend to that cannae be neglected."

"They can wait," Brian declared.

"Nay," Lady Grace replied, her voice faint. "They cannae."

Brian's eyes narrowed with displeasure. As much as Ewan wanted the opportunity to converse with her, he sensed it would be a fruitless effort if she was forced into his company.

"'Tis an admirable quality to put duty first," Ewan said smoothly. "I look forward to sitting beside ye at the evening meal. Ye will be joining us then?"

"Come evening, I'll be in the great hall with the rest of the clan, Sir Ewan." Lady Grace hesitated. She glanced again at her brother, then back at Ewan. Her mouth thinned into a tight line, resigned, as though she'd decided it was unwise to challenge her brother— and his famous temper—any further. "I shall leave it to Lady Aileen to decide where I'll be sitting."

With a pointed stare at her brother, Lady Grace turned and scuttled away. Brian shrugged, pretending to have no concern at her reply. But Ewan smiled. *Clever lass.* Clearly, she had lived with them long enough to understand the extent of Aileen's power over her husband.

A wave of sweet anticipation swept over Ewan,

along with a deep sense of relief. Lady Grace was an intriguing female, possessing more desirable qualities in a wife than he had dared to hope he could find. The corners of his mouth lifted into a smile, while his mind imagined how it would feel to pull her into his arms, press her delicate body against his chest, and kiss her pouting lips.

Then, after he'd tasted those lips, he'd lay a sensual path of kisses down her graceful neck to her breasts, nuzzle his face between those soft globes, then feather kisses behind her delectable ears. When she had softened and relaxed, he would move back to her lips, coaxing them to open so he could taste her sweetness.

He'd move his thumb slowly over her nipple until she arched into his touch, a willing temptress who—

"Haven't I fed ye enough?" the McKenna asked. "Ye've the expression of a starving man lining yer face."

Interrupting the erotic image invading his mind, Ewan glanced at Brian, knowing the man would have his bollocks on a platter for such disrespectful thoughts about his sister.

"It's been a grand feast, and I thank ye fer it, but I could eat some more," Ewan replied, mustering a smile.

Though it tasted like straw in his mouth, Ewan enthusiastically chewed the course brown bread. As he swallowed, his mind whirled, his thoughts raced.

Brash confidence and charm would not be enough to win Lady Grace's hand. It would take more and he had little time to discover exactly what *more* he would need. Yet he would not relent. Disappointments had been something Ewan had learned to accept at an early age, given his upbringing. But complete failure was never tolerated.

He needed a wife with a substantial dowry and a noble bearing. Grace McKenna Ferguson had both. She was also fair of face, appeared to possess above average intelligence and a quiet spirit. As Ewan had watched her glide across the room earlier he felt as though he'd been punched in the gut and handed his heart's desire, both at the same time.

Now all he had to do was convince her to be his bride.

Grace closed her eyes and clenched her fists, the rounded fingernails digging into her palms. Mortification flooded through her, making her first hot and then cold. She concentrated on putting one foot in front of the other, trying to shut down her mind so she could escape the hall with her dignity. Or what remained of it.

Her body tense, she went in search of her sister-in-law. She found Aileen in the solar, sitting in the faint sunlight, mending one of her husband's shirts.

"Ye seem upset."

"I am." Grace sighed and unclenched her fist. "'Tis foolish, I know. I suppose I was merely caught off guard by my brother's actions and have allowed it to rattle me."

Aileen released a long-suffering sigh. "What's my bullheaded husband gone and done now?"

"He told me that Sir Ewan is in search of a wife and that I would be a good choice," Grace replied. She heard the annoyance in her voice, but couldn't hold it at bay.

"Truly?"

"Aye."

Aileen's fingers went idle and she allowed the shirt to drop onto her lap. It draped her swollen belly like a banner, emphasizing the girth. "That is a surprise."

"Ye knew nothing of this plan?"

"Nay." Aileen took the jug of sweet wine from the table at her side and poured them each a goblet.

Grace accepted hers, yet felt too restless to drink. "Why did ye not warn me that Sir Ewan was coming?"

"I dinnae know either. Fie, I was struck near speechless when I saw the man standing in our hall. I know he and Brian fought together fer the king's cause, but I never thought to see Ewan Gilroy under my roof."

"Why?"

Aileen gave her a secretive smile. "Yer brother is a jealous, possessive man. I dinnae think he would look kindly upon a man who once kidnapped me."

Grace rolled her eyes, assuming her sister-in-law was having a bit of fun at her expense. "Stop teasing, Aileen."

"I'm not. Honest." She got a thoughtful, faraway look on her face before adding, "I was, in truth, held captive by Ewan Gilroy. 'Twas a long time ago, and in the end all was put to rights. But it's not something one easily forgets."

"I should say not."

Aileen smiled, then took a dainty sip of her wine. "Tell me, what was yer impression of Sir Ewan?"

"He's very sure of himself," Grace huffed.

"An admirable trait in a man."

"Not always." Grace fiddled with the goblet in her hand, then set it down. "I dinnae know what Brian was thinking, suggesting a match between us. He knows I willnae remarry. I only wish to be left in peace. Is that so very wrong?"

"Yer brother is well aware of yer feelings on the matter, but he willnae accept yer decision to remain unwed until ye have placed yerself behind convent walls," Aileen said mildly. "Surely ye know that, for Sir Ewan is not the first man Brian has offered to ye."

True. Yet somehow this time it felt different. Very different. Grace didn't understand why she should feel such intense emotion. Aileen was right—Brian had proposed other possible matches to her before.

But never to a man as handsome and appealing as Sir Ewan Gilroy.

There was something undefinable about him, something that fairly knocked the breath out of her lungs when she stood near him. And it appalled her. She didn't want to feel an attraction for him. And she was ashamed that she could be so easily impressed by a handsome face. Was she truly that shallow? That lonely?

Brian appeared. He stepped into the solar, sparing not a glance for Grace, but heading directly for his wife. Grace moved forward to intercept her brother. Enough was enough. If she did not find a way to exert some control over the situation, she'd find herself wed to Sir Ewan before the week was done.

"Ye ambushed me, Brian," Grace said, quite loudly. "'Twas mortifying to have ye propose a match so publicly. It took a great effort to keep my composure."

Brian's back stiffened, yet he did not turn to face her until after he had properly kissed his wife. "My dear little sister," he replied, his tone reproachful. "Is it so very wrong of me to want yer happiness?"

"We agreed it would be my decision." Grace dragged in a deep breath. "Ye said it when the Macgregor made an offer and again when Sir Alfred broached the idea of an alliance between our clans. What makes things so different with Ewan Gilroy?"

Brian's expression didn't soften. "He's a fine man. He'll do right by ye."

"He's near as handsome as I remember him," Aileen mused. "I bet there's many a lass who sighs with longing the first time she sets eyes upon him."

"Aye, and there appears to be plenty of charm to go along with those good looks," Grace replied wryly. "It makes no difference. I'm not interested in having another husband."

Grace noticed her brother's brow tighten. She wondered if he had heard her, for his attention was centered utterly upon Aileen. "Ye think Gilroy handsome, wife?"

"I do. Though he cannae hold a candle to yer rugged appeal, milord," Aileen replied, bestowing her husband with a saucy wink, successfully deflecting the temper brewing in his eyes. "Why are ye considering him as a husband fer Grace?"

Brian folded his arms. "He is a worthy man. Grace would be blessed to have such a husband. Though I expect him to know his place and be respectful of other men's wives."

Grace could not contain a small smile as she watched her proud brother refuse to acknowledge his jealousy. Whatever this past relationship was between Aileen and Sir Ewan, it still had the power to rankle her brother. It wasn't much, but 'twas the only weapon she had at her disposal and Grace had no hesitation using it.

"Though I know not all the details, I find that I must question the honor of a man who resorts to kidnapping innocent females, no matter how worthy ye believe him to be," Grace said pointedly.

Brian favored her with a reproving frown, but it was Aileen who answered. "The incident occurred years ago, before Brian and I married. Sir Ewan seized an opportunity and I was caught in the middle. Yet when danger presented itself, he fought bravely to keep me safe, and thus I must agree that he would be a good match fer ye to consider."

A sharp slice of betrayal cut through Grace's heart. She had always believed that Aileen was on her side in the matter of a remarriage. It was an unhappy surprise to hear that Aileen, an independent thinker and an outspoken woman, would agree with her husband.

"Ye are to give him a chance, Grace," Brian commanded.

"Fer what?"

"To state his case and win yer hand."

Grace felt her back bow with indignation, yet what could she say? 'Twas not an unreasonable request. As it was, Brian was allowing her far more power than most women of her station were awarded.

And if circumstances were different, perhaps she would look more kindly upon the notion of having Sir Ewan for a husband. But it could never happen. The actions of her past defined her future. Grace had accepted it, had tried to embrace it with as much dignity as she could muster.

She must atone for her role in Alastair's death. She must devote the rest of her life to prayer and servitude to God in hopes that would be enough to forgive her sin. For she carried no remorse or regret over the deed, knowing deep in her heart, that given the chance, she wouldn't hesitate to do the same again. No living creature deserved such a harsh, painful fate, such an agonizing death.

Grace closed her eyes, willing her fluttering heart to cease tightening in her chest. Oh, how she wished she could confess her deed to Brian and Aileen! But that was impossible. A large part of the burden of her sin was the necessity of carrying it alone.

"Chin up, Grace," Aileen admonished with a sly grin. "There are far worse things than being courted by a handsome rogue."

Grace refused to smile. As a vision of Sir Ewan's sensual grin and sparkling eyes appeared in her mind, 'twas very difficult for her to think of any.

"What will ye wear this evening, milady?" Edna asked. "The blue silk? Or perhaps the red? The blue deepens the color of yer eyes. But the red brings out the bloom in yer cheeks."

Grace turned to her maid in astonishment. "Why would I change my gown?"

"For Sir Ewan. I've yet to cast eyes upon him myself, but two of the kitchen maids could not stop talking of his handsome face and form."

"Saints preserve us, not ye too, Edna." Grace drew in a deep sigh. "'Tis bad enough I have to listen to Brian and Aileen sing his praises."

Edna's lip curled. "Perhaps ye should take heed of their words. Ye might like what ye discover."

Grace heaved a deep breath. "The very last thing

I desire is to encourage Sir Ewan—not that much is required on that front. I swear he'd have me as his bride even if I possessed two heads and the temperament of a shrew."

Sadness glistened in Edna's eyes. "Will ye not at least consider him? Ye deserve a chance at happiness."

"I cannae marry him, Edna. I cannae marry any man."

Regret flared across Edna's face, followed quickly by resignation. Slowly, she placed the two gowns on the bed. She remained silent as she poured water from the pitcher into the washing bowl and brought it to Grace.

Grateful for the quiet, Grace washed her hands, face, and neck, then sat patiently while Edna loosened the pins in her hair and brushed it. For just a moment, Grace closed her eyes, enjoying the feel of the brush gliding through her long tresses, easing the tension in her neck and shoulders.

It felt heavenly.

Edna moved away, but Grace kept her eyes closed a moment longer, savoring the peace. When she opened them, Edna once again stood before her, holding up the red and blue gowns.

"It might lift yer spirits if ye wear something pretty," the maid said temptingly.

Feeling too languid to scold, Grace merely shook her head. "The only way to lift my spirits is to find a way out of this mess."

"The laird willnae force ye to wed."

Grace bit her bottom lip, hoping that was still true, but no longer as sure. "Sir Ewan is my brother's friend and fer some unknown reason he wants this alliance. 'Twould in truth be far easier fer Brian to accept the decision if Sir Ewan found me disagreeable and rejected me." Grace sat up straighter, her even mood giving way to alertness. "Do ye think that's possible?"

Edna frowned. "To make yerself unappealing to Sir Ewan?"

Grace nodded her head vigorously. "Fetch my oldest gown. Wait, nay, bring me a gown that needs washing. And the veil that has mud stains from Malcolm's dirty little fingers."

The disapproval in Edna's eyes deepened. "Ye think a bit of dirt will be enough to put him off?"

"Dinnae forget the smell. I'll be sitting beside him as he eats his meal."

Edna scrunched her nose. "'Tis a ridiculous notion, but I can tell by the tilt of yer chin that ye are determined to see it through."

"I am."

Edna stood silently for so long Grace thought she might refuse to do as she was told. But then the maid let out a lengthy sigh and shook her head with resignation. "May Laird McKenna forgive me fer encouraging ye, but I believe I have a better idea."

Grace could feel the stirring of interest and curiosity among the crowd the moment she entered the great hall. The tables and benches were filled with various retainers and clan members, the male and female voices raised in relaxed conversation. The seats at the high table were also occupied, except for her empty chair. Nervously fingering the edge of her gossamer veil, Grace moved forward.

She kept her gaze on the mighty timbers crossing

the roof as she made her way to her seat. Although she had been forewarned that she would sit beside him at the meal, 'twas still disconcerting to catch a glimpse of the broad-shouldered figure hovering near her place.

"Good evening, Lady Grace." Sir Ewan bowed.

Hearing her name, Brian glanced over at her, then quickly swung his head back for a second look. Grace ignored him. She sank regally into her seat, tipping her chin in what she hoped was a superior manner. "Sir Ewan."

Sir Ewan's blue eyes regarded her appreciatively. "Ye look beautiful. I'm honored."

Grace's heart sank. *Damnation! Sir Ewan obviously believes all this finery is for his benefit.*

Frustrated at the poor start to the evening and needing a bit of fortification, Grace reached for her wine goblet. As she lifted it to her lips and took a large swallow, the gold and silver bracelets on her wrist clanked noisily.

"Ye misunderstand, Sir Ewan. I dress only to please myself, no one else. I simply adore pretty, luxurious things," Grace said loftily, placing the goblet down. "Silks, satins, jewels, they are all essential items fer a lady's wardrobe, necessities that any worthy husband provides fer his wife."

She waved her hand dramatically, nearly poking herself in the eye with the large ring she wore on her right hand. *Drat.* She had told Edna the ring was too big, but the maid had insisted that she wear every piece of jewelry she owned. 'Twas an essential part of the plan designed to showcase a frivolous, empty-headed female.

"'Tis obvious that ye deserve only the best and finest." Sir Ewan smiled charmingly. "When I have coin to spare, I'll shower ye with gifts fit fer a queen."

"Coin to spare?" Grace lifted her brow. "My needs are to be an afterthought? I dinnae like the sound of that, Sir Ewan. Not one bit."

"We must provide fer our people first," he said gently. "As fer yer needs, well, I vow that I shall see to them far better than a cold necklace of gold and gemstone."

Grace felt an unaccustomed warmth flood her cheek. His tone was so smooth, so inviting, it made her blush. This was not going according to plan. Edna had assured her that Ewan would find her avarice repellent. Instead, he seemed to find it amusing.

Switching tactics, Grace launched her next volley, filling every bit of silence with a constant stream of the most inane chatter she could devise. The best way to make soap, the preference for beeswax candles over tallow, the difficulty in finding good weavers to make quality cloth. Whenever Sir Ewan tried to respond, or make a comment of his own, Grace rudely interrupted, dominating the conversation like a king leading an army.

After exhausting every domestic item she could think of, Grace switched to complaints. 'Twas too cold in winter, too hot in summer, too rainy in spring. She babbled as her food congealed on her trencher and her voice grew hoarse, all the while waiting for Sir Ewan's eyes to glaze over with boredom or annoyance or both.

It never happened.

Finally, when she had to take a sip of wine to ease

the dryness in her throat, he clasped his tankard of ale in his right hand and looked her dead in the eye. "Why have ye taken such a dislike to me, lass?"

The wine hit her empty stomach in a rush. "Why ever would ye say such a thing?"

"The looks."

"What looks?"

"The ones darting from yer lovely eyes telling me ye're wishing I'd fall into a deep, dark hole and disappear from the earth."

"Not the earth, good sir. Ye need only disappear from McKenna Castle."

A small tick of amusement crossed his face. "I willnae overstay my welcome. But when I leave, I plan on taking ye with me."

Grace's shoulders sagged, but she was not yet ready to admit defeat. "I should like to save ye a good deal of time and breath, Sir Ewan, and tell ye—"

"Ewan."

Grace blinked. Had she misheard him?

"I want ye to call me Ewan. Is that acceptable, Grace?"

No, 'tis not. Familiarity was the last thing Grace wanted, knowing it could make her more vulnerable to him. But her brother might object if she refused and claim she was not holding to her end of the bargain. And that could spell disaster.

She could ill afford to risk Brian's wrath, for if pushed hard enough, her brother might decide to ignore her objections and force her into the marriage. She must therefore give every appearance of being open-minded to Sir Ewan's—*Ewan's*—proposal.

"This is not the first time the possibility of a second

marriage has been raised by my brother, Ewan." She paused. He smiled when she spoke his name. A lopsided grin that was so boyishly disarming she nearly smiled back, before blinking rapidly and regaining control of her senses. "Ye do me a great honor by asking fer my hand. Yet my answer remains the same to ye as it was to the others. I wish to retreat to the convent and a life of religious reflection. I know 'tis best fer me."

She said the last forcefully, then felt a stab of worry that she had gone too far. Men did not like being told they were not in charge, in control, especially of females. Yet Ewan did not appear annoyed; his eyes were still dancing with merriment.

"They willnae allow ye all yer pretty baubles in the convent," he said innocently.

"I shall manage without them," Grace bit out.

He looked at her inquiringly, his head tilting slightly. "I've been told that silence is a virtue well regarded and sought after among the good sisters. Will that be difficult fer ye to endure day in and day out?"

Grace squirmed in her seat, though she supposed she deserved this bit of teasing. "I will strive and struggle day and night to hold my tongue."

"Or ye could avoid these restrictions completely and marry me."

"Nay," Grace gritted out.

Sir Ewan's jaw bulged as he clamped it together. She waited for the explosion of anger, but he was somehow able to conquer it.

"Women are known for changing their minds. 'Tis one of their many appealing traits." His voice dipped lower, honeyed and coaxing. "What can I do to influence yer mind, fair Grace?"

"Accept the truth, good sir. I willnae change my mind nor my answer."

She spoke each word crisply and held Ewan's eyes as she uttered them. It seemed the best way to make him understand the depth of her feelings, the extent of her determination to remain unwed.

She braced herself, fully expecting him to cast off his flirting smiles. But he surprised her with a gentle look she found even more disarming. "I enjoy a challenge, especially one from a worthy opponent. It makes victory all the more sweet, fer nothing of great worth in this life is ever easy to obtain."

"Yer pretty words have no effect on my decision."

"Aye, 'tis the deeds that matter." His eyes filled with warmth. "I willnae threaten nor cajole ye, lass. Instead, when the time is right, I'll make my appeal to yer heart. Directly from mine."

Oh, my. It took an extreme effort not to look away. Or down. To keep her eyes steadily focused on him without betraying a single ounce of emotion that was spreading through her body.

"Well, then, I suppose I cannae prevent ye from trying." Thanks to years of practice, there was no wavering in her voice. But the same could not be said of her emotions.

Grace's back went rigid. Who was this man? Somehow, he possessed the power to make her want the things she had never had. But worst still, he possessed the power to make her dream they were possible.

Chapter Five

Ewan peeled open his eyes as sunshine poured in through the narrow bedchamber window. Feeling an odd combination of exhaustion and exhilaration, he rolled to his back. With morning came the chance to achieve his most important task—marrying a lady with a substantial dowry. He had stayed up most of the night with Brian, plying his host with ale, then whiskey, in hopes of gaining some much-needed insight in wooing Grace.

Unfortunately, Ewan had not received the answers he sought. After the fifth tankard of ale and the third dram of whiskey, it was clear that Brian had no useful advice to impart. The McKenna had no idea what Ewan could possibly say, or do, to win his sister's hand in marriage.

All Brian did confirm, with a deep thread of reluctance flowing through his voice, was his promise not to force Grace into a union she did not want, fearing the wrath of his sister, but more importantly, his wife, were he to go back on his word.

Ewan's head ached—and not just from too much

ale and whiskey. 'Twas obvious that Grace was not going to be an easy conquest. Her behavior at the evening meal had confirmed her desire to remain unwed. It would take time and charm and more than a wee bit of luck to change her mind. And the only way to accomplish that was to spend as much time as possible in her company.

Yet it was clear from their conversation last night, Grace was not going to cooperate. Nay, she would do all that she could to avoid him, of that Ewan felt certain. Yet she would quickly discover he was not a man who easily accepted defeat, especially with something as important as his future. She might be a clever lass, but she'd soon learn there were few on this earth as wily as Ewan Gilroy.

Ewan threw back the covers. As his bare feet touched the hard floor, the sound of church bells rang in his ears. Fighting his way through the cloud of sleep and drink, he realized it was a call to Mass. It took a moment for the importance of that fact to sink into his skull, but when it did, he smiled. Broadly.

Where else would a devout woman who longed only to lock herself behind convent walls be found at this hour of the morning? At Mass, of course. Which was exactly where he was headed. *Aye, ye might run from me, lass, but ye cannae hide.*

Spirits bolstered, Ewan walked to a small table set below the window. Without hesitation, he plunged his head into the wooden bucket of water that had been left last night, staying submerged until the cold bit into his flesh. Feeling more awake, and completely sober, he rubbed his face and hair dry, and dressed.

He hurried down to the great hall, finding a small group of clansmen and servants gathering for the morning meal. Apparently, Brian did not command that everyone in his household attend Mass each day. Ewan hurried across the hall and out the door. Following the sound of the ringing bell, he located the chapel.

Given the number of people he had seen earlier staying in the hall, Ewan was surprised at how crowded it was inside the church. His eyes moved to the front of the chapel, searching for a glimpse of Brian's broad shoulders, but he saw neither the McKenna nor Aileen.

He did, however, locate what he sought. A petite female stood near the altar, her hands clasped in front of her, her head bent in prayer. Ewan could see Grace's profile through the fine weave of her veil. Though a woman of small stature—she barely reached his shoulder—she had a stately presence and a graceful, willowy form. She reminded him of a statue he had once seen of the Virgin Mary—elegant, refined, regal. Yet Grace was not cold marble, she was warm flesh and fighting spirit.

Weaving his way through the crowd, Ewan reached Grace's side. Her eyes were closed, her lips moving in silent prayer. To get her attention, he put his hand on her arm. She drew away immediately, then turned to him, her gray eyes startled.

"Sir Ewan!"

"Good morning, Grace."

She turned away, but not before he saw the unease revealed in her face. Seeking to reassure her, Ewan gave her arm a little squeeze. The rosary beads clasped in her hand trembled at the gesture. Fearing he was doing little to advance his cause, he released his grip. She sighed softly, taking a step away from him. Ewan grit his teeth and resisted the strong urge to move closer to her, suspecting a show of dominating force would not be well received.

The Mass began. Ewan tried to listen to the words, but his mind was too crowded with thoughts of the woman beside him. He went through the ritual of the service by rote, always a second or two behind. Grace, on the other hand, was nearly leading the congregation, her movements a step ahead of all the others, including the priest's.

Was she truly meant to live a religious life? Or had the many years of training left such a deep impression upon her that she could participate in the Mass even in her sleep?

Pondering these thoughts kept Ewan's mind focused, and he was therefore surprised to realize the priest was giving the final blessing. As they filed out of the chapel, Ewan took Grace politely by the elbow.

"Come fer a ride with me this morning after we break our fast, Grace. The sky is blue, the sun is shining, and there's nary a cloud to be seen. 'Tis a day meant to be enjoyed outdoors."

"I've work to attend," she answered. "If ye wish to tour the castle and the outlying grounds, I'm sure my brother would be happy to oblige."

He kept pace easily with her quickening steps, his hand still on her elbow. She allowed it, yet he noted that she took great care not to meet his gaze.

"I have already spent a considerable amount of time in yer brother's company," Ewan replied. "I'm in need of a change and ye're much prettier to look at, especially in this bright sunshine."

"Not today."

"Tomorrow?"

"Nay."

He stopped abruptly, increasing the pressure on her arm. She had no choice but to stop also, her frown indicating she was not pleased about it. "Ye promised to give me a chance," he entreated.

There was a flash of white in her eyes. "I never made any such promise."

Ewan released his grip and folded his arms across his chest. "Well, ye should have, lass. 'Tis the polite thing to do."

She snorted. "It is far better manners not to be badgering a helpless, defenseless woman."

"Mayhap. See, 'tis yet another reason fer ye to marry me. Ye can teach me all the pretty, fine manners ye like. Is that not what women enjoy most—reforming a man?"

She rolled her eyes heavenward, but was saved from replying by the sudden appearance of Alec. Ewan smiled at his friend and motioned for him to come closer. As he introduced the pair, he noticed they were both assessing each other, though Grace performed the task with delicate subtlety, while Alec was openly brazen.

"Tell me, good knight, have ye come to sing me Sir Ewan's praises?"

"Nay. 'Twould be a sour song, indeed, milady. One that could easily curdle milk."

"Oh?"

"He's a good, fine man, there's no mistake about it. I've trusted him with my life more times than I can count, and as I'm standing here before ye, the result is clear." Alec's lip curled. "But 'tis obvious to me that a lovely lady such as yerself can do better than being tied to a rogue like Sir Ewan."

Grace smiled, appreciating Alec's blunt humor. "Then ye agree I should reject his proposal?"

Alec leaned toward Grace and whispered, though his words were deliberately loud enough for Ewan to hear. "'Tis tempting, I'll grant ye that, but I beg ye to spare his feelings and spend at least a few days thinking it over. It will be a kindness to all his men, fer we shall bear the brunt of his wounded pride if ye turn him away so quickly."

Her expression lightened noticeably as she cast her eyes on Ewan. "I'll meet ye at the stables in an hour." Then turning to Alec, she sank to a graceful curtsy. "I am most pleased to have made yer acquaintance."

The two men remained silent as they watched Grace walk away. But the moment she was gone from sight, Ewan turned to his friend.

"I'll thank ye to cease charming my future bride," Ewan snapped, feeling a stab of resentment at how easily Grace had responded to Alec. Why could she not let her guard down like that with him?

"She seemed more than ready to walk away from ye before I stepped in," Alec replied. "'Twas embarrassing to watch."

"Liar," Ewan countered, wishing that were true. "She was at the verge of falling into my hands, like a ripe pear."

Alec raised a skeptical brow, but let the matter drop. "In any event, getting into the lady's good graces will buy ye more time to convince her brother to allow ye to wed her."

"The McKenna has already agreed to the match," Ewan replied, without thinking.

Alec grinned and slapped Ewan on the back. "Congratulations. I confess, I wasnae sure ye'd manage it. Will she be bringing the dowry ye need?"

Ewan held up his hand. "Dinnae start crying the banns just yet. I still have to get her consent."

"What?"

Ewan shrugged. "The McKennas are an odd sort. Grace must accept me as her husband or there'll be no marriage."

"I see Lady Aileen's fine hand in all of this," Alec replied, shaking his head. "She's not forgotten what happened all those years ago."

"Ye mean when she was taken?"

"Aye, by ye."

Ewan tilted his head. "As I recall, 'twas on yer horse Aileen rode, hands and feet bound and cradled within yer arms."

"'Twas yer orders that made it so." Alec cast him a rueful grin. "Why did ye think I sat in the back of the hall last night, shielded by the shadows? I'm not eager to bring myself to Lady Aileen's attention and possibly incur the wrath of her husband. The McKenna has always struck me as a man who holds tight to his own."

"Aye." The men were silent as they pondered that truth. "Now, why are ye suddenly grinning like a fool, Alec?"

"Well, I just realized that if the McKenna has agreed to the match, and all ye need do is charm yer bride to make it happen, then the deed is as good as done."

Ewan grimaced, wishing he had as much confidence in the matter as Alec. Grace was not like other women. She was bent on traveling a path that led away from him and he was perplexed over how to pursue her, how to convince her to take a chance and come with him.

What he did know, with alarming certainty, was that he would need time in order to prevail. Along with a healthy dose of luck.

Ewan was still mulling over Alec's remarks when he spied Grace entering the bailey. She had not appeared in the great hall after Mass to break her fast. He assumed instead that she had taken her meal in the women's solar, most likely to avoid him.

He stood by the stables and waited. The sun shone pleasantly on his head. He gazed up at the sky, pleased to see only a few white puffs of clouds. At least the weather was cooperating. 'Twould be interesting to see if Grace would.

When she drew near, Ewan strode forward to greet her, a winsome smile on his face. He received a curt nod before Grace brushed past him, pleasantly greeting the lad who held her horse. Before mounting, she took the animal's face between her hands and spoke to it in a low, soothing tone. Delighted, the horse pushed its nose against her chest and neighed. After a final, affectionate pat, she moved to mount the mare. Once she was seated, Ewan swung up on his stallion, who was already prancing about sideways, eager to be off.

"Ready?" Ewan inquired, refusing to react to her brisk manner.

"Nearly." She tilted her head and looked at him sideways, seeming very mysterious.

Ewan smiled indulgently. Lord only knew what sort of scheme she had devised to thwart his courtship, but whatever it was, he was not about to let it pierce his good humor.

"Ah, there ye are at last," she called out merrily. "Are ye excited fer our ride this morning?"

Ewan froze at the sound of running feet approaching. He turned just in time to see the two McKenna lads rushing into the bailey and race toward the stables.

"Ye dinnae have any objections if Malcolm joins us, do ye, Sir Ewan?" Grace asked in a voice as sweet as honey. "His pony is stout and sure-footed and can go a fair distance."

I'll just bet. Having the child along would be the perfect excuse to make this a short outing. Not to mention the impossibility of getting her alone in some secluded, romantic setting. Ewan could feel the weight of her gaze upon him, waiting for his answer. Her expression remained neutral, but he could swear there was a smirk glimmering in her eyes.

"It's not fair! I want to come, too," the smaller one whined.

"Ye cannae," Malcolm yelled to his younger brother. "Ye're too little to ride on yer own."

"I'm not!"

"Ye are!"

"I'm not!"

"Aye, ye are!"

The lad's bickering escalated in volume and intensity. Ewan looked helplessly about, searching for either of the children's parents. Or a servant. Or anyone who could lead the little monsters away.

"Hush now," Grace commanded. "Or ye'll be going nowhere except to yer chamber. Both of ye."

"Aunt Grace!" the lads wailed in unison.

"Quiet! Do ye want Sir Ewan to think ye're a pair of ill-mannered heathens?"

"Nay." The older lad's head dropped dejectedly as he pushed the toe of his boot in the dirt. "Forgive me."

"I'm sorry, too," the younger one piped up. "Now can I come?"

"Ye're too little," his brother growled.

"I am not!"

Jesus, did they never give it a rest? Ewan braced for the bickering to begin anew, but one stern look from Grace had the lads quiet as church mice. "Go and help saddle yer pony, Malcolm."

The lad broke into a sunny grin and scampered to do his aunt's bidding. The younger lad stifled a whimper with the back of his hand. "Dinnae leave me behind, Aunt Grace. Please. I beg ye."

"Och, my darling James. Ye're a strong lad, but ye're just learning how to ride. 'Twould not be safe."

The lad's bright eyes widened and silent tears began to run down his cheeks. Grace's face crumbled with sympathy. Oddly, Ewan understood how she felt, for the lad's earnest plea had tugged at his own heartstrings.

Ewan had been isolated his entire childhood. The unacknowledged bastard son of the earl was not easily accepted as a playmate or friend. Remembering well what it felt like to be left behind gave Ewan but one choice. "Ye can ride with me, young James."

The swift change in the lad's demeanor was enough to overcome the annoyance Ewan felt at being tricked into taking along a chaperone. He leaned down and scooped James up with his arm, dropping the child on his rump. All smiles, James dug his fingers into the horse's mane, settling himself in front of Ewan. Once he was certain the child was set, Ewan picked up the reins with his right hand while steadying the lad with his left.

Using the strength of his knees, Ewan wheeled his stallion around. Grace and Malcolm were mounted and ready. He led them out of the stable and through the courtyard, spying several of his men in the area. Jaws slack, mouths agape, they watched him and his companions as they rode out.

"Which way?" Ewan asked after they had cleared the castle gate.

"Follow me!" Malcolm shouted.

His pony shot out like an arrow, heading toward the distant forest. Grace and Ewan obligingly trailed behind. James twisted around, gazing into Ewan's face. "Malcolm always has to be the leader. Can ye overtake him?"

Ewan felt his chest constrict with empathy. It clearly wasn't easy for young James, being the second son. "Aye, we'll overrun him soon enough. Let's wait a wee while, until his mount tires."

Content with the answer, James leaned back trustingly against Ewan's chest. It was apparent by the lad's ease and comfort that he had ridden this way before, most likely with his father.

For a moment Ewan wondered what it would feel like to hold his own son this way. A fiery scamp, with red highlights in his hair and Grace's gray eyes. A son he could teach, and mold, a lad that would bring him joy and make him proud. Thinking about it brought a lump of emotion to Ewan's throat, along with the realization that a child was something he wanted to have in his life. Nay, not child, but children.

They rode for several miles, with Malcolm leading the way. Ewan kept a sharp eye on the lad, all the while listening with half an ear to James's running commentary about everything and anything they came across. For her part, Grace remained silent, riding just far enough ahead of him to avoid making conversation.

Not that it would have been possible to be heard above James's cheerful chattering. It took several miles, but eventually the talking gradually lessened until it finally ceased altogether. He was quiet for so long, Ewan wondered if the lad was feeling ill. No sooner had the thought entered Ewan's mind when James's head lulled to one side.

"He's fallen asleep," Grace declared.

"Must have been from all that talking," Ewan replied with a smile. "I confess, it near wore me out."

"James likes ye."

Ewan's lips twitched. "'Tis good to know that someone does."

She turned to him, as if curiosity overcame her better sense. "I dinnae dislike ye, sir, I merely prefer not becoming yer wife."

"Yer brother approves of the match."

She snorted. A loud, unladylike sound that brought a broader smile to Ewan's lips.

"Men have a habit of banding together when it benefits them."

"This marriage would be a boon to ye," he insisted.

"That's yer most biased opinion. I humbly beg to differ, though I've no doubt ye will take delight in telling me the many reasons that I am wrong."

"Aye. I could spin ye a yarn about the idyllic life that awaits ye. But I believe it's better if I tell ye the truth."

Eyes wary, she cocked her head. Pleased he had caught her attention, Ewan spoke from his heart. "The land I've been granted by the king is harsh and rugged, but I swear ye'll not find a more beautiful place in all of Scotland. I'll not lie to ye; it's not nearly as grand as the McKenna Castle, nor will it ever be. There's still work to be done on the keep and rebuilding needed in the village."

"Sounds charming."

"'Tis." Ewan smiled. He was not offended by the irony in her voice, having anticipated her determination to find fault no matter what he told her. "The villagers are good honest folk, with a proud Highland spirit and the backbone to survive. I know they'll quickly grow to respect and adore ye."

"I've no burning need to be placed on a pedestal by anyone."

"Not even by me?"

"Especially not by ye."

"Ah, lass, ye dinnae know—"

"Aunt Grace, look!" Malcolm shouted. "There's at least five rabbits running across the meadow. Can we set a trap fer them?"

Malcolm's shouting startled James awake. He sat up abruptly, the motion startling Ewan's horse. Instinctively he tightened his grip on the child, keeping him from taking a tumble.

"I want to see the rabbits," James yelled, rubbing his eyes with his closed fists.

"They've run to ground in the underbrush," Ewan explained.

"But they'll come out again," Malcolm insisted. "Then we can catch them."

"I like rabbit stew." James yawned loudly as he stretched his arm skyward. "So does Aunt Grace."

"Does she now?" Decision made, Ewan pulled up on the reins. He swung off his horse, then lifted James down. "Well, we shall have to catch a few of those fat hares to make yer aunt happy."

Grace stayed on her mare while Ewan and the boys gathered the supplies needed to set several snares. From the leather bag tied to his horse, Ewan produced a sturdy length of thin rope, which he pronounced would be perfect for a snare. With the boys practically yapping at his heels, Ewan searched for an appropriate spot to set the trap.

Eager to help, Malcolm and James dogged his steps and copied his every movement, making the task twice as long to accomplish. Yet Ewan didn't seem to mind overmuch. Grace was impressed by the patience he showed toward her nephews, the way he skillfully ceased their bickering and allowed each boy a chance to perform a task. Before long, several snares had been placed. All they need do was to return when the rabbits had been caught.

"James has found the perfect place to hide while we wait fer the rabbits to reappear," Ewan said with a smile.

He offered his hand up to her. Grace ignored it. "Could we not ride on and check the traps upon our return?" she asked, looking down at him in dismay.

"Nay, 'tis best if we stay close, to make certain another hungry animal does not steal our catch. The lads would be sorely disappointed to find the snares empty."

Their gazes locked and Grace smiled wanly. The tension that had plagued her for most of the night returned as her thoughts ran faster than a melting river. The very last thing she wanted was to be strolling through the area with Ewan at her side. It was too secluded, too private, too intimate. Well, at least she had Malcolm and James as an escort; their boisterous presence would prevent her from being completely alone with this handsome knight.

Seeing no other possibility, Grace placed her hand in the one Ewan offered. She slid from the back of her horse, grateful she was wearing leather gloves and thus could avoid contact with his bare flesh.

Once on the ground, Ewan gripped her arm to draw her attention. Her heart gave an odd lift at the amused glimmer in his eye and she braced for more of his attention.

But he didn't speak. Instead, he walked calmly beside her, taking care that the path they trod was not too narrow, making certain she avoided tripping on any large tree roots. Malcolm and James ran ahead, their feet crunching through the underbrush.

Eventually they exited the grove of trees and entered a small valley. A stream flowed through the middle, while around them fields of heather were beginning to bloom, the spicy scent bringing a familiar sense of comfort.

Ewan suddenly halted and turned toward her. Grace tried stepping around him, but he blocked her path.

"The lads," she said lamely.

"Are within our sight and hearing," Ewan insisted.

"If they aren't careful, they'll end up in that water in the blink of an eye," Grace warned. "And trust me, they are very seldom careful."

"Then I'll fish them out," Ewan replied. "I'm a strong swimmer."

"Naturally. Is there anything ye dinnae do well?"

His sharp gaze swung over her. "I'm a sore loser, Grace. Especially when I'm denied something I truly want."

His voice was edged with determination. It sent a shiver down her back, yet at the same time stiffened her resolve. She would not relent.

She bit her lip in frustration. Ewan was not easily dissuaded. His need must be dire, to be trying so hard. Most Highlanders would be humiliated at the notion of wooing a reluctant lass; they did not take kindly to having a woman doing what she wanted.

Grace let out a long, audible sigh. "I cling to the hope that ye'll soon grow as tired of hearing the same words of refusal as I am to say them."

In spite of her adamant words, Grace felt a sudden loneliness assaulting her. If only circumstances were different, she might be listening to Ewan's seductive words with an open mind. He seemed a genuine sort, doing his best to be honest while presenting a flattering portrait of himself and the life he could offer her.

"If ye are weary of refusing me, then say something else. Say yes."

"I cannae."

Her reply was lost in the wind. James yelled and Malcolm laughed. Grace turned to look, but Ewan suddenly grasped her arm and swung her toward him. Without warning, he pulled her close and kissed her, his tongue slipping between her lips. Grace's body froze.

Saints alive, what is he doing? Alastair never kissed me this way.

Emotions in turmoil, Grace tried to move away, but Ewan clearly had other ideas. His left hand grasped the nape of her neck and held her in place, while the right dropped to her hip, slipped around and cupped her buttocks. His arms felt strong and sure. His body was harder than hers, but she found security and secret enjoyment as her soft breasts pressed against his strong chest.

He pushed his tongue in farther, circling, stroking, teasing. Her heart nearly stopped as sensations filled her. Unfamiliar, yet exciting. A strange restlessness. The intoxicating taste of him, the sensual feel, the aching closeness. It was too much to comprehend, too much to understand. So she shut her mind to it and for a moment, a single, wicked, stolen moment, Grace allowed the experience to flow over her, engulf her.

Something primal beat through her body. Ewan swept his tongue across her teeth insistently, nudging her into a response. Her head was spinning as her body filled with a deep yearning, an incredible need. She was alive—painfully alive—and aware of every sensation coursing through her.

This is passion, desire.

He moaned. The low, throaty sound vibrated through her soul, sparking a well of temptation. She could feel the heat of him through the layers of their clothes. He was hard and muscular, a solid strength to her softer curves. She laced her fingers through his hair, feeling the soft, silky strands, tasting and teasing him with her tongue and mouth until she could no longer catch her breath.

With another low-throated growl, Ewan pulled away and Grace stumbled. They were both breathing heavily. He moved to embrace her again, but Grace put out her hand, holding him at arm's length.

Yet the distance failed to break the intimacy. Ewan looked at her as though he were trying to see into her mind. To decipher the secrets of her heart and learn her true feelings about their kisses. An unwelcome blush crept into her cheeks at the notion that he would discover how much she truly enjoyed it.

No doubt he had kissed dozens of women, nay, probably hundreds. And there would be many more after her. Abruptly, she turned away. Needing to occupy her hands, Grace stooped to pull a wildflower. Feeling the weight of Ewan's stare, she tore a petal from the flower and tossed it to the wind.

"Ye are destined to be mine, lass," he said. "Those kisses prove it. A wise woman would admit defeat and accept her fate calmly."

His wife. His woman. Sharing his life. And his bed. Her mind spun with the memory of his lips upon hers, distracting her in ways she dared not contemplate. Grace closed her eyes briefly to gain courage and willed herself to ignore the wicked thoughts that raced through her mind.

This was not the moment to weaken. Ewan's kisses—as pleasant and delightful as they were—meant nothing, changed nothing.

"Rabbits! We caught the rabbits!" James shouted.

Grace sagged with relief at the distraction. Sparing a brief glance at Ewan, she hurried to her nephews. Having no other choice, Ewan followed. When they arrived at the traps, the boys were fairly dancing with excitement.

Grace sighed with gratitude when Ewan turned his full attention to the hares. As the four of them mounted their horses, Grace felt more at ease and composed, confident she had successfully put the heated encounter firmly from her mind.

Indeed, by the time they arrived back at the keep, she'd convinced herself those afternoon kisses were all but forgotten.

Well, nearly forgotten.

Chapter Six

Ewan kept stealing glances at Grace throughout the evening meal. If she noticed, she gave no sign. Instead, she sat with an almost regal stillness, her shoulders square, her head erect, her gaze sharp as a falcon hunting its prey, never once glancing his way.

When asked a direct question, which he did as often as possible, Grace was forced to speak. Yet she achieved her revenge by keeping her manner annoyingly formal and distant, as though she were holding herself apart from the very air surrounding her.

None of which boded well for him. The kisses in the glen should have made a difference. As much as she might protest the contrary, Ewan knew she enjoyed them. Yet it had not softened her attitude toward him, nor opened her mind to his proposal. She was as determined to deny him as he was determined to possess her.

A stalemate.

Worst of all, his time was running out. Spring planting was starting. If he did not return home soon—with seeds to spare—many in his village would starve this winter.

At first pleased to discover that Grace was no sheep to meekly follow where she was led, Ewan now wished for a more pliable maiden. One who succumbed easily to flattery and admiration. One who did not hold her emotions so tightly. Aye, he wanted badly to break through her composure, to unlock the fire he believed burnt beneath her calm control.

"Today we hunted rabbits." Ewan glanced sideways at Grace, staring hard until she was compelled to look at him. "Tomorrow we'll go fishing."

Wide-eyed, Grace stared at him. "I dinnae know how to fish."

"No matter. I'll teach ye."

"I've no wish to learn." She cleared her throat, then tilted her head and cast him an innocent smile. "But I'll wager that Malcolm and James would relish the adventure. I'll tell them ye'll be taking them tomorrow before they go to bed. Though I fear they will be so excited they might not sleep much and that could make them a wee cranky come morning."

Ewan grinned, not bothering to suppress his laughter. He could well imagine what a handful the lads would be if they lacked proper rest. "There'll be no chaperones this time, Grace. We'll be alone. So I can woo ye properly, as is fitting fer a courting couple."

Grace turned an interesting shade of red, the blush starting on her chest and rushing upward. "Do ye never let it rest?"

"Never. I'm told 'tis part of my charm."

"Fie, I dinnae believe that for an instant."

"'Tis true. Lasses throughout the land clamor for my attention."

"Then it will not be hard fer ye to find a bride," she said in a prim tone.

"I've already found her," he said, allowing the huskiness to linger in his tone.

Grace let out an exasperated sigh and turned her attention to her trencher. She speared a small chunk of meat with the tip of her table knife and plunked it into her mouth. His gaze fixated on her lips as she chewed. They were plump and full, teasingly inviting a man to kiss them.

Tension coiled in his gut and whirled through his limbs, bringing on a reckless desire. Ewan watched her delicate fingers wrapped securely around the stem of her wine goblet, imagining them on his body. Curling into his tunic and pulling him closer. Caressing his shoulders and chest, then moving lower, across his stomach and upper thighs before reaching for the hardness between his legs.

For an instant, Ewan allowed his imagination to take him on an erotic fantasy, but the mood was shattered by the banging of tankards on the wooden tables as the men demanded more ale. When the servants hurried to appease the soldiers, Ewan turned to Grace.

"I'd like to propose a truce," he stated formally.

She looked at him as though he had two heads. "I was unaware that we were at war."

"We are trapped on opposite sides."

"And shall forever remain that way." Her expression darkened. "Our lives are not meant to intertwine."

"No one fated to live out their days locked away in a convent kisses the way you do, Grace."

She had the conscience to blush and look away, but refused to engage in further conversation. Ewan turned to his tankard and slowly drank. He knew better than to underestimate her. She was a worthy opponent. Thankfully, there were few in this world who could best him when it came to hard bargaining.

Grace was remarkably, at her core, a reasonable woman. What he needed to do was discover what she wanted out of a marriage. Quickly.

And then pray to God he could provide it to her.

Knowing it was wise to avoid Ewan, Grace broke her fast the next morning standing in a corner of the kitchen, munching on oatcakes and hard cheese. The bustling servants barely spared her a glance as they hurried to set out the meal in the great hall.

Hunger appeased, Grace retreated to the women's solar, the one place she knew Ewan would not be able to find her. Like many others, Aileen was protective of her female domain—no male entered her solar uninvited, including her husband. It was a comfortable and welcome retreat, reflecting the thought and care that had gone into creating it.

Grace's feet were cushioned as she walked across the patterned carpet positioned in the center of the chamber. One of the maids had opened the shutters and brisk air circulated throughout the room. Grace sat upon a bench set beneath the window, moving the soft cushion to the side. Tucking her legs under her, she gazed out at the newly sowed fields and the picturesque hills in the distance.

Her thoughts drifted as she looked at the landscape, wondering what lay beyond the mountains.

What would it feel like to ride out into the wilderness? To explore a world previously unknown, to journey to a place she had never been. To make a new life for herself . . . with Ewan.

Grace frowned. Where had that ridiculous thought been hiding? 'Twas foolish to dwell on things that could never be. Aye, foolish and a complete waste of time. Shaking off her unexpected melancholy, Grace reached for the box that held her sewing tools and the half-sewn tunic resting on top. Last week she had started making it for Malcolm and now seemed like the ideal time to finish it.

In due time Aileen arrived, her daughter, Katherine, trailing on her heels. Grace gave her niece a hug, her sister-in-law a warm greeting, then bowed her head attentively to the sewing she held in her lap. If luck was with her this morning, Aileen would take the hint that Grace preferred silence. The very last thing she wanted to discuss was Ewan Gilroy, especially with her thoughts and emotions so jumbled in her mind.

The scent of morning was in the air, the clean smell blowing through the window. Aileen sat at her loom, positioning her swollen belly so she could lean forward and wind the threads around the wooden dowels. Grace winced as she watched her sister-in-law lean forward, then pull back to weave the cloth. It looked dreadfully uncomfortable.

Still, Aileen kept at it. Every now and then she would pause and rub her lower back, but her hands always returned to their labor. After watching her for several minutes, Grace felt compelled to ask, "Are ye sure ye should be weaving so close to yer time? If the need is so great, I can do it, so ye can rest."

Grace rose from her bench, but Aileen waved her away. "The work keeps my hands and mind busy and helps me forget how tired I feel."

Grace frowned with concern. "Does the babe pain ye?"

"Nay, though this one kicks and squirms more than any of my others." Aileen made a soft clicking sound with her tongue. "That makes me think 'tis another boy. A lass would not be so inconsiderate of her poor mother."

"What does it feel like, carrying a babe?" Grace asked, curiosity getting the better of her.

Aileen's eyes went soft and dreamlike. "Glorious, exhausting, and miraculous, often at the same moment."

"I cannae fathom it."

Aileen's head turned sharply, her mouth curving into a mischievous grin. "Why dinnae ye accept Ewan Gilroy's proposal? Then ye can learn fer yerself precisely how it feels to have a bairn growing inside ye."

Grace felt her cheeks heat at the very suggestion. For a second, a brief momentous second, a spark of hope and excitement entered her heart, but it quickly sputtered and died. There would be no children in her future, from Ewan Gilroy or any other man.

Grace sighed and cast her eyes to the ground. If sensing a weakness or hesitation in her conviction to remain unwed, Aileen would pounce. Katherine, who had been sitting quietly by the window playing with her rag doll, chose that moment to let out a cry of dismay. Relieved at the distraction, Grace beckoned the child. Katherine came running over, her sweet face scrunched with distress.

"Look, Auntie Grace, 'tis broken." The little girl lifted her treasured doll and Grace noticed the small tear along the doll's arm.

"Dinnae pester yer aunt with that, Katherine," Aileen admonished. "I'll see to it when I'm finished with the weaving."

"'Tis no bother, Aileen. I can mend it." Reaching into the box at her feet, Grace extracted a length of thread, then carefully pulled it through her needle. Katherine watched with anxious eyes as the body of her beloved doll was stitched closed.

"Thank you, Auntie." Katherine clutched the doll to her breast, kissing the top of its head. Then she turned it into the crook of her arm, cradling the toy gently as she softly sang a lullaby.

Grace's chest felt tight as she watched her niece. The need to nurture started early in females, giving them a sense of purpose and contentment. A purpose she would never know.

"Ye've said very little about yer ride with Ewan yesterday," Aileen said, her voice edged with curiosity.

"Malcolm and James had fun," Grace replied vaguely.

"Aye. They talked of little else but the rabbits they caught."

"Which made a tasty stew," Grace hastily added.

"'Tis not a meal that I'm interested in hearing about, as ye well know." Reaching out, Aileen touched Grace's arm. "I've been impressed with Ewan, but it's not my opinion that matters. I'm anxious to hear yer thoughts, as is yer brother."

Grace stirred uneasily on the chair. She did not relish disappointing Aileen or Brian, but what they were asking was impossible. "Sir Ewan is a fine man. Charming, handsome, with a sharp wit and an easy smile. He's neither quick to anger, nor slow to forgive."

Aileen offered her a knowing look. "Fine qualities in a man, and particularly desirable in a husband."

"Aye." Grace managed an offhanded shrug. "Though they have no meaning fer me, since I am not in search of a husband."

The sudden sounds of clashing swords and masculine grunts saved Grace from any further interrogation. Curious, she turned to look out the window. Aileen soon joined her.

As they looked below into the bailey they saw a large circle of men. The air hung with a palpable sense of excitement and Grace soon understood why. Her brother stood next to his squire, who was carefully extracting the laird's sword from its scabbard. Ewan stood opposite him, claymore already in hand. 'Twas clear they were preparing to spar, just as soon as the two men currently engaged in swordplay were finished.

"Watch closely, lads," Brian shouted, as he and Ewan took to the practice field. "And ye'll learn a valuable lesson."

To the delight of the crowd, Brian swaggered around the courtyard in his usual fashion, raising his sword above his head to loosen his limbs. Ewan smiled at his opponent's antics, his eyes dark with anticipation.

The ringing was nearly deafening as the pair slammed their swords together in a series of powerful blows. They spun and pounded each other back and forth across the bailey, as the men surrounding them shouted and cheered. 'Twas not only the skill of the swordplay that drew such enthusiasm and awe from the crowd; Grace could see that the men respected Brian's and Ewan's fearlessness, the way they attacked with lethal intent, even though this was only a practice session.

Both men had discarded their tunics and fought bare-chested. Grace noticed Ewan's muscles rippling with every move he made, bulging in his upper arms and chest. He attacked without hesitation, the hardness of a determined warrior blazing from his eyes.

Suddenly, Brian let out a roar and charged, his sword held high. With a swift stroke, Ewan blocked the blow, then swung around. He caught Brian on the chin with his elbow, then whirled behind him and struck him on the arse with the flat of his weapon.

The watching men broke into gales of laughter, jeering and yelling. Twirling, Brian faced Ewan and spat a mouthful of blood on the ground. "If it's play-time ye're seeking, I'm happy to oblige."

"Ye always wield yer sword with a high swing," Ewan shouted cheerfully, wiping the sweat from his brow. "'Tis easy enough to defend against it when I know it's coming."

"Then I'll need to try something a wee bit different," Brian countered, as he swung at Ewan's legs.

Anticipating the move, Ewan jumped over the blade, throwing Brian off balance. Through sheer strength, Brian managed to stay upright. Unprepared for the swift recovery, Ewan was knocked on his back as Brian drove his shoulder into Ewan's gut.

Grabbing hold of Brian's ankle, Ewan pulled his opponent to the ground. Dust flew as the pair wrestled, rolling across the bailey. A raucous cheer went up from the men and the wagering on which man would be victorious escalated.

Scrambling back to their feet, Ewan and Brian once again reached for their weapons. Breathing hard, faces lined with dirt and sweat, they faced each other, each searching for a weakness to exploit.

"Will they ever tire?" Grace asked.

"Aye, eventually, and then a blade will slip and one will be injured." Aileen positioned herself fully in front of the window. "The match is a draw," she shouted.

All heads turned in their direction. Instinctively, Grace shrank back from the sea of male eyes, while Aileen leaned forward.

"Milady, there needs to be a clear victor," one of the men yelled.

"The sun will long be set and the torches lit before either of them bests the other," Aileen replied. "'Tis obvious they are equals in skill and tenacity. I say we declare this a draw and invite all into the great hall to toast the match with ale and whiskey."

A weak cheer was heard from a few of the men, but many more grumbled. "They dinnae seemed very taken with yer suggestion," Grace muttered from the shadows.

"I dinnae care," Aileen hissed. "I need to give Brian and Ewan a way to end this with their pride intact."

"Ye cannae believe they will truly hurt each other?"

"Accidents happen, even while practicing. They'll fight until one presses a sword against the other's throat. Whoever loses will be humiliated and that could sour their friendship and our alliance."

"Riders approach!"

The shout from the guard tower quickly put an

end to the match. Without needing to receive any orders, the warriors in the courtyard took off at a run, each man hurrying to his post. Grace saw Ewan fall in behind Brian and accompany him to the wall.

Grace and Aileen exchanged a worried gaze as they anxiously watched the hasty preparations. 'Twas hushed as all eyes, including Grace's, strained toward the road, waiting to see what colors the men approaching were wearing. She could tell from the amount of dust swirling along the path that they were sizable in number, a full complement of armed men.

Though not currently engaged in any open feuds, there were several clans that the McKennas counted more foe than friend. Grudges between clans were held for years, often passing from one generation to the next. It was thus essential to always be vigilant whenever a mounted group of warriors displaying such a show of strength rode this close to the castle.

The suspense throughout the keep was unbearable. Then Grace heard Aileen gasp, her hand reaching upward to cover her mouth. "'Tis the Sinclair colors," Aileen announced, relief filling her voice. "I can see the banners of green and gold."

Grace relaxed. Aileen was the only child of the Sinclair laird; obviously she was pleased to welcome her kinsmen. "Is yer father among the riders?"

"Aye, front and center, leading the way." Aileen smiled ruefully, amusement lighting her eyes. "I told him to wait until I sent word that the babe had safely arrived, but he's never been one to follow another's orders."

"Hmm." Grace merely smiled, not needing to comment on how much the daughter followed her sire. "I'll hurry to the kitchens to make certain a proper welcome is prepared."

"Thank ye, Grace. I know my father and his men will appreciate a good meal."

Glad to be of service, Grace made her way down to the kitchen. The cook, a stout, heavy-jowled man who clearly enjoyed the fruits of his labors, favored her with a panicked look the moment she entered his domain.

"Are we under attack?"

"Nay." Grace cleared her throat, bringing her hand to her mouth to hide her smile. "'Tis the Sinclairs who ride into the courtyard. Naturally, Lady Aileen would like a feast prepared to welcome her father and his men."

"I have fresh venison, fish, and mutton," Cook said, as he lumbered to the storeroom. "The breads are ready for the ovens, there's meat jelly from yesterday, and plenty of dried apples and pears to make some tarts."

"Do ye have enough honey?" Grace asked.

"Aye, the hives were stripped of their combs last week. But I'll need more help to prepare a feast that is worthy of our guests."

Grace nodded. "I'll send some others to assist ye, then I'll fetch the spices ye'll need."

The cook gave her a happy smile, then started shouting orders at his helpers. Grace had a few additional servants fetched before going back into the storeroom. Some of the more precious spices, such as salt, nutmeg, and cinnamon, were locked away, brought out only for special occasions. Grace assumed

Aileen would consider a visit from her father an opportune time to raid the spice supplies.

After handing Cook the spices, Grace stayed to help peel vegetables, paying no attention to the curious looks she was given by several of the women gathered around the worktable. Unlike many other ladies of her station, Grace was no stranger to menial tasks. Being raised in a convent had taught her that no chore was beneath her. In truth, Grace sometimes missed the quiet solitude that came with performing a simple, mindless job.

"I thank ye fer yer help, milady," Cook said, as he pointed a large wooden spoon in her general direction. "I couldnae have managed without ye. But ye best join the others at the high table before we bring out the food."

Grace nodded. She placed the last carrot on the pile and wiped her brow. She had never met Aileen's father and was curious to discover what sort of man would raise such an outspoken, confident female.

The fresh air in the great hall felt cool and refreshing after the heat in the kitchen. Grace breathed deeply, then quietly slid into a chair at the end of the high table. She was still arranging the folds of her gown when Ewan took the chair beside her. His hair was wet, his tunic clean. Clearly he had taken the time to bathe and change before coming to the table. Suddenly nervous, Grace glanced down at her gown, hoping she had not gotten any spots on it while working in the kitchen. The last thing she wanted was to offend Aileen's father.

Introductions were made as the food was brought into the hall. Laird Sinclair was not particularly tall and his short stature made him appear almost round, but his proud bearing proclaimed him a respected leader. There was gray in the hair at his temples and his skin was tanned from being outdoors.

He looked strong and capable, despite his years. Aileen favored her father in few ways, except for his erect bearing and confident air. Those traits had clearly been passed to his daughter.

He examined Grace with an unwavering intensity, the scrutiny making her rather self-conscious. "My sympathies at the passing of Sir Alastair," Laird Sinclair said as his gaze continued to travel over her. "Ye'll be taking a new husband soon, I expect, Lady Grace."

"No, milord, I will not," she replied through clenched teeth.

"My sister asks to return to the convent where she was raised," Brian said, helping himself to a portion of venison stew.

Laird Sinclair raised his brow. "Do ye not wish fer a home of yer own? A babe in yer arms and another grabbing at yer skirts?"

The words pierced her heart. "Alas, that shall not be my fate." She shrugged philosophically, trying to appear calm yet knowing she failed miserably.

"'Tis unnatural for a female to remain unwed," the laird said, shaking his head.

"Which is precisely why I am trying to change the lady's mind," Ewan interjected smoothly.

Laird Sinclair ceased chewing. "I should not be surprised to hear that ye're sniffing around her, Gilroy. Ye always were an ambitious cur."

"I've an eye fer beauty and an appreciation of a noble and gentle soul," Ewan protested.

Sinclair scoffed. "Ye've the need fer a bride with a rich dowry and an alliance with a powerful clan like the McKennas."

"Are ye suggesting that the lady is not incentive enough on her own?" Ewan asked, rising to his feet. "I take great offense at that insult!"

"Sit down," Sinclair said, the humor evident in his voice. "No need to preen like a peacock in front of the lass."

"Ye do me, and the lady, a grave injustice," Ewan insisted, casting a reproachful look at the older man as he once again took his seat.

"I speak honestly, as ye well know," the laird replied. "Any alliance with the McKennas becomes an indirect alliance with me, so I too have an interest in who the lass weds. I admire yer skill on the battlefield, Gilroy, and would much prefer to have ye fighting beside me than against me. But even ye'll admit that the land ye were given is in the farthest reaches of the kingdom. By the time a message reaches ye, and yer men are mustered and on the march, the battle will be long over."

"I hold and keep what is mine," Brian retorted, a warning light in his eyes. "I value the friendships I share with many clans, but I can protect my lands without the aid of any allies."

"Enough of this talk of battles!" Aileen sighed. "The war has finally ended and yet all ye men can speak of is the next one. 'Tis putting me off my food."

Both Brian and Sinclair reached for Aileen's hand at the same moment. She resisted for a second, then allowed first her husband and then her father to placate her.

The remainder of the meal passed in relative peace as everyone's attention was diverted by the fine food and ale that had been placed before them. Grace slowly let out a breath, but there was no time to relax, as Ewan began whispering in her ear.

"Did ye hear, Grace? Laird Sinclair also thinks it would be best if ye marry me."

Gracious, was there no escape from overbearing men? "He thinks that all women should be wed," she replied tartly. "And as I recall the conversation, he had a rather low opinion of me making a match with ye."

"That might have been his initial reaction," Ewan conceded. "But once he's had a chance to think it over, he'll agree I'm the best husband ye can find."

Grace shot him a sharp look before picking up her goblet. Thankfully, the talk turned to politics and the policies of King Robert. Like many independent-minded chieftains, Laird Sinclair did not approve of all of the king's actions and he never hesitated in expressing his opinion or arguing his point.

"Lady Grace, tell us what ye know of the Fergusons' troubles?" Laird Sinclair asked, staring down at the empty bowls and trays that covered the table. The savory smells of the now-eaten food still hung in the air and most were lingering over the delicious meal.

"Nothing." Grace lifted her chin and willed herself not to blush as all eyes were suddenly on her. "I am unaware of any particular difficulties."

"Och, 'tis a sad business that's plaguing the Fergusons these days. They say Roderick Ferguson is burning with resentment over not being chosen as chieftain. He's dividing the loyalties of his clan, persuading some of the men to his side."

Brian shook his head. "'Tis bad enough when the clans fight each other, but discord within a clan will tear it asunder. Mark my words, if this isn't settled soon, without too much bloodshed, it will be the undoing of the Fergusons."

Grace noticed many heads nodding in silent agreement. The mention of Roderick brought a myriad of images and emotions to mind, none of which were pleasant.

"Roderick has challenged his brother's rule," Laird Sinclair elaborated. "He claims Alastair's death was hastened by foul play and blames his brother."

"Shocking," Aileen mused.

"Aye, 'tis an unpleasant business." Laird Sinclair wiped his hands on the front of his tunic, then sent Grace a calculated look. "Were ye with yer husband in his final hours, Lady Grace?"

Grace felt her stomach jolt into a sickening twist. She was so overcome with surprise and fear that for an instant she was unable to speak. Quickly, she looked down at her trencher, not wanting anyone to glimpse the guilt she was certain was shimmering in her eyes.

Ewan slammed down his tankard, his upper lip curling into a disapproving line. "'Tis clear that speaking of her husband is a painful memory that Lady Grace prefers to forget."

Grateful for the distraction, yet feeling unworthy of Ewan's spirited defense, Grace sucked in a harsh breath. "Aye, it brings me pain and sorrow remembering Alastair's last days. His wounds were grievous and he suffered mightily. God was merciful when he called him to his side."

"What of Roderick's claims?" Laird Sinclair pressed, his voice challenging. "Do they have any merit?"

"Nay. They are baseless and rooted in jealousy," Grace replied, trying to speak calmly and with conviction. "The men elected Douglas chieftain, as is their right. Roderick divides the clan simply because he cannae accept that he was not chosen. 'Tis merely further proof that he wouldnae be a strong, selfless leader."

"Well said, lass." Ewan nodded with approval.

The protective gesture brought on a wave of calm, followed swiftly by guilt. Grace bit her lower lip. *I dinnae deserve Ewan's support.*

Sinclair shrugged. "Ye'd best be prepared for a visit from Roderick," the laird said to Brian. "He'll be seeking aid in his quest to be chieftain from even the slimmest of alliances."

Brian's nostrils flared as though he had just caught wind of a foul and offensive odor. "He'll not be getting any help from me. It pains me to hear of their troubles, yet I'm relieved to have my sister away from there. It lessens my worry knowing she's not in any danger. She is back with her family and I'll see to her protection and future. Roderick has no business involving Grace in his quarrels."

"He does not strike me as a man who cares much about right and wrong," Laird Sinclair commented.

"I'll make certain that the men know to be extra vigilant," Brian declared, once again grasping his wife's hand.

Young Bess was summoned to entertain them. Well

known for her lovely voice and witty songs, Bess executed a graceful curtsy and set to the task with obvious gusto. Needing to be alone with her thoughts, Grace seized upon the distraction, and quietly slipped away from the table the moment Bess started singing.

Chapter Seven

Grace stood in the shadows, trying to calm her racing heart and shaking hands. She despised Roderick and what he was doing to the Fergusons with every fiber of her being. His reckless, selfish quest for power was causing suffering and despair. The clan did not deserve such a dire, uncertain fate.

Guilt plagued her, for deep in her heart she felt responsible for contributing to the misery of so many good, innocent people. *If I had not aided Alastair in hastening his death, could this have been avoided?* Yet even as the disturbing thought entered her mind, Grace knew it would not have mattered. Roderick was hell-bent on leading the clan and damn the consequences.

Still, the ambiguity surrounding Alastair's passing had given Roderick the opportunity to gain a substantial foothold in his challenge for power. And that Grace knew *was* her responsibility.

"Are ye troubled?"

Grace screeched in surprise, unable to contain the

sound. Ewan stepped closer and extended a hand to steady her. "'Tis only me, Grace."

His hand tightened on her upper arm and he gently pulled her toward him. Badly in need of comfort, Grace allowed it.

"Ye startled me," she whispered, as her head rested against his broad shoulder.

For a few moments she found relief from the cold chill of dread pulling at her heart, but then reality closed in around her and she reluctantly pulled away. "The talk of Roderick has rattled me. Though I am no longer among them, I wish only peace and prosperity fer the Ferguson Clan."

"Yer concern and caring does ye proud, Grace. The clans have fought against each other and among themselves fer years, and though there are many that long fer it to stop, we know it willnae." Ewan peered keenly at her. "Ye must learn to let go of the past and look toward the future. With me."

Grace took a deep, shaking breath and placed a trembling hand to her throat. Potent emotions gripped her soul. "Wedding ye is not the answer."

Ewan seemed to consider her words carefully before speaking. "What do ye truly fear, Grace? Please, tell me."

Grace didn't reply right away. She leaned against the stone wall and crossed her arms over her chest. What did she fear? Roderick's retribution rearing its ugly head and threatening not only his clan, but the McKennas as well? Aye, that was a big worry.

As for marriage, well, she could not tell him the truth . . . that her past made her feel enormous guilt. That the only way to possibly atone for her actions was to seek a life of pious solitude and devotion, locked behind the walls of a convent.

"Dinnae press me, Ewan; I beg ye. All I can say is that I cannae be a wife to any man."

"Not even me? I'm different from most others. I want more from my wife than to take complete control of her life. I want a companion, a woman who will share in my joys and burdens, who will advise me when it's needed. A woman I can honor and cherish."

And love.

He was not foolish enough to speak the words, for he must have known that any woman would be hard-pressed to believe them upon such a short acquaintance. But he was clever enough to know that was what many females craved most of all—to be loved.

Still, Grace clearly heard that magical word—*love*—in the sincerity of his tone, the wistfulness of his expression. It brought tears to her eyes. It would have been so much easier to turn him away if he were merely searching for an advantageous alliance. If he wanted a wife for the usual reasons of property and position.

She shivered, looking away. His tender, sweet words were difficult to ignore, yet she knew that she must. "Ye need a wife with a dowry, who has a family that will accept ye. There are many others that will do."

"Nay, Grace. Ye. I only want ye." He touched her cheek, then cupped her chin, forcing her to look at him. "I cannae promise to be an ideal husband, but I will try to be all that you wish me to be, all that you need."

She had to bite her lip to hold back the smile that lightened her heart, for it was cruel to encourage him and foolish to indulge herself. "Ye are without question the boldest man in the Highlands, Ewan Gilroy."

He grinned at her. Grace felt her heart quicken and her throat go dry. She knew he was going to kiss her even before he leaned close and brushed his mouth against hers. And when he did, she forgot to breathe.

Her entire being was enraptured by the feel of his lips on hers. He put his arms around her and drew her close and Grace sighed with contentment. The sensation was so sweet, so perfect, she allowed herself to get lost in it.

The pressure on her lips increased and Grace clutched the muscular strength of Ewan's arms, lifting herself up on her toes to get closer. Boldly, she parted her lips, gasping at the feel of his velvet tongue sweeping across hers. It made her tingle and tense, bringing on a restless urgency throughout her body.

Wanting, nay needing, more, she arched forward, tilting her head and kissing him back. He answered by moving his warm hands frantically up and down her back, molding her body against his. The exquisite pleasure seemed to fill her entire being. Like a fever it seemed to overwhelm her, making her almost dizzy with exhilaration.

His breathing was fast and hard and she could feel the thickening hardness beneath his braies pressing against her belly. She closed her eyes tightly, unable to control the trembling that shook her body. Their tongues continued to dance as their kisses grew bolder and Grace felt a quiver inside her, an ache of need, the restless urgency of unfulfilled passion.

Unfulfilled. And thus it must remain.

Regretfully, she twisted her lips away. Ewan groaned low in his throat. His hands were in her hair, holding her face between his palms. When her breathing finally slowed, Grace dared to look up at him.

Ewan's eyes were glittering like fire. She recognized the intense need on his face, hardly believing that she had been the one to put it there. He wanted her. Badly. Not only for her dowry, not only for an alliance—he wanted *her*.

The knowledge rattled her. For a moment, a pang of longing for what could never be stirred inside her, but she quickly suppressed it.

"Ye will be mine one day," he murmured.

Grace shook her head. His voice was a low rumble in her ear, deep and oddly comforting. He lifted her hand to his lips and kissed her ringless fingers. For a long tense moment they stared at one another.

Somewhere in the distance Grace heard people talking. It would be unwise to be caught alone with Ewan; castle gossip could force the issue of her marriage and cause Ewan greater humiliation when she refused. "We should not be seen in so intimate a setting together," she muttered.

Grace nearly flinched beneath the kind stare he gave her, as it made her feel unworthy of his sympathy and understanding. "I'll go back to the hall first," he offered. "Then ye follow."

Not trusting her voice, Grace nodded. *He will soon forget me,* she told herself sternly. *As I will him.*

Yet she stayed rooted to the spot, her gaze following him long after he had disappeared down the lonely corridor.

* * *

Thoughts of Ewan were soon replaced by disturbing thoughts of Roderick. Knowing she was in no fit state to return to the hall, Grace instead sought a place for private reflection where she could be alone with her thoughts. Remembering a quiet area on the large curtain wall, Grace walked to the end of the corridor and began climbing the stairs.

She was slightly out of breath by the time she reached the fourth and final staircase. Lifting the hem of her gown, Grace placed her feet carefully on the slick, steep treads and stepped out onto the battlements. Normally, she disliked great heights, but the lure of this peaceful scene calmed her.

A breeze of cool air greeted her, welcomed and bracing. Grace placed her hands on the top of the gray stone wall, darkened with age, and leaned forward, taking in the spectacular view.

The newly plowed fields stretched nearly as far as the eye could see, straight rows of neat tilled earth. Beyond them were meadows and streams and to the left a vast forest. The village at the base of the long hill that surrounded the castle was a labyrinth of shops and thatch-roofed homes, most with smoke rising through the chimneys.

Even from this distance she could hear the sounds of the hammers and saws of the laboring men, could catch the faint scent of roasting meat and rich stews as the women prepared the evening meal for their families. It was a tranquil, everyday occurrence, but the hard-won peace of the moment was undeniable.

All that will change if Roderick appears.

Grace shuddered, hugging her arms tightly around her waist. She had great faith in her brother's skill, and the strength and readiness of the McKenna's warriors. There was no doubt they would protect her if Roderick dared to show his face. Nay, it wasn't the McKenna men she doubted, it was Roderick. He wouldn't fight fairly or honorably to get what he wanted.

And that put every man, woman, and child of the clan at risk.

The mere thought of it was her undoing. Instinctively, Grace dropped to her knees and bowed her head. Ever since Alastair's death she had found little comfort in prayer, but suddenly that felt like the only thing she could do.

The words were slow to fall from her lips, but soon the apprehension faded as she opened her mind and heart. Thoughts and possible action mixed with her prayers until a sense of rightness entered her soul. Her choices were few, but the decision was suddenly easy.

For the protection and safety of all those she loved, 'twas time for her to leave.

As soon as the morning meal was cleared from the great hall, Grace went in search of her brother. Though convinced of the rightness of her decision, sleep had been impossible last night. As she walked the corridor toward the laird's private study, a dull ache pounded in her temples. She had never before felt so weary. It felt as though all emotions had been drained from her and only numbness remained.

Grace was not completely certain what else she would say to Brian, beyond refusing to marry Ewan and requesting that she be escorted to the abbey by the end of the week. She only knew that she needed to present her request in a reasonable manner, thus giving her brother no other choice but to agree.

Unfortunately, Brian was not alone when she found him. Ewan was by his side, the pair of them intently studying a large map spread across the table.

"Excuse the interruption," Grace said, hastily backing away. "I shall return when ye are unoccupied."

"Nay, come in, Grace." Brian beckoned her with a waggle of his fingers. "Ewan and I were trying to locate his keep on the map."

"The property is so far north we cannae define the borders," Ewan added cheerfully.

They stared at her expectantly. Hastily, she moved forward and examined the map. "Are ye near the sea?" she asked, pointing to a fierce drawing of several sea monsters.

"Not too close," Ewan replied. "'Tis a half day's ride, which affords us the pleasure of fresh fish from the ocean's bounty with none of the dangers."

"'Tis a fine holding," Brian said pointedly.

"Indeed," Grace replied, not liking the direction of the conversation.

"Ye must see it fer yerself," Ewan said invitingly.

Grace stiffened. She could feel the sudden tension in the air and was sorry for it. But that did not prevent her from speaking.

"Alas, that willnae be possible. I've come to tell my brother that I'd like to return to the abbey by week's end," she said, deliberately keeping her voice soft and devoid of all inflection. She would not be accused of making a womanly, emotional decision.

"I'd hoped ye'd stay at least until Aileen's babe is born," Brian said.

"That willnae be happening fer at least a month, maybe longer. I need to go now."

Brian sighed heavily. "Are ye certain?"

"I am. 'Tis what I told ye I meant to do from the beginning and I've not changed my mind." Grace felt her cheeks warm. "Sir Ewan is also aware of my decision."

From across the table she felt the force of Ewan's disappointed gaze. She met his stare with imploring eyes, willing him to understand, and accept, her decision.

True, she had not shared with him her intention to leave so soon, but she had never once led him to believe she would accept his marriage proposal. And yet, Ewan still stared at her dumbfounded. The tension that gripped him was obvious and she felt a pang of regret.

Ewan was a good, decent man. She had no wish to cause him any upset. But the outcome was inevitable. 'Twas time—nay past time—for her to shed the ties to the outside world. Delaying it would serve no useful purpose.

"I'll not lie and say I'm pleased," Brian said, with a deep note of regret in his voice.

Grace lowered her gaze. She had never seen her brother so disappointed and she was distressed to be the cause of it.

"I hope in time ye'll understand," Grace replied solemnly.

It was impossible to remain calm while looking at Ewan, so Grace deliberately avoided his gaze. Then, having said what she came to tell her brother, she sank into a low curtsy, all the while ignoring the tiny voice inside her head that warned she was making a mistake, she was throwing away her only chance at true happiness with both hands. Legs shaking, she strode out the door and purposefully down the hall, telling herself she felt grateful to have gotten her way.

If only the taste of victory were sweet, instead of filled with bitterness.

The room was deadly silent after Grace left. Ewan glanced at Brian for answers, but the McKenna shrugged his shoulders helplessly.

"I gave her my word that she could choose and thus she has made her decision. She'll leave fer the abbey at the end of the week."

Damnation! He'd been close, so close. Ewan had nearly tasted victory, a triumph made all the more sweet because Grace would have been his bride. When he started this quest Ewan was honest enough to admit he would have married any woman in order to secure the well-being of his people.

But now he wanted more. He wanted a woman he admired, a woman he could grow to love. He wanted Grace. But she didn't want him.

Time. That was what he needed. She was thawing toward him, even allowing herself to be charmed a bit, he was certain of it. If only he had a wee bit more time, he could change her mind.

"Drink."

Ewan looked down at the tankard Brian offered, resisting the urge to grab it, throw it against the wall and shout out his frustrations. Instead, he tipped the vessel to his lips and drained it. Without being invited, he refilled it and took another long sip. Perhaps if he drank enough tankards, the sting of defeat would not feel so sharp.

"No matter what she says, I cannae believe it's what she truly wants," Ewan muttered.

"I'm as disappointed as ye," Brian insisted. "Grace was raised in that abbey, knowing almost nothing of the outside world. She speaks little of her life as Ferguson's wife, but I think she found some contentment. I thought once she tasted the freedom of being mistress of her own castle, she would again want her own home. I truly believed if anyone could get her to change her mind it would be ye."

Ewan made a slashing motion with his fist, his frustrations spilling over. "God's bones! She prefers the life of a nun to a life with me. 'Tis a bitter pill to swallow."

Brian stroked his chin thoughtfully. "She'll need an escort to the abbey," he said mildly. "Especially with all this talk of Roderick Ferguson and his quest to rule his clan. I'll take no chance with her safety."

Ewan failed to hide his impatience at the obvious remark. "Aye, 'tis yer duty to protect her from the marauders that travel the roads."

"But my men need training and we've started new fortifications to the south wall. I cannae spare enough of them to make a proper escort."

Ewan paused, his disappointment turning to curiosity. "Ye think to stall her leaving by denying Grace a contingent of men? I doubt that will work and I know it will anger yer wife if she believes ye are being devious."

"Aileen understands the importance of maintaining a castle's defenses."

"She'll not be fooled," Ewan warned.

"I would never be such a lack-wit as to try and pull the wool over my wife's eyes." Brian smiled. "I dinnae have the men to spare, but ye do. Do ye think ye are up to the task of leading Grace's escort? It's at least a four-day ride from here."

Ewan blew out a loud breath and then his lips parted into a wide grin. "Five or six days, depending on the route taken."

"Now that's the spirit. What do ye say, Ewan? Will ye do it?"

"With pleasure," Ewan replied, certain the gratitude he felt was shining in his eyes.

The day dawned gray and damp as Grace prepared to leave the castle. A variety of horses, carts, and men assembled near the stables as all was made ready. In addition to the packhorses that carried the food and tents they would need for the journey, there were carts carrying supplies to the nuns. Grace had seen to that packing personally, ensuring her presence would be an asset and not the burden of yet another mouth to feed at the convent.

A gust of wind swirled as the sky darkened ominously and the clouds loomed full and low.

"Ye could wait until tomorrow or the next day fer the weather to clear," Aileen suggested, as she stepped gingerly into the courtyard.

Grace shook her head. Delaying would only make it harder. "The rain will keep the dust at bay," she reasoned. "Besides, the horses prefer riding on a cool day."

"'Tis not the comfort of the horses I care about," Aileen grumbled. "But I'm hardly surprised by yer answer. Despite yer pretty face and gentle voice, ye are as stubborn as every other McKenna that walks the earth."

"I shall miss ye also, Aileen." Grace reached over and hugged her sister-in-law tightly. "Very much."

She felt a tug upon her sleeve and glanced down. Malcolm stood at her side, his face cautious. "When will I see ye again?" he asked.

Grace bit her tongue, holding back the temptation to lie. "Not fer a very long time, I'm afraid. Why, ye'll most likely be a man full grown the next time I set eyes on ye."

Grace expected the lad to swagger at the notion, but instead his brow knit together in a frown.

"Why do ye have to leave?" James asked with a sniffle. "Don't ye like us anymore?"

"I love ye!" Grace proclaimed. "All of ye. But my place is at the abbey."

"I dinnae want ye to go," Katherine cried, flinging herself forward. She clasped her arms around Grace's knees and held on tightly.

"Oh, dearest." Helplessly, Grace searched for assistance. Heaving an impatient sigh, her brother came forward. It took him a few moments to pry Katherine's fingers open. The moment he succeeded, he lifted the little girl into his arms. She hung on to him, burying her face in his shoulder.

"I dinnae suppose that ye'll be changing yer mind?" Brian asked, his mouth turning into a grim line when she shook her head. "Then I'll be wishing ye Godspeed on yer journey, Sister. Always remember ye've a home here with us, if ye ever have the need."

Brian's arm felt as hard as granite when he hugged her. "Thank ye. Fer everything," Grace whispered in his ear, before pulling away.

She wanted to say more, but could not, as the words congealed into a cold lump in her throat. Tears filled her eyes as she mounted her palfrey. Grace brushed them away with her gloved hand and forced a smile. She would not have her family's final memory be of her riding away with red, weepy eyes and a grim expression.

I'm doing what must be done, she admonished herself, as she adjusted her seat and picked up the reins. It offered little relief to the hollowness she felt, to the sudden jolt of fear and uncertainty, but 'twas all she had. Clinging to the solitary thought, Grace positioned her mount in line with the others.

Ewan had not come to say his farewells. In fact, she had not seen much of him all week, ever since she had announced that she was leaving. *'Tis better this way,* she told herself. Yet the feelings of disappointment that flooded her were something she could not deny. Though she could, and did, struggle to ignore them.

The mood lightened as the line of travelers started moving through the bailey. Dogs began barking and children ran alongside, shouting and waving. Malcolm and James joined in, elbowing one another aside for a better view, though Grace noticed Katherine stayed in her father's arms.

When they reached the drawbridge, Grace turned and raised her hand in a farewell salute. Her vision was blurred by the unwanted tears that sprang to her eyes, but she did not right herself and face forward again until the bailey was no longer in her sights.

It took a full quarter mile until Grace had her emotions in check. Then, and only then, did she take a few moments to survey her escort. For her protection, she had been placed in the middle of the line. A group of soldiers scouted ahead while the packhorses and carts were set at the rear. Grace hoped that Edna was comfortable riding among the luggage. Her maid had insisted she make the journey, though she would return at a later time to McKenna land.

Grace's mount twisted its head and for the first time she noticed how tightly the guard had hemmed her in between them. She glanced at the men who rode on either side and realized she did not know them. That was, of course, no great surprise; not all of the McKenna retainers were known to her.

Yet as she took a few minutes to closely examine the others in her entourage, she realized there was not one man she recognized. Startled, she pulled herself up, squinted and strained to see the soldiers at the front of the line.

Nay, it cannae be!

Grace's back stiffened as she caught sight of the man leading her escort. Telling herself she was being fanciful, Grace tamped down the flutter of alarm that rose in her stomach. But her worst fears were confirmed when the leader turned to the man on his left and she caught a clear look at his profile. There was no mistaking those features and that tall, straight bearing.

Saints alive, it's Ewan!

Without missing a beat, Grace urged her palfrey forward, breaking through the ranks, ignoring the shouts of the men who reluctantly allowed her through.

"I dinnae understand," she muttered when she reached Ewan's side. "Why are ye leading these men?"

"'Tis simple. I'm leaving and ye needed an escort. It seemed logical to combine the two."

"Nay!"

"Aye!"

"Was this yer idea?" Grace asked, trying to sound calm and failing completely. "Or do I see my brother's meddling hand in this officious plan?"

"The McKenna thought it a fine idea, but I heartily agreed." Ewan offered her a cocksure grin, his white teeth flashing. "Ye'll not be rid of me so easily or quickly, Grace."

She shot him a look of bored indifference that fooled neither of them. A part of her balked at falling so compliantly into this little scheme, cooked up by her brother and his good friend, but her choices were few. If she refused Ewan's escort, Brian could delay her departure for weeks, if not months. It had been difficult enough leaving the first time; she doubted she would be able to do it a second.

Being duped was not a pleasant feeling, but Grace decided she must rely on her inner conviction and faith. A few additional days in Ewan's company would change nothing. Yet as she looked ahead to the path they were taking, she added a prayer for the good weather necessary to hasten their journey and end it as quickly as possible.

Chapter Eight

The scenery changed little as they broke through the McKenna woods, though the sound of thunder rumbling in the distance had Ewan and his men looking toward the sky. Feeling the same sort of prevailing tension he experienced when preparing to face an enemy in battle, Ewan urged his mount forward, pulling alongside Grace.

"If we keep to this steady pace, we should reach Glenmore Keep before the rain strikes. We can take shelter there fer the night."

"Hmmm."

"Of course we can stop fer a short rest, if ye feel the need. Just say the word and I'll have Alec scout for a safe, private spot."

Grace clamped her lips together in a tight line and shook her head.

"Are ye hungry? I've oatcakes and dried fruit and there's a flask of wine in my saddlebags."

Grace pushed a tendril of hair off her cheek and sniffed delicately. Ewan waited, but it soon become clear she wasn't going to answer.

"Jesus, are ye ever going to speak to me again, Grace?"

Her back stiffened. She took in a deep breath, then turned and stared at him with wide gray eyes. "I highly doubt ye'd be wanting to hear what I have to say."

"Grace, please, be reasonable."

"Dinnae ye dare start acting indignant, Sir Ewan. We both know my displeasure with ye is more than warranted."

"How so? I did a favor fer a good friend, by offering my sword and men to protect his sister on her journey. Is that so very wrong?"

"Och! Dinnae pretend to be a chivalrous hero coming to the rescue of a helpless maiden. Yer actions are wholly self-serving."

"I hadn't realized what a suspicious nature ye have, Grace. 'Tis refreshing, really, to discover ye do have a fault or two."

"I've more than one. And I'd be cursing yer deception with vigor if I knew any appropriate words."

"Shall I teach ye a few? It might make ye feel better."

Grace lifted her eyes to the clouds, but he caught sight of the grin she tried to hide. Heartened, Ewan smiled at her. She pretended to be unaware, but he was not discouraged. Bit by bit he would wear down her resistance. 'Twould be a four-day journey to the abbey that could easily stretch to five or six if the weather worsened and the roads became muddy.

Kicking his horse forward, Ewan glanced at the sky and silently prayed for rain.

* * *

They reached Glenmore Keep as dusk was falling. Laird Kilkinney was not in residence, yet upon being told that the McKenna's sister rode with them, the gates were open in welcome. The laird's nephew, Simon, stood in the bailey as they entered. A short, stout, balding man of middle years, he cast a glowing smile in Grace's direction and hurried over to assist her from her mount.

The sight of those beefy hands clasped around Grace's waist had Ewan gritting his teeth and tightening his grip on the reins. When the man had the boldness to reach out and touch the edge of her veil, Ewan was hard-pressed not to succumb to the urge to pull his sword and run it through Simon's protruding belly.

"Steady." Alec's calm voice cut through Ewan's rising agitation. "We've come in peace, remember."

Ewan let out a snort. "What do ye know of him?" he asked, his eyes never leaving Grace's slight form as she stood beside their host.

"Nothing. Kilkinney fought with the Bruce, but I never heard any talk of his nephew."

Ewan spat. "By the looks of him, he was left at home to oversee the lands while others went to war."

"Aye. He hardly looks like a fighting man, strutting and posturing like a damn peacock. He's no threat to Lady Grace or us," Alec concluded cheerfully.

"I'll be the one to make that judgment," Ewan snapped. "In the meantime, tell the men to keep a sharp eye. I want to make certain nothing odd is afoot. This place gives me an uneasy feeling."

Ewan's gaze drifted to the gray stone steps and the dark wooden door that Grace and Simon had just passed through. With an aggravated sigh, he followed quickly behind them, arriving in the great hall as Simon was assisting Grace to a bench set before the fire.

Two large hounds ceased their scavenging in the rushes and lifted their heads. Ewan reached for the hilt of his sword as one lumbered curiously toward Grace. He was nearly at her side when he heard a high-pitched scream.

"Get away, ye dirty beast!" Simon shrieked, wrinkling his nose in distaste. "Och, I do beg yer pardon, Lady Grace. I hope this mangy cur dinnae frighten ye too badly."

"I'm used to dogs freely roaming the castle," Grace replied, a light of humor in her eyes. She scratched the dog affectionately behind the ears and he obligingly rested his head in her lap.

Simon's startled expression soon turned envious, and Ewan could easily imagine the other man fantasying about switching places with the beast. *Over my dead body.*

"Aye, it takes something much fiercer to distress Lady Grace," Ewan interjected.

Simon's brows knitted together, puffing his jowls and narrowing his eyes. "Who are ye?"

"Sir Ewan Gilroy, commander of Lady Grace's escort," Ewan replied, watching with pleasure as Simon flinched at his thundering tone.

"Ye and yer men are welcome to set up camp within the bailey," Simon grudgingly offered. "Lady Grace will naturally be given our guest chamber in the north tower."

Ewan's gut tightened. Unless the weather was bitterly cold, 'twas not uncommon for unexpected guests to sleep in the courtyard. Keeps of this size seldom had enough space in their great hall to house others as most of the servants and soldiers already slept in the hall.

Yet Ewan had no intention of laying his head down that far away from Grace. Especially with a host like Simon ogling her so blatantly.

"Yer hospitality is appreciated, sir," Grace said, with a winsome smile.

"'Tis my pleasure, milady," Simon replied, his chest puffing with importance.

Then, before Ewan realized his intent, Simon lifted Grace's hand to his face and noisily kissed it. Ewan's sword was out of the scabbard in a thrice.

"Ewan, no!"

Grace reached out and touched his arm. The contact brought him back from the pounding rage. He narrowed his gaze on the slack-jawed Simon. "Lady Grace is under my protection," he snarled.

Simon's nostril's flared. "The lady is completely safe under *my* roof, Gilroy."

Ewan's reply was a feral glare that brought a flash of alarm to Simon's ruddy face, followed by a pathetic, helpless gaze directed toward Grace. *Coward.*

"I confess my throat is parched," Grace interjected hastily. "Might I trouble ye fer a drink?"

"Of course! I do beg yer pardon, milady. This unpleasantness has caused my manners to go missing." Simon shot Ewan an accusatory glare, then turned and bellowed for a servant.

The moment he was otherwise occupied, Grace leveled her full attention on Ewan. "Sit," she hissed beneath her breath.

Ewan opened his mouth to protest, but Grace glowered at him and shook her head in warning.

Grumbling, he followed her order, placing himself so close beside her on the bench their thighs touched.

He heard her startled gasp and felt her muscles flex against his. A bolt of heat seared his loins, sending a wave of lust through his entire body. The luscious lavender scent of her hair teased his nostrils. How could she smell so enticing after riding all day? Ewan was certain his own flesh wafted the odors of sweat and horse.

Grace wiggled away, then primly adjusted the skirt of her gown around her. The pink color rose high on her cheeks, but she refused to look at him. He exhaled briskly in an effort to bring his lusting body under control. It didn't help.

"Behave," she admonished.

Ewan glanced over at her, amused by the command. Her show of spirit and inner strength aroused him even more. Her eyes sparkled, vital and alive; her mouth took on a pouting countenance that begged for a kiss.

As if reading his thoughts, Grace narrowed her eyes suspiciously at him for a moment, then whirled to face Simon, who was now directing a bevy of servants. In addition to the ale and wine Grace had requested, platters of artfully arranged food appeared. Meat pies, cured tongue, roasted birds, hard and soft cheeses, dark crusted bread, custard tarts, and stewed fruit were all set on a table that had been brought over and placed in front of them.

"Ye must forgive our humble offerings," Simon fussed. "Had I known of yer pending arrival, Lady Grace, I would have held the evening meal so ye could partake of some hot dishes as well."

"'Tis more food than I could eat in a week," Grace replied in amazement. "Thank ye."

Without being invited, Ewan reached for a roasted capon. He ripped off the leg with one hand and sank his teeth into the succulent meat, while casually placing his other hand possessively at the base of Grace's spine.

"I also had food prepared fer yer men, Gilroy," Simon said, nodding his head toward the trestle table set on the far side of the hall. 'Twas clear Ewan was expected to remove himself and sit with his men. Not likely. He made a noncommittal grunt and reached for another piece of capon.

"Ye are the very model of consideration, Simon," Grace said. "I shall make certain to mention yer kindness when I next correspond with my brother."

Simon fairly beamed. "My uncle will be most pleased."

Ewan snorted. *Fuss and bother, what a pile of horseshit! Can she not see the man is a preening lack-wit?* Moodily, Ewan shoved another bite of capon in his mouth, barely tasting the succulent bird.

Unable to take his gaze off Grace, Ewan sulked through the remainder of the meal. While not precisely encouraging the attention, Grace allowed Simon to keep her fully occupied in conversation. Ewan could have been a stone statue for all the regard either of them paid him. Deciding he'd had enough, Ewan tossed a picked clean capon bone on the table and stood.

"We'd best get some sleep," he announced.

Both Grace and Simon turned simultaneously.

"Now?" Simon whined.

"Aye." He gave Simon a hard look. "We've a long way to travel on the morrow. Lady Grace needs her rest."

Simon bared his teeth back, but thankfully Grace had already risen. Ewan met her gaze, but she gave away none of her thoughts or feelings. "At least she still remembers how to follow orders," Ewan grumbled to himself as they left the hall.

Instead of delegating the task to one of his servants, Simon insisted on escorting Grace to her chamber himself. Determined not to give Simon a moment alone with Grace, an uninvited Ewan trailed along.

Clearly annoyed, Simon somehow squeezed himself beside Grace as they climbed the narrow staircase and stayed by her side until they reached her chamber. As Ewan watched, the other man made an exaggerated bow to her. Grimacing, he caught the bold, assessing stare Simon dared to bestow upon Grace just before finally taking his leave and retreating down the corridor.

"I'm placing a guard outside yer bedchamber door," Ewan stated flatly the moment they were alone.

Grace placed her hands upon her hips and smiled. "There's no need. Besides, Simon might take offense at the gesture."

"I dinnae care one wit about what Simon thinks," Ewan huffed. "The man bears watching. I swore to protect ye and I take that oath most seriously."

"He's harmless," Grace insisted.

"Ye are too trusting."

"Simon fancies himself a sophisticated gentleman, a courtier with refined tastes and sensibilities."

Ewan looked suspiciously at her. "And that appeals to ye?"

"Well, he did spend the entire evening singing my praises. He said repeatedly that I was a priceless treasure, a woman possessing a face and figure as soft and alluring as the angels in heaven."

"Pure rubbish."

Grace dropped her hands and straightened her spine and Ewan belatedly realized he had inadvertently insulted her. Feeling contrite, he tempered his expression. "Simon mostly enjoys hearing the sound of his own voice. He wouldnae recognize a true beauty like yers even if it reared up and bit him on the arse."

Grace smiled sheepishly. "Forgive me. When yer face clouds like a rumbling thunderstorm, I cannae resist teasing ye."

"My man stays outside yer chamber."

"'Twill be as ye command, Sir Ewan."

"Aye, and dinnae forget it, lass."

Acknowledging his concern for Grace's safety would afford him little sleep, Ewan decided he would be the one to guard her bedchamber door. He constructed a makeshift pallet out of a thin blanket and his cloak, laying it across the threshold. Grousing to himself about how he should be sleeping on the other side of the door, Ewan squirmed to find a position that wouldn't leave him stiff and aching come morning.

Ears attuned to the sounds of an unfamiliar household, Ewan drifted into a very light sleep. A cloudy edge of a dream invaded his mind; a redheaded beauty with a winsome smile and sparkling gray eyes first beckoned, then pushed him away. He strained forward, eager and desperate to capture this elusive prize. 'Twas close, so close . . . *ewagh*.

Ewan came fully awake as the distinct sound of a creaking wooden floorboard alerted him to the presence of another. Body on edge, his first instinct was to spring forward, weapons drawn, but he caught himself before yielding to that warrior urge.

Feigning the deep, even breaths of slumber, Ewan opened his eyes a crack and peered into the darkness. Menacing shadows appeared. A trick of the moonlight? Ewan squinted harder and caught sight of a barrel-chested man lurking at the end of the corridor. *Simon.*

Yet Ewan's feeling of vindication at his correct assessment of their host's true character was short-lived as Simon moved forward. Didn't the man notice him guarding the door?

Steadying his breath, Ewan waited. Simon continued to advance. Ewan could see no weapon, but a dirk could easily be concealed within the fold of Simon's clothing. The moment the other man was within reach, Ewan caught the edge of his tunic and pulled. Careening off balance, Simon landed with a thud on the wooden planks. Wasting no time, Ewan swung wide, his closed fist connecting with Simon's jaw.

"Holy hell!" Simon gasped.

Moving with surprising speed for such a large man, Simon twisted and tried to elbow Ewan in the gut. Ewan leaned to the side and the blow glanced off his ribs. Recovering, he caught Simon's arm and wrenched it behind his back.

"Ye appear to be lost," Ewan hissed, yanking the arm higher.

"Arghh." Simon's moans echoed through the corridor. "Let me go, ye ignorant bastard!"

"Not until ye explain yerself."

"What are ye doing here? Ye should be in the bailey, sleeping with yer men."

Ewan felt a strong urge to choke the fool. Lord only knew what might have happened if he had followed Simon's dictates and left Grace on her own. "I'm here to protect my lady from worms like ye."

Simon stiffened. "Release me at once."

"Or what?" Ewan challenged.

"Lady Grace will regret it."

"Bugger that!" Ewan's upper lip curled in a snarl. He gave Simon's arm one more hard jerk, then pushed the man away. "Off with ye! Run back to yer chamber before I change my mind and gut ye like a fish."

"Ye know naught of what ye speak. Lady Grace favored me with smiles and coy glances all evening. 'Tis obvious the lovely widow would welcome me into her bed."

Ewan raked him with a glare that could start a bonfire. Such blatant disrespect toward a woman was unacceptable, and directing it at Grace added even more rage to Ewan's growing ire. "Ye're dreaming. The lady has no interest in ye at all. She was merely being polite."

Simon curled his lip. "Jealous?"

"Of ye?" Ewan threw back his head and laughed. "Not in this lifetime."

Simon stood shakily on his feet, his hand clutching his shoulder. "Ye forget who ye are addressing, Gilroy. My men outnumber yers twenty to one."

"Dinnae ye mean yer uncle's men?" Ewan taunted.

"Ye dare to insult me?"

"I speak the truth. 'Tis not my fault if ye find it hard to stomach."

Simon glared with outrage, his breath coming in quick, short pants. "Ye'll regret those words one day, Gilroy. As well as yer actions tonight."

Ewan shrugged as Simon walked past him. "I highly doubt it."

He counted far better men than Simon Kilkinney as his enemy. He had survived being outcast by his own father and hunted as an outlaw by his half brother. Any threats from Simon were puny by comparison. Still, he remained on guard as Simon stalked away, nursing his aching jaw and wounded pride.

Ewan paused and glanced at the door, expecting it to open at any moment, for no one could sleep peacefully through that ruckus. Yet minutes ticked by and nothing happened. Pressing his ear against the heavy oak, Ewan strained to listen, yet heard no sounds from the chamber.

Ewan smiled. Once again, Grace had succeeded in surprising him.

Aye, 'twould be a long night, but well worth it if it meant keeping Grace safe. Ewan squatted, then sat, grateful his mind and body had been trained for years to go without rest. He propped his back and head against the thick wooden door, and with a resigned sigh, waited for the dawn.

Grace rose with the sun the following morning, glad that Edna was there to help her get ready. Initially she had resisted taking Edna on this journey, but the maid had insisted and Grace was thankful for her presence, for she afforded a much-needed dose of female companionship.

"The gray or the blue, milady?" Edna asked, holding up the two gowns.

"Gray," Grace replied, yawning. Though the bed had been comfortable and the mattress free of vermin, she had not slept well. Her mind was still attempting to reconcile the fact that Ewan was leading her escort and she would be forced into his company for the next few days.

And then there had been that commotion outside her chamber door in the wee hours of the morning, which had broken the fretful slumber she had managed. Her natural inclination had been to investigate, but then she remembered that Ewan was standing guard outside her door.

Odd, how she trusted him implicitly with her safety. Yet with not much else.

As she made her way down to the great hall, Grace decided she would not speak of the incident to Simon. His cloying, overbearing manner had been a bit tedious last evening, though she had wickedly taken a small amount of pleasure in witnessing Ewan's ire.

When she arrived, Ewan separated himself from the others gathering in the hall. His expression was serious as he hastened to her side. "Don yer cloak, Grace. My men are already mounted and ready to depart."

She raised her chin and looked him straight in the eye. "Why are we rushing away?"

"Best to leave before the weather turns."

"Before Mass? Before we break our fast?" Swallowing hard so she could modulate her tone, she added quietly, "Has something occurred that I should be made aware of, Sir Ewan?"

He sighed softly, displaying a visible effort to be even-tempered. "I only wish to keep ye out of a soaking rain. Clouds are already hovering overhead."

Grace squinted, but could see only darkness through the narrow window slits that rimmed the upper stones of the hall. "Clouds? 'Tis black as pitch outside."

Ewan's look sharpened, but before he could answer, Simon drew closer. He extended his arm, his face widening in an obscene smile. "Good morning, Lady Grace. Please, allow me to guide ye to our chapel."

Grace shook her head. She had an inkling she could use a blessing this day, but she was loath to challenge Ewan. Especially given his attitude toward their host. "Regretfully, we must depart."

Simon's face fell. "Will ye not attend Mass in our chapel before breaking yer fast?"

"We've time fer neither," Ewan replied in a solemn, regretful tone, though Grace thought he looked anything but remorseful.

"Surely ye cannot expect a lady to ride all day without sustenance?" Simon shuddered. "'Tis barbaric."

"Aye, even a crude, ignorant bastard such as myself knows such things," Ewan chirped. "Yer cook most obligingly prepared a meal fer us." He held two large baskets aloft. "A feast fit fer King Robert himself, I'd say. And more than enough for the lady and her escort."

Taut white lines appeared around Simon's full lips, but Grace was in no mood to humor him. 'Twas nigh impossible to appease both men, she decided. She was done with trying.

Thankfully it was Alec who guided her toward her

horse and lifted her to her saddle. Grace noted the sky had lightened, but the clouds that Ewan had mentioned did in truth blanket the sky. 'Twould be a miracle, indeed, if they stayed dry today.

A visibly perturbed Simon followed them into the courtyard. He gave her a strained smile, and somehow managed to touch his forelock and bow. She nodded her head in what she hoped was a regal pose of gratitude. Then paying no heed to Ewan or Simon, she gathered her reins and forced her thoughts to the day ahead.

Once they cleared the gates of the keep, they rode hard, slowing the pace only when the trees and underbrush became a dense forest. Here the path continued to narrow until the riders were forced to reposition themselves into pairs. Grace glanced over, not surprised to see that Ewan rode at her side.

"I noticed Simon sporting a rather nasty-looking bruise on his jaw," Grace said by way of opening the conversation.

"Aye."

"Do ye have any clue as to how it got there?"

"I might."

She heard him shift in his saddle. "Is there anything ye wish to tell me, Ewan?"

"Yer eyes sparkle with the brilliance of the stars lighting the night sky," he crooned.

"What?"

"Och, is that not fancy enough fer ye?" He let out an exaggerated sigh, then scrunched his nose. "Yer flaxen hair is spun from the purest gold, while yer ruby lips remind me of the ripest cherries, red and sweet and begging to be tasted."

Distracted, she jerked her reins, causing her mare

to dance nervously on the path. "My hair is red, not golden, and if my lips are red it means they are cold. Have yer wits gone missing, Ewan?"

He gave her a heart-melting smile, then grabbed her reins to steady her mount. "Well, lass, now that ye're no longer in Simon's company, I though ye might be pining fer a wee bit of flattery."

Grace opened her mouth to tell him exactly what she thought of his jest, but then the overblown flattery registered in her brain and she smiled. The smile quickly grew into a giggle and then a full-blown laugh.

"Ye had no right to strike him, though I cannae deny that Simon was a pompous fool." Grace giggled again, then took a deep breath.

Amusement lit Ewan's stormy blue eyes. "'Tis good to hear ye laugh. And that is the honest truth."

She nodded, taking a strange comfort in their easy banter. There was little conversation between them after that, but the silences were almost restful and Grace felt no inclination to break them.

The anticipated rain arrived just as they stopped to break their fast. Huddled beneath a canopy of dense leaves, Grace sat upon her horse as she chewed the crusty brown bread and nibbled on the sharp cheese. Despite the dismal weather, the men were in good spirits, especially Ewan. Apparently it took more than a gloomy, cool rain to dampen the spirits of a true Highlander.

Returning to the road, they plodded onward and were rewarded by a lesser drizzle and then, as the afternoon grew longer, a rare glimpse of sun. They crossed a narrow bridge built over a fast-moving river. From there, the party rode through forests that suddenly opened into rolling hills and jagged rocks.

The sun setting on the horizon was a glorious riot of purple, red, and gold. Ewan lifted his arm suddenly and Grace gazed at where he pointed, catching sight of a large bird in the distance, wings spread wide as it wheeled, spun, and soared through the clouds.

"Magnificent," he remarked.

"Freedom," Grace whispered, almost reverently. "I wonder if the bird realizes what a boon 'tis to live untamed and wild."

Ewan shook his head. "He's free until a predator strikes and makes a meal of him."

"A disheartened thought." Grace shivered. "Though it has long been the way of the world. The weak are preyed upon by the strong."

They rode for several more miles, but as night came upon them and the temperature began to cool, the men scouted for a safe location to make camp. Tents were raised; several fires were built. A kettle was placed over the largest to boil, then a group of men set about making the evening meal.

Grace was amused to see Ewan working beside his men; skinning the hares they had trapped, chopping the vegetables from the sack of food supplies that Brian had provided, stirring and tasting the stew. They worked with no regard to rank, in an almost silent rhythm that bespoke of years of camaraderie.

What manner of man was a knight who soiled his hands with the menial labor of cooking? Who ensured that each of his retainers had an equal share of food, who treated those who served him with respect and dignity? Who inspired, rather than commanded, loyalty?

Ewan handed her a bowl. The delicious smell caused her stomach to growl. Embarrassed, Grace ducked her head, but ate heartily, feeling full and satisfied when she was done.

Ewan settled himself beside her. They sat in companionable silence for several minutes, the quiet punctuated only by the popping and hissing of the logs on the fire. A gust of wind sent a sudden chill through her bones, causing Grace to gather her cloak closer.

Ewan shifted his position, resting his thigh, warm and solid, against her own. Grace opened her mouth to protest this familiarity, then shut it without saying a word, refusing to be so mean-spirited. It *was* cold— any warmth was appreciated.

"Try this," Ewan said, passing her a cup.

Grace obligingly took a sip, then sputtered as the liquid ran like fire down her throat. "What did you put in this drink?"

"Hot water, whiskey, and a spot of honey. It warms ye first on the inside, then spreads to the skin."

"Lovely," Grace choked out, before a fit of coughing overtook her.

"Well, if ye balk at the taste, and ye're still cold, I've other ways to keep ye warm, lass."

"I'm about to enter a convent, Ewan," Grace remarked primly.

"Aye. That's why I figured ye could use the warmth. Ye'll be giving up the comfort of a man's arms forever."

"I'll survive."

"Mayhap. But will ye thrive, lass? I think not."

Grace turned away, hiding a flush. The warmth that began on her face rapidly spread through her entire body, stirring her nerves to a tingle. She could feel her heart beating, but refused to give in to the feelings that were stirring inside her.

Hastily, she jumped to her feet, stepping so close to the fire that she nearly scorched the hem of her gown. "I bid ye good night."

"Sweet dreams, Grace."

His voice sounded hoarse and sultry, filled with warmth and intimacy. Her eyes closed. Visibly shaking off the spell he was weaving around her, Grace stalked away, stepping inside her small tent. Edna lay curled in a tight ball on a pallet of blankets and furs, her gentle snores filling the space.

Not wanting to disturb the maid's much-needed rest, Grace prepared for bed on her own, electing to sleep in her linen shift. Kneeling beside her pallet, she recited her evening prayers, then climbed beneath the blankets, worried she would be unable to rest.

The fur pelt tickled her nose each time Grace shifted her position, but gradually her eyelids began to feel heavy. The tent leaked in one corner, bringing an unpleasant dampness. The chilling wind howled, Edna continued to snore, yet ironically Grace drifted off to sleep with far more ease than she had the previous night.

Chapter Nine

The following days took on a familiar pattern. They rose early each morning, broke their fast with simple fare, and started their journey. The heavy carts of supplies and food stores packed to bring to the convent made it necessary to travel at a slower pace and on wider, defined roads. By unspoken agreement they rode through the small villages without stopping, passed by manors and keeps, electing instead to sleep in their own camp.

Grace didn't mind the rougher conditions, though she did long for a proper bath. She appreciated the efforts made each night to ensure her tent was comfortable—soft pallets for her and Edna to sleep upon, extra candles to light the interior, even a chair for her to sit.

Ewan and his men were skilled hunters. There was freshly roasted meat each evening and a relaxed atmosphere of camaraderie around the campfires at night. During the day, Ewan usually rode beside her. He told her outrageous, comical tales of his boyhood and amusing anecdotes of his years serving

King Robert, all of which Grace suspected contained mere grains of truth.

No matter what the situation, the man did have a talent for making her smile.

Living this carefree nomadic life with Ewan at her side was a rare treat, a grand adventure. She awoke each morning eager to begin the day, anxious to experience whatever awaited her, delighted she would be spending time with Ewan. 'Twas only on the evening of the third day of travel that Grace realized she was in no particular hurry to reach the abbey.

The thought kept her awake for the next two nights.

Ewan made no comment about the abrupt change in her daytime demeanor, though his increased efforts to entertain her let Grace know he had noticed. She tried to avoid him as much as possible, riding beside the cart that carried Edna during the day and going directly to her tent after the evening meal.

Still, there were times when closeness was unavoidable. Her throat was parched and the water skins empty when they stopped to make camp. Intending to follow the man assigned to find water, Grace was dismayed to realize that Ewan had taken the task upon himself.

Knowing she'd look the fool if she balked at accompanying him, Grace took deep breaths to calm herself. Her muscles tensed when he took her arm, but the thickening trees soon made it impossible to walk two abreast.

As they pressed their way down the narrow path, they stumbled onto a trickling stream. Though not deep, the clear water flowed steadily. It tasted cool and refreshing on the tongue and Grace savored every swallow.

With her thirst sated, Grace filled her water skins, and retreated to sit on a large flat rock positioned at the base of a tree trunk to wait for Ewan. She surveyed the area with mild interest, noting the quiet tranquility. Beyond the forest, she could see the mountains rising around them in majestic splendor.

Sighing, Grace turned her face up to the sunlight filtering through the trees, hoping they could walk slowly on the way back to camp. She had slept poorly these past few nights—emotion and exhaustion were starting to take their toll.

A cloud passed in front of the sun, pulling Grace out of her languid state of relaxation. She turned to look at Ewan, who was crouched at the water's edge, his back toward her. She saw him pull his tunic over his head and tossed it casually on the rocky bank. Grace's eyes opened wider. Then he reached for the hem of his shirt. She let out a squeak and sprang to her feet.

"What are ye doing?" she asked.

"Washing off," he replied, without bothering to turn around. "I swear I've got a layer of dirt on me an inch thick."

"Must ye do it now?"

"I doubt I'll find a better place," he answered, cupping his hands and sloshing water over his face, neck, and bare chest. "We've each had a good long drink, and filled the water skins to near bursting. Now is the perfect time to get myself clean. Ye can turn yer head if the sight of my naked chest offends ye so much."

Grace fought back the urge to argue, clamping her mouth firmly closed. Offend her? Hardly. In truth, she was having difficulty keeping her eyes averted. Ewan's sculptured body fairly gleamed, his firm muscles glistened with water droplets that reflected the sunlight like a hundred sparkling gems.

She pulled her lower lip under her teeth. Why did men find it so effortless to remove their clothing at every opportunity? And why were they not embarrassed to be seen? Was modesty only a female trait, something innate to women? Or something only taught to women?

Ewan set his hands on the ground in front of his knees, then tipped forward and dunked his head in the water. He came up with a shout, no doubt shocked from the cold. Still laughing, his hand moved to the laces on his braies.

Grace swore she could feel her heart stop. *If he removes those, then I shall . . . I must . . . Saints alive, what shall I do?*

Thankfully, she didn't have to decide. Rubbing his hands vigorously over his face, Ewan stood. Trying to keep the relief from her eyes, Grace struggled to assume a calm expression. Drops of water flew in all directions as Ewan shook his head like a large hound. He then picked up his shirt and tunic, draped them around his neck, and moved away from the stream.

Grace flattened herself against the tree trunk as a bare-chested Ewan strode toward her. He stopped when he drew near and stepped close to her, his eyes glittering in the sunlight.

Water dripped from the ends of his hair, beading on his shoulders and chest. There were even a few droplets on his eyelashes, reflecting the blue of his eyes.

'Twas mesmerizing.

He spoke not a word, merely leaned in closer. Then

closer. Grace could feel the shock of cold as his chest pressed against hers, dampening the front of her gown. The air between them hummed with tension.

He lifted his hands, pressing them against the tree trunk on either side of her. The tingling warmth of his breath brushed against her cheek, sending a spiraling shiver down her spine. Grace caught the edges of her cloak and dug her fingers into the fabric.

He touched his lips to hers almost glancing, but that gentle touch soon grew bold. Grace shivered, but didn't move. The kiss was sweet and slow and masterful, raising gooseflesh all over her arms. He made a sound deep in his throat and ran his tongue over her teeth. She tasted the cleanness of the water he had just drunk, and tried not to groan.

His breath grew rougher. So did hers. She wanted to throw her arms around him and pull him closer, to beg him to caress her, but she restrained herself. She tensed at the feel of the hard bulge of his arousal pressed insistently against her thighs. Sweat broke out on her palms as she tried to control her rising passion.

Ewan eased the kiss to its conclusion, pulling away slowly, pressing his lips to the corners of her mouth, then rubbing them sensually across her cheek. Grace's heart pounded as the heat between her thighs rushed up through her entire body. She felt her back digging into the tree trunk and realized it was the only thing keeping her on her feet.

Ewan straightened. The smile was back in his eyes, along with a smoldering heat so intense it nearly scorched her. "Just a wee reminder of what ye'll be missing when ye lock yerself behind those convent walls," he whispered.

His hand settled on her cheek and she fought hard against the urge to turn into the caress. He moved his hand slowly, up and down, once, then twice, then one final time before breaking contact. Grace heard herself moan with objection, but Ewan never reacted. Without saying or doing anything else, he turned and walked away.

He was nearly out of her sight before Grace regained her wits. With a firm shake of her head, she calmed her erratic breathing, gathered her cloak firmly around her, and followed in his wake.

Ewan kept his eyes sharp as he stared into the darkness that surrounded the camp. Time was running out. Grace needed to change her mind about her future and agree to a marriage between them. Very soon.

He had summoned every ounce of charm he could muster these last few days, wooing her, impressing her, enticing her. There had been a few glimmers of success. She smiled more easily and was certainly more relaxed in his company. He even believed that she liked him. Yet there were times when she seemed so far away. Aye, he could be standing right beside her, yet she seemed so distant, unreachable.

He felt a small qualm of guilt strike at his conscience for his deceptive behavior. The convent was a mere four-hour ride from where they made camp. Two nights ago. Aye, he'd been leading them all in a wide circle for two days, hoping that would give him the extra time he needed to change her mind.

Ewan reached for his sword at the sound of the rustling underbrush, but it was Alec who emerged from the woods.

"Feels like rain," Alec pronounced as he came to stand beside his leader.

"Aye. I'm thinking there'll be no need for an early departure come morning." Ewan looked up at the starless night sky. "In fact, we might not be able to travel at all. If the rains fall heavily, the carts will get stuck in the mud. There's a village less than ten miles from here. We could spend the day warm and dry inside the local tavern."

"I dinnae think that Lady Grace would appreciate passing the day drinking cheap ale and wine, gambling, singing, and watching our men seek the company of prostitutes," Alec grunted.

"Maybe we can find a more genteel setting for her," Ewan mused. "I'm sure she would appreciate a day out of the saddle."

"The lady would be grateful to reach her journey's end," Alec said, turning to meet Ewan's gaze. "A circumstance that should have happened two days ago."

"All in good time," Ewan replied.

"When?"

"When I say!" 'Twas impossible not to notice the tightening around Alec's mouth, but Ewan refused to consider it.

"God's wounds, Ewan, get yer head out of yer arse! 'Tis clear that Lady Grace is unused to travel, but she's an intelligent woman. Eventually, she'll get her bearings and realize that she's seen that same grove of trees, winding stream, and low-lying hills three times. And she willnae be happy about it."

"Aye, ye're right. We should alter our course. South or north, which do ye think would be best?"

Alec let out an exasperated sigh. "We should go west, to the abbey."

"But that's less than a day's ride from here!"

"Aye."

"Nay. 'Tis too soon," Ewan replied, biting out the words. "I need a wee bit more time to convince her to be my bride."

Alec fixed him with a piercing stare. "Ye need more than time, my friend. Ye need a miracle."

Angry words of denial sprang to Ewan's lips. Yet he was a fair man and could not argue with the truth. Why was it so hard to let go of the dream? Could he possibly hold fast to it for a few more days?

"Another day," Ewan muttered under his breath. "Mayhap two."

Alec slammed his fist into the trunk of a nearby tree. "Och! Ye're the most stubborn, hardheaded man I've ever known."

"I thank ye."

"'Tis not a compliment, Ewan."

"I know." An unfamiliar pang of failure twisted in his gut. He had not felt this helpless, this powerless, since he was a lad. "What would ye have me do, Alec? I need Grace to become my wife."

Alec slowly shook his head. "Ye'll have to stand down. I know it goes against yer grain to admit defeat, but ye cannae simply will this marriage to happen. The McKenna gave his sister the right to choose and she has taken it into her head to enter a convent. Ye must honor her decision."

Guilt crashed down on him. Alec was right. He could stall no longer.

"Tomorrow we shall reach the abbey," Ewan announced, a coldness gripping his heart. 'Twas the only honorable course and he must follow it. He was certain.

Yet why did he feel such a crushing blow of regret?

They arrived at the convent as dusk started falling. Despite the light drizzle, they had traveled at a steady gait, avoiding the mud and ruts in the road. The moment they were sighted, the heavy gates of the abbey were thrown open in welcome.

Grace urged her mount forward, her face splitting into a grin as she caught sight of many familiar faces. She had been raised in this convent, and many of the girls she had been fostered with were now women, dedicated to the service of the Lord.

Her heart lifted when she curtsied before the abbess. She had been a kind and loving substitute mother to Grace and her cheerful face was a soothing balm, an affirmation that Grace had made the correct decision in coming here. Here, among these good and decent women, she could atone for her sins, she could strive to be a better person, a better Christian. She might not achieve the happiness that came from being a wife and mother, but she would be content.

Sternly, she told herself it would be enough.

"We expected ye days ago, child," the abbess declared, as she hugged Grace tightly. "I'm relieved to see that our prayers fer yer safe journey were answered."

"I am grateful to finally be here," Grace replied with a shy smile. "All is as I remember."

"Aye, we have changed little over the years."

Though she wore the simple, plain gown of a nun, the abbess possessed a regal air of authority. Grace noted that Ewan and his men bowed especially low when they were introduced. Then the men quickly unloaded her possessions and the carts of supplies she had brought. With a hushed rumble of conversation, the nuns exclaimed their pleasure over the unexpected bounty.

Task accomplished, the men returned to their horses. All except Ewan. He was waiting expectantly, his expression unreadable.

Under the abbess's watchful eye, Grace turned to him. Her heart thudded and her knees shook, yet she maintained a pretense of calm.

"'Tis time to bid ye farewell and thank ye fer yer escort, Sir Ewan."

Her voice rang with forced cheer. She had never expected it would be easy, but until this moment she had not realized how ill-prepared she truly was to forsake the outside world. And those who occupied it.

Including Ewan.

Especially Ewan.

Clasping her hands in his, Ewan regarded her solemnly. "'Tis too late fer us to begin our journey home. We'll make camp a few miles away and take our leave after sunrise. I'll say my good-byes to ye on the morrow, before we depart."

Grace felt her bottom lip start to tremble. "I shall be busy with other duties in the morning. 'Tis best if we say farewell now."

"Nay, in the morning."

Grace's chest felt tight at the thought of prolonging this good-bye. She withdrew her hand and he flinched. It seemed as though they both knew she was pulling away more than that single body part.

Ewan's eyes flared with anger. He leaned closer

and repeated in a whisper, "We shall say our farewells in the morning. Ye owe me at least that much, Grace."

He did not wait for her reply. Stalking away, he mounted his horse, yanked the reins, turned, and led his men away. Heart accelerating, Grace stood rooted to the spot for several minutes watching the cloud of dust they raised and listening to the sound of the horses' hooves fade into the distance.

Then she turned and resolutely walked through the arched doorway of the convent.

Grace didn't sleep that night.

Her mind refused to rest, and try as she might, she was unable to tuck Ewan's face and form in some distant place in her memory where it could be forgotten. Her limbs were bone tired from the journey, but that did not seem to matter. Wearily, Grace exhaled, stretching her patience, seeking inner calm. Then she turned on her narrow pallet and faced the stone wall of her simple cell, commanding herself to sleep.

It didn't work.

A gentle knock was heard. Confused, Grace looked over her shoulder. The door cautiously opened and a shadowy figure stepped into the tiny, spartan chamber. "Lady Grace? Wake up. Please."

Grace sat upright. Squinting hard, she tried to discern the features of the woman who had spoken. "Who's there?"

"Sister Joan," the shadow replied. "I'm sorry to wake ye, but 'tis important. Ye must come with me."

"What's wrong?"

"I dinnae know exactly. My quarters are the first in the hallway, so I was the one asked to summon ye."

Grace sat forward on her pallet. "The abbess has need of me at this hour of the night?" she asked incredulously, yet even as she posed the question Grace was searching for her shoes. No matter how peculiar the request, she would naturally obey.

"'Tis not the abbess, but young Charles who delivered the message. From a knight, he said."

"There's a knight here? Inside the convent?"

"Nay." Sister Joan's head lowered. "He knew that men are not allowed, so he enlisted young Charles to aid him. That lad never stays where he should and no doubt was found outside the walls. The knight insisted the matter was so urgent it could not wait until morning. He's waiting fer ye just beyond the walls."

Grace swallowed a gulp of astonishment. "The abbess agreed that I should meet him?"

"Nay. I was asked not to waken anyone except ye."

Ewan! It had to be. What other man would possess the audacity to entice a nun into a forbidden act? Besides, no one else knew she had arrived at the convent.

Grace pulled on her shoes, stood, then halted. What in the name of all that was holy was she doing? It was ludicrous to give in to Ewan's demand, possibly even dangerous.

"I dinnae know. . . ." Grace's voice trailed off in confusion as she tried to deny the strange force telling her to go to him.

"Forgive my boldness in offering an opinion, but I think it wise to see what is so important," Sister Joan said.

Grace thought another moment and then decided

the nun was right. Who knew what Ewan might do if she denied his request?

Cautiously the two women made their way through the long corridors of the abbey. Together, they lifted the heavy wooden plank securing the gate, setting it on the ground.

"I'll wait here fer ye to return," Sister Joan said kindly.

With a nod, Grace slipped outside. The clouds had cleared and the moon hung low and full. Still, it took a moment to get her bearings. It was all darkness and shadows, but then a few feet beyond the protection of the gate she could see the broad shoulders of a man. Boldly, she charged forward, but soon her steps faltered as a strange sense of foreboding gripped her.

Suddenly, the figure turned. Grace felt the fine hairs on the back of her neck raise. She debated backing away, retreating to the sanctuary of the convent, but he had already seen her.

Blessed Mother, Ewan Gilroy is a trial that will follow me for the rest of my days. Grace opened her mouth to tell him just that when a shaft of moonlight drifted across his face.

Grace gasped. 'Twas not Ewan's grinning face she beheld, but another.

Roderick!

For an instant her heart seemed to stop beating. Her mouth opened and closed several times. Stunned, she could find no words.

"Surprised to see me, milady?"

The quiet menace in Roderick's voice startled her. Mutely, Grace stared up the long muscular length of him. She had forgotten how big a man he was as he towered above her, his arms folded sternly across his broad chest. Tamping down her instinct to shrink back in fear, Grace at last found her voice.

"What are ye doing here, Roderick?"

"Why, I've come to speak with ye. We've unfinished business that cannae wait any longer."

His animosity was evident in every word. Despite her attempts not to, Grace fell back a step, her mind empty. She felt a small bead of icy sweat trickle down between her breasts, yet conscious of his arrogant stare, she fought to regain her composure.

"We can talk tomorrow, in the light of day, as is proper."

Roderick sneered. "Why the sudden need fer propriety? Ye came quick enough tonight when I summoned ye. Or were ye expecting someone else?"

"Ye know full well I wouldnae have come if I knew 'twas ye."

"Ye wound me," Roderick mocked. He drew closer, halting just in front of her.

Grace clamped her cold hands together and daringly asked, "What do ye want from me?"

Roderick did not reply at once. "I seek justice. So that I may rightfully lead my clan."

Grace felt her face flush with heat. "They elected Douglas as chieftain. They chose him, not ye."

Roderick's eyes branded her with spite and malice. "Only because they dinnae know the truth," he said with a growl.

"What truth?"

"Do ye think me a complete lack-wit?" he said, his voice laden with scorn. "Alastair was murdered and ye played a key part in the plot that Douglas devised."

"Nay, Douglas is innocent!"

"But ye are guilty," Roderick concluded, his voice triumphant.

"I . . ." Words of denial rushed to Grace's lips, but there was little she could truthfully say. Ashamed, she hung her head, but Roderick's next words chilled her to the bone.

"Ye will admit this crime in front of the entire clan, Grace, speaking word fer word what I command ye to say. Ye will tell them all that Douglas killed Alastair."

Grace felt the breath catch in her throat. The day of reckoning had come far sooner than she expected, bringing with it some very ugly consequences. "'Tis a monstrous lie and I willnae say it!"

"Yer confession is of no use to me unless my brother is implicated," Roderick insisted.

So, it was as she feared—Roderick was not here for justice for his brother. Nay, he was here for himself and he intended to use her to help him get what he wanted.

"Are ye not weary of fighting?" she asked quietly. "Do ye truly wish to cause such strife among yer clan, to weaken them, to make them vulnerable to their enemies? 'Tis bad enough when there is fighting among the clans, yet 'tis far worse when ye make war upon yer own kin."

His glare intensified. "I'll battle anyone who stands in my way."

"I willnae do it, Roderick."

He jerked her elbow hard enough to pull her to her knees. His face was a medley of shades of anger and for an instant Grace worried she would faint from fear.

"I said I would attack anyone, Grace. And that includes yer precious nuns."

Grace felt the tears prickle behind her eyes. "Ye would not dare!"

"Dinnae push me, Grace. I'm well beyond the end of my patience."

"And so ye'll make war on a group of nuns? Innocent, defenseless women?" Grace shivered. "I never believed ye'd be that much of a coward, Roderick."

Her words cut sharply in the night air. Grace regretted them instantly. Roderick's bloodlust was already boiling. 'Twas foolish to provoke him, no matter how much she detested his threats.

"I'll do whatever I must to gain my rightful place," he cried with great vehemence.

"Ye'll burn in hell, Roderick, if ye dare to strike down the Lord's servants on holy ground."

He laughed bitterly. "Ye'll be there to keep me company, Grace."

His tone was as cold as a gust of frigid Highland air. Grace pulled away and struggled to her feet. The abbey gates seemed so far away, but they were her only chance of safety, at least for the remainder of the night.

They stared at each other in the moonlight, eyeing one another like a pair of wary wolves. Grace knew she had been foolish to leave the protection of the convent, but she had no intention of compounding that mistake by being easy prey. If she could escape his clutches now, she might have a chance to avoid the fate he intended for her.

Though the trembling inside her had reached epic proportions, she forced herself to remain composed, keeping her breath calm and even. An owl hooted in the night, drawing Roderick's attention. Deciding this was the only advantage she was likely to get, Grace swiftly pivoted and began to run.

With courage born from desperation she started her nerve-wracking escape, refusing to look left or right as she scurried toward safety. Her chest heaved from her exertion, her legs trembled. As she grew closer to the gate, she increased her speed.

"Sister Joan, open the gate," Grace cried, no longer worried about waking the others. "Hurry!"

Steeling herself not to turn and waste any seconds by looking behind her, Grace continued to run. She bolted through the door, nearly knocking Sister Joan to the ground.

"Milady!" the nun yelped, as she stumbled against the door.

"Hurry, oh, hurry!" Grace sobbed, slamming the gate. She reached for the heavy plank, dragging it forward, but was unable to lift it without aid. "Help me!"

Blindly, Sister Joan followed her command and the two women successfully barred the gate. Grace pressed her back against it for good measure. Shivering, she pulled her cloak firmly around her body and waited for Roderick's assault.

Yet there was only an eerie silence. Seconds ticked by, turning gradually into minutes. *I'm safe.*

The relief was so strong it buckled Grace's knees. Quivering, she slid against the door until her rump landed on the floor. Sister Joan mimicked her actions and sat beside her. Grateful for the nun's help, Grace reached over and squeezed her hand.

Terror gave way to relief and then a tiny burst of triumph. She had outwitted Roderick! At least for the moment.

Slightly calmer, Grace reviewed the events carefully in her mind. And her sense of victory rapidly abated as she realized the truth.

The only reason she had managed to escape was because Roderick had allowed it.

Chapter Ten

The early morning sky was dark and ominous as Grace waited in the small courtyard outside the chapel. The nuns were at Mass. From there they would gather to share the morning meal and then begin their daily tasks. Offering no explanation, Grace refused to join them. She had already placed them all in terrible danger—she did not deserve the comfort of their company.

Instead, she stayed outside and paced, awaiting her fate, desperately hoping a way to protect these innocent women would be found. She was unable to see beyond the abbey gates, but the sound of approaching horses was distinct. Many horses. Ears attuned, her body stiffened in alert.

Was it Roderick or Ewan who rode with such purpose? A fit of trembling seized her and she had to fight for control. For several long moments she stared unseeingly ahead with only an occasional shiver of fear racing through her blood. She wiped her cheek as a single tear trickled down it and sniffed to hold off any more. Crying did no good; nay she was beyond it at this point.

The sounds of hoofbeats grew stronger. Grace moved her position so she could see over the gates and sharpened her gaze. A long row of riders approached. *Merciful Mary!* They were too far away to distinguish either their features or the plaids they wore.

Grace made a fervent sign of the cross and began to pray in earnest, conscious of the fierce pounding of her heart. Though it felt an eternity, it was but a few minutes before the men were close enough to identify. She dipped her chin and squinted, her eyes straining so hard her head hurt.

Finally she caught a glimpse. *God be praised!* 'Twas Ewan riding in front, leading his men. Grace had never seen a sight so welcome in all her life. She dropped to her knees and finished her prayer. Then fortified by the discovery, she regained her feet and began moving her trembling limbs forward.

The fear she had fought so hard to keep at bay caught her the moment Ewan dismounted. Disregarding any sense of propriety or decorum, Grace broke into a run and flung herself into his arms. Lashing her wrists around his neck, she held him so tightly she could hear the breath being pushed from his lungs.

"Och, lass, not so tight." He chuckled warmly. "Ye stay one night behind convent walls, then give me such a greeting. I dinnae dare imagine how ye'd react if ye were left here for a week without seeing me."

"Oh, Ewan." Her attempt at a laugh came out as a painful moan.

"Are ye cold? Ye're shaking so hard it's rattling my bones."

Grace pulled back, struggling to speak, but couldn't find her voice. Embarrassed, she turned to hide her tears from Ewan, but he caught her by the shoulders and cradled her against his chest. The final thread of her composure snapped. Curled within the safety of his arms, Grace let the tears flow. She'd tried so hard to be independent and strong, but it was all too much.

For a few minutes she allowed the feeling of protection he imparted to fully embrace her, allowed her terrifying burden to be shared. Just this once, she relinquished her fears and allowed Ewan to be strong for her.

"I was so afraid ye wouldnae come. That ye wouldnae get here in time," she whispered.

She felt him pull away just enough so he could see her face. "In time fer what?"

"To protect the abbey. To keep the nuns safe."

Ewan's gentle eyes searched her face. "Grace, ye are making no sense. Why do the nuns suddenly need protection? Who threatens them?"

"Roderick Ferguson." As she spoke his name, the desperation she had managed to hold at bay returned. "Ye must stop him, Ewan. Please, I beg ye."

"What cause does Roderick have to attack the abbey?"

Grace could feel the sweat start to trickle down the middle of her back. Confession might be good for the soul, but she was loath to reveal her shameful secret to anyone, especially Ewan. She took a shaky breath. "Me. He comes fer me."

"But why?"

Grace fixed her attention on the distant horizon, but she could feel the heavy weight of Ewan's gaze upon her. "Roderick holds me accountable for Alastair's death, claiming that he was murdered. He wants me to stand before the Ferguson Clan, admit my guilt, and say that it was all a plot devised by Douglas."

"Och, lass, no wonder ye're so distressed." Ewan pulled her into his arms and squeezed. "Roderick's lust fer power has addled his wits. No one with any sense will believe that ye are capable of such a heinous act. They will quickly see that Roderick is a fool and his words are lies."

His words pierced her heart. Ewan never hesitated in his defense of her honor, in his belief of her innocence. If only she deserved it. Reluctantly, she pulled away from the safety of his arms.

"Fool or not, Roderick will have his way. He's burning with resentment and resolves to have what he believes is his due." Grace brushed back the hair that had fallen across her eyes. "Can ye protect the abbey, Ewan? Can ye keep the nuns safe?"

Ewan was quiet for such a long time that her palms started to sweat. "I left most of my best fighting men at Tiree to defend my lands," he replied. "My small band of warriors are no match fer Roderick's troops."

"Aye." Grace hung her head in despair. Roderick had won. In order to save the nuns, she would have no choice but to go with him. The abbey was too far away for her to get word to her brother in time. Ewan had been her last hope.

She pivoted on her heel, but Ewan clasped her shoulder, preventing her from leaving. "Just because I have far fewer men, does not mean I willnae do everything I can to keep Roderick from harming the abbey. From harming ye."

Grace exhaled a long breath as her pulse began to race with hope. "But ye are outnumbered. How will ye win?"

"By being clever."

He flashed a winning smile and Grace felt her heart lighten. She believed him. Even with the odds stacked against him, she knew that Ewan would somehow emerge victorious. "Thank ye."

A sardonic smile flitted across Ewan's face. "I said that I would aid ye, and I shall. But I've one very important condition."

"Oh?"

"Once I've set a defense for the abbey, ye'll leave here and come with me to Tiree, Grace. As my wife."

Her mouth twisted bitterly. 'Twas the same question he had posed to her for nearly two weeks, yet this time it struck her hardest. Those words stirred a deep longing inside her, one she had time and again refused to acknowledge.

She conceded now that under different circumstances she would happily comply with Ewan's request. Heavens, she might have even been bold enough to suggest it herself. But he deserved a far better woman to stand beside him and share his life than she.

Though it pained her deeply, she knew that she had to reveal the truth—the whole truth. In her sleep-deprived state, the effort to maintain a clear head was exhausting, but this she knew was right. Ewan deserved an explanation, deserved to know the truth, no matter how reluctant she was to reveal it.

Grace rubbed her temples vigorously with the tips

of her fingers, almost as if trying to will the correct words into her brain. Then she took a deep breath and spoke. "Roderick has gone witless in his quest fer power. His motives are selfish and self-serving, but there is more."

Ewan cocked his head. "Grace, we shall talk of this later. I must gather my men and form a plan."

"Nay! Ye must listen, Ewan. Roderick is not a complete madman. He speaks the truth." She felt a fluttering churning in the pit of her stomach as she forced out the rest.

"I killed Alastair. I killed my husband."

Ewan could not have been more shocked if she had announced she had grown wings during the night and could now fly. *Killed her husband? Impossible!*

Yet her expression was so earnest, her distress very real. Questions rattled and collided in his brain. Why? How? When? Unprepared to hear the answers, Ewan shook them off.

Long an admirer and connoisseur of the fairer sex, Ewan had no doubts a woman was capable of murder. All he need do was look to his own mother and her behavior for that truth.

But Grace? Nay, she was different. Sweet, pure, noble.

"Is that why ye are entering the convent?" he croaked out.

She nodded her chin sharply. "'Tis selfish, I know, but I am repentant fer my sin. Perhaps if I live a good and simple life, if I pray hard and long enough, God will be merciful and forgive me."

Jesus, it is true! Ewan could hear the tremble in her

voice, see the anguished truth in her eyes. But there had to be more. More that she wasn't telling him. Did Alastair mistreat her? Beat her? Humiliate her? Forsake his marriage vows and take another to his bed? Jealousy was a powerful foe, easily turning heightened emotions into a rage. Is that how it happened? Had Grace been blinded by fury when she did the deed?

"Grace, ye must tell me exactly how this—"

"He's coming!" Grace screeched. "Listen! Do ye not hear them?"

The courtyard went deathly still. Even the wind ceased to move, heightening the distinct sound. Approaching horses! Ewan was seized by a fit of urgency.

"To me," he shouted, and his men immediately scrambled to their mounts and unsheathed their swords.

Ewan was debating whether they should face Roderick with swords drawn when he felt another presence near him. He turned and faced the abbess, who gazed up at him questioningly.

"What is happening, Sir Ewan? Why are yer men ready for battle?"

"There is trouble brewing and I propose to stop it." Seized by an unaccustomed fit of foreboding, Ewan dropped to his knee and bowed his head. "I would ask fer yer blessing in my quest."

The abbess laid her hand upon his head and closed her eyes in prayer. Ewan silently mouthed the words with her, then stood. As he turned to mount his stallion, he nearly collided with Grace.

"Here," she said, thrusting an armload of fabric at him.

Ewan drew a short breath. "What is this mess?"

"Plaids," Grace replied, bending to pick up two that had fallen. "From a few of the nuns and novices. They renounce all their worldly possessions when they enter the order, but the abbess allows those who wish it to keep a small token of their heritage."

"Grace, I dinnae see—"

"Many nuns of the order are of humble origins or orphans who know nothing of their blood kin," she interrupted breathlessly. "But others are daughters of noble families, connected to powerful clans. And there are young women who are fostered here, as I was when I was a girl, who have relatives who would avenge any harm that befalls them."

Bewildered, Ewan stared down at the cloth. He recognized most of the clan colors, even knew some of the clan chiefs, as many of them fought with King Robert.

"These men will stand with me if Roderick threatens their women," Ewan replied, understanding dawning. "I only wish there had been time to call for their support."

"Roderick does not know that," Grace said quietly.

Ewan nodded. "Aye. If I can convince him that others are already riding hard to protect the abbey, and those who reside within its walls, he will think twice about attacking. Clever, lass. This could very well turn the tide in our favor."

His confidence seemed to divert some of Grace's distress. She nodded encouragingly. "As for the rest, I understand that ye must withdraw yer offer of marriage after learning of my disgraceful past. Neither of us—"

"Withdraw?" He looked into her shameful eyes and banished any lingering misgivings. "Ye'll not slip away from me that easily, Grace. Once I've dealt with Roderick, I'll be back fer ye. Inform one of the priests to be at the ready."

She winced. "Ye cannae be serious?"

"I most certainly am. And ye'd best be waiting fer me, lass. With a welcoming smile on yer lovely face."

Ewan rode from the abbey with two columns of his men behind him and nearly a dozen plaids stuffed into his saddlebags. It was an uneasy feeling preparing to face an enemy that far outnumbered him, but this was not the first time Ewan had experienced these odds. As a young man he had spent several years successfully raiding the lands of his powerful half brother with a hand-picked group of outlaws. He knew firsthand that greater numbers were not always needed to be victorious.

But they certainly helped.

They traveled farther than Ewan expected and he realized the sound of approaching horses had been misleading—Roderick and his men were several miles away. Through the fog of a misty morning, Ewan could see the lines of men riding in tight ranks. He briefly considered, then discarded, the idea of hiding beneath the cover of the trees and ambushing the lot.

'Twould be a foolish risk that could end badly and would leave Grace, and the abbey, completely unprotected. Nay, negotiation and a wee bit of trickery would carry the day.

Eyes keen and ears alert, Ewan scouted for an open spot before raising his hand and signaling his men to stop. This action forced the approaching Roderick to do the same, though judging by the scowl on his face, he was none too pleased with the delay.

His reins dangling loosely in one hand, leaving the other free to draw his sword, Ewan approached his adversary. "Have I the honor of addressing Roderick Ferguson?"

A surprised look, followed immediately by a guarded one, darkened Roderick's bold features. "Who wants to know?"

"Sir Ewan Gilroy."

"The earl of Kirkland's bastard?"

There was no missing the disdain in Roderick's tone, but Ewan refused to be baited. He studied his foe in the bands of cloudy light that dappled through the surrounding trees. Roderick's bearing was haughty and proud, his weapons finely made. He was heavily muscled and fit and no doubt knew well how to wield the lethal sword slung over his back.

"I've heard tell that ye plan to visit the abbey on this fine morn," Ewan said.

"'Tis no business of yers where my men and I go," Roderick replied, his face hardening.

Ewan reached into the leather pouch hanging on his saddle and slowly pulled out a plaid with the Dickson colors. He next withdrew one of Clan Wallace and then the Campbells. "Protecting the defenseless has long been my business. 'Tis a trademark of a true Highlander to be passionate about keeping one's kin safe. 'Tis also very interesting, is it not, to discover how many noble clans have gifted the convent with the presence of a female relation?"

Ewan continued pulling the pieces of fabric out of his bag, until the pommel of his saddle was covered in the brightly woven designs. The visual demonstration had a profound impact. He could see the men lined up behind Roderick shift nervously on their horses. Yet Roderick barely flinched.

"This has nothing to do with ye, Gilroy. I dinnae see the Gilroy colors nor any McKlendon plaid, though I doubt either clan claims ye as their own. Take yer men and ride off and we'll speak no more of it."

Ewan tensed. "The Lady Grace is to be my bride. Be forewarned, I hold and protect what is mine."

Roderick did not betray an ounce of surprise. Instead, he reached down and patted the neck of his dancing horse, his smile gleaming much too brightly. "I warn ye to tread lightly. My brother met a gruesome end with Lady Grace as his wife."

Ewan cocked his head, feigning puzzlement. "Sir Alastair's death had naught to do with my lady. Or do ye have proof to the contrary ye wish to share?"

Ewan knew it was a risk provoking Roderick, but it was obvious if the man had any sort of proof of the deed, he would have used it, instead of threatening Grace to confess.

Roderick lifted his eyes skyward and laughed. "She is a comely lass. I've heard tell that a woman's beauty can rob a man's mind of wit and thus she has bewitched ye with her pretty smiles and innocent looks. If ye value yer life, ye'll turn tail and run as fast as yer horse can carry ye away from her."

"I need no advice from ye." Ewan allowed himself but a few words. To say more would prolong the conversation and he wanted to avoid having Roderick voice his vile allegations against Grace publicly.

Roderick stared back at him with an inscrutable expression. Ewan clenched his hand as his foe shifted in the saddle, waiting for him to draw his sword. Indeed, almost wishing for it, as it would give Ewan the chance to end it all and run him through.

But Roderick paused, seeming to weigh his options. His eyes drifted down at the plaids, then narrowed. "This is far from over, Gilroy," Roderick snarled as he turned his horse and spurred the animal into a full gallop.

His men followed, a long line of sturdy horseflesh, a budding army that would one day prove formidable. Ewan waited until the dust had settled before guiding his stallion around and heading back to the abbey.

Back to his bride.

The courtyard was empty when Ewan and his men rode through the open abbey gates. For an instant Ewan feared he had been tricked, that somehow Roderick had circled around and attacked the defenseless convent, but then the chapel door slowly creaked open. The abbess poked her head out, then turned and spoke to whoever else was hiding with her.

The women calmly filed outside, their heads bowed, their hands clasped. A tidy row of brown wrens, along with his own gray dove. He dismounted and looked over at Grace. "Milady?"

She straightened and met his gaze, her chin up,

her back stiff, as if she faced an executioner. "Has Roderick gone?"

"Fer now. But I've no doubt he'll return. 'Tis imperative that ye not be here when that happens."

"I beg yer pardon fer eavesdropping, but I overheard yer request for a priest," the abbess interjected. "If ye still desire to be wed, Father Mark is glad to oblige."

"I must speak with Sir Ewan privately," Grace insisted, her voice high and tight with agitation.

The abbess looked to him for approval and Ewan nodded. At her signal, everyone melted away.

"One of my men is riding hard to reach the Westland Keep, as it is the closest fortress," Ewan said. "The Wallace Clan will guard the abbey and speak with the other clans to ensure it is protected."

"What will ye tell them?"

"That Roderick bears an unfounded grudge against my bride and has threatened the nuns."

"'Tis a lie." She took a step closer to him and he immediately noticed the sadness in her eyes. "I am not innocent."

Ewan sighed. "The past is over, Grace. I care naught for it."

His words seemed to snap her composure. She let out a sharp shriek. "Are ye truly that desperate fer my dowry that ye'll turn a blind eye to the reality of my past? Merciful heavens, ye cannae simply ignore the truth because it doesn't suit ye, Ewan."

She paced back and forth as she spoke, flaying her arms in distress. Ewan grasped one. Turning it palm up, he gazed at the soft, delicate center and long, tapered fingers. By all the saints, this could not be the hand of a cold, bloody murderess.

"How did it happen, Grace? Did ye run him through with a dirk? Smother him with a pillow? Pay another to accomplish the deed?"

Grace froze. Her eyes widened in horror and he regretted causing her this pain, but he realized she was right. The past could not be laid to rest until they confronted it. Together.

"Alastair died by my hand," she whispered. "I, and I alone bear the guilt."

Ewan felt a rising tide of panic. Truth could be ugly and unforgiving. Was he truly prepared to hear it?

"Tell me what happened," he said gently.

She shook her head violently. "Nay, there's no point."

"Tell me."

She took a deep breath, then folded her arms. Foot tapping, she stared at him with hard eyes, but he refused to be denied. Finally, she sighed and lowered her chin.

"Alastair was gored by a wild boar while hunting," Grace said quietly. "The wound slashed his leg down to the bone in several places. It became putrid, the flesh rotting, dying. No matter what medicines were used, what care he was given, the wound would not heal.

"Roderick brought a monk from Turriff Monastery to tend him, but it made little difference. Alastair grew worse each day, each week. The fever raged, his body weakened, he was in agonizing pain. The monk wanted to amputate his leg, yet he admitted there was but a slim chance that would save his life. Alastair begged me to prevent it, begged me to allow him to die in peace, as a whole man."

"What did ye do?"

She looked at him a moment. Her eyes filled with tears, yet she made no motion to brush them away. "I stole the medicine from Brother John. Small amounts over several days, so he would not notice any was missing. Then one evening I poured it in Alastair's wine."

"Did Alastair know?"

"Aye. His mind would drift in and out of consciousness. I needed to wait for a lucid moment so I could ask him one more time, if he truly wanted to end his life. He assured me that was his final wish.

"He was so weak. I brought in extra pillows and stacked them high so he could sit upright. He couldnae reach the goblet, so I placed it in his hand." Her voice choked. The tears flowed freely now, creating a dampness on the front of her gown. "I'll never know where he found the strength to hold the vessel to his mouth, but somehow he managed. The goblet fell from his fingers the moment it was empty. I placed it on the table beside his bed."

"Did he die quickly?"

"It felt like an eternity, though in truth it was no more than twenty minutes. I knelt at his bedside, held his hand, and prayed. His breathing grew shallow, slowed, then stopped. That's when I knew it was over, when I fully realized what I had done."

Ewan closed his eyes. His sense of relief was so strong he felt guilty for harboring even a shred of doubt. From the first he had seen the kindness in Grace's heart, had glimpsed the goodness of her soul. The mere fact that she harbored such a strong sense of guilt over her actions spoke to her character.

Grace shifted her feet as she waited for Ewan's judgment, his condemnation, knowing it was going to hurt. He would be horrified, shocked, repulsed by her and her deeds. There would be no more talk of marriage. He would forsake her now, turn and stalk away.

She wanted to escape, to run away and hide, yet she knew that her past would always follow. So instead she wiped the tears from her face, the moisture dripping from her nose, straightened her spine, and squared her shoulders.

She risked a quick glance at Ewan, then she wished that she had not given in to the temptation. He was staring at her wide-eyed, his face pulled in surprise. She swore she could see the puzzle pieces moving around in his mind as he digested what she had told him.

Ewan took her hands in his and stared into her eyes. Grace's knees started to buckle when she realized there was gentleness and kindness reflected in his expression. He did not think she was a monster!

"Ye do not condemn me?" she whispered.

"I've no right to pass judgment on ye, Grace, nor to offer forgiveness. That is between ye and the good Lord. But I can say that I honestly believe ye did the right thing. Ye acted with courage and humanity. Ye dinnae allow yer husband to live in unbearable and increasing pain. Instead, ye gave Alastair precisely what he asked of ye—the gift of a peaceful death."

Grace stared at Ewan in wonder. Feelings welled up inside her. She still believed her actions had been sinful, yet the greatest part of her guilt had always been knowing she carried no regrets for what she had done. It had been a difficult, heart-wrenching choice, yet given the same set of circumstances a second time, she would make the same choice.

"He gave me his blessing," she whispered.

"What?"

It was hard to speak, because her voice had swelled so tightly with emotion. Grace swallowed and repeated the words. "As he died, Alastair opened his eyes a final time, thanked me, and gave me his blessing."

"I'm sorry," Ewan said. "I'm sorry that ye were ever put in such a moral quandary, yet I'm proud of ye, lass. For being so courageous. Proud, too, that ye finally yielded yer trust to me and revealed the truth."

Grace couldn't speak. She could only nod. He was a good man, who had treated her far better than she had ever dared hope. He opened his arms and she moved into his embrace. He was strong, solid—the kind of man who made a woman feel safe and protected.

She could feel the steady rise and fall of his chest, far calmer than her own. Ewan tilted her chin up so she could see his face. His blue eyes were searing with intensity.

Though she was expecting it, his kiss startled her. The comforting scent of his body filled her being, soothed her soul. He kissed her slowly, as if they had all the time in the world to savor each moment, brushing her mouth gently with his, moving back and forth so slowly it ignited a fire low in her belly.

"Grace," he breathed, slipping one hand around her neck. The deep, husky sound of his voice made every nerve within her dance on end. He kissed her again, deeply, and when he was done she was shaking from head to toe.

Ewan drew his head back, his strong hand still cupping the back of her neck. He searched her face intently and he must have been pleased with what he found, for he smiled broadly.

"So, I'll ask ye one final time. Will ye wed me, Grace?"

The moment hovered between them, full of possibilities. It stretched into a future that Grace never believed was possible and she felt humbled by it. A second chance. 'Twas here, within her grasp. All she need do was reach for it.

Did she dare?

"Aye, I'll marry ye, Ewan. And I vow that I shall honor ye, care fer ye, and work tirelessly to please ye. And I shall do everything within my power to be the best wife in all the land."

Chapter Eleven

Grace's fervent vow to be the best wife in all the land was put to the test immediately. And by the fourth night of her married life, she had true doubts in her ability to fulfill that promise. Or retain her sanity. All that she thought she knew was false; all that she believed to be true made no sense. And somehow in the confusion of it all, Ewan had become a stranger to her.

She had been filled with hope as she stood beside him in front of the chapel doors and recited her vows, clutching a wilting bouquet of wildflowers that one of the novices had presented to her.

A rather solemn gathering of women from the convent and Ewan's soldiers gathered to witness the event. Father Mark led the brief service, his face pale, his hands slightly trembling. Grace was uncertain if that was a result of the priest's age or his opinion of her hasty, unexpected marriage.

No matter. The deed was soon accomplished, a blessing delivered, and then Ewan vanished, shouting at his men to stand guard. Tensions mounted as everyone waited for the Campbells to arrive, secretly fearing that Roderick might decide to return.

A hearty cheer went up when the captain of the Campbell guard led his men through the abbey gates. It was the only demonstration of merriment the entire day and Grace repeatedly told herself that was not a reflection of her wedding, but rather a reaction to the relief they all felt. With the arrival of the Campbells, the danger that Roderick had posed was no longer an imminent threat.

Freed of his obligation to protect the abbey, Ewan elected to depart, despite the lateness of the hour. Grace would have appreciated being asked her opinion of this plan, but as there was no chance for a private discussion, she decided not to voice her objections. They set out at a grueling pace, spending the first night camped on the edge of a small river, the second in a glen surrounded by tall trees, the third in a shallow valley.

And each night, Grace slept alone.

The situation left her completely dumbfounded. She was not so vain as to exaggerate her feminine appeal, but she knew that Ewan found her desirable. His kisses before they were wed had been passionate and eager. She had felt the physical proof of his desire pressing hotly against her on more than one occasion, had seen a gleam of seduction in his eyes directed her way.

Yet somehow, once she became his wife all that changed. Ewan was polite, respectful, and decidedly distant. He rode with his men, took his meals surrounded by them, conversed with them. Grace was always included—protected on all sides when they traveled, given the warmest spot in front of the evening fire, encouraged to join in the mealtime conversation.

Yet she was rarely alone with her husband, most notably throughout the long night. It was a disturbing situation that she pondered for hours each day as they rode through the hills and valleys, pressing farther north and home to Tiree. It nagged at her mind constantly as she wondered how things had gone so wrong.

Wondered, too, how she could fix them.

Weary from another long day in the saddle, Grace entered her tent, Edna by her side. Candles and lanterns had been lit, bathing the interior in a soft, golden glow. Grace slowly drew off her leather gloves and surveyed her surroundings, immediately noting that someone had made an effort to improve the crude furnishings and make the tent more inviting. Ewan?

Her heart surged with hope at the notion, but she realistically dismissed it. Most likely it was Alec who had gone to the trouble of making her comfortable—and he had done a fine job.

Three large rugs cushioned the majority of the dirt floor while lengths of gossamer fabric had been draped from the pole supports to cover the canvas walls. They added a splash of color and elegance and a surprising air of romance. There was a table and two chairs in one corner and a raised bed covered in luxurious furs in another.

"How did they ever find a bed that size around here?" Edna asked in astonishment. "And how did they get something that large through the much smaller tent opening?"

Grace eyed the tent flap and shrugged. "They must have erected the tent around it."

She stepped forward, running her fingers over the soft pelts, then pushed downward, testing the firmness of the straw mattress. Perfect. Firm, yet there was some give. Two pillows, side by side, were placed at the top of the bed. Grace inhaled. The intimate setting brought on a rush of longing, and a stark reminder of what was missing in her marriage. Turning away, she caught sight of the final item filling the tent—a round, wooden tub.

"Och, how marvelous," she cried. Though it had only been a week, it felt far longer since she had been able to take a proper bath. She had made due with washing from a basin of cold water each morning and evening. Adequate, but not ideal.

Edna eyed the tub dubiously. "Ye cannae be thinking of bathing in here? Ye'll catch yer death of cold."

"Not if the water is heated," Grace replied. "It will warm me through."

"Ye've a husband now to keep ye warm," Edna clucked.

Aye, a husband. A husband who has little interest in sharing my bed.

Ewan had not openly confessed his regret at their marriage to her, but his actions spoke for themselves. Thinking about it brought a sinking sensation to the pit of Grace's stomach. Feeling agitated, she twisted a bit of fabric at the end of her sleeve until it grew tight around her wrist, bringing numbness to her hand.

Why had everything changed so suddenly? When Father Mark had said the final blessing at their marriage ceremony, an odd sense of rebirth had washed over Grace. If not for Ewan, she would have spent the rest of her days locked behind the walls of the abbey.

Instead, she was being given the hope of a new life and a partner with which to share it.

Abruptly she let go of the fabric. Her fingers tingled as the blood once again rushed through her veins.

"I believe a hot bath is exactly what I need to shake off this melancholy," Grace said decisively. "Instruct my husband's man-at-arms to have the tub filled with hot water as soon as possible."

Edna snorted with disapproval, but a glare from Grace had the maid following orders, though she grumbled with every step.

In little more than an hour a seemingly endless line of men arrived, a bucket of hot water in each hand. In no time the tub was more than half full. Billowing clouds of steam rose invitingly from the water and moved through the tent.

As Edna continued fretting and clucking her tongue in worried disapproval, Grace disrobed, then twisted her hair into a knot and pinned it atop her head. The sides of the tent shook as a breeze blew. Feeling chilled, Grace scrambled to the tub.

Gingerly, she dipped her toe into the water, gasping at the heat. Knowing she would get no sympathy from Edna, Grace stalled for time. She scampered back to her small trunk, impatiently shuffling through the contents until she found a sack of dried herbs.

She tossed them into the water, grit her teeth, stepped into the tub, and quickly sat down. The water rose to her shoulders. Hunching forward, Grace tucked her knees under her chin and took a deep breath while she waited for the temperature to become bearable.

"Shall I scrub yer back?" Edna asked.

"Nay," Grace answered, trying to keep her teeth from chattering. 'Twas odd that the extreme heat would cause such a reaction, but she knew the water would cool and be far more comfortable soon. "Just leave the pot of soap and washrag within my reach."

All was pleasantly quiet after Edna left. Reveling in the warmth as it seeped into her bones, Grace rested her arms on the top of the tub, leaned her head back, and closed her eyes. The pleasant scent of sage and lavender permeated the steam that danced upward from the water, assaulting her nostrils and further relaxing her.

"Is all to yer satisfaction, Grace?"

At the sound of Ewan's voice, her head snapped up. Instinctively she brought her arms forward to modestly cover her breasts, sending a wave of water sloshing over the edge of the tub. She opened her mouth to shout at him to leave, but then stopped. They were married. He had every right to see her naked body.

Grace slowly unfurled her closed fists. Drowning out the small voice of doubt in her mind, she lowered her arms, then brazenly arched her back. She felt the cool air immediately on her exposed breasts, felt her nipples pucker. Yet she refused to sink below and hide herself.

Ewan spoke not a word. He stood still as a stone and stared, his eyes first widening in surprise and then narrowing. In disapproval? Disgust? Desire?

Perplexed, she watched him, anxious and fearful of his next move. The awful thought that he regretted their marriage, regretted having her as his wife, intruded and Grace nearly allowed herself to shrink beneath the water.

Their eyes met and locked. Grace swore she could see his Adam's apple dip as he swallowed. His reaction gave her courage.

"Alas, the tub is too small to share, but I invite ye to partake of it when I'm done. The water will still be warm and fairly clean." Teasingly, she lifted the washrag and began soaping her breasts, using long, massaging strokes.

He cleared his throat. Even from this distance Grace could swear she saw beads of sweat on his brow. His eyes were bright now and intent on her every move. *Should I rise from the tub and walk toward him? Or should I wait for him to come to me?*

As Grace was uncertain she possessed the nerve to be so brazen, it was more of a rhetorical question. Her heart was fluttering in her chest, her breath was coming fast, and for the first time in more years than she could recall, she felt alive with excitement.

She shut her eyes and gathered her composure. If she could not bolster the nerve to go to him, then she must figure out a way to get him to come to her. Now. Before the moment was forever lost.

Ewan was speechless. His mind swirled with erotic thoughts as he beheld Grace's lush, moist, coral lips, her sensual smile, and glittering eyes. Who was this seductive creature who met his gaze with a bold challenge and unflinching eyes? Who stroked her creamy flesh so invitingly, teasing all his senses, driving him near to madness?

The bulk of her hair was pinned atop her head, but several long tendrils of it had escaped to curl enticingly about her neck and shoulders. He smashed his lips together tightly as he imagined pressing them against that vulnerable spot on her neck, then traveling lower. Licking, tasting, biting.

Desperation pressed in on him. All he could think about was taking her in his arms and kissing her. He wanted to feel her next to him, her breasts flattening against his chest. He wanted to rub his aroused flesh against her softness, to kiss her creamy, pink skin everywhere. To trace the pouting cleft of her sex, first with his fingers and then with his tongue. To make her whimper with need, cry out in satisfaction.

His groin tightened as lust unfurled deep in his gut. She was beguiling. Bewitching. And all his.

Yet he could not claim her. Not yet. Not here.

These past few days had been as near to hell on earth as Ewan could imagine. Wed to the woman of his dreams, yet unable to consummate the union. He had struggled mightily with his conscience over that decision, but honor had prevailed.

Grace was a noble lady, gently born and gently reared. No matter that she was a widow and not an untried maiden, no true lady deserved to be taken in a crude tent after enduring hours of hard riding in the cool, misty rain.

Nay, Grace deserved a proper bed, with feather ticking and scented, silken sheets. A blazing fire, a candlelit chamber, and above all privacy. She deserved romance as well as passion, respect as well as desire. Ewan wanted much more than a swift, crude coupling with her—he wanted to gain her trust, enflame her senses, and win her loyalty.

Leave! Now! It was the only possible course of action if he had any hope of keeping his vow to wait until the proper moment to consummate this marriage. All he need do was turn around and start walking.

A moment passed. And then another.

He didn't move.

"I've missed ye, Ewan," she said quietly.

He felt his brow furrow in puzzlement. "I've been by yer side each day."

She shrugged, making the water ripple in the tub. It lapped against her nipples. He followed the movement, imagining what that creamy flesh would taste like in his mouth, how the nipple would harden and pebble when he teased it with his tongue.

"Aye, yer body has been beside me, but yer laughter and teasing smiles are gone," she said. "Ye're distant and vague. Most days I feel as though I'm intruding upon yer life and it saddens me."

Ewan blinked in surprise. She spoke the words plainly, without accusation or self-pity. Guilt swamped him. He had vowed to make her happy, not bring her distress.

"Ye are my lady wife. I respect and honor ye above all others."

"But ye do not want me," she whispered hoarsely.

"Not want ye! Christ's bones, all I think about is ye." Losing the tight grip on his emotions, Ewan strode purposely forward. As he neared the tub he was enveloped in the heady scent of lavender, sage, and woman.

"Do ye regret our marriage, Ewan?"

"Nay!"

Grace's head dropped back and she cast him a

woeful look. "Then will ye at least give me a proper kiss?" she asked solemnly.

Her inviting request sent a bolt of lightning through his gut. Succumbing to the hunger too long denied, Ewan growled and reached for her. Pulling her wet body from the tub, he scooped Grace into his arms, savoring the feel of her naked flesh sliding against his.

Ewan's lips claimed hers in a long, hard, punishing kiss. He kissed her deeply, thrusting his tongue into her warmth. A startled whimper escaped her lips and then she returned his kiss eagerly, weakening his knees with the promise of her passion.

Ripples of pleasure tore through him. He cupped her breast with his palm, thumbing the nipple. Her breath hitched as it hardened and he could feel her entire body start to quiver. He continued playing with her for a few minutes, stroking her tender flesh with reverent care and wonder.

She dug her fingers into his shoulders and arched into him, pressing against his erection until he was aching with desperate need. He slid his hands down her wet body, caressing her curving hip and thigh, then moving between her legs. She gasped and lifted her hips, offering herself to him.

'Twas pure torture. He could not bear it. Her passionate response made him forget his plan to be noble, to wait until the setting was right. Grace's excitement roused the beast inside him; one that would demand satisfaction if he allowed it to take control.

Letting out an angry growl, Ewan pulled away and drew in a labored breath. "Enough! We must stop or else I'll lose control."

Grace's head fell forward. Her breath wheezed in short bursts, warm and moist against his jaw. "I think

I would enjoy that very much," she whispered in his ear, before lowering her lips and nipping along his neck. "Feeling ye lose control."

Ewan shivered and yanked his head back. "Ye dinnae understand. We need to wait fer a proper time, a proper setting. By all the saints, ye are a lady, Grace!"

"Fie, how can that possibly matter?" Her expression turned grave. "I've no wish to hear any details of yer past female conquests, husband, yet I find it difficult to fathom that ye've never bedded a *lady* before."

Upon hearing her indignant words, the ground beneath his feet seemed to shift. He was doing this out of respect for her. Yet she seemed almost angry at the gesture.

Ewan shook his head in confusion. He felt as green as a lad with his first lass. Though instead of trying to get the female into his bed, he was working far too hard to keep her out of his bed. Bloody hell, the world truly had gone mad!

"Grace, ye are not just any lady, ye are my lady wife. I cannae take ye while my men sleep so near and we've only the thin fabric walls of this tent to muffle the sounds of our lovemaking. 'Tis disrespectful to ye."

"I had no idea ye were such a prim and proper man. Nor was I aware that yer soldiers are so sensitive," she replied tartly.

The sarcasm surprised him. She should be pleased at his sacrifice, for it was a great one. Instead she seemed . . . annoyed?

"Why do ye not understand?" he asked. "I need to protect ye, all of ye, and that includes yer reputation."

She narrowed her eyes in suspicion. "We've never

done more than kiss. How do ye know I'll make any noise when we couple?"

The wicked laugh bubbled up inside him. "Och, love, ye'll wake the heavens with yer cries of passion and mine will bring the devil himself up from Hades."

"Boastful claims, sir. Have ye any actions to prove yer words?"

'Twas not only what she said, but the saucy way she spoke that shattered Ewan's resolve. Honestly, why should he be so concerned about her delicate sensibilities when she obviously wasn't?

"If that's a challenge, Grace, then it shall be well met."

Ewan's lips met hers in a whispered kiss and then the floodgates broke. Encircling her wet form in his arms, Ewan carried his bride to the bed.

He laid her on her back and climbed above her. He bent his head and touched his mouth to her nipple. Gently at first, slowly. The moment he heard her moan of encouragement, Ewan pulled the nipple into his mouth. Flicking the tip of his tongue back and forth, he suckled greedily.

Grace's entire body jerked. Ewan moved his tongue in a steady circle. His lips and tongue teased her unmercifully, then moved lower, across her soft belly. He pushed her legs apart and Grace's fingers sank into his hair. He kissed the inside of one saintly thigh, then the other, teasingly working his way toward his ultimate goal.

Finally his lips closed around the warm, moist center of her femininity. Grace cried out. "Ewan, I . . ." Her head jerked restlessly back and forth, her hips began moving in wild abandon.

Inflamed by her response, Ewan laved the tiny

pearl nestled between her soft folds, stroking her with the urgency that was pounding through his own veins. Her taste and scent were arousing him to maddening pleasure. His cock had never felt so hard, his lust had never soared so high, so fast, so intensely.

Slowly. Slowly. A sheen of sweat broke out on his upper lip. She was wet, hot, and clearly ready for him, but he would bring her to pleasure with his mouth first. Ewan moved his tongue in a steady circle, allowing her whimpering cries and undulating hips to guide his actions.

It didn't take long. He felt her release starting to shudder through her body and he doubled his efforts. "Let it happen," he whispered. "Come fer me, Grace."

He covered her completely with his mouth and she screamed. A long, loud, high-pitched keening wail of ecstasy. The sound of it filled Ewan's heart in a way he never expected. *Mine!* Yet beneath the bolt of possessive fervor was a need to protect this woman with everything he could muster. To nurture and share this intense emotion. To love.

He shifted from between her legs. Rising to his knees, Ewan gazed down at her. Her breathing was still erratic, her eyes closed. One arm was splayed limply across her stomach, the other was resting against her forehead.

But for Ewan, the best gift of all was the sated, satisfied smile on her delectable lips.

Grace was floating. Her body felt weightless, awash in a sea of pleasure that surrounded her in total bliss. She opened her eyes and stretched her back. Moving the hand positioned across her forehead down to her chest, she laid her palm flat against her body and felt the wild beating of her heart.

That was . . . indescribable! So many thoughts and strange emotions rumbled and collided through her mind. She wanted desperately to voice them, to talk to Ewan about what had just occurred, but coherent speech was beyond her at the moment.

Craving contact, she reached out and ran her hand down his thigh. Ewan jerked at her touch, his blue eyes flaring. His breathing was heavy and unsteady. It was then she realized how rigidly he was holding himself, how hard he was struggling to stay in control.

She stared at him with fascination, her senses coming to life. "Come, husband. Let us make some real noise."

His mouth curved in a beautiful, conspiratorial smile as she reached for his tunic. It took little effort to remove his clothing, but there was no time to admire his muscular form. He pushed her against the mattress and leaned over her, bracing his elbows on either side of her head.

The hunger she saw in his eyes made her feel deliciously wanton—and powerful. Never before had she seen such desire reflected back at her from a man's eyes. It erased any of the doubts that had started creeping into her head about how much Ewan wanted her. The truth was plain to see and it made her giddy with wicked delight.

A husky sound rumbled deep in Ewan's chest as she molded her body to his. She kissed him, throwing every shred of longing she felt into the act, saying with her lips and tongue and body what words could not adequately express. He answered with another throaty moan and a hard thrust of his hips.

Boldly she nibbled at his lower lip, pulling it into her mouth and then slowly releasing it. Her fingers moved over his shoulders and muscled back, feeling the raised scars of his wounds. He was a warrior, a protector, and she knew that she could trust him with her life.

Hardly believing her daring, Grace continued her exploration, running her hands down to his trim waist, to his muscular buttocks. 'Twas a heady feeling to lie beneath such a strong man, his hard body pressed intimately against hers. Pushing the hair from his face, she smiled up at him, hoping to convey the depth of her emotions.

Her heart nearly melted when he smiled back, that boyish grin that made dimples appear in his cheeks and his eyes sparkle with mischief. Overcome with emotion, Grace swallowed, then shook her head. This was a joyful, rapturous moment between them. There was no cause for tears.

She kissed him playfully on the lips, then brought her hand down to touch the hardness between his legs. He groaned and bucked his hips. Grace smiled and stroked slowly upward with her fingertips, touching along the length of his penis.

He rumbled something in a harsh growl; Grace was too intent in her examination of his fascinating male appendage to try and understand him. She stroked him rhythmically, excited by the smooth velvet flesh, tantalized by the pulsing shaft that grew longer and thicker with every glide of her hand.

She stretched her body, pressing her breasts against the solid wall of his chest. She marveled at the feel of him, hard and heavy and solid, reveled in the heat that simmered between them. Teasingly, she rotated her hips, trapping him snuggly between her thighs. As tendrils of fire radiated through her body, she buried her fingers in his hair and drew his face close to her own.

"Kiss me," she commanded, and he eagerly complied.

Her lips grew swollen from his endless kisses. With each one she arched herself into his hardness with complete abandon, breathlessly kissing him back. Her head was swimming in a haze of trembling excitement and it felt so good, so right.

"I can wait no longer, Grace," Ewan rasped. He dropped his head and grazed her breasts with his teeth. "If ye aren't ready fer me now, then ye'll never be."

She stifled a groan and shifted her legs. Ewan pushed them wide with his knees, settling himself between them. She could feel the tip of his hard penis seeking entrance. Ears ringing with a surge of anticipation, Grace reached up and cradled Ewan's face between her hands, meeting his eyes, wanting their joining to include far more than merely their bodies. Silently, Ewan complied with her wish, allowing her to see the haze of desire shimmering in his eyes.

They stayed locked in place for a long moment and then suddenly, without any warning, he plunged into her. Tears misted her eyes—not from pain, but from joy. At the sight of them, Ewan ceased moving. "Am I hurting ye, lass?"

"Nay, oh, nay." Grace wrapped her arms around his broad shoulders. "'Tis truly glorious."

Her legs tightened and she wiggled her hips to show him she meant every word. Every part of her tingled with the feel of him stretching and filling her. Need pulsed through her, an ache that only Ewan could assuage. She caressed his back, her nails lightly trailing over the muscles as he rocked back and forth, urging him to continue. The slow thrusts quickly built in intensity. Grace raised her legs and Ewan growled, driving into her with deep, hard strokes, claiming her with a possession she found breathless.

He slid into her again and again, torturing her as he deftly maneuvered his hips. *By all the saints, the man had not exaggerated his skill or falsely boasted about his prowess.* Grace clung to him as he teased and played with her, bringing them both to the edge of release and then suddenly stopping. Prolonging the anticipation until they were both nearly out of their minds.

She felt herself reaching, straining for the pleasure that was just beyond her and then the white-hot sun burst over her. But this time it was far more beautiful, for Ewan joined her in bliss. She heard his strangled moan deep in his chest as he found his release, felt the hot, potent seed fill her womb.

He collapsed atop her, his body still pulsing inside her. She stroked his head soothingly, marveling at how utterly her life had changed, how rich and filled with promise it had become.

After a time, his harsh breathing slowed. Grace continued to pet him, wanting so much to hold and capture the moment. Yet she knew it could not last. She gave him one final hug, trying to ignore the twinge of disappointment invading her heart, knowing what would happen next.

First, he'll pull away. Next, he'll kiss my cheek. Then the tent will fill with the sound of his snores.

Ewan lifted his head. Grace tensed, bracing herself.

"The first time, my lady wife, was a mere tease." He nuzzled her neck. "Now we get serious."

Chapter Twelve

Grace woke just as the dawn began to break. All was quiet both outside and inside the tent. Turning over, she felt privileged to witness a rare sight—Ewan reposed in sleep. He was sprawled on his back, his dark hair tousled, his limbs spread wide. Though they had joined their bodies together—several times last night—this act of sleeping together felt strangely more intimate.

For here, in this moment, Ewan was truly vulnerable. His guard was relaxed, his barriers lowered. Sitting up, Grace edged closer, watching the steady rise and fall of his chest. A faint trace of stubble darkened his angular cheekbones and framed his lips, curled now in a satisfied smile. He looked surprisingly boyish, though there was a weariness to the fine lines at the corner of his eyes that could not be ignored.

He was a man with responsibilities that were never completely abandoned or forgotten, even in sleep. Grace dabbed the sudden tears in her eyes, vowing that she would not become a burden to him. She would be agreeable and gracious, kind and noble. She would be a wife that made him proud, a companion that brightened his days, a lover that emboldened his nights.

Ewan released a soft sigh and shifted, causing the woolen blanket riding his hips to drop lower. Not one to overlook an opportunity, Grace enjoyed a leisurely perusal of his body. Broad shoulders, with long, lean muscles cording his arms and chest. There was an intriguing dusting of body hair on the top of his chest that continued over his abdomen and became a thin line from his navel down to where it disappeared beneath the covers.

Grace felt the familiar fluttering inside at the sight. She studied his face, marveling at all the perfectly formed details. *Beautiful* seemed such an odd word to describe such a hardened, tough warrior, but it fit him perfectly.

Ewan let out another sigh and shifted, turning away from her onto his side. A sudden wave of desolation washed over her. Needing to reestablish their connection, Grace slowly lowered herself until she too lay on her side, facing his broad back. Carefully she smoothed her hand over the raised scar on his shoulder, then traced another one on his side.

Badges of honor, no doubt acquired in battle. They stood as a testament to his skill and courage and a stark reminder of the violence that had marred Ewan's life. 'Twas no wonder he longed for a different existence, away from war, away from conflict.

Gradually, she inched forward until she was pressed completely against him. His muscles were hard, unyielding. She skimmed her chin along the line of his shoulder and decided that she liked sharing her bed with him. Liked the feel of his warmth beside her; even the gentle sounds of his snores were a comfort.

She inhaled his scent and sighed, nuzzling her face into the wide space between his shoulder blades. Pleasure sparkled through her veins. It was strange sleeping with a man. Strange, yet wonderful.

The bed she had shared with Alastair had been large and wide. She had slept in it alone for most of their marriage, since Alastair had been off fighting with King Robert. Yet even when he was at home, they slept on opposite sides of it. There had been a distance between them that went beyond a physical separation. Alastair had been kind and affectionate and she the same, yet she never felt completely comfortable and relaxed in his presence.

Perhaps over time that might have changed. Perhaps not. Grace could never be certain. But now she had a chance to change the course of her future. She need never sleep alone again. She could lie down beside Ewan each night and wake up in the same place the following morning.

Grace smiled, deciding then and there this was something she very much wanted to continue doing— for the next fifty years or so.

Ewan woke to the feel of gentle fingers exploring his back. He grinned at the delightful sensation. 'Twas a dream come to life to feel those delicate, inquisitive fingers, made even better because they were Grace's hands. His lady wife.

Jesus—he was married. To Grace. She trusted him

with her secrets and her safety. Finally, she was his and he would do all that was necessary to keep her.

An unknown emotion curled in his gut and he closed his eyes for a moment. Happiness? Excitement? Love? The last had him nearly choking. Troubadours and virgins spoke of love. Not warriors.

Still . . . 'twas hardly the worst thing in the world to love your wife. Brian McKenna was clear proof of that fact.

An unexpected image of his mother swam before his eyes. Huddled in front of a meager fire, her hands pressed over her face as she cried silent tears. Her moans of pain as she lamented the mistake of devotedly loving a man who had turned against her, who had failed to appreciate and return that love.

Aye, loving your wife was a fine aspiration. As long as she loved you, too.

Ewan swallowed. 'Twas clear that Grace was a woman slow to trust, slow to open her heart and let a man glimpse what she held inside. Could he win her heart? Could they build a life together that included love? The idea took root in his mind and swirled around. No doubt it was a risk. But was it a risk worth taking?

Grace's breath whispered against the back of his neck and she murmured his name. A shiver of desire ran through him, diverting his thoughts. Love was something to ponder. Lust, on the other hand, was something he completely understood.

Grinning, Ewan turned onto his back. Need, mixed with yearning, filled him as he beheld his wife. Their eyes locked and for a moment he lost himself in their depths. She favored him with a sultry look that heated his blood, making his rod stand firm.

"Ride me," he suggested, his voice husky.

Her long tresses covered part of her face, yet Ewan swore he saw her blush. She hesitated, her breath coming fast. He worried he might have shocked her, then bit his tongue before he uttered an apology. She had shown him last night that her passion was equal to his own, though she was not yet completely secure in her role as a wanton female. It was his duty to encourage that behavior.

For both their sakes.

He lifted his hand to her cheek and gently stroked it with the back of his fingers. Her breathing halted when his hand moved lower, skimming over the curves of her breast. Ewan tilted his head so he could gaze into her eyes. He could almost feel the sense of doubt building within her, but he caught a glimmer of intrigue, too.

"Ride me," he whispered again.

Her answer was an incomprehensible moan. He felt her body tense, but then she slowly maneuvered herself into a sitting position. She looked at him with a mixture of anticipation and doubt, then swung a leg over his hips.

"Is this what ye wanted, husband?"

"Aye, 'tis a start."

She frowned with concentration, obviously uncertain what to do next. He thought her naïveté enchanting and her earnest expression and clear willingness to please twined around his heart.

She wiggled forward and her heavy breasts swung toward him. Lush and pink and full, they beckoned him. Groaning, Ewan lifted his torso and captured one rosy nipple in his mouth. Suckling hard, he indulged in her sweetness. Yet the more he tasted, the more he wanted.

All traces of sleep vanished. His hunger was so strong, the yearning so intense, it was nearly impossible to realize that he had already taken her three times the night before. Apparently Grace felt the same, for she pressed herself almost frantically against him, rubbing her damp thighs against his abdomen.

Fire shot through his gut as he hardened even more. His hands roamed up and down her back until he cupped her buttocks and pressed her to his throbbing heat. His hand moved over her flat stomach down toward her thighs.

Grace gasped and lifted her hips. Seizing the opportunity, Ewan shifted, placing his aching cock at the entrance to her feminine softness. Then he arched up, grabbed her hips and pulled her firmly down.

Grace screamed. Ewan shouted. The feel of her tight wetness holding him, cradling him, was almost too much to bear.

Putting her hands on his chest, Grace slid against him and then finally, finally, did as he had commanded. She rode him. Eyes closed, head tipped back, biting her lips as he thrust his hard flesh in and out of hers. Her breathing became shallow and rapid and he knew the exact moment she lost control, for it sent a surge of desire lashing through his entire being.

Every inch of his taut body began to shake as his

climax built and built. His pulse was hammering as he clung to her, drawing her closer, closer. His fists curled around her hips, clenching and unclenching. She was hot and wet and incredibly tight and as she started convulsing, he gave himself up to the glory of the moment.

Ewan's head fell back and he felt the seed pulse and pour from his body into hers. Her inner muscles convulsed around him, the sensation so intense it sent flames through his body.

Grace collapsed on top of him. He wrapped his arms around her and held her close, drawing a wealth of comfort from the feel of her warm softness. He marveled at the smooth feel of her skin, the delicate bones of her shoulders, the tantalizing scent of her hair.

In no time her breath grew soft and steady and he knew she had fallen asleep. Carefully, so as not to wake her, he shifted her onto her side, then brushed a few wisps of hair away from her brow. She sighed and snuggled into the furs. He rested his hand briefly on her shoulder before pulling a soft wool blanket around her, tucking her securely beneath its warmth.

Turning his head, Ewan could see a streak of light creeping under the tent, heralding the approach of dawn. The camp would be stirring soon. They had at least a week of travel ahead of them—if the weather did not worsen. 'Twas best to get an early start. He needed to rise and make sure that all was being taken care of properly, yet Ewan was loath to pull himself away from the comfort of the bed and the sweetness of his wife.

The wind outside the tent whirled and blew as

their breaths fell into a rhythm. Ewan's eyes drifted shut. *Five minutes. I'll rest for five minutes.*

It took no more than two before he fell into a deep, satisfying sleep.

Grace awoke long after dawn had invaded the camp. She reached across the bed merely to confirm what she already knew—she was alone. The mattress was no longer warm, her senses no longer heightened, her heart no longer simmering with awareness. Sometime during the early morning hours, Ewan had slipped away.

A myriad of emotions swirled through her. Disappointment mingled with practicality, followed swiftly by a stab of embarrassment. Normally, they broke camp with the dawn. Clearly they had waited this morning on her husband's orders, allowing her to rest. And there was no doubt that the men would know why she needed to sleep.

"Ah, so ye are awake. At last." Edna's cheery voice cut into Grace's musing. Somehow she managed to arrange her face into a smile as the maid hurried into the tent.

"Is it very late?" Grace asked, scrambling from the bed.

"Late enough. Though the men haven't minded the easy morning," Edna said, shaking out Grace's gown. "Nor the hot meal they had time to cook and eat."

Through the thin fabric walls of the tent Grace could hear the good-natured masculine banter. "Why dinnae ye wake me?" she asked as she splashed clean water on her face and rubbed her groggy eyes.

"Sir Ewan said ye were not to be disturbed," Edna bristled, smoothing the front of the gown.

"Oh." The blush was impossible to hide, so Grace didn't bother. She flexed her shoulders, amazed at the odd places various aches, soreness, and twinges aroused, then pulled in her breath while Edna laced the back of her gown. "That was very considerate of him."

"Aye, especially when he was the cause of yer exhaustion."

The maid's comment filled Grace with a healthy dose of mortification, but she tamped down the feelings. There was no need to feel any shame or embarrassment. She and Ewan were married—they had every right to indulge in their passions.

Still, she wondered if seeing Ewan this morning would be awkward. There was no time to take any extra care with her appearance, and Grace admonished Edna to hurry. Finally ready, she left the tent. A group of men lounging in front of a small fire came to their feet and moved toward her. Momentarily startled, Grace froze, but the men simply nodded their heads and began dismantling her tent.

Flushed with color, Grace scurried away, her eyes searching for Ewan. She tried to act nonchalant when she spied him on the other side of the camp, but her heartbeat picked up speed and her spirits soared. It oddly felt as though she was seeing him for the first time.

His handsome face, his charming smile, his commanding manner. The strength of his arms reminded her of the passion she had felt when she was encircled within them. But she had felt more. There had been a sense of comfort and security emanating from him, an assurance without words that somehow all would be well.

Almost as if sensing her regard, Ewan turned. He gave her a slow, searching appraisal, then favored her with a smile of solid satisfaction. Grace felt the color bloom in her cheek and quickly lowered her chin.

She waited a full minute before raising her head and when she did, Ewan caught her eye and winked. Grace struggled to keep a dignified expression, but it was impossible. All she could hope was that not too many of the others had witnessed the exchange.

"Riders approaching!" one of the guards shouted.

All activity in the camp ceased as everyone turned toward the horizon. Grace spun around and saw a line of mounted men sweeping across the flat landscape of long grass. They rode with purpose, at a clipping pace. The faint rays of morning sun illuminated the shields clasped in their arms, but the design was not one she could identify. She wove her way through the camp, coming to Ewan's side.

"Roderick?" she asked, trying to dose the flame of fear that engulfed her.

"Perhaps." Ewan squeezed her hand in comfort, then casually drew his sword. "Stand behind me. If they attack, grab Edna and run fer the tree line. Wait there until I come fer ye."

Grace felt her heart contract, but she followed the command without question. A gust of wind swirled around her head, loosening a few strands of her hastily braided hair. Grace left them alone. Peering around Ewan's broad shoulders, she waited tensely as the riders approached.

The man in the lead was of middle years, dark-haired, with a broad nose, a wide, thrusting jaw, and a weather-beaten complexion. "I dinnae recognize any of the men," she remarked hopefully.

Ewan tensed. "Roderick would not put anyone ye could identify out front if he was hoping to catch us off guard."

As they drew near, the leader pulled back his reins. His powerful horse danced impatiently, but obeyed. Grace could smell the dirt on the clothes and unwashed bodies of the men as they closed ranks behind their leader. He spurred his horse forward, walking the beast up to Ewan.

"Good morning," Ewan called out pleasantly. His smile was friendly, his eyes watchful. "I fear ye are too late to join us in breaking our fast, but we have some ale, oatcakes, and cheese we can spare, if ye and yer men are hungry."

The intruder skimmed Ewan's body with his gaze. "Who can I thank fer such a generous offer of hospitality?" he asked, his deep voice disturbing the stillness.

"I am Sir Ewan."

The leader cast an inquiring eye over all of them, then lifted his face to the wind. "I can tell from yer speech and weapons that ye're a Scot, yet I see no clan colors."

Ewan seemed to pinch back a smile. "We are Scot through and through and loyal subjects to King Robert."

"Ye fought with the Bruce?"

"Aye."

The leader nodded with approval. "Where are yer banners?"

"We carry none."

"Who are yer people?"

"My mother is a Gilroy," Ewan replied tersely.

"And yer father?"

"Is dead."

Grace felt a surge of protective resentment at the barrage of boorish questions. She wanted to stalk forward and give the leader's horse a sharp slap on the rump, sending both horse and man away. Yet aside from the cool tone, Ewan was reacting to the questions with perfect calm. Most likely because he was used to them.

"Where are ye headed?" the stranger asked.

"North. 'Tis where we make our home." Ewan gave the man a flat smile. "And who might ye be, good sir?"

"I am Laird Kilkinney." He pointed to the plaid mantle draped over his shoulder that was pinned in place with a jewel-encrusted brooch. "Damn it! The dust and dirt have faded my colors. 'Tis to be expected, I suppose, when traveling in such fierce weather."

Though he hardly looked the part, Grace could see he was telling the truth. Despite his rather disheveled state, Kilkinney radiated the confidence, authority, and privilege of a laird, if not the hygiene. She was suddenly glad she had not acted upon her earlier impulse to challenge the man.

"May I ask why ye travel with such a small guard?" Ewan inquired.

"I stopped at the shrine of the Virgin Mother to offer prayers fer the soul of my dearly departed wife. I sent most of my men ahead of me, but when the rains struck we were forced to stay the night at the shrine." He crossed his hands, relaxing them on the pommel.

"We are but a few hours' journey from my keep. In fact, ye are on my land."

"Then it is ye we must thank fer allowing us a peaceful spot to rest fer the night," Ewan said.

"Ye should have ridden a few more miles to the north and asked fer shelter at my home, Glenmore Keep." Kilkinney craned his neck, his eyes clearly searching behind Ewan. "I'm certain a soft bed would have been most welcomed by the women in yer party."

"We have the provisions to provide our own comforts," Ewan answered. He signaled and Grace stepped forward, clasping his outstretched hand. She lifted her chin and curled her fingers around his, the heat of his body sinking comfortingly into hers. "May I present my wife, Lady Grace."

Grace sank to her knee in greeting, but kept her features stiff. His rude questions aside, Laird Kilkinney appeared friendly enough, yet she could not help but notice how rigidly and alert Ewan's men stood, their backs straight, their hands fisted.

The laird tipped his head. "'Tis an honor to meet one so fair of face, milady."

"Yer gracious words make me blush, milord."

Ewan pulled Grace closer. His fingers tensed like steel within hers. "We were afforded hospitality at Glenmore Keep but a fortnight ago," he said.

The laird's expression soured. "My nephew, Simon, was in charge during my absence."

"Aye, that was the name of our host."

"I'd like to ask if the lad did me proud, but I fear the answer," the laird grumbled.

"We stayed but one evening," Grace replied.

"And left in haste," Ewan added.

The laird snorted. "I beg ye to not judge all of my clan by his behavior." His smile was fleeting yet sincere, and Grace was pleased to note the hostility had left his eyes. "Simon's a bit of a dullard."

"Sometimes there are merits to having very few relations," Ewan quipped. His remark was smooth and lighthearted, but his fingers tensed on Grace's arm.

"Well said, Sir Ewan." The laird broke into a wide grin and several of his men chuckled. Overhead, a hawk released a cry as it circled through the gray sky. Looking up, the laird frowned. "The rains will soon begin again. Ye are welcome to wait out the storm at Glenmore Keep."

Ewan paused, as though considering it, then shook his head. "I thank ye fer the offer, but we are eager to return home."

"Then I shall bid ye both Godspeed in yer travels."

Kilkinney dug his heels into his horse's flanks, circled the mount and rode away, his men in tight formation behind him. They had not gone far when Kilkinney suddenly turned, then raised his arm in salute. Ewan returned the gesture.

Grace watched the exchange in puzzlement. "Laird Kilkinney has certainly changed his tune regarding ye. I thought his questions about yer lineage were both uncalled fer and rude."

"The crown might sit firmly upon Robert's head, but there are still those who will try to knock it off. 'Tis wise to determine loyalties when meeting strangers, especially when they are on yer lands." Ewan shrugged. "We've enemies aplenty. 'Twould be foolish to let pride forsake the chance to forge a friendly acquaintance with a powerful clan."

Grace digested the comments in silence. Thanks to

her, Roderick was now a formidable foe. Avoiding new enemies was not only smart, but necessary for survival. But the comments about his birth must have rankled Ewan. He acted as though the words meant nothing, yet Grace had seen the subtle flinch, the momentary crack of bravado that revealed a vulnerability. He might display an easy, open candor and a glib tongue to one and all, but at his core, he was a guarded, private man.

Being born a bastard had shaped more of his life than he cared to acknowledge and her heart ached with sympathy. It must be interminable to always be reminded that he did not possess a clear place in the world.

Grace watched him intently, but it was obvious that Ewan had moved away from the subject and would not speak of it. "It was a relief to discover the laird was nothing like his nephew," she said.

"Aye, though I had far more choice words than *dullard* for Simon."

Grace nodded. "Considering the state the man was in when we left Glenmore Keep, it was wise to have made a good impression on the laird."

Ewan tapped his temple with his finger. "I'm always thinking and planning and plotting."

"Aye, but is any of it useful?" she teased.

"Well, now, I've got ye fer a wife, haven't I?" Ewan retorted smugly.

Grace instantly sobered and her eyes slid away from his. "That might not be to yer advantage, especially with Roderick's threat."

"Bah, Roderick is naught but a pesky flea. Every man who sets eyes on ye is jealous of my good fortune." Ewan bent his head and kissed her. "As well they should be."

"Ewan." Grace warned when he leaned in for a second kiss. "Ye are avoiding the point."

"Nay. I'm making my own." He kissed her one final time, then pulled back and grinned wickedly. "With all this ruckus, I dinnae even have a chance to properly greet my wife." Holding her gaze, he raised her hand and pressed a kiss on the pulse of her wrist. "How do ye fare this morning? Are ye well?"

Grace took a deep breath of the clean, crisp air, attempting to sweep the cobwebs from her head. It was difficult to keep her wits about her when he favored her with that smoldering look, especially after the night they had spent together.

"Ye should not have let me sleep so late," she admonished.

"Since I was the cause of keeping ye from a proper night's rest, I thought it only fair." His eyes swept over her, his gaze a tender caress. "Will ye be able to ride today?"

It took a moment for the meaning of Ewan's question to penetrate her brain. The blush that came on the heels of comprehension was impossible to halt, but Grace deflected her embarrassment with a question of her own. "Will ye?"

Ewan laughed, then lifted his fingers to her cheek. He took his time admiring her, letting his lips curve into a lazy, seductive grin. "I can sit on my horse easily enough, yet my mind will surely wander as I'll be thinking of the night to come."

The yearning in his eyes was so tantalizing Grace wanted to fling herself into his arms. Instead, she took a step closer until her breasts pressed against his chest, then tilted her head to meet his grin. His mouth was so close she could feel his warm breath against her lips. "Ah, my husband, trust me when I tell ye that yer imaginings shall pale when compared to the reality."

Hardly knowing where those bold, wicked words had sprung from, Grace kissed a stunned Ewan on the lips, then turned and scurried away. She quickly ate the oatcake Edna had saved, washing it down with a few swigs of lukewarm ale, all the while feeling her husband's eyes boring into her.

Her hand shook slightly as she lifted the cup to her lips. For days she had lamented over the lack of attention from her new husband and now that he had finally showed some interest in her, she was determined to keep it.

Even though she had no earthly idea what she was doing.

Chapter Thirteen

They traveled the rest of the day making only a few necessary stops to water the horses and answer the call of nature. Feeling responsible for their very late start, Grace made no protest at the grueling pace, even though her muscles ached and her eyelids drooped with exhaustion.

Grace kept her cloak wrapped tightly around her to keep warm, though she enviously eyed the pouch that Ewan sipped from every now and again, suspecting it was filled with whiskey. Whenever possible, she tilted her face to the sun filtering through the clouds, basking in the warm rays.

They made camp at dusk. Ewan assisted Grace from her horse, catching her by the waist and steadying her once her feet hit the ground. Her legs wobbled, but held.

The evening meal was hot and plentiful; the conversation congenial. As was his custom, Ewan sat among his men, but his eyes found Grace's across the open fire. They flickered against the dancing flames, the brightness telling her that he was eager to be alone with her.

Grace wasted no time in retiring to her tent. Though it felt like an eternity, Ewan soon joined her, the smoldering intent in his gaze making her quiver. The moment their lips touched, she melted inside. Ewan wasn't gentle, but she didn't care—she felt greedy, desperate, wild. It was a swift and fierce coupling, the merging of hungry flesh and ravenous desire. Yet it was also tender and satisfying and for Grace a reaffirmation of her wedded state.

When it was over, Ewan stretched out beside her, his chest firm at her back. She felt his fingers glide down her backbone, massaging the stiff muscles. It felt glorious.

"Are ye sore from all the riding?" he asked.

Grace smiled in the darkness. "Aye, my horse and my husband made me ache."

Ewan laughed. "Relax, lass. I'll make it better."

His hands were warm and gentle as they attacked her knotted flesh. Kneading, pressing, stroking, he concentrated on each muscle until it relaxed. Grace sighed and succumbed to the soothing rhythm, grateful for the tender, considerate ministrations.

Her eyes closed as Ewan adjusted her position, resting her head in the hollow of his shoulder. His arms cradled her, offering her comfort, warmth, and security and Grace was quickly able to fall asleep.

The following days took on a similar pattern. Days spent in the saddle, nights encircled in Ewan's arms. 'Twas as close to heaven as Grace could imagine and she relished every mile they traveled.

The men's mood lightened as the landscape

changed. They moved beyond the grand mountain ranges and dense patches of forest and climbed even higher into the hills. Here the slopes were rocky and mossy green, the air fragranced with heather, and thick white misty clouds obscured the peaks.

They rode through a thick forest of graceful, tall pines and willowy birch, then halted at the crest of a windswept ridge.

"We are nearly there," Ewan declared, stopping beside Grace.

Anxious for her first look at her new home, Grace peered through the low fog, catching a glimpse of a stone tower and curtain wall surrounding it. The mist parted as they began descending and she could see that the keep was set on the highest point at the end of a valley that boasted sparing patches of green. A small flock of sheep gathered near the shallow river under the watchful eyes of a few old men. The clean smell of fresh rain permeated the earth and the damp ground was not muddy, but tightly packed.

"It's not as grand as yer other homes," Ewan remarked carefully.

It tore at Grace's heart to hear the hesitation in Ewan's voice. "I dinnae know where ye have gotten the notion that I expect to be bathed in luxury," she replied wryly. "I was raised in a convent and planned on spending the rest of my days behind those simple walls."

"I doubt the Fergusons' hall is small or miserly. And I know the McKenna Castle is grand."

Grace felt a frisson of disappointment at the remark. Did her husband truly know her so little? Did he honestly believe she was that concerned about the size of his home and the splendor of its furnishings?

"Even from this distance I can see that yer keep is a fine holding," Grace said evenly. "It has simplicity and strength, which is far preferable to bloated grandeur."

"Ye think yer brother's castle is bloated?" Ewan smiled. "I shall be certain to mention that to him when next we meet."

Glad to have lightened Ewan's mood, Grace returned the smile, but it soon vanished as they entered the valley. Anticipation stirred when they came closer to the keep. The shepherds waved at their passing, as did the few workers toiling in the fields.

They rode single file through the portcullis and arrived in the courtyard. Keenly aware of the scrutiny, Grace dropped back the hood of her woolen cloak, better to see and be seen. A delicate shiver went through her as a cheer erupted from the crowd.

There were nearly a hundred people crammed into the bailey—men, women, and children—all eager to catch a glimpse of Ewan and his escort. There were many round-eyed glances cast her way and Grace realized that none were certain of her identity. 'Twas known that Sir Ewan had traveled south to find a bride, but the hasty nature of her wedding made it impossible to send word of their marriage.

The buzzing of talk stopped as an older woman stepped forward. She was tall and elegant, wearing a gown of crushed gold velvet. A ring of keys hung from the leather belt draped low around her waist. Her eyes were sharp and smoldering, her hair streaked with gray. Grace glanced at that uncompromising face and immediately knew it was Lady Moira, Ewan's mother.

Unlike the rest of the smiling, waving crowd, Lady Moira did not look happy. At all.

Ewan swung off his horse and embraced his mother. After exchanging a few private words, he turned and came over to Grace. Extending his hand, he assisted her off her horse, then brought her forward to introduce her.

Up close, Grace could see more of a family resemblance. Ewan had his mother's eyes and coloring, though her formality was a stark contrast to her son's easy manner.

Lady Moira's eyes swept her from head to toe, then she took a deep breath and let loose a great sigh. Momentarily shocked, Grace stiffened. Ewan cleared his throat loudly.

"Welcome." Lady Moira's greeting sounded pleasant enough, but there was a clear lack of warmth in it. And there was the tightness around her mouth that bespoke of how difficult the words were for her to speak.

Grace, taken aback by this unexpected occurrence, sank into a graceful curtsy. Then she raised her chin, tilted her head, and met that chilling glare. "I'm honored to meet ye."

Lady Moira's mouth tightened further. It hardly took much intuition to see that she did not approve of her son's choice of wife. But why?

"Ewan says that ye are a McKenna," Lady Moira said, the inflection in her voice disapproving.

"Aye."

"And a widow."

Grace nodded.

"How long were ye married?"

"Seven years."

"And in all that time ye had no bairns?" Lady Moira retorted, her eyes glittering with a disgruntled scowl.

"My husband was away from home most of our marriage, fighting fer King Robert's cause," Grace replied slowly, feeling the betraying warmth of embarrassment creep into her cheeks.

"Dinnae yer brother fight beside the Bruce?"

"He did."

"Does he have any bairns?"

"Aye, three and another on the way." The words were no sooner spoken when Grace realized the implication, but it was too late to avoid the question.

"Humph."

Grace was struck silent by the older woman's piercing stare. Disoriented, it took her a moment to realize that Lady Moira was hoping to get a reaction from her. Much as she wanted, Grace would not lower herself to argue with the woman. Nay, the best way to cope with this rude inquiry was not to react—though that was proving more difficult by the moment.

"Yer journey was long. I'm certain ye are feeling tired." Lady Moira waved her hand toward the heavy oak door of the keep. "Deirdre will show ye to yer chamber so that ye may rest."

Orders delivered, Lady Moira stepped dismissively around Grace and went directly to her son. *Blessed Mother Mary, what rudeness!* Unexpected travelers were given a more hospitable greeting. Indignantly, Grace turned to her husband, anticipating Ewan's effrontery at this treatment, but he appeared unaware that anything was amiss. He rested his arms on his mother's shoulders, then bowed his head and again spoke to her in a low tone.

"This way, if ye please, milady."

Grace turned to the young woman who had spoken and realized she must be Deirdre. She glanced from the servant to her husband, her feelings raw. She could almost feel the wedge of separation being driven between them.

Grace fought down her bitter words. Biting her lip in frustration, she ignored the knots that were twisting inside her stomach. This was neither the time nor the place to make a scene, especially when her husband's support was so questionable. Barely squelching her dismay, Grace followed the maid into the keep.

The interior of the great hall was solidly built, yet bare and dark. There were no tapestries on the wall, no fire burning brightly, no decorations of any kind, not even a pitcher filled with wildflowers. The starkness reminded her of her husband's mother—hard and unwelcoming.

"Lady Moira is not at all what I expected," Grace muttered, dismayed at the weakness in her own voice.

Deirdre lowered her head shyly. She was a comely lass, with a willowy shape, and dark, thick hair that fell to the center of her back. Her eyes were round and honest, a pretty shade of blue.

"I know it must be difficult to believe, but Lady Moira is capable of some kindness," the maid said.

Upset that she had betrayed how uncertain she felt, Grace merely nodded. It was a matter of pride that she play her role correctly, that she establish herself as the lady of the manor, in control of everything, including her feelings.

As they climbed the stone stairs, Grace willed away her gloomy thoughts. The bedchamber she was taken to was a pleasant surprise, holding comforts she had not seen in the hall, including a small tapestry hung on the longest wall.

A huge carved bed, which boasted a soft, overstuffed mattress, dominated the chamber. Velvet hangings were tied back with thick cords around each of the four posts. When the curtains were drawn, it would be a warm, private spot.

There was a knock on the door and two men carried in a tub. They were quickly followed by a line of serving women with buckets of steaming water. Grace sent Deirdre a questioning look and the maid hitched her shoulders as if to say she was equally confused.

"Sir Ewan ordered a bath fer ye, Lady Grace," one of the women explained.

Grace's eyes brightened at the thoughtful gesture. Edna soon arrived, along with Grace's trunks. In very short order, the maid had things organized to her satisfaction. Before she left, Deirdre dipped a respectful curtsy. But it was the welcome in the servant's eyes that soothed Grace. At least she had found one person in the household who was glad of her arrival. Hopefully, there would be others.

Grace rushed Edna as she assisted her with the bath and changed into a clean gown. She stood impatiently as the maid fussed over her hair and tightened the lacings on her gown, then allowed her to place a white veil on her head and secure it with a gold circlet.

Edna nodded with approval when she stepped

back to admire her handiwork. "Now ye look like a true lady of the manor."

Grace let the observation pass without comment. Earlier, while sitting in the hot bathwater, her distress and pique had cooled, replaced by a fit of apprehension. She had been raised to be meek, agreeable, and obedient, but after spending a few minutes in the company of Lady Moira, she knew those traits would not serve her best.

Grace ushered Edna out of the chamber, needing a few moments alone to compose herself. No matter how Lady Moira acted this evening, she would answer with an amiable expression and a firm attitude. She would not stoop to petty behavior or rudeness, yet neither would she allow herself to be bullied. She would be pleasant and gracious at all times.

Pinching her cheeks to bring out some color, Grace took a deep breath, steeled herself for what was to come, and strode down the short corridor. No one seemed to take note when she entered the great hall as all were occupied with their assigned tasks in preparation for the evening meal. Two young lads were diligently trying to coax a blaze in the fireplace while a group of sturdy-looking women were moving heavy wooden tables and benches into the center of the room.

Grace watched as two high-back chairs were placed in the center of the table set at the head of the room. She was not surprised the hall lacked a proper dais for the more important members of the household. From what she had seen of the overall condition of the keep, there were far more important matters to attend to first.

As the servants scurried about finishing their work,

men and women began to drift into the hall and take their places at the tables. Grace spied Lady Moira entering on the opposite side. The older woman's scowl warned Grace this first meal would not be particularly enjoyable, yet she was determined to make the best of it.

There would be time aplenty for disagreements. Time also to determine precisely why Lady Moira had such a displeased reaction to their marriage and held such a low opinion of her.

Eyeing one of the chairs, Grace headed directly toward it, knowing she needed to establish her rank in the household at this very first meal. Lady Moira's pace quickened noticeably and Grace knew Ewan's mother had realized Grace's intent. Realized and decided to try and thwart it.

They reached the table at the same moment. The glance Lady Moira bestowed upon her boded ill for a peaceful settlement. Grace felt her palms begin to moisten. The hall grew eerily silent as everyone ceased what they were doing and watched the exchange with open interest.

"Please, be seated," Grace said with civil politeness, indicating the bench next to the chair. "I'm sure Ewan would relish his mother's company during our meal."

"I always sit beside my son," Lady Moira declared with a face like thunder. "That will never change."

Grace looked her straight in the eye. "Sir Ewan conveniently has two sides, milady."

"But only two chairs," Lady Moira said. Her words gave away little emotion and Grace was impressed at her self-control.

"Aye, one for the lord and lady of the keep. I shall

ask fer a third chair to be built, so that ye may sit in comfort at *my* table."

Lady Moira raised her brows. The fire snapped, a shower of embers bursting into the air. Voices sounded from somewhere outside the hall. Yet neither woman budged.

"I fear my son has married on a whim," Lady Moira declared.

"I bring a substantial dowry and a strong clan alliance. I am not afraid of hard work and vow to do all within my power to ensure that we prosper and thrive. I shall make this a peaceful, welcoming home."

Lady Moira reached for a goblet that had been set on the table, then slowly poured herself a cup of wine. She watched Grace intently as she sipped, giving nary a hint as to what was going on behind her eyes.

"Bold words. We shall see the truth of them in the next few weeks." Lady Moira took another sip from her goblet. "If ye last that long."

Grace clenched her fist beneath the table, trying to keep a check on her rising temper. Her cheeks felt warm and she knew the rosy color betrayed her, but she vowed Lady Moira would not get the better of her, no matter how hard she pushed.

But Grace's peevish attitude vanished the minute Ewan, followed by a circle of his retainers, entered the hall. He walked among the tables, greeting all by name, his stride purposeful, confident, and assured. Grace's heart beat faster.

He moved closer to her, his arm slipping possessively around her waist. Lady Moira stared at them with undisguised disapproval.

"Ye look lovely," he whispered. "Did ye enjoy yer bath?"

"Aye, and I thank ye fer the gift of it."

"Next time I shall join ye." He leaned close, his eyes melting tenderly into hers. Her mind burned with the memory of their lovemaking, the feel of his body possessing hers, the intensity of the emotions he seemed to so easily evoke.

Caught firmly in his spell, Grace simply nodded.

"The food grows cold," Lady Moira interrupted.

"Then let the meal be served," Ewan answered, never taking his eyes off Grace. "I, fer one, am famished."

Lady Moira grumbled. Keeping his arm securely around her waist, Ewan carefully pulled out a chair for Grace. An enormous sense of relief washed over her at the gesture. Striving not to openly gloat, she took her seat. Looking none too pleased, Lady Moira hastily sat on the bench at Ewan's other side.

At Lady Moira's signal, trays of hot food were brought into the hall. Grace's stomach rumbled as the aroma of savory dishes invaded her senses. The servants each stopped in front of Lady Moira, then lifted the lids covering the trays for her inspection. The food was simply prepared, but tasty and plentiful. At Ewan's encouragement, Grace tasted everything.

The conversations around them were loud and boisterous and laughter floated on the air. Everyone appeared to be in a celebratory mood. Except for Lady Moira. As for Ewan, well, he was perfectly at ease, somehow able to totally ignore the tension swirling between his wife and his mother.

"Are ye pleased to be home, Ewan?" Grace asked.

"Aye, it feels good. Though there is much work to be done. The warmer days pass quickly; we must make the most of them."

"I am eager to begin," Grace said.

Ewan shook his head. "Nay, I dinnae expect my lady wife to toil like a servant."

"But, Ewan, of course I shall work alongside everyone else." Not wanting anyone, especially her mother-in-law, to be privy to their disagreement, Grace lowered her voice to a whisper. "I insist."

Ewan favored her with an indulgent smile and patted her hand. "I'm sure we will find something of use fer ye to do."

Mortified, Grace turned away. One of the men shouted up to Ewan, asking him to settle a wager as to which was more essential to a knight—a sword, a horse, or his armor. A chorus of male voices immediately rose in a good-natured argument as the merits of each were debated.

Grace took a small sip of her wine. Her cheeks burned crimson, a combination of embarrassment and annoyance. Not work! What exactly did Ewan expect her to do all day? Sit around and act ladylike?

With the wager among his men settled, Ewan turned his attention back to Grace. "Have ye tried the venison pie?" he asked. "'Tis Cook's specialty." Not waiting for a reply, he skewered a portion with his eating knife and held it to Grace's lips. A thick, dark gravy dripped from the chunk of meat. Grace's stomach flipped. 'Twas far too large a piece, yet feeling the eyes of many upon her, she reluctantly opened her mouth.

"I suggest ye cease feeding her like she is a babe,"

Lady Moira commented sourly. "All are likely to think she's a simpleton, incapable of eating on her own."

"'Tis romantic," Ewan argued.

"'Tis revolting," his mother countered.

Grace struggled to swallow. Merciful Mary, would the woman never sheathe her claws? Her cheeks puffed as she chewed the meat, endeavoring not to choke. It felt like sand on her tongue and her mind could only wonder what other unpleasant surprises awaited.

Thankfully, her maudlin thoughts were interrupted as the empty platters were cleared away. Additional pitchers of ale and wine were brought and the evening's entertainment began. It started with a story by Deirdre, a fine tale of knights and dragons and lost love. There was applause and shouts for another when she was finished, but the pretty maid shyly lowered her head and took her seat.

Alec distracted the crowd by tossing three eggs into the air, clumsily juggling the delicate orbs. Everyone broke into laughter as the cook began chasing the knight, screeching not to waste any food. Alec ran skillfully around the tables, tossing his pilfered eggs in the air as he moved, much to the delight of all.

Then the singing began and by the fourth ballad, Grace saw her opportunity to withdraw. 'Twas clear the celebration would last late into the night and she was simply too tired to remain. Leaning close to her singing husband, she shouted to be heard.

"I shall take my leave, now. Good night."

Ewan frowned for an instant, then nodded in understanding. Uncertain if he would follow, Grace took her time getting out of her chair. Ewan appeared to also be getting to his feet, but then his mother clasped her hand on his arm and his attention was diverted.

Tired of sparring with Lady Moira, Grace grumbled beneath her breath and kept moving. She left the hall without incident. As she climbed the stairs, she heard footsteps behind her. *He's coming!* Smiling, Grace turned. Edna screeched and nearly knocked into her.

"Och, milady, be careful. These steps are uneven and much harder to climb in this dim light."

Hiding her disappointment, Grace waved her maid away. "Go back to the hall and enjoy yerself. I'll be fine on my own."

Edna hesitated a moment, but Grace nodded and the maid complied. Grace took care as she climbed the rest of the staircase, heeding Edna's words about the uneven steps.

The sight of some of her possessions in the bedchamber eased Grace's misgivings, for they gave her a sense of belonging. She lit several candles, then began preparing for bed. She had just finished braiding her hair when Ewan entered the chamber.

She was surprised to see he was carrying a pitcher of wine and two goblets, yet even more surprised to see the pleasant grin on his face. She gave him a glower as he passed her.

Ewan either didn't notice or didn't care. She recognized that lazy slant to his smile and that sinful, sensuous expression, yet refused to be charmed. He bent his head and she knew he meant to kiss her, but before their lips touched, Grace hauled herself away.

He sighed. "'Tis my mother, isn't it?"

"How did ye ever guess?" Grace glared at him, then turned away.

Ewan tilted her chin with his fingers, forcing her

to look at him. "I know she can be grating on the nerves, but ye must try not to take her remarks so personally."

"Ha! Will ye listen to yerself. Her barbs are sharp, direct, and meant to wound. She's eager to pounce on any flaw, real or perceived. 'Tis hardly possible to feel anything but insulted and unwelcome under her constantly condemning glare." Grace took a deep breath, holding back the sudden onslaught of tears. "Why does she dislike me so much?"

Ewan at least had the good sense to look a wee bit guilty. "My mother is more angry with me than upset about ye. She dinnae want me to marry a lady. She wanted a simple village lass fer a daughter-in-law."

"One she could mold into her own image?"

Ewan shrugged. "Perhaps."

"Do ye want a wife like yer mother?"

"Nay!" Ewan protested hotly. "Christ's bones, I cannae think of anything more . . . perverted."

"Well, now, I suppose that's a relief."

Ewan set the pitcher and goblets on the table. "I'm sorry fer my mother's behavior. I suppose I'm so accustomed to her wicked tongue that I no longer notice what she says. I promise I shall speak with her in the morning."

Grace slowly shook her head. This was between her and Lady Moira. Ewan's interference might make things worse. "She's a grown woman; she can make her own amends fer her behavior."

Ewan studied Grace's face. "Ye willnae be waiting fer that to happen, I hope?"

Grace almost smiled at the worried expression on his face. "I know that yer mother's character will not soon change, nor will her propensity to judge others disappear simply because I desire it."

"Good. That's good."

Ewan leaned closer. His breath tickled her neck, but Grace shrugged her shoulders to move him away. "'Tis not only yer mother that caused me distress this evening. I take issue with ye."

"I know I've neglected ye, but—"

"Nay! I understand that ye've got duties that must be attended, especially since ye've been gone so long. What I dinnae appreciate is being told that I cannae work with the others. What do ye expect of me, Ewan?"

"I expect ye to be happy. That's all I've ever wanted." He nuzzled her ear, then bit it gently, making her squeal. "Though I've made a muck of it so far, I swear to ye that I will be a good husband."

His voice was compelling and sincere. The passionate words and affectionate gesture deflated Grace's anger. She even managed a smile as he tugged gently on the braid that tumbled down her back. Then she turned into his arms.

Ewan's lips slanted across hers with an almost desperate intensity. She shifted and allowed him to lift her in his arms. He carried her to the bed.

She watched him with hungry eyes, saying nothing as he removed his clothing, smothering her gasp of delight as he turned to face her, a thick erection jutting eagerly toward her. The soft mattress sank under his weight and she closed her eyes, breathing deeply. Her nostrils flared when she caught his beguiling, familiar scent, setting her heart racing.

There was no other man who affected her so deeply, who enticed her so completely. Aye, his skillful fingers and wicked mouth could quickly ripen her body with pleasure, but it was more than her flesh that responded to him.

It was her heart. It was her soul.

They kissed until their lips were swollen and tender, until they were gasping and arching against each other with passionate need. He entered her in one fluid motion and she cried out, moaning his name. It was wild and torrid and she relished each powerful thrust, welcoming him into her body, into her heart.

He collapsed on her slick and spent, bellowing deep breaths. Grace held him against her breast, welcoming the crushing weight, the solid strength. It gave her a strange comfort, an affirmation of the bond they had forged.

After a few minutes, Ewan rolled onto his back, pulling her along with him. She snuggled against his broad chest, listening to his steady heartbeat as he gently stroked her hair.

It will *be all right,* she told herself. *We* will *overcome these problems and find the happiness we seek.*

Then, with those thoughts echoing faintly in her mind, Grace drifted off to sleep.

Chapter Fourteen

Grace awoke alone in bed the next morning in a different frame of mind. She had but two choices—to waste her time lamenting the unfairness of Lady Moira's attitude, or devise a way to take her rightful place in the household. Neither appealed. She pulled the covers over her head and lay beneath them for a moment, contemplating how peaceful it would be to remain there for the rest of the day. Or the rest of the week.

But wallowing in self-pity was not her way, so Grace emerged from beneath the blankets. Merely thinking about Lady Moira was enough to set Grace's blood boiling. Normally she would shy away from such a bold confrontation, making the strong urge she felt to confront Lady Moira even more surprising.

What was causing this uncharacteristic response? Was it merely her pride being stung? Or was being the wife that Ewan desired so important to her that she would do whatever was necessary and damn the consequences? It was a startling revelation to realize she had such fire in her belly, such passion in her soul.

Yet as she pondered her approach to this dilemma, Grace concluded that causing undue strife among the household was not the answer. She was intelligent, clever, and patient. Her future might be at stake, yet she firmly believed she could conquer Lady Moira in a peaceful, harmonious manner. 'Twould be more difficult for her, but better for everyone else.

Her arrival at her new home might not have been what she had hoped, but there had been a cautious acceptance by nearly everyone—except Lady Moira. For now she would gracefully endure her mother-in-law and focus her efforts on becoming acquainted with the members of the household and village.

The sounds of activity from the hall below carried up the stairwell to her chamber. Grace could hear a door bang shut, benches and tables being moved on the stone floor, muffled voices giving and receiving orders.

After dressing in a simple gown, Grace walked through the hall, down a set of steps, and into a bustling kitchen. The cook, a gaunt, drawn woman with a sour face, gave her a suspicious glare.

"Was there something ye'd be needing, milady?"

Grace smiled in what she hoped was a cheery manner. "A pleasant good morning to ye. I was wondering if I could be of any help."

The cook ceased chopping, her frown deepening. "Are ye displeased with my meals?"

"Not at all." Grace smiled encouragingly, though the oddity of having such a thin cook running the kitchen bespoke of the true state of affairs. Ewan had hinted that he needed to find a wealthy wife, but she now realized the clan barely had enough food to feed themselves. "The evening meal was very tasty. I commend ye on producing such fine dishes on such short notice."

The cook gave her a tense smile, her expression apprehensive. Grace understood. The cook was loyal to Lady Moira and that lady's opinion of Grace was clear to all.

"Have ye broken yer fast yet?" Cook asked.

Grace shook her head. The cook handed her a crust of bread, a wedge of cheese, then poured her a cup of cider. Grace sat at the worktable, keeping a careful distance from the root vegetables that were being chopped with a lethal-looking knife. The cook seemed a bit annoyed at her presence, but dared not voice an objection.

"I've brought spices with me," Grace said casually, as she nibbled on her cheese. "Do ye have a proper place to keep them?"

The movement of the knife abruptly ceased. "Spices?"

Grace nodded. "Cinnamon, ginger, cloves, nutmeg, pepper."

"Pepper? Ye've brought black pepper?"

"Aye. And nearly a half barrel of salt."

Grace struggled to remain nonchalant, though the cook's astonishment and delight was contagious. Spices were expensive, precious, and sought-after commodities, especially black pepper and salt. Their addition to food elevated the taste considerably and enhanced the reputation of the individual preparing that food.

"We have a spice chest in the cellar, though little is kept inside," Cook said. "Lady Moira has the key."

That was no surprise. It was the duty of the lady of the keep to manage all aspects of the household.

"Though I know that it is well within my rights, I hesitate to demand the key from Lady Moira. I would not wish to insult my husband's mother."

Cook raised an eyebrow. "Aye, she willnae take kindly to being pushed aside."

"I shall think upon it and try to devise a way to handle the matter delicately," Grace said as she took another bite of cheese. "Did I mention that I also brought seeds? Beans, turnips, peas, parsnips, cabbage, carrots, and several others."

The cook's eyes glowed. "I could start a kitchen garden again. A few weeks back I had one of the lads repair the fence and till the soil, but had naught to plant."

"I'm sure I can spare a goodly amount of seeds to get ye started again. Some must be saved fer the fields, but I find many of these vegetables grow best in smaller plots." Grace popped the final piece of bread into her mouth, then brushed the crumbs from her fingers. "Do ye think we should ask Lady Moira's opinion before we begin?"

A bit of the excitement waned from Cook's expression, but then she drew herself up and faced Grace. "Ye are Sir Ewan's wife. If ye want a kitchen garden planted, then it must be done."

Grace nearly cried out with delight, as a rush of elation coursed through her veins. *My first victory!* "We shall speak of this later and see which lads we can find to help with the work. Young fellows do love putting their hands in the dirt and mud."

The cook smiled, then bobbed an awkward curtsy. Her mood considerably lightened, Grace headed outside. The clouds were hanging low and a chill was in the air, but no raindrops fell. It was the perfect weather to do some exploring.

There were few signs of life in the bailey at this hour of the morning. As she strolled through it, Grace saw the spot for the kitchen garden, the pens for the animals, and stables for the horses. She could hear the squawking of a few chickens, the baying of goats, and the occasional shout of a child.

As she walked, she found herself making lists in her head of things that needed to be done, improvements that should be made. A chair for Lady Moira was the first order of business, and a tapestry for the great hall should be designed and woven. The seeds must be unpacked, distributed, and planted, and the threadbare clothes for the servants replaced.

Hopefully there was some cloth available; if not it would have to be woven. Her eyes scanned the bailey for a weaving hut, disappointed not to find one. She had brought one loom with her, but others could be built. She hoped that at least a few of the women possessed the necessary skills, but if they were lacking, Grace could teach them.

All these tasks would require a great deal of time and effort, but Grace realized the challenge appealed to her. When she was mistress of Alastair's castle she had overseen the women's work, but everything ran so smoothly. The servants all knew their jobs and did them—they required little guidance from her.

But here it was different. Here she was truly needed. 'Twas an overwhelming responsibility, but one she welcomed. If not for the disagreeable presence of Lady Moira, Grace would have already begun her work.

Shaking off that gloomy thought, Grace continued

her exploring and her mental list-making. As she strolled near the kennels, a sound distracted her thoughts. Craning her neck, she looked over the chest-high stone wall. Her face broke into a smile when she caught a glimpse of the occupants. A brown and white bitch lay peacefully on her side while her litter of pups nursed.

Delighted, Grace watched them feed, amused by the sounds of contentment they made. Tummies full, jaws slack, several dozed off to sleep, but two of the bolder pups decided to play. They began climbing and wriggling over their brothers and sisters, trying to boost themselves onto their mother, but their legs were too short to carry them up her body.

Turning, the female gave them an exasperated look. She nudged them with her nose and the pair tumbled onto the others. After a few quick licks on the top of their heads, the mother stood. Frantic cries soon filled the air, as those who were still eating were now denied their meal. Rooting blindly, they fell over each other as they tried to find a nipple. The mother gave herself a long shake, from head to tail, then eyed Grace suspiciously.

"Ye've a fine brood," Grace said calmly.

The bitch moved closer, favoring her with a low, rumbling growl. Grace nodded respectfully, keeping her distance. She would have dearly loved the chance to cuddle one or two of the fat, frisky pups, but knew well the mother would not appreciate the gesture.

"Och, is that a growl I hear?" Deirdre asked as she approached the kennel, a wooden bucket in her hand.

"Aye." Grace turned with a friendly smile. "She's a protective mother, but I cannae fault her instincts to care fer her young."

"She's a fine hunter, and a favorite of Sir Ewan," Deirdre said. "The pups were born a few weeks ago and all seem healthy."

The maid cautiously opened the gate and carefully set the wooden bucket in front of the dog. The animal sniffed, then wagged her tail, yet she still stood guard, refusing to eat.

"Best if we leave her in peace," Grace suggested. "She'll not eat with us so close and she'll need her strength to take care of all those puppies."

"Lord above, can ye imagine having so many at once?"

"Nay. 'Twould drive any sane woman to drink, I'm sure of it." Grace fell in step beside the maid. As they walked away she could hear the dog heartily enjoying her meal. "What about ye, Deirdre. Do ye have any bairns?"

The maid shook her head. "I'm not married."

"Really? A pretty lass such as yerself."

Deirdre smiled and lowered her chin modestly. "Truth be told, fer years there has not been anyone to marry. Nearly all the men were killed when they refused to yield the keep to King Robert's soldiers. 'Twas a long siege, followed by a fierce battle that lasted fer days. Those that did survive swore allegiance to the king and were taken away to fight."

"Sounds dreadful."

"It was horrible." Ashen-faced with the memory, Deirdre sighed. "We barely survived the next few years, with little food and no one to protect our village."

"War is so senseless, so brutal." Grace covered Deirdre's hand with her own. "I'm sorry fer all yer suffering."

The maid sniffed, then tried to smile. "Mercifully,

that has all changed now that Sir Ewan has arrived. 'Tis good to have a knight as our leader, to protect and watch over us."

"Aye, and now there are more than enough handsome rogues in yer midst to consider fer a husband. Tell me, is there any man in particular who's caught yer fancy?" Grace said the words teasingly, but Deirdre's telltale blush let her know the remark had struck close to the truth.

"Sir Ewan has many fine-looking retainers," Deirdre said demurely. "Though I doubt they all wish to marry. Not all men do, and when that is the case, 'tis best they shy away from it."

Grace nearly stopped walking. 'Twas true that many men chaffed at the bonds of matrimony. Had Ewan been one of them? He had never made a secret of the fact that he needed her dowry. And after arriving at Tiree Keep she well understood that need. Yet she could not help but wonder if he would have chosen to remain without a wife under different circumstances.

"Fie, any man who isn't proud to have ye as his wife is a half-wit," Grace declared.

Deirdre smiled at the compliment. As they walked to the edge of the bailey, Grace could see the area that had been marked for a second wall to be built, recognizing this usual manner of defense. With a smaller garrison of soldiers to protect them, a second wall could prove the difference between victory and defeat.

This would be an expensive, time-consuming undertaking, but a necessary one. Most castles had two walls and in the strip of land between them a pattern of long, sharp wooden spikes was stuck into the ground.

Dangerous and lethal, they stood ever at the ready to shred an enemy if he managed to breach the first wall.

They turned the corner and Grace could hear the sounds of sawing and hammering, along with some cursing and good-natured arguing. It seemed as though every man was there, working on the construction of a pair of outbuildings. Including her husband. 'Twas an odd sight indeed to see a hammer, instead of a sword, in Ewan's hand and a stark reminder of how different his life was from most lairds.

As if sensing her presence, Ewan looked up and gave her a welcoming smile. Grace returned it. "I will not disturb yer work, husband, though I will ask if ye could spare a lad or two to help with the kitchen garden. Vegetables and herbs need to be planted, and the sooner that is done, the sooner they will grow."

"I'll send Arthur and Giles to ye once we have secured the roof," Ewan replied. "Just make certain someone keeps careful watch. The lads have a talent fer getting into mischief."

"I shall put Cook in charge of the work. Thank ye."

Very aware of the curious looks she was receiving from the working men, Grace dipped a respectful curtsy, then let out a yelp when Ewan grabbed her arm. He leaned his head down and kissed her soundly on the lips. "That, my dearest wife, is the proper way to say thank ye."

The men hooted and whistled and Grace blushed. "I shall strive to remember, sir," she replied with a saucy wink.

Grace returned to the great hall in a happy mood, her spirits buoyed. She passed through the front door and the women ceased talking for a few moments. They gave her a collective stare, pressed their heads together, and then the conversation once again started. Grace shuddered, thinking what Lady Moira might have told these women about her. No matter. 'Twas time to get to know the members of her household.

Deirdre made the introductions. Grace smiled and nodded a greeting, repeating each name so that she might remember them. There was uncertainty among the faces staring back at her, but that was not unexpected.

Grace also noticed several anxious glances toward the stairs leading to the kitchen and decided that was most likely where Lady Moira was this morning. Clearly, the women feared being caught talking to her.

In due course, Lady Moira emerged. She spared no greeting for Grace and immediately began assigning duties to the others. Grace decided to let the insult lie, choosing to listen rather than speak. She quietly melted into the background and observed, soon gaining a grudging respect for Lady Moira's household knowledge, though she did not agree that such a firm hand was needed with the servants.

When all was set to rights in the great hall, several of the women retreated to the storeroom. Lady Moira led the way, declaring the need for an inventory. The work had just begun when a sudden commotion drew everyone's attention. One of the women clumsily knocked over a wooden bin of oats, spilling the precious grain on the dirt floor.

Frantic, the girl dropped to her knees and started gathering the oats into a pile and scooping handfuls of them back into the bin.

"That's not fit to serve the dogs," Lady Moira bellowed. "There's bits of dirt, straw, and small rocks mixed in with the oats."

The maid's eyes welled with tears. "I . . . I . . . c-can fix it, m-milady," she said.

With tears flowing, the young servant started picking out the large pieces of straw and rocks, but it was impossible to separate them. Truth be told, the girl was making more of a mess.

Grace noticed several of the other women looked pained, but no one dared to move. Grace remembered the girl's name was Helen. She seemed a simple soul, a bit slow, mayhap even dim-witted, but earnest and eager. Her speech was thick and her eyes a tad dull, making her the ideal target for mockery.

Fearing Lady Moira's retribution, Grace knew she must intervene. Moving forward, she knelt beside Helen.

"'Twas simply a mistake," Grace said calmly. "We all make mistakes, do we not, Helen?"

"A . . . aye." The girl ceased her weeping and wiped her nose with the back of her sleeve. "I dinnae mean to make such a mess."

"I know." Grace raised her head. "We need to sift the oats to remove the large bits of debris."

"I'll get a sieve from the kitchen," Deirdre volunteered.

Grace saw the fire of anger building in Lady Moira's eyes, uncertain if it was directed at her or Helen. No matter. This poor, simpleminded creature was doing her best and Grace was determined to help her.

She showed Helen how to properly sift the oats, then stayed at her side while the girl performed the task. Her hands shook at first, but gradually her confidence built and Helen successfully finished the job.

With a grateful smile, the girl rose awkwardly to her feet. Grace felt a moment of triumph, but then

Helen stepped back and knocked over a pitcher of wine. It cracked on the hard dirt floor, spewing liquid in all directions.

Everyone gasped and leaped away. Grace quickly checked the front of her own gown, relieved to discover it was clean, then looked at the others. Most of the women were smiling and nodding their heads. Except for Lady Moira. She blinked in bewilderment, then stared down the front of her dress. It was splattered with wine and stained a deep red color.

One of the women cried out, then clasped her hand over her mouth. Grace tensed, knowing she would be unable to protect Helen now. Servants were struck for far less and it was obvious the gown was ruined.

"I should box yer ears fer this, girl," Lady Moira said in an angry voice.

Shamed, Helen bowed her head. "'Tis what I deserve, milady."

"Hmm." Lady Moira took a deep breath. Pressing her mouth into a taut line, she ineffectively brushed at the stain covering her chest. "There are some who say ye are of little account, Helen."

"Aye," Helen whispered, lowering her head even more.

"But I dinnae believe it," Lady Moira exclaimed.

"Ye have always been kind to me." She gave Lady Moira a sorrowful look. "I am truly sorry that I ruined yer gown."

Grace's brow rose in astonishment. Had her ears deceived her? Did Helen just say that Lady Moira was *kind*?

"Ye shall help the laundress clean my gown, Helen."

"I will use lye and then soapwort, milady, and scrub until the wine stain is gone," Helen promised, sounding eager.

"Take care not to tear the fabric," Lady Moira admonished.

"I will be ever so careful. And I will tell the laundress to add marjoram so the gown will smell sweet."

"Very good. Now come and help me change. Ye must wash the gown right away, before the stain has time to set."

Sparing not a glance for the others, Lady Moira sailed from the storeroom, Helen following dutifully in her wake. The rest of the women returned to their work. Grace also remained, but her mind was in a whirl, as she tried to comprehend what she had just witnessed. She was pleased that Helen had not been harshly punished, but astonished to discover that Lady Moira was capable of such compassion.

Surprised and hopeful and selfish enough to pray that one day that compassion would be cast in her direction.

By the end of the week Grace was feeling pleased over the progress and improvements that had been made. Seeds were planted, a weaving hut and looms constructed, and a brand-new chair sat at the head table on Ewan's other side. Lady Moira had naturally commented on the size and design, claiming it was not as grand as the other two chairs, but she sat upon it at every meal.

As for Ewan, well, her husband's stamina was nothing short of miraculous, for he worked alongside his men until it was too dark to see, ate a hearty supper, and then made love to her for a good part of the night.

She could see the pride he took in his holding, the care and concern he had for those under his protection. Yet underlying it all, Grace felt something was lacking. Ewan was working hard to build a legacy, yet had no legitimate name to pass along.

Grace had an idea of how to change that, but needed her brother's help to make the plan succeed. The problem lay in getting word to Brian without alerting Ewan. Happily, that opportunity came sooner than she expected, when Ewan told her he was sending a few of his men south to barter for additional supplies.

"Will the men travel on McKenna land?" she asked, stooping to push several seeds deeper into the soil. They were walking the southern fields this morning, surveying the progress.

"Most likely." Ewan tilted his head. "Why do ye ask? Are ye in need of something from yer brother?"

"Well, I'd like news of my family. The time has come and gone fer Aileen's babe to be born. I should like to know if it was a lad or a lass."

"I shall instruct the men to stop and speak with Brian."

"Wonderful! I will write a letter this evening fer them to deliver."

Ewan's eyes narrowed. "Why must ye write? Is something amiss ye wish to report to him?"

Grace was taken aback by the harshness of Ewan's tone. He seemed genuinely distressed at the idea of her writing to her brother. Why?

"It seems foolish to waste this opportunity. We sent

word to them of our marriage and I asked that Brian gift the convent with additional supplies, since I took nearly all of what I was bringing to them here, as my dowry. I would like to assure both my brother and Aileen that all is well and that I am happy. If ye wish, ye may read the letter before I seal it."

That suggestion brought an almost stoic expression to Ewan's handsome face. He said nothing, just looked straight ahead to the fields. Grace waited. Finally, he glanced her way and for a moment he looked embarrassed. Grace swallowed her cry of understanding, not wanting to further insult him.

Ewan was unable to read. Or write, most likely. Only sons of the nobles were tutored—bastards, especially those who were ignored by their fathers, as Ewan was—were not afforded that privilege.

Ewan cleared his throat. "'Tis unusual fer a woman to read and write."

Grace's heart lurched. It was so painful to see her proud husband humbled by the limitations of his birth. "I was raised to be a nun, with the hope of one day assuming the duties of the abbess. Thus I was taught to read, write, and do my sums."

He met her gaze squarely. "Those are useful skills fer a wife as well."

"Aye." She grasped his hand and squeezed. "If ye'd like, I can teach ye."

Ewan stiffened and Grace feared she had gone too far. But then he squeezed her hand in return and a sense of relief washed through her. "I would be honored. Och, be careful of the mud."

The warning came a moment too late as Grace's foot sank into the soft dirt. "Blessed Mother, these are my best slippers!"

Ewan lifted her and threw her over his shoulder. Grace let out a surprised grunt as her head landed against the center of his back. Ewan laughed and moved his hand to her hip, his touch familiar and possessive.

"Ewan, put me down," Grace commanded, though it was hard to sound forceful with her head hanging toward the ground. "My slippers are already ruined. A few more steps in this quagmire will make no difference."

"In a moment, dearest," he replied, giving her bottom a playful swat.

They went a fair distance before stopping. Laughing, Ewan set her on a moss-covered bit of ground at the bottom of a small hill. Then his hands cupped her bottom and lifted until her face was near enough for a kiss.

His mouth played over hers. Grace melted into his hardness, his strength, skimming the crease of his lips with her tongue, boldly pressing for entrance.

Ewan eagerly complied, pulling her closer, deepening their kiss. In the blink of an eye Grace found herself lying on the ground, her shoulders pressing against the moss while her husband loomed above her. She snuggled against him, savoring the feeling of his strength surrounding her, protecting her.

"I fear we are not alone," she whispered, tilting her head toward the thick bushes where she heard something rustling.

"No one will dare to disturb us."

Ewan bent his head for another kiss, but Grace pulled back and raised a brow. "What about yer mother? She seems to take joy in coming between us."

"Nay, I willnae allow my mother to make trouble in our marriage." He reached beneath her gown and smoothed his fingertips over the top of her thighs.

Driven by the need to say more, Grace banked the embers of passion smoldering inside her and pushed aside the sensual fog Ewan was creating. "By all the saints I swear yer mother looks at me as though wondering if her hands are large enough to squeeze around my throat."

Ewan's lips lifted off her shoulder. "Ye exaggerate."

"Do I? Yer mother meets me with a constant frown and a watchful stare." Grace hated how peevish she sounded, but she had to tell someone aside from Edna how she felt and Ewan appeared willing to listen.

True, some progress had been made when dealing with Lady Moira, but not nearly enough. Most importantly, Grace had realized that she had no need to be loved by the woman that was her husband's mother, but she did chafe under her palpable dislike.

"I dinnae know what else to do, Ewan. I work until I can scarcely stand up at the end of the day and all she can say to me is that wealthy ladies like to whine and complain and order everyone to do their bidding."

A lock of Ewan's hair fell over his eye. Grace swept it aside, cupped his jaw, and continued. "Yer mother does not approve of how I make soap. Nor does she like my recipe fer rabbit stew or my design fer the new looms that have just been built, or the way I've instructed the women to weave the cloth. Honestly, there are times I feel she disapproves of the way I breathe."

"I'll speak to her," Ewan promised.

"Nay."

He had made this offer before, but once again Grace was reluctant to take it, knowing this problem was hers to solve.

A soft groan sounded deep in his throat. "Why do ye tell me of these difficulties if ye dinnae want me to fix them?"

"It just felt good talking to ye about it. Does that make any sense?"

"Nay, but I've long given up trying to understand the workings of a woman's mind." He caught her hand and lifted it to his lips. "There is another way to guarantee my mother's approval. Give her a grandchild and she'll think the sun rises and sets upon ye."

Grace tilted her head and acted as though she were pondering the idea. "'Tis a most ingenious solution, good sir, yet I need someone to help with that particular chore." She parted her lips and ran her tongue teasingly around them. Ewan's nostrils flared and his grip on her hand tightened. "Might ye know of anyone interested in the task?"

Chapter Fifteen

"Old Donald says the bailey well is showing signs of drying out," Alec reported.

Frowning, Ewan shifted his feet on the scaffolding before lifting a large stone into place on the wall. "Tell Graeme to have a look."

"Graeme is off with the others at the quarry cutting more stones. They willnae return fer hours."

"Then the well must wait."

The sharp angles of Alec's face contorted with concern. "Without fresh water, we willnae be able to hold off a siege," he warned.

"Aye, and without a strong defensive wall, we willnae have the chance fer a siege. We'd be cut down in a matter of hours," Ewan snapped, wiping the sweat from his brow with the back of his hand.

The minute he had laid eyes upon Tiree, he knew he had a difficult task ahead of him, yet he had not understood the magnitude of rebuilding the keep until now. Allocating his limited resources was a constant challenge and a constant worry.

Though everyone strived to do their best, the back-breaking work was painfully slow. What Ewan really needed was a large skilled workforce to complete this job. Ditch diggers, stonecutters, masons, carpenters, and a man with the building skill and knowledge to direct them. But he had neither the time to find such men, nor the coin to pay them.

Still, when Ewan set out to accomplish something, he kept at it until he succeeded.

"Is there a particular reason ye are in such a hurry to finish the wall?" Alec asked, as he handed Ewan a heavy stone.

"Roderick Ferguson." Ewan spit out the name as though it was a foul-tasting morsel on his tongue. "It willnae be easy fer him to find us, but I have no doubt he shall try. He's hungry fer power and thinks he can use my wife to get it."

"We need to increase the guard," Alec proclaimed.

Ewan nodded. "That will help, but we must do more. There's no others near enough that we can call upon to aid us, should Roderick decide to attack. That's why I'm sending Harold and Tavish south on the morrow."

"I thought they were going fer more supplies?"

"'Tis a ruse. Oh, they will bring back more goods fer the household, but their true mission is to gather information. I want to know where Roderick is now and what he is doing."

"No doubt scheming and plotting his next course," Alec replied, voicing Ewan's greatest fear.

Grace. He had done it all for her. Damn, nearly everything he did these days was for her. Though she had asked him not to, Ewan had spoken with his mother about the way she treated his wife, commanding her to cease undermining Grace's authority and causing her grief.

Lady Moira had listened with her arms crossed tightly over her chest and a stoic expression etched upon her face. Ewan had prepared himself for a war of angry words, but his mother refused to battle.

She remained silent until he was finished and then walked away without saying a word. It was not a good sign. His mother had never taken well to being told what to do. Belatedly, Ewan realized he had in all likelihood made things worse and he regretted not doing as Grace had asked and stayed out of it.

"I could take a look at the well," Alec offered. "Mayhap the problem is easily seen."

Ewan brushed the stone powder from his hands and clapped Alec affectionately on the back. "Ye know as much about wells as ye do about building a curtain wall, my friend."

Alec laughed. "Aye, I've smashed my fingers too many times to count these past few weeks."

"As have I." Ewan held his bruised hand aloft, displaying two swollen, purple knuckles.

He was distracted from hearing Alec's reply by the sight of Grace approaching. She looked especially comely today. As was his custom, he had left their bed before dawn, while she still slept, thus this was his first glimpse of his wife today.

His gaze fastened on her, taking in every subtle nuance of her appearance, from the tightly woven braids pinned to her head to the sturdy leather boots on her feet.

She walked with purpose, her skirts billowing out behind her. As if suddenly aware that she was being observed, Grace lifted her chin and met his gaze, giving him a sweet smile that warmed his heart.

He waved and she moved faster. Grace halted at

the base of the ladder leading to the scaffolding and glanced up. "Have ye a moment to spare?"

"Fer ye? Always." He flashed a wicked smile, enjoying the sight of her modest blush. "Climb up so we can talk."

Ewan saw her hesitate. Then she took a deep breath, gathered her skirts in one hand and slowly began to climb. When she reached the top of the ladder, he held out his hand to her. She eyed it for a moment, then took it, and he suddenly remembered she was leery of heights.

He watched her silently as she looked out to the valley below and the forest beyond. The apprehension on her face soon turned to appreciation. Ewan felt a twinge of pride in both his home and his wife, for he knew that not every female would appreciate the rugged beauty of this unyielding land.

"We are running low on meat," Grace said, tearing her gaze away from the scenery. "Will ye or yer men be able to hunt today?"

Ewan looked at the low-hanging clouds rolling toward them. The woodland creatures would run to ground in the wet weather, making hunting a more difficult task. But if food was needed, then he must provide it.

"Instead of chopping down trees in the forest this afternoon, I shall tell the men to hunt fer small game."

"But do ye not need the wood to help build the wall?"

"Aye, but that can wait if we've got hungry bellies to feed."

"Cook will be relieved to hear it."

"She's been doing a fine job with so little supplies and so many mouths to feed."

Grace nodded. "Ye must tell her. Praise from ye will lighten the burden of her work."

Ewan knew the truth of those words and was ashamed for not having thought of it himself. Having other important matters on his mind was no excuse. He had learned long ago that even a small bit of praise yielded great results. And it cost nothing to give. "I shall make it my business to speak with Cook tonight, after the evening meal."

Grace smiled. "I need to get to the weaving hut to try and fix one of the spindles on the looms."

Ewan watched her carefully descend the ladder, his eyes trained upon her every move until she was once again on the ground. Turning back to the wall, he noticed the sly grin on Alec's face.

"What?"

"I never thought I'd live to see the day ye would moon over a lass like a lovesick calf."

"Ye're daft!"

"Nay, I can see it in yer eyes. Ye cannae bear to be apart from her, even fer a few hours."

Ewan sputtered a protest, then caught himself. It was true. He preferred Grace's company to anyone else's and missed her when he was parted from her, even for short bursts of time. Seeing a smile on her lovely face or a brightness in her eyes never failed to warm his own heart.

He often thought of her when he finished a task, hoping the result would please her. At the oddest moments of the day, he would find himself thinking how lucky he was, how blessed he was to have convinced her to be his wife. His fear of harm befalling her was a knot in his belly, a worry that plagued him.

Uppermost in his mind was a solid determination to keep her safe.

And their physical relationship, well that was extraordinary. And not merely because it had been such a long time since he had taken a woman to his bed. There was something open and honest and raw between them. 'Twas different from anything he had ever experienced. He wondered each day if it would lessen, if the intensity would fade. But instead of those emotions withering, they had grown stronger.

Was that love?

The thought intrigued him. But even more intriguing was the possibility that someday Grace would have these same feelings about him.

As was the usual occurrence, the hall fell silent once the morning meal had been cleared and the stone floor swept clean. Taking advantage of a rare day of sunshine, Grace set herself in front of the meager fire, her sewing basket at her feet. The previous day she had sketched out a design for a tapestry she wanted to create for the main hall and today she wanted to fill in the details.

The Battle of Bannockburn seemed a fitting subject, for it was King Robert's greatest victory and the final battle that had secured his crown. Naturally, the king would be depicted in all his royal glory, but at his side Grace would place Ewan. This might be a slight exaggeration of events, for even she doubted that her husband had fought directly at the king's side.

Yet there was no denying that Ewan had participated in this most important battle. Ewan's illegitimate birth might have robbed him of his heritage and left him without a true place in the world, but Grace was determined to create and preserve a legacy for her husband.

The tapestry was but one part of her plan. For the other part—the more important part—Grace had to rely upon the king. And her brother. She had already taken steps to enlist Brian's aid. The letter she had sent with Ewan's men to her brother outlined her plan and the part she needed him to play in this delicate matter.

Ewan deserved to be a chief, to lead a clan. But that clan would need a name—a strong, proud name. Thus Grace had requested that her brother intercede and ask the king to approve the formation of a new clan. Once permission was granted, Ewan would have the chance to name his clan and all would take that name as their own.

Slowly, Grace unwound the parchment with the tapestry design. She stared at it thoughtfully for a full minute, then added more trees to the forest of Tor Wood, where King Robert had gathered his army, and more horses and Scottish foot soldiers. 'Twas yet another inaccuracy, an exaggeration of the truth as the English forces had outnumbered the Scots by nearly three to one. Yet it was the Scots who had carried the day.

Pleased with this altered design, Grace rolled the parchment, secured it with a ribbon, and put it in her basket. The weaving and embroidering of the tapestry would have to wait. There were tears in many of Ewan's garments, as well as her own. Grace reached into her basket of threads, searching for the best color match to begin her mending, when a kitten leapt in front of her.

For a moment they stared at each other, each startled and unsure. The animal was jet black, with a tiny single spot of white upon its skinny chest. The bright sunlight glittered off its fur, the clear green eyes glowed. It meowed in greeting, then swished its tail.

Charmed by the kitten's friendly manner, Grace smiled. "Now where did ye come from, little one?"

The shy kitten dipped its head, then suddenly straightened and took a wild leap onto the pile of clothes Grace was waiting to mend. Scrambling excitedly, the animal burrowed under the clothes, spinning frantically on its back. Paws in the air, tail twitching with glee, the kitten played with a loose bit of thread hanging from one of the garments, pulling it between its teeth.

"Oh, fer heaven sakes," Grace muttered with a laugh, pulling the shirt away.

Surprised, the kitten released the thread. Excitedly it twisted, turned, and then righted itself. Crouching low, it stalked the shirt, but just as it was ready to pounce, the sound of approaching female voices could be heard. Frightened, the kitten sprang forward and skidded, becoming entangled in the hem of Grace's gown.

"Good morning, milady." The women called out a pleasant greeting that Grace returned with a smile.

Curious, the kitten poked its face out, then boldly took a few steps. Grace waited for the maids to spy her little friend, but when they did, their reaction was not at all what she expected.

"A black cat!" Margaret cried in alarm, her hands fluttering in agitation.

The maid backed away hastily, nearly falling over in the process. Two others paled noticeably while the remainder made the sign of the cross. All looked horrified.

"'Tis only a harmless kitten," Grace insisted, giving the women an imploring look. "I doubt that he—or she—will bite."

She reached down, untangled the animal's claws from her gown, and lifted it onto her lap. The kitten squirmed for a moment, sniffed Grace's hand, then rubbed its head against her fingertips.

"Everyone knows a black cat is the spawn of the devil," Mauve said fearfully. "It should have been drowned at birth to keep away the evil spirits."

"Nonsense!" Grace placed a protective hand over the nestling kitten. Almost as if knowing it was the topic of conversation, the kitten stood on its legs and arched its back. "This is one of God's innocent creatures, free of sin and evil. We need not fear it."

Unconvinced, the women shifted uncomfortably from one foot to the other. Grace's emotions flared at this unjust reaction, but soon relented at the sight of their true fear. Casually, she lowered the kitten to the floor. Almost as if sensing the hostile environment, it scurried away.

The tension immediately vanished and smiles once again returned to the women's faces.

"We are off to pick brambles," Deirdre said. "Mauve knows a secret spot where they grow in abundance."

"If we get enough, Cook says she'll make cobbler tonight," Mauve exclaimed.

"Will ye come with us, milady?" Margaret asked shyly.

Pleased to be asked, and to have the attention shifted away from the hapless black kitten, Grace abandoned her needlework and joined the women. They took a path behind the keep and climbed a steep hill, pulling their skirts away from the branches and thistles. A flock of birds flew into the wind, wheeling and turning gracefully. Grace lifted her hand to shade her eyes against the bright sunshine to watch them, marveling at their beauty, and wondering if she should add a few to her tapestry design.

When they reached the summit, Grace was surprised to see Lady Moira among the women. It took but a few moments for her mother-in-law to spy Grace. When she did, her brow wrinkled in a frown. Grace braced herself, waiting for a cutting remark, but Lady Moira turned away without speaking.

Goodness, I am becoming so insignificant that I no longer warrant her censure. Uncertain if that was a good or bad thing, Grace elected to ignore the matter entirely and instead concentrate on enjoying herself. The bushes were scratchy and thorny and it took a bit of effort to first find the ripe berries and then pick them without snagging one's clothing.

"Ah, now here's a prime specimen." Grace held up a plump berry of the darkest hue.

Several of the maids *oohed* in appreciation. Grace moved to place the prize in her basket when she was suddenly seized by a whiff of mischief. With a crafty smile, she whisked the berry up to her face and popped the morsel into her mouth.

"Milady!" Deirdre sounded shocked.

Grace broke into laughter. "Aye, there's fun in the picking but greater enjoyment in the eating."

"Lady Moira willnae approve," Margaret whispered in a worried tone.

"Then we must make certain she doesnae see us," Grace replied.

Eyes wide, the maids exchanged glances. Then following her lead, each woman grabbed a berry and promptly ate it. Several of the maids giggled behind their hands as they chewed while darting speculative glances at Lady Moira.

"We must not eat too many," Grace admonished.

"Aye, we must save the bulk of our harvest to share with the others," Deirdre said piously.

"Nay, there is more than enough here fer all to enjoy." Grace glanced over her shoulder. "My concern is that if we eat too many our juice-stained lips and teeth will give us away to Lady Moira."

The announcement brought a fresh gale of giggles, along with a suspicious glare from Lady Moira. Grace returned her mother-in-law's stern look with an innocent shrug, then cautioned the others to be quiet. The group noticeably increased their efforts as they picked, each occasionally giving in to the temptation of eating a berry. Grace decided the berries tasted even better because they were forbidden fruit.

As Grace lifted another plump morsel to her mouth, she heard something rustling in the hedge. Curious, she leaned down, but saw nothing that could be causing the disturbance. Shaking her head, she returned her attention to the berry picking. The noise returned, much louder, and then suddenly a large boar emerged from the thick underbrush.

It stood and stared at them, its sharp yellowed tusks gleaming, its long snout raised as it sniffed the air. For an instant no one moved. Then one of the maids began to whimper. The beast instantly gravitated toward the sound and began pawing at the ground as if getting ready to charge.

"Silence!" Lady Moira demanded. "Yer crying is drawing his attention."

"He must have been foraging fer berries on the other side of the bushes," Grace whispered.

"It matters not where he came from," Lady Moira snapped. "What we need to be concerned about is getting rid of it. Does anyone have a weapon?"

"I have a dirk," Grace admitted.

"Ye cannae kill a beast of that size with a knife," Lady Moira muttered in annoyance.

"I was not intending to slay it," Grace retorted. "I was merely answering yer question."

"We need to reach higher ground," Lady Moira said calmly. "The animal cannae attack us if we are in a tree."

"A tree!" Grace screeched. "'Tis a far sprint to reach any trees."

"I cannae climb a tree," Deirdre wailed. A few others sniffled in agreement.

"Can we outrun it?" Grace asked. "I know these creatures have poor eyesight. If we scatter in different directions, we could confuse it long enough to escape."

"Ye'll not get very far if he cuts yer legs with those sharp tusks," Lady Moira answered. "And once it attacks, it will not cease until it kills its prey."

The boar snorted loudly and shook its head. Lady Moira barely seemed to breathe as she stared the gruesome animal in the eye. Grace swallowed in fear. How could the woman remain so calm in the face of such danger?

"We need to make a decision quickly or else he's going to make it fer us," Grace stated anxiously.

"All right." Lady Moira slowly set her basket of fruit on the ground. "At my signal, I want each of ye to run fer the trees."

"Lord save us," Deirdre cried.

Grace swallowed the lump of fear in her throat. "Lady Moira is right. The nasty thing cannae follow all of us."

"Run! Now!" Lady Moira shouted.

At the sound, the boar turned. Grace began to run, but a scream, followed by a crashing noise, drew her attention. She turned and saw Lady Moira sprawled on the ground, the boar charging toward her.

Terrified, Grace knew she had to act. Pulling back her arm, she threw her basket of berries. Time seemed to cease as it flew through the air, berries flying in all directions. Miraculously, it somehow landed on the animal's head.

"Hey, ye witless beast," Grace yelled. "Where do ye think ye're going?"

Stunned, the boar halted and spun around in confusion. Shocked her ploy had worked, Grace stumbled backward. The beast seized the moment and charged her, bellowing and squealing. Grace screamed too as she regained her footing and took off at a run. Her heart pounded against her chest and her mouth grew dry with fear.

Hoping to confuse the animal further, Grace veered from side to side as she moved. She could hear the other women shrieking and shouting, but she dared not spare the time or energy to look behind her, for she also heard the angry snorts of the relentless boar coming hard on her heels.

She spied a sturdy tree ahead and went directly

toward it, leaping onto the lowest branch. Her arms burned as she struggled to pull herself onto the limb, praying it was strong enough to support her weight, knowing that if she fell to the ground now, the boar would shred her flesh.

Shaking in terror, she considered climbing higher, but the animal roared in anger and rammed the tree trunk. The rough bark dug into her palms and her grip faltered as the entire tree shook. Screeching, Grace straddled the limb and wrapped her arms tightly around the trunk. The breath she had been holding came out in a gushing sob and the boar circled the tree, preparing to strike again.

Her mind flashed with the memory of Alastair's wounds, his leg badly cut and mangled. Those mortal wounds had been inflicted by a boar. If a warrior like Alastair, a man who hunted with skill and accuracy, could be cut down by such a beast, what chance did she have of surviving?

The thunder of hoofbeats and shouting penetrated her terrified mind. Nerves tingling, she gazed out and saw a group of riders making a dangerous headlong gallop up the hill. From her perch in the tree she had no difficulty recognizing the horse or the rider in the lead.

Ewan!

"Have care," she yelled. "There's an angry boar at the base of this tree."

Ewan slowed his mount, then reached behind his shoulder. Grace expected him to pull his sword, but instead he produced a heavy crossbow. Using his strong thighs to guide the still-moving horse, Ewan held the crossbow in both hands, aimed, and let loose an arrow.

It struck the boar with unerring accuracy. The boar squealed in anger and rammed the tree harder. Ewan quickly fired off two more shots, each finding its mark. The beast let out a final squeal, then fell. Clutching the trunk tighter, Grace willed her trembling to stop as she stared down at the unmoving animal.

"Are there any others?" Ewan shouted as he reined in his horse beside the tree.

"The maids . . . yer mother . . ." Grace babbled.

"Nay, lass, are there any other boars?" he said gently.

"Oh. We dinnae see any others. Do they hunt in packs?"

"Not usually, but I'll have the men check the area." Ewan extended his arm.

Grace swallowed and tried to slow her harried breathing. Her hand shook as she reached out and grabbed onto him, basking in the feel of his solid strength. He settled her in front of him, then laid his hand on her shoulder and eased her back against his chest. His arms closed tightly around her, surrounding her in quiet warmth. Catching her breath with a shudder, she burrowed into him, basking in the security of his comforting embrace.

Safe, I am safe.

Ewan slowly maneuvered his mount around the dead boar and rode up the hill. The horse picked his way carefully through the thick bushes and rocky ground. Grace could see the rest of Ewan's men combing the hillside on horseback, assisting the other women.

"Have ye found everyone?" Ewan asked, as they pulled alongside Alec.

The warrior nodded. Deirdre was perched in front of him, looking perfectly at ease nestled in the shelter of his arms. "None are harmed, though there are brambles scattered all over the hillside," Alec said.

Deirdre swung around, hitting Alec in the chin with the top of her head. "We had little care fer the berries when we were fleeing fer our lives."

"Aye, 'tis a miracle ye are all in one piece." Alec rubbed his jaw, then leaned forward and buried his face in her hair. Deirdre giggled.

"My mother?" Ewan asked.

"She is safe, though all the others can speak of is how bravely Grace acted to save her," Alec answered.

"'Tis true," Deirdre confirmed. "Lady Grace was magnificent."

The two men looked at her in utter disbelief. Grace shrugged and rubbed her fingers over her eyes.

"Where is my mother now?" Ewan asked.

"She insisted on riding her own mount and forced young Duncan to relinquish his horse," Alec answered.

Deirdre clucked her tongue in sympathy. "Poor lad. 'Tis unmanly to have to give up yer horse, and to a woman, no less."

"That's not even the worst of it." Alec chuckled. "Lady Moira insisted that the men collect all the berries that were spilled. Most are on their hands and knees right now."

"A rich berry sauce tastes heavenly when eaten with roasted boar," Deirdre said with a smile.

Grace nearly choked. "I dinnae think I could eat

one bite of the beast. Not after staring into those ferocious yellow eyes."

"Ye'll feel differently once ye catch a tempting whiff of the roasted meat," Ewan commented, rubbing her shoulder.

Lacking the strength to argue, Grace set her head against Ewan's broad shoulder and closed her eyes. And they remained closed until they reached the keep.

Chapter Sixteen

When they reached the bailey, Ewan set Grace down first, then dismounted. Dozens of curious faces gathered around, anxious to hear the tale of what had happened. Grace managed a small smile, trying to assure them that all was well.

"Ye're hurt," Ewan exclaimed.

"Am I?" Dazed, Grace glanced down at her arm, barely registering the sight of blood. "Odd, I dinnae feel any pain."

Grace gasped as Ewan swung her into his arms. With long purposeful strides, he carried her into the keep and up the winding stone staircase.

"Ewan, I—"

"Hush, love. Save yer strength."

"But I'm not—" Ewan cradled her against his chest, muffling the rest of her words. Grace decided it was a waste of breath to argue. Besides, it felt delightful to be held in her husband's arms.

He reached the landing and hurried down the short corridor. Their bedchamber door was slightly ajar and he kicked it wide, the sound reverberating through the hallway.

"Ewan, ye are making too much of a fuss," Grace insisted as he placed her gently on the bed.

"The wound has opened," he replied. "It needs tending." Ewan went to the door and shouted for help. It took a few minutes for someone to answer his call. Grace could not see who had come, but could hear him muttering orders to them.

She shifted her position to get a better look and felt a bit of throbbing in her arm. Her gaze dropped to the blood seeping through her sleeve.

"Did ye bring the whiskey?" Ewan asked.

"Aye, along with my herbs. Will the wound need stitching?"

Grace's head jerked forward. Stitching? Truly? She looked again at her blood-soaked arm. "Dinnae be ridiculous; my wound does not need to be sewn. A simple poultice will aid the healing."

Ewan touched the back of his hand to her brow. "I fear the wound may become infected. Ye have no fever, but clearly yer wits must have been addled."

Grace bristled with indignity. "That's a most unkind thing to say."

"Is it? Ye risked yer life to save my mother's."

"I did?"

"Aye. Do ye not remember? The boar was set to charge her, but ye drew it away. 'Twas all the other women could talk about." He poured a dram of whiskey into a tankard and pressed it into Grace's hands. "Drink."

Grace took a small sip, then a larger swallow, wincing as the liquid hit her belly with a burning fire. She truly did not know why Ewan was making such a fuss, but the more whiskey she drank, the less she cared.

The healer carefully pushed back Grace's sleeve and examined the wound. Deirdre arrived with a basin of water and Margaret followed with a wooden bowl. She held it steadily while the healer mixed a secret concoction, the smell so cloying it tickled Grace's nose, causing her to sneeze. Once. Twice. Three times.

"Did she catch a chill?" Ewan asked worriedly, pushing his way through the women to grasp her other hand.

Mother Mary, what was wrong with him? "I dinnae take a swim in the loch, Ewan," Grace admonished, rolling her eyes. "I ran from a boar and climbed a tree. How does that cause a chill?"

Ewan shrugged helplessly. Grace saw the other women exchange a quick, private smile. "Me thinks 'twould be best if ye wait outside, Sir Ewan," the healer said.

Giving him no time to protest, the old woman shooed him from the chamber. As much as she appreciated his concern, Grace soon agreed it was far calmer without him present. The healer's hands were gentle and efficient as she tended the wound and Grace gradually felt herself starting to relax.

This tranquil mood was interrupted by a commotion in the doorway. A path was cleared around the bed as a woman entered the chamber. Lady Moira! Grace's wound once again began to throb.

Her squinting eyes swung toward Grace. "I suppose ye expect me to be grateful fer what ye did today?"

Hitching herself up on her elbows, Grace faced

her nemesis. "When I heard ye scream, I reacted without thought." She shut her eyes and bit her tongue, but it was too late to recall the words.

Lady Moira nodded sharply. "I assumed as much. 'Tis the main reason I'll not feel beholding to ye."

Grace cracked open one eye. The whiskey Ewan had given her was making her head woolly and her tongue loose. "Why do ye dislike me so much? I'm from a respectable family. I've brought a handsome dowry, the promise of fealty from my clan, supplies that are needed and appreciated. I care fer yer son and do all that I can to make him happy."

"Ye're soft."

"Nay!" Grace protested, pulling herself away from the pillows and sitting upright. "I work as hard as everyone else, taking pride in all that is accomplished."

Lady Moira sniffed. "He pampers ye."

"He tries and I find it gallant and endearing." A flicker of guilt burned in her cheeks. Ewan did try to spoil her and aye, she appreciated all his considerate gestures. "I do my share. Ye dinnae have to like me or call me *daughter* or even be my friend, though I would be pleased if ye did any of those things. But ye need to respect me. As I respect ye."

Lady Moira cocked a brow at her. "I still say ye dinnae deserve such a fine man as my Ewan."

Grace shrugged. "Deserve or not, I've got him and I shall do whatever is necessary and fight to keep him. Ye'd best remember that, milady."

Feeling exhausted, Grace fell back upon the bed and closed her eyes. And in doing so, she missed the grudging smile of respect on Lady Moira's face.

* * *

Ewan's mount nickered and tossed his mane as they crested the hill. Ewan could well understand his horse's pleasure. The animal was muddied, weary, and overheated, but had caught a familiar scent—home. No doubt the horse was anticipating an invigorating rubdown, a hearty meal, a well-deserved rest.

As was Ewan.

He and Alec had left before sunrise and would be returning in near darkness. The outer wall of the keep had finally been completed and Ewan was anxious to begin construction of the second wall while the days were longer and filled with warmth. Though not as wide as the first wall, this new defense would require more stone than the quarry they were using could produce.

Thus he and Alec had set out in search of a new quarry to mine. They had found one, but it lay a full day's ride from Tiree, a journey that would take even longer given the rough terrain and lack of roads for the wagons to travel.

Yet somehow these additional challenges did not dishearten Ewan. Nay, he was buoyed by the fact they had located the stone and convinced the obstacles they faced to retrieve it would be met.

His mother had once told him that those in love always saw the world in a rosy light. The bitterness in her voice had belied the sentiment of those words and he had not truly understood their meaning. Until now.

It had come on as a gradual realization, yet Ewan finally admitted to himself that his heart had indeed chosen to love Grace. And that emotion colored all that surrounded him. No problem appeared insurmountable, no crisis unsolvable, no task impossible.

With Grace at his side there was nothing that could not be accomplished. The love he felt for her calmed him, centered him, made him a better man. He embraced it. Yet he kept it to himself. At least for now.

It was not something he wished to dwell upon, yet his mind had difficulty turning away from it. He was waiting for the right time, the best circumstance to reveal his feelings to his wife. A part of him wanted to tell her the moment he saw her again, but he held back. Grace deserved more. She deserved something memorable, romantic.

Women, gentle creatures that they were, prized such gestures and men had been making fools of themselves for centuries attempting to appease them. Ewan never believed he would be one of those men, but amazingly he took pride in that knowledge. It made him happy to acknowledge it. Made him happy too, imagining that when he told her, he would hear the same words back from her sweet lips.

I love ye, Ewan.

Feeling a rising swell of excitement, Ewan growled low in his throat. Alec, riding beside him, tossed him a startled glance, then raised a questioning brow. Ewan ignored it and leaned forward in the saddle, urging his mount to a faster pace.

Home. They were nearly home.

Ewan reined in his horse and cocked his head, slowing to a walk as they entered the forest. Wind rustled through the leaves and branches of the trees. The rush of water flowed over the rocks in a stream. He startled when a flock of birds suddenly flew from the tree above him, and then he finally heard what had caused him to stop in the first place—the sounds and smells of an encampment.

Ewan kneed his mount to a trot and Alec followed

behind. A cold numbness trickled down his spine as they cautiously approached a small clearing. Keeping themselves safely hidden in the thick forest, the pair silently observed the activity in the glen.

"I only see a tinker's cart and one man," Alec whispered. "And all he's doing is sitting upon that fallen log, staring off in the distance."

"Aye, but it could still be some sort of trap," Ewan cautioned. "Ye stay here while I go and speak with him."

Ewan urged his horse forward. At the sound, the man raised his head. Ewan could see his body stiffen, but he did not reach for a weapon.

Ewan understood the fear. The tinker was trespassing. Courtesy demanded that he ask permission, and offer the laird a small payment, before making camp in the woods, just as he would require approval to barter and sell his wares.

"Good day to you, sir," the man said, his voice thin and reedy. He was tall and gaunt and most likely hungry, judging by his pale coloring.

"Ye are squatting on my land," Ewan challenged.

The man's eyes widened. "A thousand pardons, Sir Knight. I meant no offense."

Ewan's gaze shifted around the small campsite. "Ye would be welcomed in our village to sell yer wares."

The tinker's head bowed. "Alas, nearly all my goods have been sold. We travel south in search of more."

The words were humble, but something felt wrong. Ewan's hand slowly reached for his sword handle. "Ye're trembling, man. Why?"

"Nerves," he whispered.

"An innocent man fears nothing."

"My family sleeps yonder." The tinker waved toward

the enclosed cart. "My wife gave birth last night to a fine son. They are both sleeping. I want no trouble, milord. Please, allow me to pay ye fer the privilege of staying on yer land."

The tinker fumbled in his tunic, eventually extracting what he sought. Arm shaking, he held out his open hand. Interest peaked, Ewan leaned down to get a closer look. Resting in the palm of the tinker's hand was a gold ring.

Ewan's chest constricted. The ring was beautiful, boasting a design unlike any he had ever seen. Delicate and refined, it resembled golden threads intricately woven together. The workmanship was flawless; clearly this had been created by a master jeweler.

It was exactly what he had been hoping to find for Grace. No woman alive could doubt the depth of a man's feelings when she beheld such fine craftsmanship. Seeing it upon her finger every day would be a constant reminder to Grace of how much he loved and cherished her.

Mesmerized, Ewan plucked the ring from the tinker's hand and held it up to the sunlight. It was heavier than it appeared, further substantiating its value. "'Tis magnificent," he muttered.

The stiffness in the tinker's shoulders visibly relaxed. "I am glad that it pleases ye. I hope that—"

The tinker suddenly began to sway. Then his eyes rolled back in his head and he fell to the ground in a heap. Moving swiftly, Ewan vaulted from his horse, pulled his sword, and knelt beside the fallen man, bracing for an attack.

Alec appeared, charging from under the cover of the trees. Sword drawn, he let out a shrill battle cry, but there were none to answer. "What happened?" he asked.

Ewan lowered his sword. "I dinnae know. One moment the tinker was speaking to me and the next he collapsed."

"The way he fell, I thought an arrow had struck him," Alec confessed.

"As did I." Ewan drew closer to the prostrated man. His breathing was shallow and labored, his face beaded with sweat. There were red, angry-looking fever pustules on his neck and in his scalp. "He's not been shot," Ewan exclaimed. "He's weak with sickness."

The tinker's eyes slowly opened. "Forgive me. I should have warned ye to stay away." His eyes began to close. He gasped, twitched, and took one final shuddering breath.

"God Almighty, he's dead!" Alec shouted.

"Aye, stay back," Ewan warned. "Ride to the tree line and wait there until I call fer ye."

Ewan sprang to his feet and ran to the tinker's enclosed cart. Heart beating with escalating fear, he ripped aside the cloth that hung over the doorway and stepped inside. A rising tide of stench assaulted him, the odor so strong and offensive he started gagging. *Bloody hell!*

Holding his forearm over his face, Ewan peered into the dimly lit space. The newborn babe the tinker had spoken of was nowhere to be seen. Instead there were four bodies pressed together on a single pallet, one female and three children, their limbs and faces grotesquely bloated from sickness and death.

Ewan backed away from the cart, nearly tripping in his haste to retreat. An illness such as this could kill an entire village quicker and more effectively than an invading army. He must contain the disease before it spread any further.

"Build a fire," Ewan ordered Alec grimly. "We must burn everything."

Grace carefully climbed the stone steps to her bedchamber. She had seen Ewan enter the keep and head for the stairs earlier. She assumed he was preparing to have a tankard of ale and then wash away the dirt and grime of the day, as was his usual custom, before coming down to partake of the evening meal.

A week had passed since Ewan and Alec returned from their successful quest to locate another stone quarry and in that time she had noticed a subtle change in her husband. Ewan seemed distracted. Worried. She knew his thoughts were occupied by many important matters, but she sensed there was something else bothering him. Something he refused to talk about.

She had asked him several times if anything was troubling him, but he had deflected her questions with a forced cheeriness and assurances that all was perfectly fine. Which raised her suspicions higher.

Well, no longer. Today she was determined to discover the reason for his uncharacteristic behavior.

The bedchamber door was slightly ajar when she arrived. Ewan stood alone in the room, looking out a window. Grace stepped into the chamber and closed the door behind her.

"I would like to talk with ye, Ewan," Grace said formally. 'Twas not the tone she would have preferred to use, but she decided it would be the most effective.

However, Ewan remained silent and continued staring out the window.

"'Tis important," she added in a somewhat pleading tone.

At last he turned, yet still he said nothing. Growing impatient, Grace stepped forward. The moment she touched his shoulder, Ewan staggered, then suddenly slumped to the floor. Astonished, Grace glanced at the pitcher of ale, but it was nearly full. He wasn't drunk—was he?

Curious, she dropped to her knees beside him. "Ewan?" She shook his shoulder, belatedly realizing it felt unusually warm, even through the layers of his clothing.

Alarmed, Grace placed her hand on his forehead. He was burning! She wrenched her hand away, the fear inside her mounting. Ewan's teeth started chattering and his body began to tremble as though shivers were racing through it, yet he could hardly be cold.

Nay, he was sick—terribly sick.

She jumped to her feet and raced from the chamber, searching for help. She ran down the stairs so quickly she nearly lost her footing, reaching the hall out of breath and no doubt looking frantic.

Grace paused. Several of the retainers were gathered near the fire, polishing their swords. Two maids were sweeping the floors, another was laying fresh rushes. Lady Moira was speaking with Cook, most likely reviewing the evening's menu.

As much as she wanted to scream with worry and fear, Grace knew it was important not to create a panic. Even the hint of a grave illness would cause concern.

"Lady Moira, Alec, may I speak with ye a moment, please?"

Alec obediently set his sword aside and came to her. Lady Moira frowned in annoyance at the interruption, but she must have seen or sensed Grace's agitation, for she too obeyed the command.

Wordlessly, Grace turned and hurried back up the staircase. A clearly curious Alec and put-out Lady Moira followed. Grace paused when they reached the door of her bedchamber, knowing she needed to prepare them.

"Ewan has taken ill. I need help getting him into bed." Grace swung the door open.

"Dear Lord!" Lady Moira made a quick sign of the cross when she saw Ewan prone upon the floor, then rushed to her son's side.

It took all three of them to move Ewan's body to the bed. Once there, Grace and Lady Moira quickly stripped him of his clothes.

"Do ye have any idea what ails him?" Grace asked, smoothing her hand over his damp, hot flesh.

Lady Moira shook her head. "Ewan never gets sick. He has always had a strong constitution, even as a young lad."

"I fear I might know what is wrong." Alec's handsome face was taut and drawn. "As we returned from our journey to the new quarry last week, we chanced upon a tinker and his family in the forest. We discovered too late that the man was ill. His family had all succumbed to the sickness and he soon followed. Ewan had close contact with him, while commanding that I keep my distance. I suppose that is the reason why I, too, have not been struck down."

"Why did Ewan not tell me?" Grace cried.

Alec shrugged his shoulders helplessly. "I'm sure he dinnae want to worry ye."

"I've seen this type of illness before, when I was a child," Lady Moira interjected, her voice quavering. "It strikes swiftly and mercilessly. Most who contract it die within a few days."

Despite her resolve, tears rose to Grace's eyes. *Ewan will not die! He will not!* "Burn his clothes, Alec, but dinnae let anyone see ye doing it."

Alec's brow deepened with worry, but then he nodded and followed her orders.

"We must have water, the coldest ye can find," Lady Moira said.

Asking no questions, Grace followed her mother-in-law's dictates, fetching the water from the well herself. They bathed Ewan together, each woman lost in her own concern.

"We need a healer," Grace said when they were finished. "Shall I summon the woman who tended my arm?"

"Nay, she cares for those with broken limbs and wounds that need stitching. She will be of little help with fevers," Lady Moira replied. "Besides, she is a frightful gossip. We need someone we can trust, someone who willnae tell the others of Ewan's condition."

"Who?"

A thoughtful frown knitted Lady Moira's brow. "Deirdre's grandmother, Agnes, has some skill and can hold her tongue. She nursed many villagers through the winter fevers. I will send fer her."

When the healer arrived, Grace hovered over Agnes, intently watching everything she did. "'Tis a powerful sickness that has struck down Sir Ewan," Agnes said as she studied her patient.

"Will he survive?" Lady Moira asked.

The healer shook her head. "'Tis too soon to know."

"What do we do? How do we help him?" Grace asked, her heart sinking.

"Watch him carefully. Keep his body cool, bathing not only his forehead, but his arms, chest, and legs. 'Tis the best way I know of to fight the fever." Agnes hesitated, clearing her throat. "If boils form, send fer me immediately, and I will lance them."

"I'll not leave him. I shall tend him day and night," Grace said, brushing her hand lovingly across his brow.

"I will help," Lady Moira announced. "One needs faith and strength to battle this illness and I thank God that Ewan possesses both."

The deep resolve in the older woman's voice gave Grace a beacon of hope. They did not agree on much, but there was no questioning the depth of love Lady Moira held for her son. She would fight as hard as Grace to save Ewan's life.

Over the next three days and nights Ewan's condition deteriorated rapidly. He drifted in and out of consciousness, writhing with convulsions as his fever burned stronger. One night, helpless to keep him still and quiet, Grace crawled on top of him, trying to stop the deep tremors.

Ewan refused to allow it. He gripped her shoulders with a force that astonished her and tried to throw her off. Grace cried out, but refused to relent as Ewan ranted incoherently. Gradually, his hold eased and then his arms fell to his side. Though labored, his breaths came in a constant rhythm.

Exhausted herself, Grace collapsed atop him. Her lips moved in silent prayer as the tears flowed. The life seemed to be draining out of him and there was little she could do to stop it. Finding comfort by imitating the cadence of his breathing, Grace soon drifted off to sleep.

She awoke with a start when she heard a strangled sob behind her and turned. Lady Moira stood in the doorway, her face pale with emotion. "He's getting worse."

"Nay." Grace shook her head vehemently. "His will is strong. He fights hard to live and thus he shall."

Lady Moira wiped the tears from her eyes. "Ye have been with him all day and most of the night. Go lie down fer a few hours. I'll stay and watch over him."

Reluctantly, Grace obeyed, though her rest was short and fitful. Another day passed. Ewan's condition remained the same. He pushed away the broth and water they tried to get down his throat; he thrashed and struck out when they bathed his fevered body.

Every now and again delirium would take control of his mind. His fever-brightened eyes would open, then quickly cloud with confusion before they closed.

He babbled and ranted too, shouting commands as though he were in the midst of a great battle, muttering sweet words of flattery to a nameless female, confessing the pain and humiliations he felt as others taunted him for his illegitimate birth.

Hearing him voice his fears and pain was a window into his soul and Grace found herself near tears at those times. He had suffered greatly, yet refused to be cowed. Her heart ached for his pain, but her admiration for his courage grew by leaps and bounds.

Hour after hour, Grace would sit at his bedside, watching his chest inhale and exhale. She would talk to him, the sound of her own voice helping to ease the loneliness and keep the stranglehold of fear at bay.

If Ewan dies . . . nay, I willnae allow myself to consider such a thing!

The healer visited often, always trying a new mixture of herbs and medicine that seemed to help initially, but the soothing effects wore off quickly and Ewan was once again thrust into the storm of illness. Lady Moira nursed him as diligently as Grace and the two women bonded over their mutual love for their patient.

Grace changed the bed linens every day and when he was quiet, she shaved the beard on his face and washed his hair. Lady Moira at first objected to this grooming, calling it foolish and nonsensical, but Grace insisted. Having him clean-shaven and neat made Ewan look more like himself—handsome, boyish, and appealing. Seeing him thus gave her comfort—and hope.

Speculation as to why Sir Ewan remained abed took root inside the castle and fear spread throughout the village. Realizing it was impossible to keep Ewan's illness a secret, Grace admitted to Deirdre that he had caught a chill, yet she was deliberately vague about the severity of his symptoms.

There were two things, however, that gave Grace hope for his recovery. The dreaded boils she checked for every few hours never appeared on Ewan's body.

And no others showed any signs of contracting the disease.

Then, finally, after nine days and as many sleepless nights, Ewan's fever began to recede. Grace sat on the bed gently stroking his brow, then squealed when he caught her arm and pulled her down beside him. His unfocused gaze rested on her a moment and then he frowned.

"Grace, my love, why are there such dark circles under yer eyes?"

His voice was hoarse and weak, no doubt from all the shouting he had done when the fever had raged so potently. But his voice truly was the most wondrous sound Grace had ever heard. He was alive!

The relief was so overwhelming she burst into sobs. Ewan stirred and she felt his touch on her cheek as he wiped away the tears. Through the blurry moisture, she saw him struggling to sit upright. Her emotions forgotten, Grace rushed to help him, propping several pillows behind him.

His face was ashen against the dark furs, his cheeks sunken. He had lost weight and much of his strength, but none of that mattered.

He had survived. In time, he would fully recover. Her lips moved swiftly in a silent prayer of thanks. Then she opened the chamber door and shouted the news to one and all.

Chapter Seventeen

Ewan was drifting, floating. He struggled to pull himself down to solid ground, away from this dream-like state. His eyelids fluttered, but he lacked the strength to lift them fully. Pulling them open as far as he was able, he squinted through half-closed eyes as he surveyed his surroundings.

He knew this place. 'Twas his bedchamber. His hand touched the ground beneath him. Soft. A mattress. He was lying in his bed. Alone. Nay, Grace was here. He had seen her, spoken to her. But now she was gone? Or had he dreamt it?

His vision was blurry, his head pounding, his throat felt burnt and raw. Closing his eyes, Ewan searched his memory. Heat. Unbearable heat. He had been on fire, with angry flames engulfing him, surrounding him and scorching his flesh.

Yet through the pain he remembered feeling the gentle touch of cool cloths bathing his body, the sound of soft words of comfort being whispered to him. It had eased his suffering, calmed his agitation. By concentrating on the familiar tone of that female voice, he had been able to escape from the agony that was gripping his entire body.

Grace. His beloved wife. He called out to her now, shocked at how weak and reedy his voice sounded. Dread cramped his stomach, followed swiftly by pangs of hunger. When had he last eaten? He could not recall.

He tried to collect his thoughts, to revive his memory. More stones had been needed to build the second wall around the keep. He and Alec had journeyed to find a new quarry and upon their return they had discovered the tinker in the woods. Ewan clenched his jaw at the memory of the bodies he had found. The tinker, his wife, their children, all victims of a fearful illness.

Ewan tried turning to his side as a wave of nausea hit, but was barely able to move. *God's bones, he was weaker than a newborn.*

Ewan took a deep breath and tried again to clear his mind, swearing at the confusion that swirled around him. Footsteps sounded in the hallway, outside his chamber. Finally he would get some answers!

Yet while the sounds persisted, no one opened the door. Ewan called out. There was no reply. Bloody hell, his voice was too weak to be heard. He tried again, yet failed to get anyone's attention. Exhausted by the effort, he struggled to keep his eyes open, but a great weariness overcame him and sleep took control.

Hours later, he woke. This time his head was clearer, though his tongue felt swollen, his stomach queasy, and he badly needed to relieve himself. Ewan cautiously turned his head. All was darkness, then he caught the movement of light in the corner.

"Ewan?" He felt a cool, steady hand on his brow. "Here, drink this." A goblet was placed to his lips. The liquid was sweet and soothing as it slid down his parched throat, though his tongue still felt rough and oversized.

He opened his eyes fully, wincing at the light that now filled the chamber. The shadow of a woman stood beside his bed. He tried to see her face, but the light hurt his eyes.

"Grace?"

"Oh, Ewan, my love, I'm here."

My love? Am I once again dreaming?

"What's wrong with me? I feel as though I've been trampled by a column of horses."

"Ye have been ill with a dreadful fever. But it has passed and ye are recovering."

"How long have I been in bed?"

"Nine days."

Ewan swore. "Has anyone else taken ill?"

"No one. We have all been spared from this dreadful scourge." Upon hearing that no others had suffered, a surge of relief spread through Ewan's veins, bolstering his pitiful strength. "Did Alec tell ye about the tinker and his family?"

"He did. We have all said prayers fer the souls of the departed. Nay, Ewan, do not try to rise." Grace placed her hand upon his shoulder and pushed him back against the pillows. "Save yer strength so ye can stay awake and eat something."

He nearly smiled. She sounded so unlike herself— arrogant and in command. "Dearest wife, I must rise from this bed to answer nature's call. I implore ye to either help me or get out of my way."

Lips pursed, Grace stepped to the side. Ewan rose shakily from the bed, every limb in his body protesting the movement. Grace immediately placed her arm around his waist. As much as he would have liked to straighten and stand on his own, he knew that was impossible.

Slowly, Grace guided him to the chamber pot, and when he was finished she helped him back. Ewan leaned heavily on her, grateful for the support. After but a few steps, the muscles in his legs trembled so badly he feared they would crumble.

Ewan's chest heaved with exertion once he returned to the bed. Grace quickly plumped several pillows and helped ease him into a sitting position. He let his eyes drift closed.

"Ye need a full week of rest and lots of good, rich food inside ye before ye can leave this bed," Grace cautioned. "If not, ye'll be falling down and knocking yer thick skull upon the ground."

"Aye." He licked his dry lips and opened his eyes. She was right. His body was ravaged by the effects of the sickness and needed time to heal.

He saw Grace nearly wilt in relief at his compliance. Caring for him so diligently, nursing him through such a brutal illness had taken its toll on her strength. He felt guilty for causing her such worry, yet grateful for her devotion, uncertain if he would have survived without her tender care.

A moment later, his mother bustled into the chamber, carrying a tray of food. She passed it over to Grace, then drew near. Lady Moira stood beside his bed, hands on her hips, her stare never wavering.

"I see that ye have decided to rejoin the living," she said gruffly. "'Tis past time."

Then, to Ewan's utter shock, he saw her eyes moisten with tears.

"I dinnae mean to be such a bother," he remarked softly.

She wiped her eyes, then smiled. "Ye were far more than a mere bother, my son. Ye were a royal pain in the arse."

"Milady," Grace exclaimed. "Can ye not at least wait until Ewan has eaten some of the hot food ye brought before starting to scold him?"

"As his wife, 'tis ye who should be blistering his ears fer the fright he gave us all," Lady Moira replied. "Day and night she nursed ye, Ewan, barely eating, hardly sleeping, refusing to leave yer side. I was expecting her to drop at any moment, but apparently she's a lot stronger than she looks."

"Ye helped, too," Grace said in a low voice.

"Aye, I did my part. But ye did the yeoman's work."

Ewan shook his head in confusion. His wife and mother working together in harmony? Had his fever returned? Was he hallucinating such a miraculous occurrence?

"We both worked tirelessly," Grace insisted.

"And have each more than earned a rest. I'm fer bed," Lady Moira proclaimed. She turned to leave, thought better of it, then bent down and gave him a swift kiss on the forehead. "I'll see ye on the morrow."

Still in shock over the sight of his mother's softened features and quivering voice, Ewan gazed at his wife. She looked exhausted. Her face was pale, further accenting the dark circles beneath her eyes. Apparently his mother had not exaggerated Grace's devotion and determination to make him well. She had given much of herself to aid him. 'Twas both a humbling and heartwarming realization.

"Would ye like to try and eat something?" Grace asked.

"I am hungry."

She smiled broadly at his answer and lifted the tray his mother had brought. As Grace came closer, Ewan's stomach rumbled at the enticing aromas. She fussed with the covers and his pillows, then settled the tray in front of him.

"Do ye need my help?" she asked.

Ewan gave her a hesitant look. The idea of being fed by his wife was completely emasculating. Yet would he appear more manly with food dribbling down his chin and falling onto his chest from an unsteady hand?

"Let me try on my own first," he said.

She nodded. Ewan scooped a small portion of the rich broth onto his spoon and brought it slowly to his mouth. Absurdly proud not to have spilled any, he took a sip. It tasted like heaven on his tongue. Hunger building, he reached for another spoonful, this time snaring a small chunk of meat.

"Eat slowly," Grace cautioned. "Ye've had nothing in yer stomach fer days except some broth and watered-down ale."

Ewan obediently complied. After half the soup was gone, Grace dropped some pieces of torn bread into the bowl. Ewan eagerly ate those broth-soaked chunks, scraping his bowl when he was finished.

"May I have some water?" he asked as Grace took the tray away.

"Are ye thirsty?"

"Nay, not to drink. To wash."

Grace looked horrified. "Ye cannae possibly have a bath so soon."

"Not a bath, just a wash. The stench of illness engulfs me."

Her features were suddenly stricken. "I washed and shaved ye as often as I could," she whispered.

"Ah, lass, ye did a fine job and I thank ye fer it." He reached for her hand and squeezed it gently. The last thing he wanted was to appear ungrateful and demanding. But once expressed, Ewan's need to clean himself grew.

Grace sniffled and gave him a watery smile. "I suppose it's a good sign that ye are feeling the need to be clean. 'Tis late and the castle sleeps, but a small fire still burns in the great hall. I will heat some water there and return shortly."

Ewan must have dozed while he waited. When he next opened his eyes, Grace was once again at his side. She laid a strip of cloth in the washbasin, then lifted a pitcher and poured a steady stream of hot water over it.

This time Ewan did not refuse his wife's assistance. He lay contentedly against the pillows as she dampened his skin and swabbed it with a soapy cloth. Wetting a fresh cloth with clean water, she wiped the soap off, then dried him with a warm towel.

When she finished, Grace leaned down to kiss his cheek. Though still feeling weak, Ewan seized the opportunity and pulled her close. Grace gasped and lost her balance, tumbling onto the bed. When she lifted her chin, her face was mere inches from his own.

Precisely where he wanted it.

This might not be the memorable, romantic moment

he had envisioned, but the ordeal he had just survived made Ewan realize how precious and fragile life could be, even in times of peace. He could wait no longer to tell her what was in his heart.

"I love ye, Grace," he whispered.

"Ewan?"

"Aye, ye heard right. I love ye. I have fer a long time. Ye are special, lass. Courageous and loyal, smart and kind. Ye claimed my heart so thoroughly that I cannae imagine being without ye, fer ye are the person that gives my life meaning.

"Ye can lighten my mood with a simple smile, fire my blood with a single glance. I should have told ye sooner, but I was waiting fer the right moment. I wanted it to be special, unique, something that ye would always remember. Something that ye would hopefully treasure."

Her eyes rounded in astonishment. She lifted her fingers and traced his lips, almost as though she hadn't believed the words that had just spilled from them. For a very long minute she remained silent, holding his eyes in a look.

No matter. One day she would share in these wondrous feelings. One day she would say the words back to him.

"Ye love me, Ewan?"

"I do, Grace, with all my being." Ewan leaned against his pillows and cupped her cheek. "Yer jaw has fallen open and I dinnae know what that means. Does this news displease ye?"

"Nay, Ewan." Grace reached out to touch his face, then hesitated. "I am humbled by yer tenderness, by the gift of yer love. I, too, have feelings fer ye. They sneak up on me and when they strike, the need to be near ye goes so deep that I feel it in my bones. The intensity overwhelms me, almost frightens me it's so strong.

"There's something inside ye that calls to me, that touches me in a way I dinnae completely understand. All I know is that it is a feeling unlike any I've ever known. Ye have unlocked the secrets of my heart, Ewan Gilroy. I trust ye, I need ye, I care more about ye than I do myself. Is that love?"

"Aye, I believe so."

Ewan felt his chest constrict so tightly with emotions it crowded his ribs. His heart hungered for her. His soul rejoiced in her. More than anything, he wanted to hold her in his arms and make love to her, affirming this emotional bond in the most primal, physical manner.

But alas, his weakened and depleted body would not allow it.

"Och, my love, now I know that ye are truly recovering when I see that spark of desire returning to yer eyes," Grace said with a laugh.

"Even though ye know it will come to naught?" Ewan grumbled, and Grace giggled again.

She brushed a lock of hair off his forehead and stared deeply into his eyes. "I can wait. There are days, weeks, months, years ahead to be spent in each other's arms. I believe that with all my heart."

Her words mollified him, for the future she envisioned brought Ewan joy. He, too, could imagine it. Time spent together, both in and out of bed. Love, laughter, joy.

Ewan pulled Grace down so she lay beside him. Having her near, her softness pressed against him, settled him. Belly full, mind clear, heart contented, Ewan relished the gift of calm that descended inside him.

* * *

Grace awoke with a jolt, startled by the clanging of a bell. *Is it time fer Mass already?* Jerking upright, she quickly realized that she was not at the convent, but rather in her own home, in her own bed, lying beside her husband.

She looked down and saw she was wearing her chemise. Though she had no recollection of it, she must have removed her gown sometime during the night before crawling into bed with Ewan.

The bell continued to ring. Ewan stirred sluggishly. Concerned, Grace touched his forehead. The flesh felt cool and dry. The fever had not returned, praise God.

Without even the pretense of a knock, the bedchamber door burst open and Alec came barreling through it. He held a sword in one hand, but his scabbard was missing. His hair was disheveled and his tunic askew, indicating that he had hastily dressed.

"Riders approach," he declared.

Ewan moved so quickly Grace felt the mattress shifting when he sat upright. "How many?"

Alec grimaced. "Too many to count."

"Is everyone from the village inside the walls?" Ewan asked.

Alec lowered his chin and shook his head. "There wasnae time."

"Shit!" Ewan swung his legs over the side of the bed, but the moment he stood on his feet, he began to sway.

"Ewan, ye cannae go outside," Grace cried, reaching out to steady her husband.

"She's right," Alec interjected. "I'll go to the battlements and report back to ye."

"I'm coming with ye," Grace insisted.

She scrambled from the bed before either man could protest, pulled a fur from the pile of covers and wrapped herself in it. Barefooted, Grace climbed the stairs. The stones felt cold on her toes, the chill seeping into her bones, but she did not even pause to catch her breath until she reached the ramparts.

She walked until she found a section where she could see out without getting too close to the edge. Apprehensively looking over the wall, Grace hugged herself tightly when she beheld the sight that greeted her.

Soldiers were swarming all over the valley like a hive of angry bees, surrounding the keep on three sides. Some were still atop their horses, shields displayed and swords drawn. Others were busy erecting tents, building cooking fires and setting up camp. It would have been an impressive sight, were it not so terrifying.

"It looks like they're preparing fer a siege," Grace croaked.

"Aye, and doing a fine job of it," Alec answered grimly.

She searched among the men on horseback, straining to see their leader, though in her heart she already knew his identity.

"Can ye see the banners they fly?" Alec asked, pointing toward the pennants that snapped and fluttered in the wind.

"Aye, 'tis Roderick's colors flanking that large tent. It must be meant fer him." Grace's chest ached. This time Roderick was not leaving until he got what he came for—her.

"Why does he pursue ye, milady?"

Had the situation not been so dire, Grace might have smiled with appreciation at Alec's perceptive question. "Roderick believes that I can help him disgrace his brother and thus aid his quest to become chief of his clan." Grace shivered. "But I cannae."

Swallowing her fear, Grace turned away. As she walked from the ramparts, she could hear the panic starting to catch in the bailey below. The clanging of metal, shouting of orders, the steady tread of running feet. There were cries of hysteria from a few of the women and sobs of fright from the children.

Her hands had barely stopped shaking when she arrived back at her bedchamber. Ewan had somehow managed to partially dress himself, but his face was pale and his brow moist from the effort. He listened silently as Alec made his report.

"What of our defenses?" Ewan asked.

Alec rubbed his chin. "Our food and water supplies are adequate. We can last at least two months, mayhap longer, depending on how many of the villagers made it inside the walls."

Ewan's brow creased with worry. "The south wall?"

"Should hold if it's not bombarded. I dinnae see any catapults or ladders in the encampment, but they can easily be built. There are plenty of good trees in our forest that can be cut down and Roderick has more than enough men to put to the task."

Grace shivered. She had never been involved in a siege, but had heard enough tales of them to be scared. Along with fear, they brought suffering and despair to those forced to endure them.

As supplies ran out and starvation ensued, many would be forced to eat anything they could get their hands on—rats, dogs, cats, even horses. Disease would spread, hastened by dead animal and human body parts that were hurled by the attackers over the walls.

'Twas not only the physical suffering, but the mental anguish, the sense of hopelessness that gripped a person as the siege continued and those around them died. Given the size of Roderick's army, their only chance of survival lay in holding out until help arrived from an ally. But they were so far away!

Grace glanced at Ewan and Alec. Their heads were pressed close as they spoke, yet there was no mistaking the worry they each carried.

"What if we simply give Roderick what he wants?" Grace said softly. "Me."

Ewan reared his head back in shock, his expression fierce. Ignoring her, and her suggestion, he turned to Alec. "Ready the men and weapons. Position the archers on the battlements and have my mother do a complete inventory of all our food supplies. I also need to know which villagers are still outside the walls."

Alec nodded, then left to carry out the orders.

Ewan kept his back toward her, saying nothing as he continued to dress. She retrieved her rumpled gown from the floor and did the same, finishing first.

Grace stifled a gasp when Ewan finally turned. He looked pale and sweaty and ready to keel over.

"Ye should be in bed, resting, Ewan. Ye are not yet well."

"I dinnae have time to be ill, Grace. I must find a way to defeat Roderick or we are all doomed."

Grace forced herself to keep her trembling under control. This was all her fault. She was the reason they were all in peril, subjected to Roderick's mad schemes. Ewan was their leader, yet she truly felt it was her responsibility to somehow set things to rights.

"Perhaps if I met with Roderick privately and told him the truth about Alastair's death—"

"Nay!" Ewan shouted. "I know ye have suffered with guilt these many months, Grace. But ye must accept the fact that Alastair died by his own hand. Ye might have helped provide the means, but it was Alastair's choice. That's the truth. That's the truth that ye must tell Roderick. And trust me, Grace, it's a truth that no one in the Ferguson Clan will want to hear."

"Oh, Ewan, dinnae ye see? This will end it once and for all. The truth will set us free. If not we will forever be at odds with Roderick."

Ewan moved closer, his eyes blazing with determination. "Speaking to Roderick about what happened that night will only make matters worse. I'm certain of it. I forbid ye to say anything to anyone about Alastair's death. Do ye understand?"

Grace swallowed hard. "It pains me greatly to reveal this act, and my part in it, but I have no choice. 'Tis all I can think of to try and save us."

Ewan bit back a curse. "No matter what ye say to him, Roderick will find a way to place the blame on ye and make himself a hero to his clan in the process."

Grace wrung her hands. "What can we do? We cannae allow Roderick and his army to camp outside our gates fer months. They'll hunt in our forest, ruin our crops. They'll retaliate against the unfortunate villagers who did not make it inside the keep. And those of us that are behind the walls, well, they shall starve and torment us. I could not live with myself if so many innocent folk were harmed on my account."

Ewan crossed his arms. "Do ye have so little faith in me, Grace?"

She placed her palm against his chest and felt the strong beat of his heart. "There is no finer man, no greater warrior in all of Scotland than ye, Ewan. That I truly believe with all my heart. But even ye cannae perform miracles."

"Just watch me, Grace." Ewan lifted his brow. "I shall never easily relinquish what is mine."

Stepping around her, Ewan strode from the chamber with a confident swagger. Grace stood alone, her heart stuttering with fear and confusion.

"Mother of God, aren't we the pair?" she whispered.

Chapter Eighteen

"Are ye sure ye know what ye're doing?" Alec asked, as Roderick Ferguson rode through the open portcullis, flanked on each side by a monk and a priest.

"He comes under a flag of truce," Ewan answered, narrowing his eyes at the approaching trio and wondering at Roderick's choice of escort. He would have expected him to arrive with two of his most seasoned warriors at his side, as a show of strength. Not two men of God.

"A promise of a truce hardly means that Roderick will act with honor," Alec retorted.

"I know. He's a man filled with guile. But hearing his terms will give us a chance to decide how to best him and buy us some much-needed time."

"Do ye think young Duncan was able to slip by Roderick's troops?" Alec inquired.

"I'm hopeful. It has been hours since the lad rode off and we've yet to hear of his capture."

"Aye, Roderick would waste no time in letting us

know our messenger had been caught, and with him, any chance of getting word to our allies."

Ewan curled his lip. There was but a slight chance that Duncan would reach the McKenna's in time to make a difference in this struggle with Roderick. Yet they had to try. Duncan was a smart and courageous lad. He had volunteered to ride for help and after a brief debate, Ewan had allowed it. If the worst came to pass and they were defeated, well, at least the truth would be known and their deaths avenged. Brian McKenna would make certain of it.

"We must stall fer time," Ewan said.

"Then I suppose it is wise to hear what Roderick wants," Alec conceded.

"I already know what the man wants," Ewan snarled. "He means to take Grace from me and use her to bolster his own position in his clan. But he willnae take her, at least not while there is breath left in my body."

Ewan straightened his spine, knowing all eyes were trained upon him. Most of his people had not seen him for nearly a fortnight—all knew he had been gravely ill. 'Twas essential that he appear strong and in command, as they were looking for him to keep them safe. Roderick, on the other hand, would be searching for a weakness.

Roderick raised his arm, demonstrating that he was unarmed, then slowly dismounted. The monk and priest did the same. Ewan approached.

"I've come with these holy men on a matter of most importance," Roderick proclaimed.

Ewan pierced his foe with the full weight of a disbelieving stare. "Ye have an army at yer back that is camped at my gates. That seems more like an act of war to me."

Roderick grinned. "My men ride with me everywhere I travel." He lifted his head, then twisted his body, eyeing all those who stood in the bailey. "Where is yer wife? Hiding somewhere within the keep?"

The casual mention of Grace had Ewan itching to reach for his sword and run it through Roderick's smirking face. But he would not be so easily baited.

"I am here, Roderick," a female voice shouted.

The sea of people parted, and Grace stepped forward, her head held high.

Sweet Jesus! Ewan had told Grace to stay out of sight and here she was, parading herself in front of their enemy like a prized catch. Though angry at her disobedience, Ewan also felt a burst of pride at her courage. His wife was no meek lass.

"As this concerns ye, Lady Grace, it is important that ye are present."

"Ye risk much by coming here, Roderick," Grace declared.

Roderick tossed a glare in her direction, then postured himself in the center of the bailey. "Good people of Tiree, I have come to yer home in good faith, seeking justice fer my kin. My brother Alastair's death has long been shrouded in mystery. I have prayed and fasted fer many long months while seeking answers and spiritual guidance, and in my grief I have consulted with these two holy men.

"They, too, have prayed fer answers and by Divine Providence have finally been able to determine the reason fer my unease, the cause of my distress."

Roderick gave a dramatic pause, and then shouted, "Witchcraft!"

There was a loud gasp from the crowd. Ewan could see people exchanging fearful looks as speculation erupted among the masses. Most turned their attention toward Grace, confusion mixed with frightened judgment on their faces.

"What are ye saying?" Grace asked, straightening her shoulders under the heavy scrutiny of all those surrounding her.

The set of Roderick's mouth hardened and his eyes assumed an accusatory stare. "I accuse ye, Lady Grace, of practicing the dark arts, of using yer unholy knowledge to hasten the death of my brother, Alastair."

Of all the things Ewan had been trying to prepare for, this was totally unexpected. But the menace in Roderick's eyes let him know his foe was deadly serious. For the first time since Roderick and his army appeared at the gates, Ewan felt real fear.

"That is the most ridiculous thing I've ever heard," Ewan protested hotly.

"Sir Ewan, we ask that ye not make light of such a serious charge," the priest said with great indignity.

Ewan could not stop himself from taking an aggressive step forward. "My wife is a woman of noble birth. Raised in a convent, devoted to her faith. Who dares to cast such aspersions on her character? What proof do ye present? Where are the witnesses to such a heinous crime?"

Many of the servants and villagers began stomping their feet in support and Ewan felt himself start to calm. This preposterous charge would amount to naught. Roderick's final, desperate attempt had no proof, no facts. It was bound to fail.

"Witches are too clever by half to leave evidence of their crimes," the monk said.

"There has been no crime," Ewan insisted.

"Witchcraft is a crime, an abomination against God and man," the monk proclaimed. "We must first determine if Lady Grace is indeed a female who freely practices Satan's vile arts. Father Harold and I have both been trained to recognize this unholy skill in others and have much experience in detecting the witches who dare to live among decent folk."

"No doubt ye take great delight in wielding this power by frightening and threatening innocent women," Ewan scoffed.

Father Harold's face contorted into haughty puzzlement. "Nay, Sir Ewan. We have been called to do God's work and thus have vanquished evil and saved the souls of hundreds of unsuspecting mortals. We are here to save the good people of Tiree Keep, to protect them and ensure they are safe from witchery."

"Father Harold speaks the truth," Roderick said. "We have come to save the innocent. Will ye not aid us in this righteous cause?"

Ewan felt his temper explode. "I willnae. Now get yer arse out of my bailey, Roderick, before I ignore that flag of truce and run my sword through·yer blackened heart."

"True blood shall tell in times of adversity," the priest cried. "Ye are a man born in sin, Ewan Gilroy, and yer attitude in this grave matter bears witness to yer birth."

Ewan ground his teeth in frustration. "I say again,

ye have no case of witchery against my wife. No proof."

"Then ye willnae object if we question her?" The priest craned his neck to get a better view of Grace. "If Lady Grace is innocent, then there is nothing to fear. She will come to no harm. In truth, she will clear her name of this most serious charge."

Ewan refused to mask his disgust. "I forbid it."

The monk and priest exchanged a guarded look. "We will examine her for a physical deformity or abnormalities to see if she possesses a witch's mark. And if one is found, we must prick it, to see if it brings her pain. If it does not, then we know it is a true sign of Satan. Ye may be present during the examination if ye wish."

Ewan's hand clenched. He imagined his fist connecting with the end of the priest's bulbous nose and blood spewing far enough to hit the monk and Roderick right in the eye.

"I've seen and stroked and kissed every inch of my wife's lovely flesh in candlelight and sunlight. I can assure ye all, there is no witch's mark."

His lighthearted comments brought a nervous laugh from the crowd, yet he could feel their anxiety, their uncertainty. The charge of witchcraft from not one but two holy men was difficult to ignore. Roderick had planned this carefully.

The monk shifted on his feet. "What of Lady Grace's familiar? We've heard tell of a black cat with whom she shares an unnatural fondness."

Ewan's head jerked forward. "What? I've never seen her with a cat, black or otherwise."

Roderick extended his arm and spun around in a slow circle. Stopping suddenly, he pointed at one of the maids. Her head was bowed so low Ewan could not see her features, yet he could see the trembling of her limbs.

"Ye there, lass, speak up," Roderick commanded. "Tell us what ye know of this matter."

Eyes wide with terror, the maid tried to scramble back into the crowd.

"Ye have nothing to fear," the monk assured her. "God protects those who reveal the truth."

Out of the corner of his eye, Ewan saw Grace flinch and his heart plummeted.

"I did, in truth, befriend a black cat," Grace admitted, stepping aside to shield the maid from their view. "'Twas a kitten, actually, and in no way evil."

The monk eyed her shrewdly. "We will examine this creature also and make that determination ourselves."

Grace slowly shook her head. "'Tis bad enough that ye falsely accuse me. I'll not allow ye to torture a defenseless animal. Besides, I have not seen the kitten fer weeks."

Momentarily stymied, the priest and monk looked toward Roderick.

"We could perform a water test," Roderick offered as casually as though he were suggesting a leisurely ride through the forest.

Beside him, Alec made a strangled cry of protest, bolstering Ewan's own outrage.

"Nay!" Ewan shouted. "Ye'll not be tying Grace's hands to her feet and then tossing her in the loch."

"But the innocent will sink while the guilty remain afloat," Roderick insisted. "A sure sign of a witch."

"The courts and the church disapprove of this method," Alec countered.

Father Harold shook his head. "It can be used in addition to other evidence gathered by the accuser."

"But there is more," the monk added. "Even as we speak of this evil, Lady Grace stands so tall and proud. 'Tis known that witches rarely weep. The mere fact that she does not cry displays damning evidence of her guilt."

Father Harold tried to take a step in Grace's direction, but Ewan thrust up his arm and blocked his path. "If ye value yer life, ye will keep yer distance from my wife."

After viewing Ewan's rigid gaze, the priest wisely decided against the notion.

"We are not surprised that ye dinnae believe these charges, Sir Ewan," the monk interjected. "The lass has bewitched ye."

"Aye." A flare of malice gleamed in Roderick's eyes. "It is not uncommon for those surrounded by the demon spawn to be bewitched by their power. Yer passionate defense of Lady Grace naturally calls into question yer own judgment. A witch drains a person of all reason and sense. That could very well be the case in this situation."

Ewan's lip curled. His pulse was pounding loudly in his ears, driving his anger to unimaginable heights. Enough! The longer he allowed these men to voice their vile untruths, the greater the possibility that others might believe the charges. Or at least start to question the truth.

His people would need strength and solidarity to survive a long siege. Strife among themselves would weaken their position, which was precisely what Roderick hoped to achieve.

"Ye have said yer peace and spewed yer lies and now ye will leave," Ewan commanded.

"Nothing has been settled," Father Harold whined.

"Aye, it has," Ewan barked out, pulling his sword. "I'll have my patience tried no further. Ye will climb back upon yer mounts and ride out of here before it gives way. I swear before one and all that I'll not be responsible fer my actions if ye dinnae heed this warning."

"We have come under a banner of truce," the monk cried in a desperate voice.

"Aye, but I can guarantee that ye'll not be leaving under it unless ye move quickly," Ewan threatened.

White-faced, the priest and monk scurried away, but Roderick held his ground. "This is far from over," he declared with a flare of malice in his eyes. "I willnae be denied the justice I seek."

"Ye seek vengeance, and I'll not allow ye to satisfy it with my wife, on my land, in my home." Ewan felt his entire body tighten with rage, then suddenly his head swam with a wave of dizziness. *Damnation!* The aftermath of the fever still held him in weakness, but it would be foolhardy to allow Roderick to see it. Pulling from the dregs of his strength, Ewan announced, "The next time we meet, it shall be in battle."

The bailey was painfully quiet as Roderick, the priest, and the monk rode from it. The moment they were clear of the gate, the keep was shut tight and Grace finally allowed the breath she had been holding to escape.

Witchcraft? The notion was so preposterous that when Roderick had initially shouted it, she had not believed he was serious. But that emotion was quickly dispelled when the priest and monk had started making accusations and discussing how they would examine her to arrive at their verdict. In a fog she had listened to the ridiculous charges, hardly believing her ears.

And then she had cast her eyes at Roderick. It was not the fierce, almost mad intentions reflected in his eyes that frightened her the most, but rather the ghost of a smile that touched his lips when her gaze met his. For in that moment Grace finally understood the depths he was prepared to go.

She felt herself begin to shake at the memory. Legs unsteady, she walked toward Ewan. He pulled her into his arms and held her close, running his hand up and down her back. Though she still felt worried and confused, she was not afraid. She knew she was safe in Ewan's arms.

"Well, this is a damn fine mess." Lady Moira stood near, eyeing them both shrewdly. "Though I'll admit I'm not surprised that Grace has brought such turmoil into our midst."

"I'm asking ye to keep a civil tongue in yer head, Mother. We've enough grief without ye adding kindling to the fire."

Lady Moira huffed, but held her silence. Grace paid no attention, for there was no time for her to be distressed by her mother-in-law's brisk disapproval. Not when their very survival hung in the balance.

Arms still entwined, Grace and Ewan made their way to the great hall, with Lady Moira, Alec, and a slew of others following in their wake. A ripple of murmurs circled through the crowd as they passed.

"Do ye think they believe these horrible lies?" Grace whispered.

"Nay," Ewan swiftly replied. "Though it has only been a short time, ye have proven to them that ye are a good woman, with a kind heart. They willnae forsake ye."

Encouraging words, yet it was impossible for Grace to miss the steady glances of curiosity and uncertainty that were tossed her way. Alec, too, sensed the tension and he moved to protectively flank her on the other side. Grace smiled wanly at the knight in thanks.

Once in the hall, Ewan gathered a group of his soldiers around him. Expressions solemn, the men listened, then offered opinions and advice.

"Roderick demands we turn my lady wife over to him and that pious pair for judgment, but I shall never release her into their corrupt hands."

"If ye dinnae do as they ask, they will storm our walls," Alec said.

"Or lay siege to the keep," another said. "We willnae last long."

"The McKenna will come to our aid," Ewan insisted.

"Aye, we can count on his support," Alec agreed. "Though it will not come swiftly. Many could die before it arrives."

Grace forced down the lump in her throat. The thought of so many suffering because of her was unbearable. "I am innocent of this charge," she said, as all eyes turned in her direction. "I do not fear their examination."

"Ye should, milady," Alec said bluntly. "'Tis plain as day that they have already decided ye are guilty."

"Witches are not simply put to death," Ewan said grimly. "They are burnt. 'Tis the law and considered the only appropriate punishment for those who practice the black arts."

The room felt as though it were spinning around Grace. She knew this, of course, but the agony and cruelty of such a death was almost beyond comprehension.

"There is another way," Alec said.

"Aye, trial by single combat." Ewan leaned back in his chair and crossed his arms. "I will challenge that Grace is innocent of the crimes she is accused and prove it with my sword."

Grace's stomach turned, the fear creeping steadily into the back of her throat. She had seen Ewan's skill on the practice field and knew he was a formidable opponent. But Roderick was equally skilled and had not just arisen from nearly a fortnight in a sickbed.

Feigning a kiss, Grace leaned over and pressed her lips to Ewan's ear. "Ye are in no condition to fight," she whispered.

He stroked her arm gently and Grace nearly burst into tears. "Our choices are few, Grace. Of all of them, I believe this one to be the best."

As much as she longed to protest, Grace knew Ewan was right. She hid her heartbreak by turning toward the fireplace, but there she caught Lady Moira's eye. The older woman glared at her with undisguised anger. Grace could hardly fault the emotion, for it was one she also felt.

There was a rumble of protests from men seated around him, but Ewan held up his hand and it ceased.

"I shall champion Lady Grace and fight fer her honor," Alec declared, stepping forward and drawing his sword.

For an instant Grace felt the hope inside her quicken, but one look at Ewan's scowling face made it sputter and die, like a candle in a brisk wind.

"She is my wife," Ewan insisted. "'Tis my duty to protect her. We shall send a message to Father Harold, asking him to sit in judgment of the trial. He seems the sort of pompous arse that would relish the task."

Grace nearly groaned out loud at Ewan's declaration. *Stubborn, prideful warrior!* The sweating sickness had stolen more than his strength; it has also taken what remained of his good sense. It was near impossible to hold back her distress, yet she bit her lip until she tasted blood, not wanting to shame her husband by publicly challenging his decision.

Alec had no such qualms. His protests rang loud and clear, but they were met with a forceful command to be silent. Clearly frustrated, Alec shot Ewan one final glare before turning his back and stomping from the hall, his booted footsteps echoing on the stone floor.

Lady Moira next approached. Grace saw Ewan's fierce expression and felt a twinge of pity for her mother-in-law.

"Ewan, ye must see reason," Lady Moira began. "Ye cannae—"

"Aye, I can and I will!" Ewan slammed his fist on the wooden table so forcefully the tankards rattled. "This is my keep, my wife, my fight! Is that understood?"

The hall went deadly silent. Lady Moira's jaw firmed and the rest of her features tensed, but she clamped her lips shut. If the situation had not been so dire, Grace might have taken a small bit of pleasure from the moment.

But the truth was, she agreed with her mother-in-law. And that did not bode well at all.

As promised, Ewan issued the challenge to Roderick the next morning. The reply came quickly and the trial was set for the following day. Ewan immediately took to the practice field.

Grace stood and watched him, a silent Lady Moira at her side. At first, it had not been so bad. Ewan moved nimbly and struck with accuracy. But he quickly grew tired and it was evident that his strength was ebbing.

Frustrated with himself, he shouted at his sparring partner to come at him with all his strength, but the man hesitated. With a sinking feeling Grace realized that unless Ewan was able to strike a fatal blow at the start, Roderick would win.

Unable to watch any longer, Grace turned away, then gasped. Lady Moira's eyes were trained upon her, intense and purposeful. A shiver crossed Grace's neck. They had come to an understanding while nursing Ewan through his fever, but any hint of that previous pleasantry between them was now gone. Most likely forever, especially if Ewan was killed.

Ewan killed! The mere thought of it sent a wave of nausea and fear crashing through every pore of Grace's body.

"He cannae fight," Lady Moira said flatly. "Roderick will cut him to ribbons."

"I know." The fear pressed against Grace's chest, heavy as a boulder on a mountain. "I have talked to

Ewan until I am blue in the face, trying to make him see reason. Begging him to withdraw from the combat, demanding that he delay it fer several days to gain more of his strength, pressing him to allow Alec to fight in his stead. He refuses to listen, refuses to change his mind." Grace hung her head in despair. "I dinnae know what else to do."

Shockingly, Lady Moira offered a comforting hand, placing it on Grace's shoulder. Desperate for solace, she did not immediately pull back from her mother-in-law's touch.

"I believe that ye care fer my son." Lady Moira's voice became deeper and more somber. "Am I right?"

"Aye. I love him. With all my heart."

"Then ye must save him."

"How?"

"By leaving here before the trial."

Chapter Nineteen

That night it rained. A steady onslaught of pelting water that intensified with each hour, soaking the ground, blinding those foolish enough to try and move through it. By early morning the banks of the river had overflowed, flooding a section of Roderick's camp. Grace smiled broadly when she heard the news, her heart lightening at the sound of the continuing rain beating against the roof of the keep.

Under a banner of white, a messenger from Roderick's camp was received, verifying what all knew—the combat would have to be postponed.

"Tomorrow," Ewan agreed.

"Nay, the day after if the weather remains harsh," Grace boldly insisted, not caring that the messenger stared at her with suspicious eyes.

No doubt Roderick, Father Harold, and the monk were telling their men that she had used sorcery to conjure this storm and thus avoid her fate. Let them believe what they wanted. She would dance naked on the battlements to give Ewan any advantage in this contest.

But alas, fate was a cruel mistress. It teased her with the promise of fairness and then quickly snatched it away. By the afternoon, the rain had ceased, the water had receded back to the river, and the sun shone brightly.

There would be no more delays. The trial by combat would take place the following morning.

All through the long day, Grace pondered the merits of the daring plan Lady Moira had proposed to her, wondering if she had the courage to enact it. Grace fought to conceal her growing distress from Ewan, but he was so preoccupied with preparing for his battle with Roderick that he barely noticed.

She faced the coming of the night with dread. The hours flew too quickly and then suddenly the evening meal had ended and she was alone with Ewan in their bedchamber. Wanting to avoid climbing into the bed as long as possible, Grace turned her back to it and gazed out the window.

It was a moonless night, but the night sky was clear of clouds and sparkling with countless stars. Lost in her troubling thoughts, Grace allowed her mind to drift. A gentle touch on her shoulder brought forth a squeal of surprise.

"'Tis only me, lass," Ewan said.

Her face went tight, the lines in her forehead deepening. Ewan wrapped his arms around her waist and pulled her back against his chest. Her entire body melted into him and she savored the feel of him surrounding her.

Longing pulled at her heart. She loved him so!

Grace wiped at her eyes, then felt his lips pressing on her neck.

"Ye need to rest, Ewan. To save yer strength fer the morning."

He reared back. Grace could feel the emotions roiling in him. Slowly, she turned to face him. Ewan placed his fingers beneath her chin. Then holding her in place, he kissed her fiercely.

He was avoiding the obvious, refusing to discuss what lay ahead. Perhaps that was best. Perhaps the only way to survive the next few hours was to surrender to the most pleasant distraction they could devise.

Grace raised her arms and clasped them around Ewan's neck and returned his kiss, allowing him to feel the need that was shuddering through her. He pressed her against the wall and the rough stone dug into her back.

Her flesh was hot everywhere he touched. Ewan's hands moved over her and she wantonly arched forward. He whispered endearments in her ear and she reached down, cradling his arousal. He groaned, kissing her wildly, plunging his tongue deep into her mouth as though he could not get enough of her, as if he desperately needed to be a part of her.

Heart sobbing, Grace lifted her legs, hooking them around Ewan's calves. He accepted her invitation, placing his hands on her hips and moving her higher against the wall until she was in a most vulnerable position. She rocked forward and he entered her in one brusque movement, filling her, touching her in the deepest recess of her heart.

"Ewan!"

He tightened his hold and she did the same. Clinging together, in love and passion and desperation, they moved their bodies, each holding nothing back, each giving totally and completely of themselves.

They shuddered at the same time as they lost control, crying out in satisfaction. Grace pressed her palm against Ewan's chest, over his heart, while she felt his body throbbing inside her, his seed spilling against her womb.

"See, my love," Ewan whispered wickedly in her ear as he slowly lowered her to her feet. "I am no longer as weak as a kitten."

"Nay, good sir. Ye are as strong as a lion." Grace looked away, her heart breaking. "And just as arrogant."

He laughed. "I hope that I've given ye a child tonight."

"Oh, Ewan."

Grace's throat tightened. Would either of them even live long enough to see if their lovemaking had indeed produced a babe? The question haunted her.

"If all does not go well tomorrow . . . If Roderick bests me—"

Grace's breath hitched on a sob and she pressed her fingers against Ewan's lips. "Dinnae say such a thing."

"Hush, now." Ewan rocked her in his arms for a few moments, then pulled back to look into her eyes. "We must both be strong, Grace, and practical. I believe I can win and I pray that I do, but if Roderick somehow emerges victorious, then ye must plead yer belly. It will buy ye some time before they carry out the sentence. Enough time, I pray, fer word to reach yer brother."

"They willnae care that I might be carrying a

child," she lamented. "Instead, it would bring them joy to kill the devil's spawn along with the witch."

A shuttered look came over Ewan's face. He lifted her once again in his arms and carried her to their bed. He placed her beneath the covers and then climbed in beside her.

Grace clutched her fingers around the blanket, gripping it so hard her hand began to throb. Ewan reached down and drew her fingers into his palm. "Ye must banish these maudlin thoughts fer they will surely muddle our minds," he declared.

"Aye, and give us nightmares," Grace retorted with an edge of sarcasm.

Amazingly, he smiled. "Sleep, my dearest. I shall hold ye close and keep the demons away."

"I love ye, Ewan."

"And I ye."

Grace obediently closed her eyes and feigned sleep. The minutes dragged as she waited anxiously to hear the steady rhythm of Ewan's breaths, telling her that he had fallen asleep. When they came, she slowly opened her eyes.

She studied him then, stroking his hair, committing to memory every angle of his features, every line of his handsome face. If God was merciful, she would see him again. And if not . . .

Nay, that did not bear thinking. She would savor these final moments with joy in her heart, basking in the richness and wonder of Ewan's love.

Time passed. Ewan slept and Grace remained at his side until the very last moment. Then she reluctantly pulled herself from the bed. With shaking fingers, she dressed in her plainest gown, thankful she owned at least one garment that laced up the front. She covered her hair with a dark veil, fearing a white one might be more easily seen, and fastened her cloak around her shoulders.

She turned her back on the bed, yet unable to resist, Grace risked a final glance at her beloved before pinching out the candles. Her breath hitched with emotion and unshed tears, but she refused to cry.

Love required sacrifice and sometimes that included making the difficult, unthinkable choice. Ewan had not hesitated to place his own life above hers, because he loved her. She owed him the same dedication.

Grace muttered a short prayer for him as she hurried out of the chamber, pulling the door closed behind her. Roderick's siege had brought far more than the usual number of people inside the keep. The great hall was near bursting with sleeping folk, but Grace slipped past them all. She hurried across the bailey, startling when she heard a sharp bang.

At the sound, Grace felt her heartbeat quicken. She twirled, pressing herself against the wall and forcing herself to count slowly to fifty before taking another step. Her fingers ached from being held so tightly fisted, but the pain kept her mind alert.

Holding her breath, she listened intently. Hearing nothing but the usual sounds of the night, Grace walked forward. As she reached the stables, Lady Moira stepped from the shadows. Though she was expecting her, the movement startled Grace and she nearly screamed.

"Quiet!" Lady Moira hissed. "Or ye'll ruin all."

Grace felt the edge of panic close her throat. She swallowed hard and tried to speak. "Will I be making this journey alone?"

When Lady Moira had proposed this daring plan, she had said she would try to find an escort for Grace. But she had not guaranteed that she would be successful.

"Garrett will accompany ye. He's just a lad, but he knows the roads better than most and feels confident he can eventually find his way to McKenna land."

Grace nodded, though the words were hardly encouraging. "How will we get past the gate?"

"Leave that to me," Moira whispered. She fumbled in the pocket of her gown, brought out a small leather purse, and pressed it into Grace's hands. "There's some coin and a brooch inside. It will help pay yer way, at least fer a time."

"Pay my way?"

Moira snorted. "If ye keep to the foothills, ye've a fair chance of escaping. But if ye are caught, ye might be able to bribe yer way to freedom. I dinnae believe that all of Roderick's men are unquestionably loyal to him."

"Which way should we head?"

Moira hunched her shoulders. "North would be safer, but it is a wild and untamed land. Go west and then south. If ye are pursued, they will expect ye to be going to yer brother, so ye must take a different path. Cross into England if ye must, then find a convent and seek sanctuary. Tell no one of yer true identity."

"What will ye say to Ewan?"

"Nothing. He'll not be pleased to find that ye have fled from the keep. I shall be as shocked and horrified as all the others when they discover that ye are missing."

The answer made sense and yet Grace detected

something else in Lady Moira's voice, a speck of warmth, a tinge of regret. Was that possible? "I must ask, milady, are ye doing this only fer Ewan's sake?"

Moira huffed. "Are ye a witch?"

Grace gasped. "What?"

"Ye heard me. Are ye a witch?"

"No!" Grace cried adamantly.

Moira nodded. "Then ye dinnae deserve to be burned alive."

It was hardly a declaration of affection, yet for some odd reason the pressure in Grace's chest seemed to ease. With Lady Moira's assistance, Grace mounted the mare. She leaned low over the animal's neck, tucking her veil close to her face.

Lady Moira led the horse away from the stable and the tension once again began to creep through Grace's body. They had gone but a few feet when the snap of a twig made both women jump. Heart pounding at a frantic pace, Grace turned to find Ewan standing behind them, a lit torch in one hand.

He loomed over his mother, his eyes as hard as the ground he stood upon. Then he glared at Grace.

"And just where do ye think ye are going on this fine night, my dearest wife?"

There was a gasp, followed quickly by a muttered curse. The gasp was from Grace, the curse from his mother. How fitting. Though the light was dim, Ewan could see that both women had gone pale.

Lady Moira pushed herself forward. "'Tis best this way, Ewan. We all know it."

"Is that so, Mother? Ye send my wife off to her death and ye believe that it is fer the best?"

His mother actually shrank beneath the tone he used, but his rage was too focused for him to care.

"Better my death than yers, Ewan," Grace interjected, her voice quivering with emotion.

"Not while my heart still beats." Ewan ground his teeth and let loose several choice curses. "Now get down off that horse."

Head bowed, Grace obeyed. The moment her feet touched the ground, Ewan hooked her upper arm and dragged her toward him.

"I wasnae going to Roderick's camp," she said quietly. "I was escaping to the south, hoping to make my way to Brian's castle."

"Escaping? A woman alone? Ye would have been attacked within the hour."

Grace huffed out a long breath. "Garrett was to be my guide and escort. I wasnae traveling alone."

"A lad of fourteen and a woman." Ewan placed his hand on his hip, bowed his head and shook it. "How were ye going to avoid Roderick's soldiers?"

"We planned to circle around the encampment."

Ewan barely suppressed a snort of annoyance. "Making yerselves a prime target fer any hungry animal prowling fer a meal."

But Grace did not back down. "I've no time to placate yer manly pride, Ewan. We both know that my brother is the only man powerful enough to save me. And if I am gone from here, then all of ye will be safe."

It rankled that her words were true. The McKenna could offer her greater protection. Ewan would have sent Grace there himself, if he believed she could arrive without coming to great harm. But the very idea was fraught with danger.

"Ye put us all at great risk with this stunt, Grace," Ewan said. "Roderick would not have simply packed up his soldiers and left if I told him ye were gone from the keep. Nay, he would have pounded our walls and attacked, showing no mercy, giving no quarter. Once he had destroyed us, he would have left in pursuit of ye."

Her face registered surprise and then dismay. "Forgive me, Ewan. I dinnae realize—"

"Yer heart is in the right place, lass." Ewan looked beyond Grace's bowed head and glowered at his mother. "I know this was not yer idea."

His mother glowered right back at him. "I did this to save ye, to keep ye from being hacked to pieces by that brute Roderick."

Ewan threw up his arms in frustration, swinging wide the torch he held. The light danced in a wild frenzy. "Christ Almighty, does no one in the castle believe I can fight?"

"Dinnae shout at yer mother fer loving ye, Ewan," Grace lectured. "She cared fer ye while ye were ill. She knows how much of yer strength the sickness stole."

Ewan's chest burned with indignation. Aye, he had been gravely ill and was not yet at full strength, but did they have to remind him of it every waking minute? 'Twas enough to rattle a man's confidence and make him second-guess his abilities.

"Well then, since I'm such a weakling I'd best be off to my bed. Ye are coming with me, Grace, so I can keep an eye on ye." Ewan glared at his mother, then dragged a hand over his face. "Lord knows, if I dinnae get some rest, then ye both will have no cause to worry about my strength, since I'll be asleep on my feet when I face Roderick in the morning."

Ewan stood in the doorway of the great hall, Alec by his side, waiting for the signal to enter the bailey. It took all his willpower not to pace with restless agitation, but instead to stand still and composed. The ale he had drunk and the meat he had eaten earlier to give him strength churned in his stomach, and he swallowed hard to keep down the bile that rose in his throat.

"Advance!" Father Harold shouted to be heard among the gathering crowd. Most were Ewan's people, but some of Roderick's soldiers had also been allowed in to witness the trial.

Taking a deep breath, Ewan strode out into the sunlight and through the outer fringes of the mob gathered in a circle. He raised his eyes to where Grace was positioned on the small tower rampart, flanked by the monk on one side and one of Roderick's guards on the other. She looked tiny and vulnerable, her eyes moist with emotion.

Ewan's heart leapt and he felt a sharp pain seize him. "If I fall," he muttered to Alec.

"Ye'll not be defeated," his friend insisted.

"Aye, but if the unthinkable happens . . ."

"I willnae be able to save her," Alec said regretfully, speaking the truth they both knew.

"I know." Unable to utter the words, Ewan stared

hard at his friend, willing him to understand what must happen if Roderick prevailed.

Alec slowly nodded. "I give ye my word, I shall not stand by and watch her be burned alive. By my hand, she will have a swift and merciful death."

"Thank ye." Ewan clenched his own hand into a tight fist. He had always been an independent man and hated asking anything of others. But he had responsibilities that followed him beyond the grave and he needed to know they would be fulfilled. "My mother?"

"She'll be too proud to accept my help, but I vow to keep Lady Moira safe," Alec replied. He grasped Ewan's forearm and held on tightly. "But enough of this maudlin talk! There's no need fer it. Ye shall win, Ewan. I've fought beside ye fer too many years not to know of yer skill with a sword and yer cunning in a fight."

"I'm not at full strength," Ewan admitted.

"Perhaps, but ye've battled, and won, when ye have gone days without food or sleep. This is not much different."

Ewan grunted. He appreciated Alec's confidence, but this *was* different. Aside from his weakened physical state, his emotions were in turmoil, knowing what would befall those he loved most if he failed.

Alec cast him a sidelong, meaningful glare. "Ye've one other thing to consider. There is truth on yer side and justice in yer cause. Roderick's accusations are false. Lady Grace is not a witch."

Aye, there was that fact. Though Ewan knew the innocent often suffered while the guilty went free. Trust in God, and fate, was all well and good, but that was tempered in the reality of the unfairness of life.

When he reached the edge of the inner circle, Ewan drew his sword. A gust of wind howled through the bailey, sending a shiver snaking down his spine. It all seemed so unreal, yet here he stood ready to defend his wife—or die trying.

Roderick entered from the opposite side. The crowds thronged in, each person hoping for a better view. Ewan was pleased to note they did not exhibit the usual bloodthirsty excitement that was often found at these events. A testament to their affection and regard for him and Grace, he hoped.

Or a grave fear over their own fate should he lose.

Father Harold stepped forward. With pompous importance, he unfurled a thick roll of parchment, cleared his throat, and began reading.

"Whereas, the Lady Grace has been charged with the grievous crime of performing acts of witchcraft, specifically regarding the death of her first husband, Sir Alastair Ferguson, and she has refused an examination of her person to verify or deny those claims, by the consent of her accuser, Sir Roderick Ferguson, and in accordance with ecclesiastical law, her guilt, or innocence, shall be decided in a trial of combat.

"Due to the serious nature of the crime, no quarter will be given. This shall be a battle to the death. Noble champions, do ye both agree to abide by these terms and conditions?"

"Aye! I battle fer justice and the church," Roderick proclaimed.

"And I fight to prove Lady Grace's innocence," Ewan shouted forcefully.

The crowd erupted in cheers. Several of Ewan's men came forward and slapped him encouragingly on the back and shoulders before returning to the sidelines.

"God go with ye, Sir Ewan," Alec yelled, and the crowd cheered louder.

Cheering ringing in his ears, Ewan followed Roderick into the middle of the makeshift arena. They started cautiously circling, each man sizing the other, searching for a weakness. Ewan immediately noted that Roderick was a half head taller, with a heavily muscled torso and wide shoulders. Ewan hoped the extra bulk would prove a disadvantage, as often men of this size were slower in their movements.

Yet Roderick would be no easy opponent. Ewan was well aware that he would have to employ every ounce of cunning and skill he could conjure in order to defeat him.

Ewan yelled, filling the bailey with a wild battle cry, then surged forward, hoping to startle Roderick by attacking, rather than waiting to make a defensive stand. The crowd cried out as one when swords clashed. At the contact, a sharp, biting pain traveled down Ewan's shoulder, but he ignored it and pressed on.

The rush of excitement, coupled with a dose of fear shielded him from the worst of his discomfort, but he knew that would soon fade. His only hope was to attack hard and fast, disarming Roderick and striking a fatal blow before his strength completely faded.

To that end he lifted his blade in a quick flurry of thrusts, hammering down on Roderick. The other man successfully blocked the blows, alternating with his sword and shield, then whirled around and went on the attack.

Ewan managed to sidestep the charge, putting

Roderick off balance and causing him to stumble and fall to the ground. But before Ewan could press this advantage, Roderick leapt to his feet. He came up swinging violently, catching Ewan on his left side, cutting through the protective leather jerkin he wore down to his tender flesh.

Ewan gritted his teeth as a fresh assault of pain ripped through him and the acrid scent of blood flooded his nostrils. Relentlessly, Roderick struck again, this time from the right.

The crowd groaned as the gash hit its mark and a fresh well of blood gushed from a second serious wound. The blow rocked him and Ewan felt his strength beginning to fail. Biting back the surge of bile that filled his mouth, Ewan took another swing at Roderick.

His blade was met with a crushing blow that sent another jolt of pain down his arm. Roderick leaned into him, pressing forward until his sword was mere inches from Ewan's face. For several long moments the combatants stared at each other, each straining to win the advantage.

Ewan could see the fury and deadly intent in Roderick's glare, along with his desperation. The latter gave him hope. Grunting, Ewan dug in his heels and heaved forward, using the entire weight of his body. The force broke the deadlock, successfully pushing Roderick back.

But there was barely time for Ewan to catch his breath. Roderick lifted his sword over his head and brought it down in a powerful blow. Just before it landed, Ewan raised his arm to deflect it. Snarling, Roderick twisted around and began to strike. Blow after blow rained down upon Ewan's sword and shield and he staggered back from the relentless assault.

Stay on yer damn feet! Legs unsteady, Ewan felt himself starting to sway. *God Almighty, I'm done fer it now.*

Tightening his jaw, he made a last desperate effort, swinging his sword directly at Roderick's skull. His opponent jerked his head back. Regretfully, the blow barely glanced his scalp. Suddenly, there was a sharp clanging in Ewan's ears and he felt himself starting to fall. Arms flaying, he realized desperately there was no way to stop the motion. Pain exploded through every part of his body as he hit the hard dirt.

His nostrils filled with the distinct odor of blood. Roderick's? His? *Most likely mine,* Ewan decided. He extended his left arm, searching frantically for his shield, hoping he could position it in time to avoid being hacked to bits.

He could see Roderick looming over him, his sword raised high above his head. Ewan watched it all as though he were in a dream. This would be the deathblow, a strike that would most likely sever his head from his shoulders. Gravely weakened, he felt no fear as he braced himself for this final blow, but then suddenly he heard a woman sob his name.

Grace! An image of her beloved face swam before his eyes. His wife, the person he loved more than life itself. Her guilt would be confirmed if he lost, her death assured. She would die being falsely proclaimed a witch and no one would be able to save her. Only he had that power.

Blinking, Ewan could see Roderick's sword descending and somehow, someway, he found the strength to roll out of its path. Reaching into his boot, Ewan drew his dirk, and hurled it with every ounce of strength that remained in his weakened body.

The dagger found its mark with unerring accuracy, lodging cleanly in the middle of Roderick's throat. He reeled backward, his eyes glazed in shock as a spray of blood spurted into the air.

The cheers from the crowd were deafening, but Ewan blocked out the sound as he fought to maintain his wits. He watched Roderick fall, then counted ten long breaths as he waited for the verdict.

"The Lady Grace is innocent!"

Only after the full impact of those words penetrated Ewan's brain did he allow the darkness to finally overtake him.

"Blessed Mother have mercy," Grace choked.

The proclamation of her innocence should have been a tremendous relief, but her mind was filled with the horrifying sight of watching a dazed, bleeding Ewan fall. She leaned as far as possible over the low tower railing, nearly tumbling over it as she strained to catch a glimpse of him.

He lay still upon the ground, blood flowing from the wounds on his sides. Ignoring the monk and the burly soldier who stood guard over her, Grace turned, lifted the hem of her gown, and started running. Along the ramparts, down the staircase, across the great hall.

She burst into the bailey, pushing her way through the crowd. Victory was thick in the air and many cheered as she passed, but Grace had no time to savor the moment.

Ewan was hurt, bleeding, possibly dying.

"Oh, my love." Grace knelt in the dirt and gently lifted his head, cradling it in her lap. "There's so much blood."

"Most of it was Roderick's," Alec replied grimly.

"Not all," Grace retorted. Lifting her gown, she tore at the fine linen underskirt, then bound the strips around Ewan's waist. "Have the men fetch a litter."

"He'll want to walk off the field of battle," Alec said. "'Tis a matter of honor."

"He's too weak." Grace hovered protectively over Ewan's body as she waited for the stretcher to be brought. "This is hardly a dishonorable way to depart. My husband has more than proven his honor with his courage and skill this day."

Grace noticed several of the men around them nod in agreement as they hoisted the litter and carried him off. Grace kept her hand tightly curled around Ewan's as they walked through the bailey into the great hall, then up the staircase to their bedchamber.

Lady Moira was waiting for them when they arrived, her eyes suspiciously red. She had summoned both healers and the women quickly set about their work. Though it was difficult for her, Grace stepped aside and allowed the healers to tend to Ewan.

When they were done, Grace sat on the edge of the bed and gazed down at her husband. Bruised, battered, yet alive. She ran her fingers gently over the bandages. The healers insisted the wounds looked far worse than they were and that Ewan would recover, yet still she fretted.

Grace's hand trembled and she stared down at him through a haze of tears. Then she saw Ewan's eyelids start to flutter and she hastily wiped away her tears.

The last thing she wanted was for Ewan to awaken to a weeping wife.

He blinked several times as he brought his surroundings into focus. She knew the moment he recognized her, for his face broke into a wide smile.

"I told ye not to worry, Grace," he croaked.

"Aye, ye did, and I vow that I shall never question yer word fer the rest of my days."

Chapter Twenty

As the healers had promised, Ewan recovered quickly from his wounds. By the second day he was either pestering Grace to allow him out of bed, or trying to cajole her into joining him in it. Though his restlessness was exhausting at times, Grace would not have traded it for anything in the world.

Indeed, she discovered she liked the challenge of keeping Ewan entertained and quiet at the same time. She recited all the stories she could remember, and made up a few more on the spot. She sang when he asked and blushed when he lavishly praised her voice, for she knew it was only passable and hardly as melodious as many other women's.

She played chess with him, though neither of them truly understood the intricacies of the game. She began teaching him to read and write and was pleased with his excitement in learning and quick progress. It was a quiet, peaceful time and Grace relished every moment of it, for she had the one thing she thoroughly enjoyed—Ewan's undivided attention.

On a rainy spring morning, arms loaded with a

tray of food, Grace pushed their bedchamber door open with her hip, entered the room, and then pulled in a sharp breath. Ewan stood at the window, fully dressed.

"Ewan!"

He held up his hand to quiet her, then surprised her by grinning. "Dinnae start blustering at me, Grace. The healer said I could get out of bed today. In fact, she suggested some fresh air and a walk around the bailey would hasten my recovery."

"In the pouring rain?"

Ewan shifted on his feet. "Nay, when the rains cease."

Grace eyed him suspiciously. "I hope that ye are being honest with me, Ewan. If not, I'll be forced to tell yer mother that ye've left the sickbed too soon."

Ewan grimaced. As threats go, it was a strong one, for there was no one more tenacious than Lady Moira in the entire keep. "Well, mayhap the walk about the bailey was my idea," Ewan hedged.

Grace set down her tray. "I've not spent the better part of a week caring fer ye only to see those wounds become infected. Now, come and eat and then we shall discuss yer activities fer the day."

Looking contrite, Ewan did as she asked. When he finished his meal, he began playfully stroking her hand, then lifted it and brought it to his lips. A chill of desire skittered down her back. Grace could feel her cheeks flush and she squirmed in her seat.

"If ye truly think it best that I not go outside, I can think of a far better way to spend the morning," Ewan said huskily.

"I'll just bet ye can," she replied primly, though amusement rang in her voice.

Ewan's hearty laugh came out on a strong breath and it warmed the flesh of Grace's hand. She answered him with a smile of her own.

"I have something fer ye, Grace."

"Oh?" Catching the spirit of the game, Grace moistened her lips and leaned tantalizingly forward. But her sensual haze was abruptly shattered when Ewan reached down and pulled something from the pocket of his trews.

Brows furrowed, Grace looked at the gold ring Ewan held between his thumb and forefinger. It was delicate and refined, of a quality she had never before seen.

"I want ye to wear this ring and every time ye look at it remember how much I love and cherish ye."

Grace gulped. "Wherever did ye find such a magnificent piece of jewelry?"

Ewan bowed his head. "The tinker offered it to me as payment fer staying on our land just before he succumbed to the fever. Given the circumstances, I was not sure I wanted to give it to ye, but after seeing it again I knew it was meant to be yers."

Her throat was starting to swell shut with emotion, but Grace swallowed back the lump. No matter how long she lived she would always remember, and cherish, the look of love and reverence shining from Ewan's eyes as he slipped the ring on her finger.

"This is truly the finest gift I have ever received," Grace said, holding her hand up to the rainy daylight and admiring the way it sparkled on her finger.

Ewan grinned with pleasure. "I hoped that ye would like it. The gold is delicate and beautiful and just like ye, a treasure that can never be truly measured."

Grace shook her head slowly. "'Tis not the quality of the gold that gives it such value, though it is a fine piece. 'Tis the love that goes along with it that means the most to me, Ewan."

A crease appeared between Ewan's brow and he cocked his head. "Dammit wife, if I had known that, then I would have had the smithy forge a ring out of iron."

"And I would have loved it as much." Grace wrinkled her nose and laughed. "Well, almost as much."

The weeks and months passed. The weather grew warmer, the crops grew tall, and peace reigned throughout the land. Ewan awoke each morning with a deep sense of purpose, thankful for the happiness that surrounded him and all the blessings in his life.

On this fine summer afternoon, Ewan stood beside the small tower that housed the keep's chapel, a sanctuary he had built as a gift to his wife. The harvest would begin soon and he had decided a prayer of thanks was in order.

His attention was drawn to the bailey and his heart swelled as he saw Grace make her way toward him. No matter what time of day or where he stood, Ewan's heart never failed to quicken whenever he beheld his wife. The love he felt for her had continued growing until it settled around him like a warm fur.

He noticed that Grace carried a letter in her hand, no doubt from her sister-in-law, Aileen. A McKenna messenger had arrived earlier, bringing all the news. Thanks to Grace's diligent instructions, Ewan was now able to read the correspondence sent to him and conduct business like a true lord of the realm. As such, he did not begrudge his wife her private letters, and though he never demanded it, she always eventually shared the contents with him.

"Have ye good news to tell me?" Ewan asked when Grace joined him.

She folded her arms. "Not exactly."

"Is something amiss with Aileen?"

"This letter is not from Aileen. 'Tis sent by the king."

Ewan tilted his head to one side. "King Robert? Why would he be writing to ye?"

Grace's face grew pale. At the sight, Ewan felt as though someone had just punched the breath from his chest. Mind racing, he snatched the parchment from her hand. His eyes quickly scanned the document, though his brain had difficulty comprehending the words, as it was written with a flourishing script.

He glanced up at Grace. She looked so guilty that the beat of his pulse soared with worry. He had feared the charge of witchcraft had somehow again reared its ugly head, but from what he could understand of it, the missive referred to the creation of a new clan. *Why on earth would that cause Grace such misery?*

"Months ago, I wrote to the king, asking him to sanction the formation of a new clan, our clan," Grace revealed.

"Aye, that much I understand."

He placed a comforting arm around her and she buried her head into his shoulder. "Please forgive me, Ewan. I've made such a mess of it. I should have asked ye first, but I thought it would be a grand surprise."

Grace started to sniffle and then to his utter shock and dismay, she burst into tears. Ewan grimaced. He wished King Robert were standing before him so he could shout at the man for causing his beloved such distress.

"It does not matter if he refused to grant yer request," Ewan said in a soothing voice.

"Och, but he has agreed, the daft man." Grace pulled back, held the parchment aloft, and shook it until it rattled in the wind. "And he has seized the honor of naming this clan himself and passing that name along to all of us."

Ewan grew still. He had taken his mother's name, since his father had refused to give him his, but the Gilroys had disowned his mother when she had birthed a child out of wedlock—they had never acknowledged Ewan as one of their own. To have a name in his own right, and a clan that followed it, was something Ewan had never dreamed possible.

He took the missive from Grace's hand and began reading it again, this time more slowly. The lines in his brow deepened as he concentrated on every word. "Henceforth I shall be known as . . ." Ewan paused and repeated the full name in his head.

"Ewan MacEwan," Grace interjected with a groan. "Bloody hell!"

"Aye." Grace wiped at the tears on her cheeks, then took a deep breath. "He might have chosen Fitz instead. Fitzgilroy. That has a fine ring to it."

"Nay, it sounds too English."

"MacGilroy?" Grace offered.

"Nay, the Gilroys would not be pleased to have that name given to me or any others, as the king very well knows." Ewan felt the corners of his mouth curl into a smile. "I am proud that King Robert has seen fit to bestow this honor upon me. And every time I am called by my new name, I shall be reminded of my king's wicked sense of humor."

Grace sniffled. "Then ye are not angry with me?"

"Nay. I'm humbled by yer thoughtfulness and elated at the outcome. I never thought to lead a clan that bears my name, and thanks to ye, it has happened. Now, dry yer tears, lass. There's no need to be so emotional over such a happy matter."

She slipped her arm around his waist and leaned against him. "I cannae help it. I've heard that it is a common occurrence fer a woman in my condition to be bursting into tears fer no good reason," she said softly.

It took but a moment for her words to sink in to Ewan's brain. Startled, his eyes widened as his heart began to pick up speed.

"What are ye telling me, Grace? Does this mean that ye are . . ." Ewan swallowed hard.

"Carrying yer babe?" She gave him a watery smile. "Aye."

"Clever lass." Ewan leaned down and nuzzled her cheek. "Ye run my household, deal with my cantankerous mother, share my burdens, offer me sound advice, warm my bed, love me far more than I deserve, and now this joyous news. I am the luckiest man on earth, fer ye are, without question, the best wife in all the land."

"Aye, I most certainly am," Grace agreed, turning her head to receive his kiss. "And ye had best never forget it!"

Epilogue

Eight years later

Grace snuggled against Ewan's chest, her head burrowed in the cup of his shoulder, his arm holding her body close to his. A shout, followed by a loud whisper and a chorus of giggles, broke through her slumber, pulling her away from her blissful rest. Blearily, she lifted her head and cracked open one eye.

Dim light filtered through the narrow window, letting her know the morning had barely started. The noise came again, a wee bit louder.

"Yer children are awake," she said, cuddling into her husband's warmth, searching for that elusive sleepy, delicious feeling. But the whispers grew louder still and Grace knew it would only be a matter of time before their bedchamber door was pushed open. "Bid them enter, Ewan. Best to see what mischief they are planning before it gets out of hand."

"Hmm?" Ewan flung his hand across his brow. "Did ye say something, wife?"

"We are under attack," she stated, feeling not a qualm of guilt for her words.

"What?"

Ewan sprung from the bed and reached for his sword. Fully prepared for that reaction, Grace stayed his hand. Then she knelt on the edge of the bed, curved her arm around his shoulder, kissed his ear, and whispered, "'Tis yer bairns who storm our chamber door, good sir. I beg ye to let them in before they do any damage to themselves. Or the keep."

Ewan swore and reached for his trews. "The dawn has barely broken. What in the bloody hell are they doing up so early?"

Grace smiled and searched among the rumpled sheets for her nightgown, finding it bunched beneath the covers at the foot of the bed. "How can ye have possibly forgotten that Brian and Aileen are due to arrive today? 'Tis all that Cameron and Kyle can talk about. They even taught our young Alec to say Uncle Brian. At least I think that's what the lad is trying to say."

Ewan rubbed his face briskly with his palms, then raked a hand through his hair. "I told ye it was a mistake to let the bairns know of the visit and once again I am proved right."

Grace shrugged into her nightgown, then laughed and pressed her cheek against his. "'Twas yer mother who told them and that was only because she couldnae contain her delight at Brian's agreement to foster James with us."

"It is a proud moment fer us to have the honor of training yer nephew. He could easily have been sent to a more powerful or prestigious clan."

"My brother is wise enough to realize James will learn everything he needs to know, and more, from ye."

Ewan bowed his head. "Yer faith in me is humbling, Grace."

"I love ye, Ewan. I believe in ye. And I always shall."

She twisted forward, intending to bestow a warm, passionate kiss upon him, but a loud thud at the chamber door, followed by a high-pitched wail, interrupted her plan. Ewan heaved a heavy sigh. Barefooted, he walked across the chamber and opened the door.

The howling instantly stopped as the three children tumbled into the room. Spying their mother on the bed, they ran to her. Opening both arms wide, Grace embraced the trio. She could feel her throat closing up, her heart nearly bursting with love. It felt like a miracle every time she held one of her sons close. Mother to three healthy, mischievous lads. She could scarcely believe it.

Ewan approached the bed, then made the mistake of sitting upon it. The boys immediately jumped on him. Ewan let out a roar, eliciting squeals of excitement. The boys attacked from all sides, climbing on his back, pulling on his shoulders, pushing against his chest.

"Help me, Grace," Ewan yelled, as he carefully flipped Kyle over his head and then pulled Cameron off his shoulder.

For a moment she watched him with their children, reveling in the sight. Ewan was relaxed and smiling—happy. Seeing him thusly brought her own happiness to greater heights.

"'Tis exactly what ye deserve," Grace replied, poking her husband in the ribs. "Eight years married and three sons. Now, if ye had the good sense to give me a daughter, she would no doubt be rushing to yer defense right now."

"What do ye say, lads?" Ewan asked, as he rolled onto his back. "Would ye like to have a wee sister of yer very own?"

"Aye! And another brother," Cameron replied.

"Nay, three brothers," Kyle shouted, not to be outdone by his older sibling.

"Did ye hear that, wife? We've a great deal of work to be done to achieve that goal."

"Four more bairns," Grace declared with exaggerated outrage, wincing in sympathy as Cameron launched himself into Ewan's lap, barely missing landing on the area necessary for producing those children. "There won't be a stone left standing in the keep if we have that many children."

"Our lads are merely energetic," Ewan insisted. He caught Kyle in midair as the lad tried to catapult himself off the bed. "And high-spirited."

"Aye, and full of the devil," Grace smirked. "Just like their father."

"Och, so this is where ye've all gotten to, ye little scamps," Lady Moira declared as she strode through the half-open door. "I've got two servants scouring the keep looking fer ye."

"Guess what? We're going to have a baby sister," Cameron announced eagerly.

"And three more brothers," Kyle added.

Lady Moira raised her brow hopefully. Blushing, Grace lowered her chin and shook her head. "I'm not increasing."

"Yet," Ewan added with a roguish grin.

"A sister and three brothers." Lady Moira's mouth

twisted into an ironic grin. "Well now, I can assure ye that willnae happen if ye allow this unruly bunch to crowd into yer chamber at all hours of the day and night."

The lads, in response to a sharp gesture from their grandmother, scrambled down from the bed. Grace sighed with envy. Lady Moira was able to control the boys better than either she or Ewan. It wasn't as though she indulged them—nay, Lady Moira was strict and demanding. Yet the boys adored her and were always eager to please their grandmother and do her bidding.

It was an insight her mother-in-law had yet to share with her, but Grace remained hopeful she would one day learn that secret. Her relationship with Ewan's mother had tempered and strengthened over the years, especially since the arrival of the children. There were still occasions when the two women clashed opinions, but they had learned that a cordial compromise was far more pleasant than open warfare.

"I'm hungry," Cameron announced, sidling up to his father.

"'Tis far too early to be pestering the servants fer a meal," Lady Moira replied. "Especially when they are all busy preparing fer yer uncle Brian's visit."

"My tummy is growling," Kyle insisted. "Can ye hear it?"

"There is some bread and cheese—"

"I have a basket of dried fruit—"

Grace and Ewan spoke at the same time, yet one stern look from Lady Moira left them both silent. She tilted her head at a regal angle and observed them all for a long moment before speaking.

"Make some space on that table, Cameron," she

directed. "Kyle, help yer brother, Alec, onto the chair. And all three of ye must wash yer hands thoroughly before eating. I'll carry over the basin of water, while yer father fetches the food."

"Could ye not bring the lads into the hall and feed them there, Mother?" Ewan asked.

"Nay. I'll not be leaving ye alone in a cozy bedchamber with yer lovely wife when ye've got that gleam in yer eye," Lady Moira declared primly. "Grace has too much to do this morning making certain that all is ready fer her brother's visit. Ye'll have to wait until nightfall to start working on that granddaughter fer me."

Ewan rolled his eyes, yet wisely decided not to argue with his mother. He scooped Alec out of his chair, sat down, then placed the boy on his lap. After making certain each of the boys had a portion of food, Ewan began munching on a crusty piece of bread.

Grace smiled as she looked around the crowded, noisy table, her gaze lingering on Ewan. Her heart softened. How had she gotten so lucky? She had expected to live the remainder of her life inside the walls of a convent in a quiet, contemplative environment.

Instead, she had been thrust inside the center of a firestorm of chaos. A husband and bairns, a home of her own, a place where she loved and was loved in return. Somehow it had all been magically bestowed upon her, a blessing she had never even dared to dream.

Aye, dreams truly were magical. But life, well, life was far better, especially when the dreams you never dared to imagine came true.